THE ONE THAT GOT AWAY

ANNABEL KANTARIA

ONE PLACE. MANY STORIES

HarperCollins
PUBLISHERS
Since 1817

HQ
An imprint of HarperCollinsPublishers Ltd.
1 London Bridge Street
London SE1 9GF

This paperback edition 2017

2
First published in Great Britain by
HQ, an imprint of HarperCollinsPublishers Ltd. 2017

Copyright © Annabel Kantaria 2017

Annabel Kantaria asserts the moral right to be
identified as the author of this work.
A catalogue record for this book is
available from the British Library.

ISBN: 978-1-84845-512-2

Printed and bound by
CPI Group, Croydon CR0 4YY

Born in 1971, **Annabel Kantaria** is a British author and journalist who's written prolifically for publications throughout the Middle East. She lives in Dubai with her husband and two children. *The One That Got Away* is her third novel.

Natu Kantaria – a light in our lives;
forever in our hearts

ONE

Stella

'Just give me five minutes,' I tell the cabbie as we pull up outside the wine bar.

'First date?'

'School reunion.'

He winces, cheeks sucked in. 'Rather you than me. Take as long as you like, love. It's your money.' He unfurls the *Evening Standard* across the steering wheel and hunkers down in his seat. Above my head, the meter blinks and I stare at the glass frontage of the bar. I'm out on a limb, far from my comfort zone, and unfamiliar these days with this regenerated area south of the river. But I was born not far from here: it should feel like coming home, not entering a different country.

Outside, there's a drizzle falling. Behind the windows of the bar, I can see the rain-smeared shapes of people standing: bright colours, short dresses, high heels. It's hard to tell if these people are even part of the reunion – how would I know what my schoolmates look like now; what fifteen years has done to their faces and silhouettes? Still, short dresses don't seem the ticket. I'm in jeans, heels, cashmere. Neutral colours; no effort.

Tyres swish as cars pass by on the wet street and I think for a second about telling the cabbie I've made a mistake; got the wrong night. Whatever bravado it was that made me click 'going' on the school reunion page is now long gone. What am I doing here? I blame it on Martin Johnson: it's he who thought up the reunion; he who set up the Facebook page that brought life to this freak show, but the irony is I don't even remember who he is.

For the hundredth time, I try out the sound of his name on my tongue. Quite possibly it's a name I used to know; to hear; to say on a regular basis. Did I like him? Did we sit next to each other; did he tease me in the playground? Was it he who famously tripped up the deputy headmistress causing her to fall outside the school hall?

I can't picture the person behind the name, and the stamp-sized adult face on Facebook doesn't bring to mind the image of the child I must once have known. What comes to mind, though, as I think about the names of the children I do remember, is the cabbage-and-dumpling smell of the school dining hall; the interminable tick of the classroom clock; the peeling beige paint of the corridors; the din of the electric bell; the constant hitching of over-the-knee socks; and the thick nylon weight of the navy blazer that coated us, one and all.

On my phone, I flick to the reunion page to check again who else has confirmed. It's a long list of names, many familiar, but most of whom I've not spared a thought for since the day I left school. I didn't stay in touch and I wonder if anyone even remembers me. I wasn't particularly gregarious; kept myself to myself, wrapped up in my cooking, neither fashionable nor cool.

Which reminds me: what am I doing here? It's really not my scene and I bet I'm not the only one – yet not a single person's clicked 'not going'; not one person has dared openly to refuse this olive branch stretching across the decades. And, without a doubt, it's George Wolsey – whom I see is happily, confidently, brazenly 'going' – who is the biggest draw.

Whatever Martin Johnson might like to think, it's George Wolsey – along with his wife, Ness – who's the glue of this event. It's because of him that people will come tonight. Housewives, accountants and social media consultants; 'mummy' bloggers, shop managers and men who work in IT – they'll all be here to bask in a little of their glorious classmate's success; they'll come just to be able to tell the people they hang out with that they're going out tonight with 'you know, George Wolsey? Of Wolsey Associates?' Self-effacing smile. 'Yes, him! We were at school together.'

My classmates and I are, I realise, some of the favoured few who knew George Wolsey before he became successful – before the celebrity lifestyle and the gorgeous Richmond house, the magazine spreads and the paparazzi shots. We're a select group that knows his secrets.

Some of us, more than others.

I wonder if he's there already.

George.

On the pavement, the sound of unsteady heels makes me

turn and I see two women, clutching each other's arm and sheltering under one umbrella, approach the door. I know them. They were close at school – like me, they hung on the outer peripherals of cool, but they didn't seem to care – they stuck together. Tonight they're noticeably heavier, tarted up, and they look happy; excited. They're giggling, and I picture them half an hour ago in the cluttered family kitchen of one of their homes, generous glasses of white wine in their hands as they down a bottle for Dutch courage. Am I jealous?

Oh please.

The women wrench open the heavy door and step inside the bar. I hear a snatch of music, laughter, but not George's voice. My thoughts slide towards Ness – also officially 'going'. Perhaps it's because of her, not George, that butterflies are dancing in my stomach. But it's all history now, water under the bridge, and I need to make a stand.

'OK,' I say to the driver. 'I'm ready.'

'Sure?'

I pass over some notes, slither out of the cab and pull open the door to the bar before I have time to change my mind.

TWO

I'm up at the bar, my back to the room, listening to a woman I used to sit next to in French class tell me about the successes of her three marvellous children when George and Ness arrive. I suppose I've been there for forty-five minutes – an hour tops. I hear the door open and the bar seems to stop, to pause, as everyone turns to see the golden couple walk in. My peers may deny it, but they've all googled him; everyone in the room knows who George is these days. There's a collective intake of breath as my classmates absorb the fact that George and Ness are actually here: that George Wolsey really did click on the 'going' button and that he and his picture-perfect teenage sweetheart wife really have come to see them. I know what every single one of them is thinking: *OMG, I have to get a selfie with him.*

George breaks the pause. His voice rings around the wine bar, somehow drowning out the music which, up to this point, has been abrasive. I turn to face the room.

'Hey! Long time!' he says in that affable voice I remember from the sixth form, and I see his smile, the way it envelops everyone in the bar, making them feel wanted, included, valuable: a missing part of George's wonderful life. He rubs his hands together and his voice takes on the tone of a game-show host. 'So how's everyone tonight?' Seeing what happens next reminds me of the day we placed a little pile of iron filings next to a magnet at school. Vroom. George is surrounded.

I turn back to my companion.

'So tell me again about the music lessons. How exactly did you decide on clarinet instead of oboe?' She's only too happy to explain the process of choosing the right instrument for your child and the lesser known benefits of learning music at a young age but I notice that, as she answers, she keeps a keen eye on George and Ness, and it makes me want to kick her in the shin. We get through a few more minutes of football and ballet and how the eldest son's in the top maths set then my companion suddenly whispers, 'OMG. He's coming over!'

For a second, I actually think she means her son.

'No!' she giggles, giving me a nudge. She flicks back her hair. 'George Wolsey!'

'Stella Simons?' George's voice is right behind me so I take a breath and turn to face him, a pleasant smile on my face as I absorb the sight of George Wolsey aged thirty-three. His teeth are straightened and whitened; his skin tanned, possibly from an Indian Ocean hideaway, or maybe from a bottle. Either way, it's clear he's a rich man in his prime; a man who knows he looks good.

'Hello, George,' I say.

'Stella! It *is* you! I'm *so* glad you're here!' George leans in with a waft of cologne, and I close my eyes and tilt my cheekbone to touch his in the most impersonal of air kisses but, as his mouth comes into the proximity of my ear, he whispers, 'I'd know that arse anywhere.' His hand touches the small of my back and I feel the heat of his breath in my ear.

Now, there are many ways this reunion could have gone; many ways in which George could have behaved with me after an absence of fifteen years but, given the fact that he hasn't seen me for a decade and a half – not to mention the terms on which we last parted – a comment about my backside is not what I'm expecting and, honest to God, it throws me.

'Lovely to see you,' I say. 'But, if you'll excuse me—' I nod vaguely at the room '—I was just about to…'

I skirt past George and launch myself into the bar. It's not a wise move: I end up face to face with Ness. At first glance, she looks like an even better, glossier version of her beautiful self – the best possible Ness there could be – but there's something slightly out of kilter from how I remember her face looking and I realise in an instant that it's Botox, and quite possibly some fillers, too, that's changed her contours. Ness's teeth gleam like a row of Japanese pearls and I clock, too, her perfect nails. Ness's complexion is glowing but, up close, I see how much make-up she's wearing and there's a brittleness about her eyes. It's not this, though, that everyone notices: it's her hair. Ness's magnificent hair has a life of its own and I see now that it's even more impressive than it used to be. In another world, I'd ask her what her secret is.

She looks me up and down, this vision of perfection that is Ness Wolsey, then she speaks.

'Stella! How lovely!'

She leans in for one of those girlie hugs around the neck and I get a whiff of some rose-based perfume as her cheek brushes mine. The scent is nauseatingly sweet.

'It's been – what? Fifteen years?'

I don't grace this with a reply: it's the fifteen-year reunion, after all, and the bar is full of banners and silver balloons proclaiming the fact. 'So how's life treating you?' she continues. 'You always *were* going to run the world. Did you succeed?' Her voice is smooth, but I see a vein pulsing in her neck. She knows what happened – of course she knows.

'I'm good, thanks,' I say. 'I'm in catering.'

'You always were baking cakes,' she laughs. 'Lucky you to do something you enjoy.'

'Yes. I'm doing fine. No complaints.' I don't tell her the name of my company – a name she'll definitely recognise. Neither do I mention that it's the largest private catering company in London; that its annual turnover could wipe out the debt of a small country. 'And, well – congratulations to you,' I say. 'You've… done well.' I force a little laugh to detract from the fact that we both know the only thing she did well was to marry George.

Ness takes a swig from her wine glass and I notice two things: first, that it's a small glass and, second, that she's nearly halfway through it. She's barely swallowed her mouthful when George swoops, grabs the glass out of her hand, and replaces it with a glass of sparkling water, making me think 'alcohol problem? Interesting.' George heads back to the bar without saying a word and Ness, unfazed, gives a little shrug.

'I'm good, thanks.' She smiles, and her pretty dimples blink at me, taking me straight back to those dark days in the sixth form. I smell medical disinfectant, see the shine of steel, feel the stiffness of a green gown against my skin. 'It's all good.' She nods towards George, back at the bar, and gives a little sigh. 'Been married fourteen years now. You know how it is.' She pauses, glances at my left hand. 'So, how about you? Got anyone special these days?'

I smile. 'Not at the moment.'

Ness puts her hand on my arm as if she understands how desperate I must be. 'Don't worry,' she says. 'We'll find you someone. The right one's out there somewhere. You just haven't found him yet.' She pauses. 'Maybe there's even someone here for you tonight.' Ness rolls her eyes around the bar taking in what she presumably sees as a cast of men with whom I at least have some shared history.

'Maybe,' I say, seeing a room full of married thirty-three-year-olds in Friday-night casualwear, 'but I'm afraid I won't have a chance to find out. My taxi's waiting. Have a lovely evening.'

I practically run out of the door.

THREE

George

'Yes!' says the woman Stell was talking to at the bar. 'So he's been picked for the rugby squad and now we're hoping he'll make the First XV!'

I'm standing with my back to the bar, leaning my elbows against the counter so I can scan the room for Stella while absorbing the chit-chat from this woman who clearly fancies me but is yet to realise that talking about her kids isn't the way to get me to fuck her. My eyes roam the crowded room; I'm searching for *that* arse in those jeans, and the cling of cashmere on those incredible tits. Failing to see Stell, I turn my attention back to the woman at the bar.

'There's a lot to be said for playing sport at that age,' I tell her with a smile. 'Keeps them out of mischief. Not that I'd know!'

Where the hell is Stell?

'But you don't have any children of your own?' The woman pauses, drops her voice a notch and I see her eyes gleaming, keen to absorb any confidences I might want to share. 'I hope there isn't a…'

'A problem?' I ask smoothly. I drop my gaze then look back at her. 'I suppose there is…'

She leans in, all ears, and I look at the floor in an attempt to keep my face straight. She's so close I can smell the scent of her skin; feel the warmth coming off her. It would be so easy – *so* easy – to lead her round to the car park out the back for a quickie. Not that I would, of course; not with Ness here. Just hypothetically. I look up and search for her hand. I take it in mine, look her in the eyes and blink, as if holding back tears. 'I suppose there is a problem,' I say quietly.

'I'm here if you need to talk,' she breathes, inching her face even closer to mine and squeezing my hand. Now I can smell the wine on her breath; see the little dots of mascara gathered beneath her lower lash line. I lean in even further and whisper into her ear, my lips touching her skin; teasing.

'Well, it's just that…' I pause. 'I'm not sure I'm doing it right.' I step back and hold my other fist at hip height and thrust my pelvis suggestively a couple of times towards her. 'Know what I mean?' I give her a big wink.

I watch her expression change as she realises she's been had, then I burst out laughing as she turns away, embarrassed.

'Oh, for God's sake, George!'

'Come here!' I say, pulling her in for a hug. 'Just kidding. Just a bit of banter!' I kiss her hair, enjoying the scent of it and the soft feel of her in my arms, then I let her go, clinking my glass to hers. 'Cheers, darling! You have a great night!'

I saunter across the bar, slapping people on the back and shaking hands as I go, working my way over to Ness. She's with a group of girls – women, I suppose now – she used to hang out with at school: the popular ones; the netball team; the pretty ones; the smart ones. This was her crowd. She looks good. She's in her element; the queen of them all.

'All right, sweetheart?' I ask, giving her a showy kiss on the cheek and snaking my arm around her waist. 'I trust these lovely ladies are keeping you entertained?'

'Yeah, all good. You?'

'Just going to the little boys' room.'

I unwind my arm and slip through the double doors that lead to the bathroom. There, in the service corridor, even though it's muted, I can still hear the racket from the pub; the screech of voices straining to be heard over other voices; the thump of the music in the background. The floor's slightly sticky and, under it all, there's the smell of old coats and stale beer. I pull out my phone and message Stell.

'Where are you?'

I wait but, when she doesn't reply, I type again. 'I can't see you.'

I'm still there in the hallway, staring at the phone, when the door to the pub kicks open. Ness, her glass in her hand, is framed in the doorway, her hair backlit and slightly wild, and she looks for a second like a modern-day Medusa. Neither of us moves. Then, quickly, I slide my phone back into my trouser pocket, knowing as I do so, that there's guilt written all over my face.

'I'm just going to the loo,' I say to her, 'then we're leaving.'

'But I was just…'

'No buts. I'm done here.'

FOUR

Stella

Back in Hampstead, I wave to the doorman and press the button for the lift. My phone chimes as I step into it and I ignore it: I've long stopped bothering to try to get a connection on the ride up to my apartment. The lift pings and I shove the key in my front door and breathe in that familiar bergamot smell of home.

I kick off my heels and saunter into the bedroom to change before pouring myself a glass of wine and collapsing onto the sofa. The blinds are open and I can see the glittering lights and sodium glow of London stretching beyond the blackness of Hampstead Heath. I lean back and relax, circling my ankles and enjoying being home. My phone chimes again. I look. It's a Facebook message from George. Two in fact.

George Wolsey.

I stare at the name for a minute. I've never seen his name on my phone or in my inbox. It used to be letters. Paper envelopes or folded pieces of paper with my name written in his scruffy, boy-writing. Birthday cards. Postcards. Once, a Valentine's card. The sight of his name in my inbox makes me feel as though we're travellers – astronauts who've made it from a distant galaxy in which technology doesn't exist.

Oh, George. Good at school. A sportsman. Quietly good-looking. Average intelligence. Excess confidence. A bit of bluster. He played the game. But even I wouldn't have picked him out to be the most successful product of our year. He didn't even go to university – he got offers, yes, but he changed his mind after getting a summer job at an advertising agency. From what I've read about him, I imagine that he lived and breathed the business; worked his way up, charming people left, right and centre. And now – now if you sing a tune from an ad – any ad that you hear on television or radio – the chances are that Wolsey Associates is responsible.

But that's not why George is in the media; that's not why we read interviews about him and see the odd picture of him rubbing shoulders with pop stars, artists, 'it' girls and actors at various black-tie events. No, what George is most known for these days is the pro bono work and the fundraising initiatives his agency does for children's charities. It's all about corporate responsibility for George now. As I said: he plays the game.

But what game is it he's playing tonight? I open the first message. Where are you?

And then the second one. I can't see you.

I put the phone down and take another sip of wine. Should I reply? Why not? Why not let him know that I left him? Typing with my thumb, balancing my phone in the same hand, I write back. At home.

Before I close Facebook and put the phone down, George has answered. You left already? I wanted to see to you.

You saw me.

I wanted to speak to you. Properly. Why did you leave?

'None of your business,' I say to the apartment. I put the phone down and head back to the kitchen for some cheese to accompany my wine. I have a salty Old Amsterdam and some Beaufort D'Ete, which I take out of the fridge almost reverentially. The phone pings again, and then again and again. I take my time cutting the cheese and arranging it on a plate. I pick up a crisp linen napkin and top up my wine glass. Back on the sofa, I put my plate on a side table and pick up my phone.

Stell?

Looking good, by the way.

'Gee thanks,' I say out loud. I think for a minute about sending George a witty reply but decide not to in the end. There's nothing to be gained from reopening this path of communication. George has been out of my life for fifteen years and I've done just splendidly without him.

I take my cheese and wine into the bathroom and turn on the taps, adding a generous slug of bath oil. I peel off my sweater, my jeans, my underwear and my jewellery and climb into the bath, letting the warm, oily water slide over my skin. I close my eyes and picture the bar I've come from this evening. What's happening at the reunion now? I wonder. Has it become wild, even the quiet ones drunk and dancing, or did everyone leave early, rushing back to partners, children and the thought of an early-morning start for rugby practice? Who's George talking to? Is he doing the rounds, dutifully remembering everyone's interests and quirks, or sitting morosely at the bar nursing a whisky as he messages me? And where's Ness in all this? I sip my wine and enjoy my cheese, happy to be alone in the peace of my bathroom.

The phone rings: an unknown number. It can only be George. The sod.

'You're married!' I tell the phone without connecting the call. I place it on the side of the bath and sink my head below the surface of the water, from where I can no longer hear it ringing.

FIVE

Stella

Please pick up. I need to talk to you.

The message comes in as soon as I turn on my phone the next morning. I put the handset down on the duvet and sigh. George will know, of course, that I've read it, thanks to the magic of Facebook. But what's he after? What's he looking for? He has everything he could want in terms of success. What does he want with me now, after all these years? I sigh again and pick up the phone. If it were anyone else, any other married man, I wouldn't have given the message a second look.

About what? I type. I hesitate, then press send.

His tiny face appears next to the message immediately: he was watching the screen. Can I call you?

Another sigh from me. I don't have the energy for this.

A pause. We're worth more than this, Stell. Come on, for old time's sake.

Stell.

I feel like I'm standing on a cliff top, teetering on the brink of something dangerous. I could step back: a part of me is curious, a part of me is defiant and – I close my eyes as I admit this to myself – a part of me is flattered. With a sigh, I twist around and open the bottom drawer of the bedside cabinet, groping around underneath the books, the hand creams, the foot lotions and the pedicure socks until I feel and grasp a hardback notebook.

It's old and worn, its corners frayed, the spine breaking, yet it's as familiar to me as my own hand. Slowly, I open it and turn the pages, looking at the pictures I stuck in fifteen years ago, the Sellotape now yellowed and peeling. The wedding dresses – so dated, so naïve – cut out of bridal magazines; the sickly, tiered wedding cakes, dusted with pastel-coloured flowers; the pencil sketches of my dream wedding dress; the photographs of apartments cut from property magazines; the pages of calculations I'd done to work out how much rent George and I could afford depending on what our starting salaries might be; and then – I know it's coming before I get there – the page of signatures I'd practised.

Stella Wolsey. Stella Wolsey. Stella Wolsey. SW. SW. SW.

A double-page spread of looping, blue-ink Stella Wolsey.

Lying back on my pillows, I let the book drop and exhale slowly.

It's been a long time since I've thought about George. Yes, I see the odd thing in the paper about the success of his advertising firm, about the good deeds his company does, but it's not as if I sit there and read them word for word. I'm interested, but not that interested. That boat has sailed.

I let the memories wash over me. George and Stella. We go back to 1987. Picture two mums at a school coffee morning, keen to make friends. Two mums whose five-year-olds are thrown together through their mums' friendship. George – my first school friend. George holding my hand as we walk into school each day. George playing with me, standing up for me, choosing me to be his partner for everything. George and Stella; Stella and George. And me taking his friendship for granted. All the push and shove, the posturing and the fights of the junior school playground passing me by as George takes care of me.

Passing the 11+ together. Getting into the same school. Laughing at our new uniforms, our blazer sleeves too long, my shoes looking ridiculously big at the end of my skinny legs. Me knocking for George in the mornings, us doing our homework together on the bus, George's hand touching mine as we work out our maths problems, check each other's answers, and test each other on our French vocabulary. And then, from the bus stop, going our separate ways at school: for the first time ever, in separate classes, with separate friends, but still looking out for each other; still caring.

I suppose it was inevitable I'd think he was mine. A part of me probably always thought we'd end up together. And, as we turned fifteen, I started to see George in a different light. He was handsome, strong, popular. A party was the turning point; Sophie's sixteenth birthday. In a dark living room full of couples slow-dancing, smooching and kissing, George grabbed my hand and pulled me close, his warm hands inside my top, sliding over my skin. I could smell beer on his breath, taste cigarettes as, for the first time, his mouth found mine.

'Come on, Stell. Come upstairs with me,' he'd whispered, his voice thick with beer. 'I want you.' And I'd gone. Just like that. I let him lead me by the hand up the stairs to Sophie's brother's bedroom, peel off my jeans and take my virginity on a pile of coats.

And from then on George and I both were and were not a couple. We didn't date – we didn't ever speak of what we did – but, at every party, study date or get-together at which we found ourselves, I let him take me upstairs. In my mind we were a couple. It was never official. It was never, like, 'George & Stell' but everyone knew, of course they did: how could they not?

'I love you, Stell,' George would moan, burying his head in my shoulder as he came inside me on Friday night and Saturday night, sometimes on Tuesday night or Thursday night, or behind the Art block on a Wednesday lunchtime, too. 'You're the best.' And I was happy with my lot: studying for my exams, being quietly adored by George.

But, while I assumed our love would take on the natural trajectory of an adult relationship – assumed that George and I would stay together, make it official, get married, have children – what actually happened was that I got pregnant, and George fell for Ness.

Pretty, sexy, bubbly Ness.

Lying back on my pillows, I close my eyes. The phone pings but I ignore it. I need to open this box of memories; the one I sealed tightly aged eighteen. I need to see how I feel about it now.

George didn't want to know.

I recall the smell of the clinic. The terror of walking in alone and telling the nurse I was pregnant. I flinch as I feel the cold smear of gel on my belly and the probe moving over my skin.

'Eight weeks,' the nurse had said. 'That's good.'

It didn't take long. I remember the ceiling. Forty-six tiles. I didn't even stay overnight; just told my parents I was shopping in London. Hobbled home pale and shaky, pretended I had an upset stomach and went to bed for the rest of the day.

Done and dusted.

Meanwhile, George and Ness… love's young dream.

Allegedly.

The phone rings and who knows why I do, but I pick up.

SIX

George

I'm awake before the alarm, a ball of morning energy. While Ness stretches luxuriously, her hair cascading over the pillows like some fairy-tale princess, I leap out of bed and zip downstairs to make the coffee, singing out loud as I take the steps two at a time.

'Morning, darling,' I say, bounding back upstairs, presenting the cup to Ness like a trophy. 'Ta-da!'

'Oh wow,' she says. 'What happened? Did someone win the lottery?'

'Nothing! I just felt like spoiling my lovely wife. What's wrong with that?' I lean down and kiss her forehead. In the bathroom, I take a sip of my coffee and look at my reflection in the mirror: not bad for thirty-three – I regularly get mistaken for much younger. I like to think the boyish light is still in my eyes, and that the lines that are slowly starting to appear add character rather than age. I smile at myself, pleased with the decision I made to get my teeth professionally whitened. It really does make a difference. I run a hand through the hair on my temples, turning so the light catches it: there's no grey there yet, but I'm not scared of the day it does start to appear: I've always fancied being a silver fox; a bit of a George Clooney. I rub the bristles on my jawline – even though I haven't shaved for a couple of days, there's no grey there, either – then I gently massage a few drops of shaving oil all over my face, to pep up the circulation and plump up my skin.

I can't stop whistling in the shower, then, with the towel slung around my hips, I pull out my best suit and newest shirt. I match my cufflinks to my shirt and agonise over my tie: bold and bright, or classic? I hold each up in turn, turning this way and that to see which best brings out the light in my eyes. I suppose it's not surprising that Ness looks up from her own mirror.

'Important meeting?' she asks, head cocked to one side, hairdryer in hand.

'Yep. Which tie?'

She points to the bright one. 'Need me for lunch?'

'Oh – thanks, but no. It's pretty much in the bag.'

'OK.' She shrugs and turns back to her hair but I can tell from the jerkiness in her movements that she's thinking; irked perhaps. She usually comes to these lunches: I joke that she's my client-magnet, though we both know she's really just an ornament at the table. I tut silently to myself, my head in the wardrobe as I look for my belt: *Didn't think that one through, did you, George?* I slide my belt through its loops and fasten it, then I go over to Ness and put my hands on her shoulders, looking at her in the mirror. She puts down the hairdryer and her eyes meet the reflection of mine.

'It's a cert. I didn't want to bore you with it.'

'It's fine.'

'Sure?'

'Yep.' She fiddles with a pot on the dressing table, unscrewing and screwing its cap. Then she sucks her teeth. 'Will you be late tonight?'

I turn and cross the room, my back to her as I pick up my suit jacket and slip it on, find my wallet and slide it into my trouser pocket.

''Fraid so. Didn't I mention it?'

'No. You didn't.'

At the door, I pause and turn to look at her. 'Yeah. Potential new client. Drinks in the West End.' I shrug. 'Sorry, hon. He chose the location. But it's not dinner. I'll be home as soon as I can. Don't worry about cooking,' I add. 'I'll pick up something on my way.'

'OK,' she says.

Our eyes meet across the bed and hang together for a weighted moment – a moment in which I wonder if she's on to me – how could she be? – then I smile.

'I'll be home as soon as I can. Have a good day, babe.'

SEVEN

Stella

It's jeans again. So shoot me: they look good. I take a final look in the mirror, pick up my handbag and leave the apartment. While I'm walking to the pub, I wonder how long it'll take George to come up from Richmond; what he's told Ness he's doing tonight. My steps ring out as I stride down the road, sounding more confident than I feel. With every strike of heel on pavement, I ask myself, *What are you doing? What exactly are you hoping to achieve with this?*

I'm usually very clear on my motives. It's my USP; who I am. From buying a sandwich to launching a new menu, I never do anything without knowing exactly what it is and why I'm doing it. Informed. Decisive.

But today I'm confused. How has this man from whom I haven't heard for fifteen years persuaded me to meet him in a pub? Am I really such a pushover? Have I seriously been waiting fifteen years to receive a call from George Wolsey? I don't think so, yet one week ago he was nothing to me and now I'm walking to the pub to meet him: go figure.

But there's more to my unease than feeling disconcerted by how easily George has blasted his way through my defences: he's married, and there's a part of me that senses his intentions are not entirely pure.

When it comes to George, my sixth sense always used to be right.

I stop and pretend to look in the window of an estate agent, my eyes roaming over the properties for sale until they focus on my own reflection in the glass. It's the pull of the past, I tell myself. That's all it is. Yes, he may have been not just 'the one' but 'the one and only' fifteen years ago (I cringe as I see in my mind's eye the page of 'Stella Wolsey' signatures), but a decade and a half has passed. I've moved on: I'm a successful woman in my own right.

Yes, I nod to myself in the glass: all this is about is a shared past; an understandable desire to link with a person who knew me years ago – nothing more. I have so much history with George. He used to know me better than anyone else on the planet. He still knows that part of me; you can't take that away. We saw each other every day of our childhoods. It's got to be worth something.

It's got to be worth an hour in the pub with a glass of wine. Hasn't it?

I used the word 'desire' back there. I noticed that.

I turn and walk on.

*

The pub is popular, well known for its food. Up a creaky staircase, six quirky bedrooms turn it into a boutique hotel. George is there before me, a bottle of wine on the table, and a whisky in his hand. He looks smart in a suit with a garish tie and he's picked – as I knew he would – one of the discreet alcoves at the back of the bar; a place where we're least likely to be disturbed. He doesn't stand up to greet me. I slide onto the bench seat opposite him and he reaches for my hand across the table.

'Hey. Thanks for coming.'

I let him squeeze my hand for a moment before withdrawing it. His skin feels cool, softer than I remember. Hands that don't do dishes.

'You're welcome.'

George looks at me. Takes me all in, and I watch him. His thirties really do suit him.

'You look amazing,' he says eventually. I'm glad to hear it but I'm not going to tell him that.

'Thanks.' I look pointedly at the wine bottle. 'I'd love a glass.'

'I'm so sorry!' George bustles into action. 'Forgive me.' He pours two glasses then pushes one towards me. I pick it up and inhale the scent of the wine. A good one; probably the most expensive on the wine list. We clink glasses and I take a slow sip, roll it around my mouth, swallow and exhale.

'Nice.'

George nods.

'So – how are things? How's Ness?' I ask after it becomes clear he's not going to speak. He's looking a little starstruck, to be honest.

'She's good, thanks,' he says.

'No kids?' I know it's below the belt, but… as I said: part-defiant.

He closes his eyes and shakes his head slowly. 'No.'

I take a sip of wine.

'And how about you?' he asks. 'You went into catering, I gather?'

'Yes.'

He names my firm. 'Impressive.'

'But I don't cook so much these days.'

'No. I imagine not,' he says.

'I'm in the office, running the business. I have a good team that does the work on the ground for me now.'

'How do you feel about that?'

'It's a new challenge. I like that. And I get to sit down a bit.'

George laughs. 'You always did like a challenge.'

'And how about you?' I ask. 'How's business?'

'Can't complain.' There's a pause. 'Our success means I have more of a chance to do stuff for charities. You know, fundraising. Awareness campaigns. Have you heard about our annual charity drive? It's global. Involves all our clients. Last year we raised nearly a million quid.'

'Fantastic. Yeah. I see the odd thing in the paper.' It's an understatement. You'd have to be living under a rock not to be aware of Wolsey Associates' global charity drive.

George looks up, a smile lighting up his face. 'You read some of the articles?'

I exhale. 'Oh, you know… I speed-read the odd one now and then.'

'I always imagine you reading the articles when they come out.' He looks so earnest it's embarrassing. 'I don't know. I guess I just hoped you would be interested.'

'In your business?'

'In me.'

I look at George, searching for clues that he's joking – a twitch of his mouth, a shake in his shoulders – but he just looks beaten.

'George,' I say. 'That ship sailed years ago.'

'Did it?'

I look at the table. The silence extends. I pick at the drinks mat. Already it's wet with condensation from the wine glass.

'So, was there a reason you wanted to meet?' I ask eventually. 'It's just… you know… nothing for fifteen years and then… ?'

George looks up and smiles at me. It's a warm smile. Not the public smile that wins over his clients, but an intimate smile, a smile just for me, and I'm not expecting it. I raise my chin and look levelly at him. Hurt me once, that's my bad luck, but you will not hurt me twice.

'Stell,' he says softly. And, just like that, the universe ruptures. A gaping black hole opens in front of me. No warning; no way to prepare myself. I've forgotten what it feels like to hear George's voice say 'Stell' and I plummet head first into the black hole and land on that pile of coats in Sophie's brother's bedroom, George's breath hot in my ear. I've almost burrowed through the drinks mat with my nail.

'I've been thinking about you,' George says. 'A lot.'

I wait, heart hammering.

'I don't mean just this week. I've been thinking about you for a long time.' George's voice is quiet. 'Always, actually.'

I can barely breathe. 'You could have got in touch. Before you got married.'

'I didn't know how it would be received. I mean…'

The air goes out of my lungs. This is the closest he's ever come to speaking about the pregnancy, the abortion, the way he left me. I didn't hear from him after I told him I was pregnant. My memory: his feet clattering on the stairs, the front door slamming shut and George out of my life. I look down at the table, compose myself, then raise my eyes to his.

'You mean… ?'

'Well. We didn't leave it in a very good place, really, did we?'

'I didn't leave anything, George. It was you who did the leaving.' What I don't say, although it's running through my head on ticker tape, is: *We could have made it work. We could have kept the baby.*

George holds up a hand. 'I know. I know. And I've kicked myself for it every day since. But, Stell, I was young. Scared. Terrified! I didn't know what to do.'

'And I did?'

He has the decency to stay quiet.

'Let me just get this straight,' I say. 'I was eighteen, about to take my A levels, and pregnant. As you well know, I couldn't tell my parents. Yet you left me to sort out – and go through – an abortion on my own. An abortion, George.' I let the word sink in. 'And, for the record, I didn't know what to do either.'

George closes his eyes and exhales. 'I'm so sorry, Stell. If I could do it all again. If I could turn back time…'

'You'd what?'

'I'd…'

'What? Come with me to the doctor? Pay for the abortion? Hold my hand while they sucked the baby out of me? Not get together with *her*?' I eyeball him, daring him to be honest.

There's a silence, George looks down, then back at me. 'What I'd do, Stell, is stay with you. I'd stay with you. Marry you. Have the baby with you. I've always held a candle for you, Stell.'

I slide out of the booth, pick up my bag and leave.

EIGHT

George

As the dust settles after Stell's exit, I close my eyes and exhale. *That didn't go well, did it?* I don't know: was I naïve to imagine she'd jump back into my arms if I said the right words?

And it's not as if I lied. Not really. Over the years, I've imagined what my son would have been like: I have. I've looked at my own baby pictures and imagined a boy with my eyes and my smile – his hair perhaps darker like Stell's or maybe lighter like Ness's. I've imagined him toddling along next to me on his cute little chubby legs, asking questions about what I do; I've pictured myself showing him off around the office on Family Day, carting him around on my shoulders as the women coo over him. I've imagined kicking a ball around the garden with him, rough-and-tumbling him on the sofa; changing nappies like a pro; getting adoring glances in the supermarket – all those sorts of things that parents do. I'd like it: I'm sure I would. I just wasn't ready for it at eighteen, but now?

Now I believe I am.

I pour myself the last of the wine and sigh. In my jacket

pocket I'm all too aware of the two key cards to one of the bedrooms upstairs. I fish them out and put them on the table: shame.

So, now what? I run my fingertip around the rim of the wine glass, wondering if it'll sing if I go fast enough. Stell fascinates me. She always has. But how do I get to her now she's walked out on me twice? She always was a tough cookie but that's what I like: she pushes me away and I come back for more. She's not easy, but I'm not giving up. Chasing Stell makes me feel alive – it's harmless and it's not as if Ness is pregnant yet. I'll rein it all in when she gets pregnant – I will – but, for now, something's missing in my life and I could do with something to put the fire back in my veins.

'Challenge accepted, Miss Simons,' I say out loud. I polish off the wine in two swigs, then I pull out my phone and speed-dial Ness.

'Hey.'

'Hey!' She sounds surprised.

'What are you up to?'

'I was going to watch a bit of TV and take a bath.'

'Well, change of plan. My client cancelled. I'm on my way. Any chance you can rustle up a bit of dinner and we could…' I leave it hanging, leaving her with the thought that I might shag her later.

'OK.'

'I'll be home inside the hour.' I pause. 'Love you.'

'Love you, too.'

NINE

Stella

Hand on heart, it feels good to walk out on George. It feels like the moment I've had coming for the last fifteen years. Admittedly, it's not as bad as being left pregnant aged eighteen, but leaving him at that table feels symbolic. It feels like retribution. Closure.

I go back to my life, focus on my work, get on with running the little part of the world for which I'm responsible. Occasionally, in spare moments on the Tube or in a taxi queue, I think about George; I practise saying his name in my head and think about what he told me. It takes me time to come to terms with my new knowledge; time to absorb the fact that George didn't get over me. There was a time when I longed to hear that he loved me, but now the words are out there, rolling around in the present day, they sound wrong. George is married and I've moved on. I don't need George in my life.

But.

This is not any married man we're talking about. This is George.

My George.

He said we should have had the baby.

I go about my business and I tell myself that it's all very well that George still feels something for me but that's his problem, not mine. George is not available, and I don't do married men. Besides, I've made my stance clear: I've walked out on him twice now. The serendipity of that is not lost on me.

It could all end there. It should all end there.

But George has both the money and the tenacity for grand gestures. The day after I leave him in the pub, my secretary knocks on my office door. It's almost lunchtime and my day's one of pretty much back-to-back meetings. I've worked out how much time I need to prepare for each meeting and asked not to be disturbed. I'm irritated when I look up to wave her in. She's carrying a box out in front of her as if it's full of live puppies.

'What is it?' I'm short with her, trying not to lose the thread of my thoughts.

'A delivery,' she says. 'Gourmet Lunch Co.'

'Not mine.' I turn back to the computer.

'It's got your name on it.' She checks the label, reads out my name, company name and address. 'I'll leave it here.' She places it on my desk, along with a set of office cutlery, and leaves.

When the door's shut, I open the box. The smell that releases makes my mouth water. Inside, there are a couple of chargrilled chicken skewers arranged on a salad of lentil, feta and aubergine.

I turn back to my work and my phone buzzes. George. **Did lunch arrive?**

My lips twitch. I don't want to smile, not even to myself, but who bar George would send food to the boss of a catering company? Only he would know me well enough to guess I rarely make time for my own lunch.

Why did you send it?

I want to take care of you.

I don't need taking care of.

Everyone needs taking care of.

Maybe when I was 18 but not now.

Touché.

I don't reply.

I'm saying sorry, George types.

I put my phone on silent and get back to work. But George doesn't stop with one lunch. Food continues to arrive on a daily basis. Once, I pick up the fork, tempted to eat, but there's something about putting food that George has chosen for me in my mouth that feels as if I'm letting him in; accepting something that I can't allow myself to accept. I'm the feeder, not him. I tell my secretary to consider the deliveries hers.

Next comes a parcel delivered by hand. My assistant places it on my desk with a raised eyebrow and I look at the rectangular package, wrapped in luxurious paper. The cream silk ribbon is perfectly tied. It can only have come from George, though I imagine he didn't wrap it himself. All morning, I leave the parcel on my desk, wondering whether to send it back, but then, around lunchtime, my resolve weakens and I gently tug the end of the ribbon to release the folds of paper. I'm expecting something new and shiny but, beneath the paper, my fingers touch something that's softer, more worn: a used copy of a novel I loved as a teenager.

Sitting at my desk, I flick through the familiar pages, remembering the excitement with which I'd read the story for the first time. There's a bookmark inside and I know before I turn to that page what I'll find: it marks a paragraph about love I'd read aloud to George when we were seventeen. It's only later, when I'm flicking through the book again that afternoon, that I realise the copy George has sent is a first edition. I place it reverentially back on my desk and nod. I'm impressed. The book is a thoughtful gift yet I don't know if I should thank him. Well, of course I should thank him. But I know what George is like. If he sees any weakness in me, any chink in my armour, he'll storm into it like the rugby player he used to be. I stick with simple.

Thanks for the book, I text him.

You're welcome, he replies, and I just know that he's smiling.

*

The next day, I'm wrapping things up at work when my phone buzzes. The sound's loud in the silence of the office. It's late – dark outside – and everyone's gone home. I check the screen: an unknown number. I stare at it for a second, weighing up whether or not to pick up. It could be a new client, or perhaps a cold call. I'm about to leave and I don't want to get into a long conversation. Even as I think all this, the phone stops buzzing. I put it back on the desk, but it starts up again almost immediately.

I pick up. 'Stella Simons speaking… Hello?'

The line crackles a little, then a female voice comes on. 'Stella! Hello! How are you?' Pause. 'It's Ness.'

I lean back in my seat, lift my chin and squint my eyes at the blackness outside the office window. 'Hello.'

'It was lovely to see you the other night,' says Ness. 'Really nice.'

I give a polite laugh.

'Wasn't it amazing to see how everyone's turned out?' she says. 'And yourself – of course! I've googled your company now.' She laughs. 'I didn't realise that was you! Marvellous! I always knew you'd go far!'

Another small laugh from me.

'I can't believe it's been fifteen years!' Ness continues. 'Gosh, did you see Julia and Sarah? It's incredible that they're still friends! And that their children are friends too! Do you still see anyone from school?'

'No.'

'No, we neither. We don't have time, really, to be fair…' Her voice trails off and I wonder if we're thinking the same thing: namely, that Ness's time is dedicated almost entirely to looking good on George's arm.

'So…' she says, and I close my eyes, sensing that she's finally coming to the point. 'Do you think you'll, um, stay in touch with George now you've reconnected?' And, as she asks this, I realise the reason that she's called is because she's worried. Insecure. I open my mouth to reply but she doesn't give me a chance to speak.

'It was *so* amazing to catch up with you after so long,' she says. 'George and I were both so happy to see you!' She doesn't sound that happy. 'I mean… after, you know, what happened all those years ago…' Her voice isn't as confident now. She stops and clears her throat, then her words come out in a rush. 'But I wanted you to know that George and I – we're, well, we're good. Really good.' She waits, but I don't respond. 'I mean,' she continues, 'I know it must have been hard for you. At the time, and all that. But it was a long time ago! We were children. Nothing but children!' Her laugh rattles down the phone line. 'But, you know, difficult decisions were made and we stuck with them. You sleep in the bed you make! Literally!' She falls silent for a second. 'Look. I just wanted to say that all that happened back then: I'm sorry. It must have been horrific for you. But I want you to know it wasn't for nothing.' She pauses again and I really am struck dumb. 'Yes. That's what I want to say. If it makes you feel better, it wasn't for nothing. I still love him.' Her intonation makes it sound like she has more to say and I wait but then Ness says, 'Stella? Are you there?'

'That's lovely,' I say. But look, I don't mean to be rude… if you'll excuse me, I really have to…' I don't bother finishing the sentence. 'Goodbye,' I say, and cut the line.

*

Some time later, George suggests we meet for a drink in London. I'm surprised he's so brazen.

Far too busy, I write. **A crazy day of meetings all over town.** And it's true.

Another time, he writes.

But, the next morning, as I'm moving about my apartment gathering my things for the day, George messages to tell me he's arranged a car for me for the day.

Outside the building, I find a sleek Mercedes with a smartly dressed driver and, again, I'm impressed. It's actually exactly what I need to get me through the day. Reluctantly, I allow the driver to open the door for me and I climb in with my bag and sink into the coolness of the leather seat. I'm annoyed I didn't think of hiring a car myself: it's presumably just an Uber of some sort. Damn it, he's good. I sit in the back of the car, feeling like this is the most delightful thing in the world as the driver pulls into the traffic, and I toy with my phone: common decency says I should thank George, but you have to understand that I really don't want to encourage him. I've said before: I don't do married men. And that means I don't encourage them either. I'm flattered by his attempts to win me over, but there's more to it than that: a part of me is curious to see just how far he'll take this without any encouragement.

A part of me doesn't want him to stop.

TEN

George

Around 10 a.m. I stick my head out of my office and call my assistant. I've been in the office since 8.30 and haven't done a shred of work.

'Rachel! Can I borrow you for a minute?'

She looks up from her desk. 'Shall I bring any client files?'

'No. Just yourself and the project book.'

She raises her eyebrows and goes over to the filing cabinet where she keeps what we call the 'Project X' book.

I pace my office while I wait for her. There are other things I should be thinking about but the need to conquer Stell is consuming me; it's all I can think about, night and day. I'm treating her as if she's a major client I need to win over. And, in a way, she is.

Rachel closes the door behind her. 'How did it go down? The car?'

'He didn't say.' I'm chewing on a little flap of skin at the edge of my nail, careful not to let slip that it's a woman I'm trying to impress. 'They have to have liked it, though. Right?'

'I should imagine so. And the other things? The book? Did the world's pickiest CEO realise it was a first edition?'

'Yes, he said thank you.'

Rachel smiles. 'Good. It took for ever to track that down. So – now what's the plan? Maybe it's time you tried to have a one-to-one meeting?'

I sigh. 'I've tried. I just keep getting blanks.'

'Maybe they're just not interested. Maybe they're going with someone else, or they don't need advertising at this stage.' Rachel sighs. 'Come on, George, it's not as if we need their business specifically. Maybe it's time to draw a line under this one.' Rachel looks at me then and, as she reads my expression, her face softens. She cocks her head to one side.

'Who is it? Is it really a potential client?'

I close my eyes and exhale.

'Is it a woman?'

I shake my head. 'Just someone I was at school with.'

'And you need to settle an old score? Getting their business would mean a lot to you?'

I smile. 'Something like that.'

A look passes between us. I know that she knows I'm lying. I'm sure she suspects it's a woman. It wouldn't be the first time she's had to cover for me when Ness calls. But she's way too professional to admit it.

'Right,' she says, opening the notebook. 'Let's see. What have we done so far? What else can we do? Opera tickets? Theatre?'

I go over to the window and stare out, my hands in my pockets. 'You know what, Rach? I think you're right. I think it's time I tried for another face-to-face meeting.'

ELEVEN

Stella

I'm going to be in your neck of the woods for work on Thursday evening. Fancy meeting for a drink?

I look at the message George has sent. In the format of a yes/no question, it's brave, risking as it does a direct rejection. It's the second time he's asked me to meet him since I left him in the pub and I don't feel that, in the subsequent weeks, I've given him much to go on. He's got balls, I give him that.

I put the phone down and let my thoughts roam. There's no way George is going to be in Hampstead for work. I know enough about him to know that his life is highly unlikely to involve him coming up here at any point. I've googled him, of course I have.

I'm going to be in your neck of the woods for work on Thursday evening. Fancy meeting for a drink?

I pick up the phone. Sure, I type. But perhaps, too, this is the moment it all starts to go wrong. Perhaps this is the tipping point of this story because I know, as I agree to meet George, that my own intentions are greyer than four-day snow.

I don't know how this is going to play out. It's not like me at all.

*

I have to leave work earlier than usual in order to make it back to Hampstead in time for eight, but that's the only concession I make to the evening's arrangements. The perversity of the meeting place is not lost on me: we'd both save time if I just suggested we meet in the West End, but I want George to have to put himself out a little. I go straight to the pub from work. Today, I've had meetings all day – a sponsorship deal and a couple of big corporate accounts – so I'm in a suit, heels, stockings. I don't let myself examine why I decide to let George see me dressed like this instead of nipping home to change: I don't want to know my motivations. I walk faster to distract myself, the clip of my heels ringing out against the noise of the traffic.

He's in the same booth as he was last time; again, a bottle of wine on the table. I note that this time two glasses are poured and it occurs to me that, last time we met, he might have thought that I wouldn't turn up. When he sees me, a smile washes over his face and he stands to greet me; gives me a hug, pulls back and kisses my cheek. Not an air kiss. A proper kiss. Lips on skin. My eyes close. Unintentionally.

I slide onto the bench opposite him and slip out of my suit jacket. Underneath, I'm wearing a sleeveless silk blouse.

'Wow,' says George. 'You look… different.' He's not seen

me in glasses before. I lower my gaze and look at him over the narrow tortoiseshell rims.

'I'm not sure if that's a compliment or not.' I stretch my arms up over my head to release my hair, which has been in a bun all day, and shake it out over my shoulders. It's a flirty move and it surprises me that I do it. 'So, how are you?' I say.

'*Comme ci, comme ça.*' George gives a Gallic shrug. I can feel his eyes on me, sliding over the bare skin of my arms and my throat.

We make small talk for a while, but below the words lies a subtext. The important discussion is non-verbal. Decisions are being made. When I can take it no more, I shift in my seat.

'George,' I say. 'Why are you here with me?'

He leans back in his seat and exhales. 'We're… having a drink?' His face lights up as he smiles.

'No. I don't mean that. I mean why are you here in Hampstead – miles from your home, from your wife – having a drink with me? I know you weren't up here for work. Give me some credit.' I see from his expression that I'm right. 'What do you want from me?'

He has the grace to give me a coy look. 'I think we both know the answer to that.'

I close my eyes, then open them again. I'm going to give decency one last shot. 'But you have Ness,' I say. 'She's beautiful. She always was the beautiful one.'

George's face collapses. 'Oh, Stell… is that what you think?'

I shrug. 'This isn't about what I think. It's about what you're doing here.'

'I know. I know how it looks. "I'm a lucky man; why risk it?" and all that, but…'

'But what? You chose. You had your choice, and you chose Ness.'

'Stell. That's unfair.'

'Is it? Really?'

George closes his eyes. When he opens them again, he starts to speak. 'I'm not happy, Stell. The marriage isn't in a good place.' He shakes his head. 'Marriage!' he snorts. 'I say "marriage" as if what Ness and I have resembles that in any way, shape or form.' He waits but I don't say anything so he carries on. I'm running my finger along the grain of the table while he talks. 'It used to be good, when it was just the two of us and we had nothing. But she changed the moment the money started rolling in. She has no career. She's nothing but "Mrs George – Mrs Advertising". She does nothing all day except pamper herself so she looks good. She's like a footballer's wife. What do you call them? A WAG. Totally vacant.' He knocks his knuckles against his temple. 'Nothing there. It's taken over who she is, Stell; it's all about her image, how she looks. I've forgotten what the real Ness even used to be like.'

I let his words settle, then I say, 'I see.' I'm not going to pass judgement on anyone else's marriage, and I'm certainly not going to sit here criticising Ness with her husband, tempting as it is.

'Ironic, isn't it,' George says when he realises I'm not going to say anything else, 'that my success is only public? Everyone thinks I'm this huge success but, privately, I'm falling apart. If only they could see what goes on at home. It's like the Cold War.' George puts his head in his hands. 'I just don't know what to do.'

The word 'divorce' springs to mind but it's not my place to say it. I give George a weak smile. I will not get involved in other people's marital spats.

'I can't leave her,' says George. 'What would she do without me? I'm her provider.'

I look at the table.

'I know, I know,' says George. 'I'm too soft. Everyone tells me that.' He sighs. 'What I want from life has changed. I'm learning that sometimes things that look the best on the outside aren't perhaps the best on the inside.' George looks meaningfully at me and, despite the backhanded nature of this compliment, I can't look away. He reaches for my hand across the table and the touch of his skin on mine fascinates me. Gently, he strokes the palm of my hand with his thumb. We stare at each other, communicating on a level that has no words. Then I pull my hand away and smile brightly.

'So, how's business?' I ask. The conversation moves on. We finish the wine, drink another bottle; stick to safer topics. George flirts a little, and I don't stop him. Around 10 p.m., he reaches for my hand again, and I let him take it. He leans towards me, his eyes searching my face.

'Stell,' he says, and I know what's coming. I realise now that I've known all along why I picked this pub below the boutique hotel the first time; why I came here tonight, what I've known all along was inevitable. 'Stell,' he says again. 'I want you. Come upstairs with me.'

Right words, wrong order, but I forgive him the slip – it's been seventeen years since that night, after all. I look into George's eyes, those hazel eyes I used to know so well. I search them and I see regret, desire, and, if I'm not mistaken, love.

'Please?' he asks.

I lower my eyes. Inhale. Exhale, then I look back up at him.

George slides a key card across the table. 'Go now. I'll come up in five.'

It's not stealing if it should always have been yours. I take the key card and head for the stairs.

TWELVE

George

There's no time for me to reflect on what happened with Stell: the very next day is my wedding anniversary and Ness, it turns out, has booked us a romantic dinner *à deux* sliding down the Thames on a luxury river cruiser. She's even arranged a cake. It's coming towards us now: a chocolate gateau held majestically aloft by a beaming waitress. Ness moves a candle out of the way and takes my hand across the table.

'I hope you don't mind.' She smiles. 'This is why I've been trying to stop you ordering dessert. I thought they'd never bring it out.'

I squeeze her hand. 'Of course I don't mind.' But I do. I hate showy, public displays of affection: the forced happiness. The hope – followed, inevitably, by the disappointment. It's just so married; so 'meh'.

'I know you wanted a quiet dinner, but – well, it's fourteen years!' Ness is pleased with herself. Has she done this because she knows I'll hate it, or do I just think that because I know I deserve to be punished?

The waitress arrives, places the cake reverentially in the

centre of the table, arranges a knife, two plates, and there it is: 'George & Ness' entwined in dark chocolate italics across a slab of white chocolate atop the cake. Naff, naff, naff.

'Congratulations,' says the waitress. 'Happy anniversary.'

Our fellow diners turn quietly back to their own dinners.

'Shall I?' I ask, picking up the knife.

'Just a little.'

I cut two slices, one marginally smaller than the other, and pass one to Ness.

'Happy anniversary, darling.'

'Happy anniversary. Another year survived.' Ness laughs.

'It's good,' she says, after tasting the cake, and she's right – it is. Gooey, moist and utterly delicious. I wolf it down.

'Did you ever imagine we'd get to fourteen years?' Ness asks.

I look at her. 'What kind of a question is that?'

'It's not that difficult. Back then – when we were eighteen – did you ever imagine us this far down the line? Or did you just think about the present? You know, a bit of fun for the time being. Not really imagine the far distant future?'

'I don't know,' I say. 'What about you? Did you?'

Ness plays with the cake on her plate, pushing it about with her dainty little cake fork. Then she looks up at me.

'Yes, of course I did. When I got married, I knew – hoped! – it was for life. You don't enter into marriage imagining it's not going to be for ever. Do you?'

'Of course not. So, in answer to your question: yes. I did.' I smile at her. 'What's brought all this on?'

She sighs. 'Oh nothing.' She picks up her wine glass and

holds it to her cheek before draining it in one. 'Right, where's the bathroom?'

While she's gone, I pull out my phone. I'm desperate to speak to Stell; find out what she's thinking after last night. The sex blew me away. When I message her, she replies immediately and I type frantically, knowing I only have a couple of minutes. Last night clearly broke some sort of barrier between us but I don't know if she sees it as a one-off, or the start of something new. I try to lead her on, to goad her into talking about it, but her responses are frustratingly ambiguous. Each reply she sends leaves me desperate for more and, for five, maybe ten, minutes, I lose track of where I am and why. When I look up from the screen, I realise that Ness hasn't come back.

Gotta go, I type reluctantly to Stell, while hoping that my disappearing might leave her wanting more, then I stand and look around for Ness. I can't see her in the dining room, so I push open the door to the deck and see her, finally, standing at the railings, staring out at the water. She looks completely, unbearably, alone.

I slip my arms around her waist from behind, getting a face full of hair as I do so, and squeeze her against me, feeling the softness of her waist, where it dips in under her breasts.

'Hey, gorgeous. Do you come here often?' I whisper in her ear, as I nibble her ear lobe. She's stiff for a moment and then I feel her relax into me.

'I was waiting for you,' I tell her, but she sighs and closes her eyes.

'I needed some air,' she says.

'It's lovely out here, isn't it?'

'Yes. London's so beautiful. You get such a different perspective from the river.'

I rest my chin on her shoulder so my eyes are the same level as hers and I get the same view she's getting. She's right. London is beautiful at night. The moon's not quite full and it reflects off the water as the boat moves along, barely breaking the surface. We stand in silence for a few minutes and suddenly I'm imagining that it's Stell in my arms, not Ness. That we'll go home together and it's Stell I'll make love to, Stell who'll be the mother of my child. Oh God, could that ever be possible?

'I love you, Mrs Wolsey,' I say.

Ness gives a tiny laugh. 'I love you too, Mr Wolsey.'

'We'll be docking soon,' I say. 'Come inside. Let's have coffee.'

We walk back in with our arms around each other.

THIRTEEN

Stella

The evening in the pub with George is the beginning, of course, of an affair. More than that: a love affair.

But, love or no love, it means the start of a series of meetings in discreet London hotels. For my own convenience as much as for his, I stop asking George to come all the way to Hampstead. We start meeting in central London. Snatched moments: lunchtimes; afternoons. We have our favourite meeting places as well as what rapidly becomes a 'regular' little boutique hotel in Mayfair, where we act out the pretence that we're married. The hotel realises, I imagine, what's really going on, but the staff play along happily enough. George buys a second phone; pays cash at the hotel. If it wasn't such a cliché, it might be funny.

I'm surprised by how right everything feels. For the first time since I was a teenager, I slowly give myself up to love, enjoying the feeling of well-being with which it infuses me; lapping up the knowledge that I am loved.

But there's a sticking point. An elephant in the room.

He's not mine.

I try not to think about Ness. I'm not the one, after all,

who stood at the altar and promised to be faithful. I don't know how George does it, but, if I concentrate hard enough, if I squeeze my eyes shut when I'm lying in his arms and if I focus on the rhythm of his breathing and inhale the scent of his skin, I can just about pretend that Ness doesn't exist; I can force her from my mind and inhabit a world in which, for an hour or two, for a stolen evening here and there, it's just George and me.

I can lie entwined with George, and imagine that he really is mine.

As he always should have been.

I try not to dwell on how right I feel in George's arms; about how our bodies remember from all those years ago how well they fit together. I really try not to. I throw myself into work; I have client meetings, I'm driving our expansion into corporate clients. It's during this period that I land some brilliant new accounts. People notice. Professionally, I'm on fire.

But then, insidiously, the alien feeling that I no longer want to be alone creeps into my consciousness like the lavender-infused curls of steam I'm watching rise above my bath one evening. I've a glass of wine balanced on the edge of the tub and the radio on a chill-out station – this bath routine is my favourite part of the day, but tonight there it is: the notion that it would be absolutely right for George to be pottering about in the bedroom. Just like that, the thought pops into my head and then, once it's thought, I can't un-think it. I sink under the surface of the water and imagine George coming into the bathroom; I imagine him plucking a warm towel off the rack and holding it out to me. Me stepping into it, George enveloping me with it, then scooping me up and carrying me into the bedroom and, as I imagine this scene, my whole body relaxes.

But this – this feeling that George should not just be in my apartment but in my life – is disconcerting. I'm a loner. Don't get me wrong: I can deal with people well enough but, at the end of the day, I like my own space. Sharing my life is not something I've dreamed of since I was eighteen years old: ironically enough, not since I was a schoolgirl imagining her life with George Wolsey – and that was presumably just because I knew no better. It's quite ridiculous if I think about it that, aged thirty-three, I've gone full loop. I have to be careful when I'm at work, not to daydream of how this life together might play out, but I'm not very successful. Like a creeping fog, George seeps into my day-to-day thoughts.

I picture a house in the country. Not an old heap with rattly single-glazing and leaky pipes but a barn conversion, perhaps, modernised inside. Lots of light and space; the kitchen glossy white; an office for each of us to work from home a couple of days a week. I've always wanted to write a book. The business is ticking over nicely. I could easily take a step back and make time to write. I see myself facing an expansive view of green fields; sucking the end of a pen as I think about my next sentence. But I also picture a small cottage by the sea, roses tangled around peeling blue window frames; a golden retriever running ahead of George and I on the cold, hard sand. Sometimes I imagine a luxury apartment on the river, its picture windows overlooking the glittering lights of the Thames as George and I stand on the terrace on a Friday evening nursing ice-cold gin and tonics. It doesn't matter, I realise, where we live: the important ingredient of this fantasy is George. George and Stell, back together, growing old together. George and Stell together for ever.

Trying to focus on my work, I see George, in jeans and a black sweater, padding into my home office mid-morning with a cup of freshly brewed coffee and 'that' look in his eye… I snap my attention back to the computer screen but it's minutes before my mind wanders again, this time down the corridor of the barn conversion, to an annexe off our bedroom where there might be… I breathe in deeply – it's not too late!… a little nursery. White, with accents of colour. Blue or pink? I don't mind.

I don't know what sex our baby would have been.

I like to think a boy. A tiny version of George, his face crumpled and new.

But I'm no marriage-wrecker. *Walk away*, I tell myself. *Walk away now.*

FOURTEEN

George

We meet, one night, for dinner. An unobtrusive restaurant that I know, with lighting so low it takes a minute for our eyes to adjust, and a lot of red velvet and ostentatious décor. There aren't many tables, but plenty of very private booths. At first glance, the restaurant doesn't look busy but, as we walk through, it becomes apparent that almost all of the booths contain couples – many of them, I imagine, here purely to snatch time away from prying eyes. It's that kind of place to be honest: much as I'd love to show off that I'm with Stell, I'm hardly in a position to go somewhere conspicuous – not with the chance that I might be recognised.

Stell's energy is off-kilter tonight; nothing I can put my finger on – she's just not her usual self. I follow her into our booth, squishing onto the bench seat alongside her, and my hand finds its usual place on her leg under the table. I stroke up and down her thigh through the thin fabric of her skirt, feeling the line of her stocking as the waitress asks if we'd like any drinks to start.

'Champagne!' I say, pointing to a good label on the wine list.

'Champagne?' Stell raises her eyebrows at me once the waitress has gone.

'What?' I raise mine back at her, mock innocence.

'Are we celebrating something?'

I put my hand on the side of Stell's face, pull her towards me and touch my lips to hers. The scent of her makes me tremble with the memory of being inside her.

'Us,' I say. 'We're celebrating us.'

She pulls away just enough so her lips move against my mouth.

'There is no "us", George,' she says quietly. 'You know that.'

I kiss her again, tasting her bottom lip with the tip of my tongue. 'But there is. We're here. Now. Or am I dreaming?'

She pulls away properly this time; smooths my hand off her skirt, suddenly prim. 'George. Please. You and me? We're an illusion. Smoke and mirrors. We don't exist in the outside world.'

I smile. 'Of course we do. We're here, aren't we?' I pinch my arm. 'Ouch. See?'

Stell sighs and shakes her head. 'You know what I mean.'

'Here we are!' says the waitress, presenting the champagne bottle with a flourish. I nod. 'Would you like me to open it?'

'Yes please,' I say, and we watch patiently while she fiddles to remove the foil, then twists the bottle until the cork works its way loose. She pops it discreetly, then carefully fills two flutes, making sure they don't bubble over. I slip my hand back onto Stell's leg under the table and give it a squeeze, but she doesn't look at me.

'I'll just get a cooler for that,' says the waitress, so we wait, once more, till she's back and the bottle's settled in an ice bucket. I pick up a flute and hand it to Stell, then I raise my glass to her.

'To us.'

'To smoke and mirrors, and the illusion of us,' she says.

I take a sip. 'One day, Stell. One day we'll have it all and, together, we'll be glorious.' I don't know where they come from but, once the words are out there, I like them. I give a little nod to confirm I mean them, but Stell rolls her eyes.

'Oh, spare me the advertising talk. We both know exactly what this is.' She looks pointedly at the other couples hiding in booths. 'Let's not make it out to be more than it is, George. It's all it ever was with you and me: sex. In secret.'

'No. You're wrong. You're so wrong.'

'How am I wrong? Tell me!' There's fire in her eyes; a challenge. 'Why are we hidden away in this sleazy restaurant? Why aren't we at the theatre, at some fantastic society party, or out with your friends?' She slumps back on the seat. 'You don't have to answer that. The least you can do is give me the honour of not pretending this is anything more than it is.'

'But Stell…' I'm at a loss for words. This was supposed to be a romantic night out, not a battle. I put my hand on hers. 'Is this our first fight?'

'It's not a fight, George. It's just me calling a spade a spade and you being a prat. I'm under no illusions here.' She takes a glug of champagne. 'I'm your mistress. Nothing more.'

'But…'

'But what?' She spins to face me. 'But you're going to

leave Ness? Oh please! Spare me the crap! It's not going to happen. Let's not pretend it is. This—' she nods her head to the room '—this is all we have. All we'll ever have. This and seedy hotel rooms.'

'They're jolly nice hotel rooms!'

'You know what I mean, "Mr Jones"!' She pauses, takes a breath and I see she's summoning her strength. 'And you know what?' she says, quieter now; self-assured. 'I'm worth more than this.' Another pause. 'I can't – I won't – go on like this.' A breath. 'I think we should end it.'

I stare at her, appalled. 'No. No-no-no. I've not got this far with you to end it before it gets off the ground.'

'What gets off the ground? What exactly? What do you have in mind here? Because I'm not seeing it. I'm seeing you married to Ness and me running around to your beck and call and, frankly, that's not who I am.'

I take her hand. I can't lose her now.

'Stell. Princess. Look at me. Look me in the eye and listen to me. My marriage is dead. It has been for years. Ness and me, we… we live separate lives. We sleep in different rooms.' I imagine this scenario as I talk, convincing myself as I go that this is how it really is. It's as if I'm telling a story. 'Yes! Different rooms. And, if you want to know: it was me who moved out of the bedroom, not her.'

'Really?' She wants to believe me. I can see that she really wants to believe me.

'Anyway, the point is,' I say, warming to my theme, 'I want you to know that this is not about you. Yes, you may be the catalyst that makes me actually get up and want to do something about it, but Ness and I started down this road long before you came on the scene; long before the school reunion.' I laugh. 'God, Stell. When I saw your name under "Going" – wow. I was like a kid waiting for Christmas to come. And then – seeing you there at the bar! I couldn't get over to you fast enough.'

'And then I left.'

I close my eyes, remembering how I'd searched for Stell. How the colour had leached out of the evening when I'd realised that she'd gone. 'Yes,' I say. 'And then you left.'

'Sorry,' she says, and I realise that she's softening; that I'm starting to win her over. 'I didn't know what to make of that "arse" thing,' she says. 'I don't do affairs. I just don't.'

'And nor should you, my princess. Listen, sitting here tonight, I promise you it won't be for much longer. All right? But please don't leave me. I know it's not nice, what we're doing, and I know it's not "you". I know you're worth more, so much more. It's far from perfect, but it won't be for ever.' I lift her chin so I'm looking into her eyes. 'But what is it they say? All's fair in love and war?'

She stares at me, her eyes searching mine.

'Did you say *love*?' she whispers.

I kiss my finger and touch it to her lips. 'Yes, princess,' I whisper back. 'I said love.'

God, I'm good.

FIFTEEN

Stella

As far as my colleagues are concerned, there's nothing unusual about me being the last one left in the office. At 6.15 p.m., my assistant pops her head around the door.

'Don't stay too late, birthday girl!' she says. She hesitates a fraction in the doorway and, although I can see she wants to, she knows better than to ask if I have plans. I wonder if she's thinking she should invite me out for a drink herself: again, she knows better. The remnants of the birthday cake the team made for me sit on the meeting table.

I smile and shake my head. 'I won't. Just finishing up here.'

'Good. 'Night then!' she says.

''Night.'

I wait for her to leave the building before snapping into action. All day I've had an overnight bag stashed under my desk. I take out my make-up bag and, in the bathroom, I go over my face, carefully touching up my foundation, darkening my eyeshadow and, finally, painting my lips siren red. I lock my office door on the way back in, and close all the blinds. My dress – bought specially for the occasion – hangs in a dust cover on the back of the door. Feeling not unlike a schoolgirl changing into her miniskirt in the school loos, I slip out of my suit and pants and into the dress, smoothing it over my bare hips as I step into the shoes I bought to match. Finally, I apply my signature scent to the pulse points on my wrists and throat, then I spray it liberally into the air above my head and let the cloud of fragrance envelop me, scenting my hair and clothes. George has, I know, an exceptional olfactory memory.

Finally, I take a look at my reflection in the glass of the office door and give myself a little nod: I'll do. It's the first time I've made such an effort specifically for George. But then I'm impressed with the way he's managed my birthday. First, he remembered. Had he forgotten, I wouldn't have said a thing – I'm not one to make a fuss of these things – but he remembered. And he's made all the arrangements for tonight himself.

'Wear something nice, Stell,' he said, 'I'm taking you somewhere special.'

That's all I could extract from him, even in those vulnerable post-coital moments when his brain turns to mush. I wonder how far this is going. Is tonight to be the night we finally get to sleep a full night in each other's arms? We've talked about it – dreamed about it – yet never done it. Will he manage to get away?

My phone beeps and I see that the car George has arranged to take me to the mystery destination is waiting. I gather up my things and lock the office before slipping into the car.

'Evening,' I say to the driver. 'Do you know where we're going?'

'Yep,' he says, misunderstanding my meaning, and I realise I don't want him to know that I don't know where I'm going myself, so I sit silently, trying to second-guess my destination at every junction. The car finally pulls up outside a smart hotel adjacent to Hyde Park.

'Here we are, miss,' says the driver. I reach for my purse. 'Don't worry. It's on account,' he says and I feel a surge of gratitude to George. This is how dating should be. My heels click on the marble as I walk into the lobby and my hair – blow-dried at lunchtime – bounces with every step. I feel like a film star and I'm expecting George to appear stage left or right, beaming and ready to escort me to dinner, but I don't see him so I wander towards a cluster of tables and perch on a seat, where I people-watch while I wait. Hellos and goodbyes play out; airport taxis pull up and leave; bellboys whisk luggage from car to reception and back again. Aware then that time is passing, I check my watch: 7.20 p.m. The table's booked for 7.30 and George told me it was important we were on time. I message him but the message isn't read. I can see that George hasn't been online for thirty minutes. Is he on the Underground? It seems unlikely; he's more of a taxi guy. I check my phone obsessively until 7.25, when I stand up and walk over to reception.

'Hello. You have a restaurant reservation for Stella Simons tonight… can you tell me which restaurant it's in?' I love that the receptionist doesn't raise an eyebrow about why I might have a reservation and not know where: she simply picks up the phone and finds out, then directs me down to the signature restaurant – the one that's spearheaded by 'that' celebrity chef who's currently generating much buzz and column inches for his unique style. Since I'd arrived at the hotel, I'd hoped it might be that one that George had booked, but I would never presume. *Nice.*

At the entrance to the restaurant, they're expecting me.

'Miss Simons?' asks the maître d', then escorts me to an anteroom, where I'm introduced to two well-dressed couples clutching glasses of champagne. Until this moment, I've held out hope that maybe George is waiting for me at the restaurant, perhaps with some sort of surprise lined up. The surprise, unfortunately, is that he's not here. A waiter hands me a flute of champagne.

'One more guest?' the maître d' asks the waiter quietly. He looks at his watch. 'We wait a few more minutes, but…'

I smile vaguely at the other couples and give a little shrug. It's not me who's late.

The maître d' moves to the front of the room.

'Welcome to the Chef's Table experience,' he says reverentially. 'Tonight we have for you a very special experience. A *unique* experience. You will start the evening with a tour of the kitchens, during which you can see and experience for yourselves the high-octane atmosphere of a Michelin-starred kitchen. Then we will take you to the chef's table where you will be joined by our executive chef, who has prepared a special eight-course tasting menu for your enjoyment. We have, too, a dedicated sommelier for you tonight who has paired each dish with a wine from our cellars.' The two couples make excited faces at each other and I check my phone one more time: George is still offline. The maître d' rubs his hands together, then turns to me. 'Madam… the other guest… your companion… will be here soon?'

I shrug. 'I'm sorry. I hope so…' I hold up my phone as if they all can see George is offline. 'He's not responding. But he's never late, so…'

The maître d' nods. 'We will wait five minutes.'

The other couples turn to each other and start to make small talk. I put my phone to my ear and move away from the group with a smile, disinterested in where they work and how much they're looking forward to this evening. While they chat, I pace. Honestly: it's excruciating. I'm relieved when the maître d' steps forward with a pained look on his face. He gives a little bow.

'I hope you don't mind if we begin. The kitchen is expecting us now and it's important that we…'

'It's fine,' I say. 'Please. Let's start. I'm sure my companion will be here any second.'

As we walk around the kitchen, looking into pots and listening to the executive chef detail a little about the history and conception of each dish, my mind's not on cooking but on George; I'm half expecting his hand on my hip at any moment as he steps up behind me and joins the tour. A shiver runs through me as I picture him realising that I'm not wearing any underwear.

'This is a recipe I initially learned from my grandmother,' a chef is telling us as he hands around tiny saucers of rabbit. I throw the morsel in my mouth in one go, registering subconsciously how the meat's so tender it practically dissolves on my tongue. I'm not a fan of game, but the taste is exquisite.

Why isn't George here? Has something happened to him? He wouldn't miss an experience like this through choice. He must either be caught up in traffic or some sort of security alert, sick, or have had an accident. I balance my phone in my hand beneath the saucer, waiting to feel the buzz of a message come in, yet I'm surprised when it finally does. Even though the chef is speaking, I ditch the saucer on a countertop and pull up the message. Princess. I'm so sorry. I'm not going to make it. Will make it up to you. Promise. X

The group moves ahead as I type my reply.

What happened? Are you OK?

I'm fine. It's Ness. She's sick. I have to go. Will try to message later.

Ness.

My heart's suddenly hammering and I see red. I know it's a cliché but I really do. The room seems to recede as my vision clouds. I shove my phone back into my bag without gracing George's text with a reply, and I go over to the group, a bright smile on my face. I should have been an actress.

'I'm so sorry,' I say loudly so everyone can hear me over the bustle and noise of the kitchen. 'I'm going to have to leave. My partner isn't able to make it after all. Have a lovely evening!'

'Oh no!' says one of the women. She turns away from the group and I can see she looks genuinely concerned. But the pity in her eyes hurts me more than George's no-show. 'Why don't you stay?' she says. 'You're here now and we won't bite!'

'Well, only the food!' says the other woman. They giggle.

'Thanks, but it's fine. I'll reschedule.'

'Aww, come on!' The first woman tries to grab my arm and pull me over but I shrug her off.

'It's fine. Really. All the more for you. Have a lovely evening.'

I spin on my heel and leave the kitchen. I stop briefly in the anteroom, where the waiter's tidying up the champagne glasses.

'Did my companion guarantee the booking with a credit card?'

'Yes… yes, it's policy.'

'He can't make it, so please charge whatever cancellation fee you need to his card, thank you.'

'I'm afraid at such late notice, you will be charged the full price.' The waiter shakes his head apologetically.

'That's fine,' I say. 'And, while you're at it, please send the group a bottle of champagne. That one we had earlier? Just add it to the bill, thanks.'

I walk back through the hotel lobby and signal for a black cab, barely registering the activity going on around me. My mind's racing: I'm remembering Ness's phone call to me after the reunion; the warning tone in her voice: 'Will you stay in touch, do you think?'

While the taxi weaves its way through Friday-night London traffic, I open Facebook on my mobile, and there, in among the notifications, I find Ness's message: 'Happy birthday, Stella! Hope you're having a lovely evening! Xx'

Sick? She's not sick: she's clever. *George!* I think. *How can you be so gullible?* And then, as the taxi draws up outside my apartment block, I remember a simple fact that sends me to the wine bottle before I even take my shoes off: he's not mine. Ness has every right to pull rank on my birthday because George is not mine.

SIXTEEN

George

When I put the key in the lock, I don't know whether I'm worried about Ness or angry with her for making me miss Stell's birthday dinner. I'd told her I had a very important 'client dinner'.

'Please can you come?' she'd said. 'I've been throwing up all day and I… I just need you.'

'I can't, hon. I'm sorry, but these people are in town for one night only.'

'Can you send someone else?'

'I would if I could, hon, but it's me they want.'

'George, please? I need you.' Her voice was hoarse from vomiting.

'Is there no one else you can call? Just till I get home?'

She'd gone quiet then, and I'd caught myself: am I such a monster that I won't go to my sick wife when she needs me? Because I'm out with my lover? I'd paced the office, torn between burning desire to see Stell and the duty I felt to go home to Ness.

'I'm sorry. Of course I'll come. You're right. I'll get Adam to go to the dinner. I'm sure the client won't mind and – well, if they do…'

'. . . if they do, perhaps they're not the sort of client you want.'

'Exactly.'

And so I stop at Waitrose on the way home and pick up a bunch of guilt flowers for Ness.

'Honey!' I call as I push open the door but there's no reply. The light's on in the living room so I look there first and, bingo, there she is, sprawled, fast asleep on the sofa, her hair spread all over the cushions. I stand over her for a minute, wondering whether to wake her up or just make her more comfortable there on the sofa, when I notice something in her hand and my whole body stiffens. A pregnancy test.

'Oh my God! Ness! Is it? What is it? Are we… ?' I squeeze my hands into fists, not sure whether to take the test from her hands or wait for her to tell me. Ness's eyes snap open and she pushes her hair out of her eyes as she struggles to sit up, her hand clamping back around the test. Slowly, she registers me standing there and her face breaks into a huge smile. She holds the test out to me.

'Here, look.'

'What is it? What does it mean?'

'Read it!'

So I look at the test, and I see that it says one word and one word only: 'Pregnant'.

'Oh my God! Ness! Does this mean… ?'

She nods.

'Oh my God! There's no doubt?'

'Well. You can get false negatives, but I don't think you get false positives, so…'

'I'm going to be a dad?'

'Yes.'

I fling myself down on the sofa next to her and scoop her into my arms, hugging her to me and kissing her face and her hair. She clings on to me.

'You're happy about this?' she asks.

'Of course I'm happy! Why wouldn't I be happy?' I swear I want a baby more than she does; I long to see that little crumpled face that looks like a brand-new, old-age version of me. 'Oh my God, oh my God. I can't believe it! You clever thing! How?'

'George! You know exactly how!'

'But – when?'

'You remember that night your client cancelled? I reckon it was then.'

'But why now?'

'Oh I don't know, George! Stop analysing it! Maybe the time's right. Maybe the stars aligned and a pink unicorn sprinkled some fairy dust over our house. I don't know.'

I look at her and maybe I'm imagining it but already there seems to be a radiance about her. Suddenly I feel very protective of her. She's carrying the most precious cargo in the world: my child.

'Come on,' I say. 'Let's get you to bed. You need your sleep now, more than ever. You both do.' I take her hand

and lead her up to the bedroom where we fall asleep in each other's arms.

At the very back of my mind, behind everything else, just one dark cloud: Stell.

SEVENTEEN

Stella

I don't contact George again after my birthday. He texts a little – though not as much as I'd have imagined, to be honest – but I delete his messages as soon as they come in, without even reading them. Was he the one let down on his birthday? Humiliated in front of strangers?

Instead, I spend all weekend alone. When the chips are down, you can rely only on yourself in this life. *Remember that!* I tell myself. Walking on the heath and passing time in coffee shops, I take the full blame for the debacle of my birthday night and berate myself with every step. George was played by Ness. This I see, and he's an idiot not to see. But there's a reason why I never get involved with married men and it's just as valid with George as it is with anyone else. Yes, he was my George and yes, he should be my George, but he's married. End of.

'It's sleazy, Stella, it's seedy and it's *not you*!' I say out loud lying on my sofa on Sunday afternoon. 'I don't care who he is, it stops now.' I get out my old notebook with the wedding dresses and the signatures and throw it in the bin without looking at it, then I toast my decision with a glass of good wine and some olives and start to feel a little better.

By the time I return to work early on Monday morning, I'm almost myself again, excited about what the coming working week will bring as I head towards the office, and then I see him – George – standing outside the office door looking absolutely freezing despite his winter coat. My first instinct is to run into his arms, then I remember what he did and I want to dodge him and walk the other way but he's looking out for me and already he's seen me. I stop and look at him.

'What brings you here?'

He takes a step towards me, his hands held out. 'Stella. Stell. Please.' I notice that his knuckles are rudely red next to the white of his fingers. His nose, too, is red, and his face is pinched with cold. He stamps his feet on the pavement, his breath coming out in clouds.

'Please what?' I say.

'Please don't be like this.'

'Like what?'

'Like this!'

'I'm not being like anything. I'm just trying to unlock the office. It's eight o'clock on Monday morning, and I have a company to run – as do you.' While I fumble for the keys in my bag, George tries to pull me round and hug me but I stand stiffly, my face averted. He lets his arms drop.

'I'm sorry about your birthday,' he says. 'You've no idea how sorry I am, but I couldn't help it.'

'OK,' I say, unlocking the door. 'Have a good day.'

'Is this it?' he asks. 'Is this how it's going to be?' His voice is sodden with sadness and something catches in my chest.

I turn to face him. 'How's Ness?'

A micro-pause. 'She's much better, thanks.'

'What was wrong?'

'She was sick. Vomiting. A bug, I guess.'

'Did you see her throw up?'

George flinches. 'What?'

'She wished me a happy birthday on Facebook that morning. She said, "hope you're having a lovely evening – kiss, kiss".'

'You can't read anything into that!'

I shrug. 'Whatever.'

'She was sick, Stell. Don't be like this.'

'Like what?' I know it sounds arrogant to assume that Ness feigned sickness to stop him seeing me on my birthday – especially when she doesn't know about our affair – but I know I'm right.

'You know she's already warned me off you?' I say. 'She called me after the reunion. Did you know that?'

'What?'

'You heard me. She's not stupid. Did you actually see her throw up? Did you see vomit come out of her mouth? Even once?'

George shakes his head slowly. 'Look. Whatever you're implying, you're wrong. Trust me.'

We stare at each other and I realise there's something he's not telling me; that there's more to this and that, in our little trio, I'm the only one who doesn't know. I look away.

'Look. I don't know what's going on with you and Ness, and I don't care. It's none of my business. But just know that she's manipulating you. Don't be gullible. That's all I'm saying.'

Saying the words out loud, I feel so mean; so petty. 'Why am I even standing here on the pavement discussing with you whether or not your wife was sick? The point is you say I'm your "everything" but I'm not. Not at all. I'm only your "everything" when it suits you. As I said before, it's not who I am. This is not my life and I will not continue like this!' I'm embarrassed to realise I'm shouting.

'Stell. I'm sorry. I stuffed up.' He's scuffing the pavement with his toe.

'Let's just say I've learned my lesson,' I say. 'That's all. Now I have to get to work. Have a good day.'

I give George a peck on his cold cheek, then I open the door and step inside the office reception. I try to shut the door behind me but he holds it.

'Stell, please.'

We tussle for a moment and, again, I'm struck with how undignified this is. Never in my life have I aspired to be a woman who tussles with her lover on the doorstep of her office. I peel George's cold fingers off the door.

'Let go, please, George. I need to get into work. Goodbye.'

I shut the door in his face.

EIGHTEEN

George

Stell stops taking my calls and refuses to answer my messages. She doesn't even check Facebook – all my messages sit there unread. It's as if she's blocked me from her life – and of course that makes me desperate. Like an addict, I check all my social media obsessively, monitoring whether or not she's online. If she is, I never catch her.

So I try to focus on Ness, but the initial excitement about the pregnancy starts to wear thin: she's capricious, sick a lot, tired all the time, and lets me know in no uncertain terms that I can forget about sex until she starts to feel better. It's too early for a scan so we don't even have one of those grainy pictures to look at. Sometimes I wonder if I imagined the whole thing.

Meantime, on the long evenings in front of the television when Ness is in bed, I can't stop thinking about Stell. Do I love her? I want her. I want to possess her. I want to be the most important thing in her life. I *need* to be the most important thing in her life; I need her to look at me as if I'm her sun, her moon and her stars. I'm obsessed with her. Is that love? I think so.

And then another thought: what if it was Stell, not Ness, having my baby? The thought makes me catch my breath. I close my eyes and imagine me and Stella in bed, my hands sliding over the tautness of her swollen belly, feeling the movements of my child under her skin. I imagine making love gently, gently to a pregnant Stella.

I'm not religious, but I say a little prayer. *Please, God. Somehow.*

And then reality slams me in the face. The love of my life is expecting me to leave my wife, but my wife is pregnant. I know I've sunk low sometimes, but leaving a pregnant woman? I can't do it.

So what can I do? How can I buy myself time?

Could I tell Stell that Ness is sick? Something that means I have to stay with her for a few more months to 'support' her and 'help' her? I stare blankly into the middle distance, tapping my forehead as I work through my ideas. If Ness was allegedly going for regular treatments, I could even come to her antenatal appointments. I'd come out of it smelling like roses on both sides.

And then the solution hits me: cancer.

A curable one, of course: I wouldn't want to give Stell the impression Ness is dying. I don't want to tempt fate. But yes: cancer's a good bet. A small one, caught early but requiring seven or eight months of treatment.

Sad face: *I'm so sorry, Stell, but I can't leave her right now.*

Yes, it's perfect. I give myself a silent high-five.

And so, I wait outside Stell's office again. All afternoon, I sit in the Greek-run sandwich shop across the road, one eye on my coffee, one on the office door. But, as afternoon turns to evening and darkness sets in, I start to wonder if she's even there. Then, around eight, just as I'm about to give up, I see the door open and, finally, it's her. I sprint across the street.

'Stell!'

'How long have you been waiting?' Stell locks the office door as she speaks, her eyes not meeting mine.

'Since half-four.' I nod at the sandwich shop. 'I was in there quite a bit. Great coffee. Kept me awake.' Instinctively, I reach to touch her arm, but she jerks it away from me and starts to walk down the pavement towards the Tube station. I dash to catch up.

'Stell. Wait!'

'What? I told you how it's going to be. I don't do affairs.'

'I know. Please come with me. Come for a quick drink. I need to talk to you.'

'About what?'

'About stuff.'

'What sort of stuff?'

'There's something I need to tell you. About Ness.'

She stops and turns, a flash of hope in her face. 'What is it? Have you left her?'

I swallow. 'Not here. Come with me.' I tug at her arm, and am surprised that she lets me guide her by the elbow to the nearest bar. We stand awkwardly as I order drinks. Below ground is a second bar that's quieter. Like a couple on a first date, we each carry our own glass down the spiral staircase, and I lead Stell over to a table. We're the only people there yet suddenly the room seems tiny – claustrophobic – and the walls close in on me, the paint a dark red that makes me think of torture, burning and hellfire.

We settle, then I pick up my drink, well aware that, should she ever find out about Ness's pregnancy or my lies, it could very well be the last time I ever have a drink with her. I look at her: at her glossy hair, her eyes, the cool paleness of her skin, the long legs slanted to cross under the table. I stare at her, taking it all in: I can't lose her. I can't.

Neither can I tell her the truth.

I lift my glass. 'Cheers.'

We clink glasses but Stell puts hers straight back down. She's on the edge of her seat, her coat still on, a smile playing around those gorgeous lips.

'So. Tell me,' she says. 'What about you and Ness?' Her tone is playful and I know she's waiting for me to say that I've left her; that I've moved out and started divorce proceedings.

I rub the back of my neck. 'Stell. This time without you has been hell. It's made me realise that it's you I love; it's you I want to spend the rest of my life with.'

She raises her eyebrows at me but doesn't say anything. I have her attention. I drop my voice and reach for her hand. 'I want everything with you: the wedding, the house, growing old together… you know it was always supposed to be…'

'A baby?' Her voice is a whisper. 'Do you want a baby with me?'

I close my eyes. 'Yes. I want to have a baby with you.'

Stell sits perfectly still. I can see she's holding her breath. I pull her into my arms and stroke her hair. 'I can't stop thinking about you. I need you in my life. We'll make it happen, I promise.' I pause. 'Please remember that. Because there's something else I have to tell you. And it's not good.'

She exhales. 'OK?'

'I'm going to leave Ness. That is one hundred per cent certain.' I pause. 'But the bad news is it might take a bit longer than I thought.'

'How come?' Stell takes a sip of her drink and puts her glass down hard. A little wine slops onto the table. I stare at the splash on the dark wood of the table, and then I start to speak in a monotone.

'She found a lump in her breast. She's had a mammogram and a scan and it's not looking good.'

'Oh my God.' Stell presses her hand over her mouth. 'I'm so sorry.'

'The doctor was very concerned,' I say. 'They're going to do a biopsy.' Stell's hanging on to my every word.

'We're hoping it's early stages,' I say, almost convincing myself. 'But the main thing is, she's in the right hands now.' I hope she doesn't question me further. What I've now said is the sum total of my knowledge about breast cancer.

Stell's nodding. 'That's good. There's a good chance of beating it if you catch it early.'

'I know. I'm trying to keep her spirits up but obviously there are a lot of unknown quantities at this stage. The point is I just feel I would be a real schmuck to leave her right now. I just couldn't live with myself. I think the doctor said that if treatment was needed, it would likely go on for a few months. So I need to be around for a while longer.

Take her to appointments and look after her if she's sick at home. She's got no one else.'

As I say this, I'm thinking ahead to when the baby's born. Then what will I do? I'll worry about that later. Solutions always magic up from somewhere. The point is that, for now, I've staved off a crisis. And Stell is reacting just as I hoped she would.

'Is this why you couldn't come for my birthday?'

I nod. 'Exactly. She'd just found out. She was in pieces. Understandably.'

She puts her hand on mine. 'It's OK,' she says. 'I get it. You'd be a monster not to stay.'

'Thank you, princess,' I say. 'Just say you'll be there for me. Say you want me. That's all I need to hear from you. We'll get through this, I promise.' I lift her chin so I'm staring into her eyes.

'Yes,' Stell whispers, and I touch my lips to hers.

'I love you,' she says.

Bullet dodged, Wolsey. Bullet dodged.

NINETEEN

Stella

I practically skip to the Tube station. OK, I feel bad for Ness, but I don't have the slightest doubt she'll make a full recovery. As George says, she caught it early and she's getting treatment. Knowing George, it will be with the best private doctors around.

But the news about Ness pales into insignificance when I think about the other things that George said. As I strap-hang home, the train throwing me about as it speeds through its tunnels, I'm barely aware of my surroundings. All I can think of is George's words.

I want to have a baby with you.

These are the words I longed to hear, alone in my bedroom at eighteen with a ball of cells multiplying in my belly. They've been a long time coming and they fall on me like balm, unlocking something that lies deep inside me. While I try consciously not to nourish it, this seed George has planted starts to take root.

I want to have a baby with you.

I push it away but it comes back, bigger and stronger:

I want to have a baby with you.

*

We're soon running at full speed again. If George is attending appointments with Ness, he shields me from them. We barely speak about her, and he never misses dates he's arranged with me. Meanwhile, since the night he told me about her lump, something's changed: we're closer. I no longer feel like a mistress stealing moments, but a wife-in-waiting. We make love with our eyes open, drinking in each other's face, and I feel like I can see into George's soul. I feel myself softening; a sense of ice melting. I'm less obsessive at work – I delegate more while I let myself daydream about what it might be like to have a family.

Even George notices a difference in me. I'm kinder, more pliable and I start to feel that this life, this love, really could be mine. It's like a shedding of layers – the layers of protection I've worn since the day George walked out on me. I start smiling at strangers. I find myself looking at other people's children, noticing for the first time not their raucous screams but the joy in their smiles, the pearly whiteness of their tiny teeth and the pudginess of their squidgy little hands.

One lunchtime I'm in Boots, being jostled by the lunchtime crowd. The heating's up too high; industrial fans are blasting hot air into the store. I'm sweating under my coat and suit, the air's too dry on my skin, and my hair's gone static. I find myself in the vitamins section. Before I know it, I'm holding a jar of folic acid supplements in my hand and wondering if I should buy them. I feel naughty, like I'm a teenager caught by my mum with a packet of condoms in my hand. Folic acid is for those respectable women who plan babies – to date it's never featured in my life plans, but George's words have pierced me deep inside: I can't stop thinking about getting pregnant and, if I have a baby, I want it to have the best chances in life. I'm passionate about this: an apology, perhaps, to the baby whose life I prevented from starting.

I stand still, people pushing past me down the narrow aisle, and I remember the feeling of those first days of pregnancy: the tingling breasts, the unshakeable feeling that there was something growing in my belly. Back then, it caused nothing but horror but, now, I long to feel it again. I smile to myself: this time I'll do it right. I put the tablets in my basket and take them to the checkout, where I catch the cashier's eye. She doesn't say anything, but she smiles, and I know she knows. I feel like I'm joining a secret club.

Maybe now the time is right.

TWENTY

George

Stell's late to our hotel one day and I loiter about the room wondering what to do. It crosses my mind to wait, naked, on the bed but, as I'm undoing my trousers, I think maybe that's too presumptuous. So I stand at the window, watching the street below, but the angle's not right for me to see the hotel entrance so I can't see if she's arriving.

Time stretches. I make an espresso, clicking a pod into the machine and inhaling the aroma as the machine vibrates and coffee splashes into the cup. When I hear the click of the door – half an hour late – I'm pacing the room. I turn and catch my breath as she wafts in: that face; that hair; those eyes; those lips – where Ness has curves, Stell is all drama, edges and adrenalin. My cock stiffens.

'Princess!' I cross the room in two strides and stop in front of her. She makes no apology, no explanation, for her tardiness – neither do I want her to. We stand, centimetres apart, for a moment, taking each other in, then I lean in, push her hair back from her face and kiss her softly on the lips. 'How are you?'

She doesn't reply, just steps around me without speaking

and starts to undress, slowly removing her clothes in what I'm sure is a tease show until she's left only in stockings and heels. Then she lies back on the bed and starts to touch herself, her hands sliding over and into the flesh I'm desperate to taste. All the while she does it, she's watching me with her eyes half closed, moaning. I move to join her, my hands on my belt buckle, but she shakes her head.

'Oh no. Not yet.'

Dear God, she makes me watch until I can't bear it, then, finally, she rolls onto her front and slips a pillow under her hips.

'Fuck me.'

I realise, as I come, gasping, inside her, that in the heat of the moment I forgot to use a condom.

As we lie together afterwards, I stroke her taut belly, so different to Ness's, which, while I can't yet feel the bump, is starting to thicken. 'Oh God, Stell, I'm so sorry.'

She smiles. 'Are you really? You said you wanted a baby with me.'

Before I can reply, she jumps out of bed and heads into the bathroom and I lie there contemplating how I'd cope with both my wife and my lover pregnant. If you sat me down and made me pick one of them at this point, I'm pretty sure I'd pick Ness. Not so much through love but because she's carrying my child and it's the right thing to do. Just think of the bad press I'd get for leaving her pregnant. But, wow, if Stell was pregnant too, it would change everything. The thought is both terrifying and and exciting.

I'm this far into my thoughts when she reappears wrapped in

a towel. I watch as she steps back into her clothes. She sits on the edge of the bed as she rolls her stockings back up her legs – usually she makes a show of it for me – it's often a sticking point that delays my return to the office but today she does it matter-of-factly, turning her body so I can't see the stretch of her legs as she eases the stockings up her thighs and I wonder if she's cross with me about the condom; if it's reminded her of that awful time when we were eighteen. Sometimes she's so difficult to read. She re-buttons her blouse and slips back into her skirt. Then she stands in front of the mirror and puts her hair back up ready to return to the office. I'm still naked on the bed watching her – drinking her in – my hands behind my head.

'I've got a proposition for you,' she says.

'Go on.' My body tenses. It's amazing what you can think in a fraction of a second. I imagine her asking if she can run away with me; emigrate to New Zealand and start a new life where nobody knows who we are.

'Would you like to stay over at mine one night?' Her tone is casual and she says it to the mirror, not to my face. I'm not sure I heard right. She's never, ever invited me to stay over. On the contrary, she's made it clear that her apartment is her space and hers alone; that she doesn't want anyone else 'polluting the energy' or some such crap. I push myself up onto my elbows.

'Did you just say what I think you did?'

'Maybe. What did you think I said?'

'Did you… Did you just invite me to sleep at your place?'

Stell pushes the final pin into her hair and turns to face me. 'I believe I just did, Mr Wolsey. So what do you think?'

I jump up and put my arms around her, even though I'm naked.

'Yes!'

'No excuses this time.'

'Absolutely. I will move heaven and earth to make it happen,' I say. 'Just watch me.'

TWENTY-ONE

Stella

I leave work on time the night that George is due to stay over. Earlier that week he'd started to tell me what plans he'd put in place to buy us our night together. We were in bed in the hotel, and I was lying half on top of him. I held my hand over his mouth.

'I don't want to know.'

'Fine,' he'd said, struggling to free his head from under my hand. 'Just know that it's foolproof. There's nothing – *nothing* – she can do to get me to go home.' He'd taken my finger in his mouth and given it a gentle bite. I rolled off him.

'Good.'

George reached out an arm and pulled me back towards him. 'Nothing short of an act of God will get me out of your bed once I'm in it.'

Now, as I take a cab back to Hampstead, I run through the preparations I've made. I should have an hour at home before George arrives. The groceries will have been delivered during the day – the concierge will have let the delivery guy in; ditto the flowers, which I briefed the florist to arrange 'casually' around the apartment, like they've just been thrown into vases. The cleaner will have been, and the place should be gleaming even more than usual. In my bag, I have a paper bag of fresh rose petals to scatter in the bathtub, and there's a bottle of champagne in the fridge. It's a complicated dish I'm cooking for supper, but I've done a dummy run so I know exactly how to time it. It's crucial that everything tonight is one hundred per cent easy and natural. Everything about tonight will say to George: this – this luxury, this easiness, this sexiness – could be yours, with a baby thrown in as well. You could have it every day.

Up in my apartment, I change into cropped blue jeans and a cream silk shirt. My feet are bare on the parquet floor; my long hair loose. Let Ness dress like a show pony in her bright colours and designer dresses, but I know what George likes. There are crisp white sheets on the bed; the duvet looks pristine, like a hotel. I light the scented candles I've scattered throughout the bedroom and the en suite and nod at the soft light they throw around the room.

Back in the hallway, I walk over to the front door and turn to face the apartment, imagining how George will see it for the first time: the small entrance hall facing the doors to the bedrooms; turn the corner, then the huge expanse of parquet flooring that decks the open-plan living, dining and kitchen area. White paintwork, cream sofas and curtains; the only splashes of colour coming from the carefully chosen art that hangs on the walls, and one feature wall in a shade of grey so rich it verges on teal. I don't know what George's house is like, but I imagine it's all to Ness's taste. Some may call mine a cold apartment. I appreciate that, but it's very me: clean, uncluttered, no drama.

I wonder what it'll look like with George inside it.

TWENTY-TWO

George

I ring the bell of Stell's building bang on eight and wait, stamping my feet in the cold, for the porter to buzz me in. Then I take the lift up and pause for a moment as the doors open at Stell's floor. The hallway is opulent in a way you usually only see in five-star hotels. A thick rug sits on a polished marble floor, the lines of its pattern leading the eye towards just the one walnut front door. Discreet spotlights highlight architectural flower arrangements that sit on incidental tables, and the smell – the smell is, for lack of a better word, 'rich'. I've never been a fan of apartment living – I prefer the kookiness of a period house – but I can't help be impressed. Stell owns this place; I'm sure she once said she bought it outright.

I pad across the carpet and tap at the door, holding myself still as I listen for the sound of her walking towards it on the other side. I take a couple of deep breaths, trying to slow my heartbeat, then, suddenly, she opens the door.

'Hey,' she says. 'You made it. Come in.' She's barefoot in jeans and holding a glass of white wine. She smiles, then walks back down the hallway. I drop my bag in the hall and follow her, catching her by the waist before she turns the corner into what I presume will be the living area.

'Hey! Where's my kiss?'

She turns in my arms and kisses me gently, holding her wine glass carefully out of the way. Her shirt rises and my hands find the soft, bare skin of her waist. She pulls away.

'Come.' She turns and leads me down the hall.

On the threshold of the living room, I stop, genuinely stunned. The blinds are open and the lighting's low so I can see the lights of the city twinkling outside.

'Wow. It's amazing!' I go to the window and put my hands up to the glass to see better outside. 'What a view!'

Stell smiles. 'Good, isn't it? What can I get you to drink?'

'Whatever you're having.'

The kitchen is open-plan. Stell pulls champagne out of the fridge. 'I thought we could toast our first night together?'

'Perfect.'

'Here – let me.' I hold out my hand for the bottle but Stell shakes her head.

'No. Tonight you're my guest. Sit down. Relax and enjoy. I'll make you work later!' She winks at me lasciviously, then pulls two glasses out of the freezer and deftly opens the champagne.

'Cheers,' she says, as we clink the glasses.

'To waking up tomorrow morning with the most beautiful woman in the world in my arms.'

Stell laughs. 'Are you OK sitting here while I do a few bits in the kitchen? I thought we'd get dinner over quickly so we have the rest of the evening…'

She tips some stuffed olives and cashew nuts into a dish and places them on the counter next to me. I think back: have I told her that they're my favourite? That I never get them at home because Ness is allergic? Maybe not. Stell pads about in the kitchen, a tea towel slung over her shoulder. I can't get used to seeing her in this domestic role. It's like seeing a whole new facet of her and, for the first time – ever if I'm honest – I wonder what it would be like to be married to Stell. Would every night be like this?

'How was your day?' she asks so I prolong the fantasy by telling her a funny anecdote about something that happened in the office today, just as I would to Ness. When I finish, I throw a cashew into the air and catch it in my mouth. Stell gives me a sideways look that's not totally approving.

'Right,' she says. 'I think we're ready for the starters.'

'What can I do? Can I carry something?'

She hands me the wine and two fresh glasses. 'Pop these on the table while I plate up the starter.'

My phone rings. I kill it without even looking at the screen. 'Sorry.'

We take our places at the dining table.

'Thank you,' I say. 'This looks wonderful.' And I'm not lying. She could serve roadkill tonight and I'd eat it gratefully.

'I hope so. *Bon appetit*.'

I'm not even one mouthful into the starter when my phone rings again. I kill it again without looking, but still, now I'm wondering who it is who wants to get hold of me so urgently at this time.

'Mmm. It's delicious.' I take another forkful and chew appreciatively. My phone rings again and I sit back and stare aggressively at it, my lips pressed together.

'Sod's Law,' I say. 'I'm sorry.'

'Take it,' Stell says.

'Do you mind?'

'Of course not.'

I look at the screen: it's Ness. I've promised Stell nothing will get in the way tonight. I cut the call.

'Work,' I say, returning my attention to Stell. 'Is this one of your signature dishes? It's incredible. The flavours are exquisite.'

'It's not. I developed this one just for you, tonight. And thank you.'

My phone buzzes. I look at it. What in God's name does she want?

'Maybe you should check it,' Stell says. 'Sounds like it might be important.'

I look at her, sizing up whether or not she means it; whether she might be doing that thing of saying one thing and meaning the opposite.

'If it's going to bother us till you answer it,' she says, 'then get it over with. Please.'

'Thanks.' I stand up and walk over to the window to read the message and the bottom falls out of my stomach. I stifle a gasp.

'What is it?' Stell asks. 'What's happened?'

I turn to her, turning the phone from her so she can't see the text. 'Oh my God. Nothing. Nothing like that. But I'm sorry. You're right. It's important. A crisis at work. I need to deal with it now. I need to make a call. How do you open this?' I struggle to open the balcony door, my hands shaking. Stell opens it and lets me out.

I wait till the door's firmly closed before dialling Ness.

TWENTY-THREE

Stella

I'm pissed off, to be honest. This dinner really isn't panning out to be the fantasy of George and Stella. True, it's probably the reality of life with George; it's probably Ness's reality – it kind of comes with the territory given his position and, for a minute, I feel a strange affinity with Ness; what it must be like to live with George's unexplained absences and obsession with work.

But tonight's about fantasy not reality. I thought we both understood that.

I sit back at the table and wait. Outside, I can see George running his hand through his hair as he paces up and down. Then he clicks off the call and stands still for a second. I see his hand move up to his eyes and I realise that he's wiping away tears. He closes his eyes and draws in a deep breath and then another, his hands steadying himself on the railing, and I get up abruptly and go into the kitchen area, feeling like I've seen something I shouldn't have. My back is to George when he steps back into the room.

'Everything all right?' I ask, my voice disappearing largely into the oven, where I'm pretending to check the dinner. There's no answer. I close the oven door, stand up and turn around. George is standing just inside the balcony door. His face is impassive but he's rubbing his chin. He's ashen. I look at his eyes: he definitely shed tears out there.

'What's happened? Is everything OK?'

George closes his eyes, draws in a deep breath, then releases it. 'Major crisis with one of our key accounts,' he says. He shakes his head. 'Shit's really hit the fan. Heads will roll over this. I can't afford to lose this account, which may well happen if I don't get in there and sort it out myself.'

'If you want to leave…'

'I'm so sorry. Look. I'll finish dinner as you've made such an effort. But then, yes, I'm afraid we're going to have to reschedule our sleepover – it's going to be an all-nighter.' He smiles as he says this, as if it's in any way funny to compare ourselves to schoolchildren. Then he comes back over to the table, sits down and replaces his napkin on his lap. I stand still in the kitchen.

'Come on,' he says. 'Let's at least eat together. You've gone to so much trouble.'

Slowly, I take my place opposite George but I can't eat. I watch him chew a couple more mouthfuls of his starter, his mind clearly not on me, the food or the evening. His breathing's shallow and he's chewing too fast. Even the sound of him eating irritates me. The mood's ruined.

'Look, George,' I say, 'why don't you just go now? If you have to go, surely the earlier the better…'

He puts down his cutlery. 'Would you mind?'

'Of course not. If you need to go: go. I don't want half of you.'

'Thanks, princess,' he says, pushing his chair back. 'I owe you.'

I stand up, too, and he gives me an awkward hug and brushes his lips to mine, his mind not even on that. A handful of seconds and he's gone with his bag, the apartment still reverberating from the bang of the front door. I turn and walk slowly back to the living area to clear the plates and turn off the oven, and that's when I see it: his phone. On the dining table.

It's as if the breath is squeezed out of me; my heart's suddenly running like a steam train. I know I don't have long. He'll be back as soon as he realises. I give him till he gets to the street. I stare at the phone. Should I trust him? Believe what he's told me? I don't need to think for long. This is self-preservation; that's all it is. I pick up the phone with shaking fingers and type in George's passcode – the year of our birth. Even as I tap the icon for Messages, I hear the lift ping as George arrives back at my floor. The top message is from Ness:

Darling. I'm bleeding. I think I'm losing the baby. I need you. Please come.

I stare at the screen, willing the words to form a different sentence, willing them to change, but they remain there in black on grey and, deep inside me, something shatters.

TWENTY-FOUR

Stella

Sorry, darling, it's really messy. Bear with me. Could take a while. Love you. X

This is the sum total of what I hear from George for nearly two weeks. I don't know what he imagines I think about his absence, but he doesn't bother to explain further; doesn't try to make even a snatched phone call. I'm supposed to assume, I suppose, that the work is all-consuming; that he has time for nothing except his client. Several times I pick up the phone to call him myself: I want to catch him out; to catch him before he's had time to prepare his lies. But every time I pick up the phone I put it back down: I need to see how he handles this.

What will he tell me?

So I wait and, as I wait, I'm haunted by the image of George standing on my balcony, brushing away his tears. Day and night, it pops into my head unbidden, causing me to catch my breath. Would you cry if the wife you planned to leave was losing a baby you didn't want? Would you?

I can't bear to follow this thought to its logical conclusion.

I think back to the school reunion. Was Ness pregnant

then? I remember the glass of white wine in her hand; how George had swept in and taken it from her. Maybe she was pregnant even then; George not controlling her, but keeping an eye on her. Oh God, maybe they'd even been trying. Now I come to think about it, I've no idea why they haven't had kids after fourteen years of marriage. Maybe they'd been having trouble for years and suddenly it clicked.

There are things I need to hide from myself; thoughts that rear up in my head and I push back down before I can examine them.

Maybe they'd been having fertility treatment.

Don't go there, Stella. Really, don't go there.

But the fact remains that she was pregnant even while George was wooing me with gifts. She was pregnant while he was sleeping with me; pregnant while he was telling me.

She was pregnant when he told me he wants my baby.

I jump up and pace my office, staring out at the street below. I'm on my fifth coffee of the day and my nerves are shot.

Get a grip! I tell myself. He's not sleeping with Ness. He told me that himself. They have separate bedrooms. I try to clutch at this, but my thoughts spread like a vine, snaking through my consciousness as they throw up more questions than they can answer: if it wasn't planned, was their sex a drunken accident; the baby the unplanned result of a spontaneous, accidental shag? Did she seduce him to try and trap him? Is it even his? For a moment I feel a leap of hope, but then I'm back to the image imprinted on my retina of George brushing away his tears on the balcony. Who the father is is almost immaterial: what matters is that he cried when he thought she was losing his baby.

And then there's my birthday – the thought of this hits me in the solar plexus.

Maybe she *was* sick that night: morning sickness, not cancer.

The air goes out of me. I just know that he lied about her having a tumour.

I can barely breathe. He told me the treatment would last about six months – he was planning to stay with her until the baby is born. The vile nature of his lie makes my knees buckle. I stop eating and, for the first time ever, take time off work, telling my assistant I'm sick. I lie, listless, on the sofa at home and do nothing but wait – I wait to see what George will finally tell me. Whether he'll admit to the pregnancy; the miscarriage; the fact that he's still sleeping with Ness.

He doesn't.

What he does do is ask to see me again. The first message I get from George after I've learned that the wife he no longer sleeps with was pregnant with his baby is a request to meet him for a couple of hours in a hotel. Not even a request, really, just a note: 12 p.m. Wednesday? Same place? Can't wait.

I stare at the message in disbelief but then I catch myself: you can't say these things over Messenger. Perhaps he's going to do the decent thing and tell me everything in person. I pull myself up into a sitting position.

Looking forward to it, I write.

And I am.

TWENTY-FIVE

George

I stare out of the hotel room window while I wait for Stell. Usually I have a Pavlovian reaction to this room – an instant hard-on – but today, for the first time, and quite understandably, it's not happening. It's been a completely shitty fortnight: one I'd never wish on my worst enemy. Aside from watching Ness go through the miscarriage and then a precautionary D and C, I've had mixed feelings: there's sadness – of course there's sadness – but there's relief, too: relief that I'm off the hook. And the relief makes me feel guilty.

I've left the door on the latch and I turn when I hear Stell push it open.

'Hey,' she says, standing on the threshold.

'Hey.' I cross the room and take her in my arms. The scent of her is like balm on my soul and I hold her longer and tighter than I usually would.

'I've missed you.' I kiss her softly for a second or two, but she pulls away and sits on the bed. I sit down next to her like a nervous teenager. It's the first time I've felt awkward with her and I don't know why.

'How's work?' Stell says. 'You got everything sorted?'

For a second, I wonder how she can talk about work after the disaster of a fortnight I've had – then I remember she doesn't know.

'Oh that. Yes. All sorted. I'm sorry. I was dealing with it 24/7.'

'It's fine. Did you manage to keep the account?'

'Yeah. By a whisker.'

'The charm of George Wolsey!' Stell gives a little laugh and I echo it.

'Yes. The charm of George Wolsey!'

'So,' she says, 'how's Ness?'

I don't miss a beat. 'Well! There's good news, actually!'

'Oh really?' Stell looks up at me.

'Yes. False alarm. The tumour was benign! Sorry I didn't get a chance to tell you sooner. We found out while I was dealing with everything at work. Sod's Law, eh? Like buses. Everything comes at once.'

'Oh fantastic. I'm glad she's OK.' Stell traces the stripes on the silk throw with her finger. 'But you had to go through all that worry… it must have been awful.'

'It was.'

'You look tired.'

'I am. There's not a lot gets me down but, hand on heart, it was a difficult time.'

Silence.

'George. Can I ask you something?' Stell goes over to the window then turns to face me.

'Yes – yes of course.' Something in her tone makes me nervous. I get up, too, and shuffle through the magazines on the coffee table. Thick magazines with stiff paper. Corporate stuff. Luxury travel. Luxury lifestyle.

'Do you still sleep with Ness?'

I look at her and our eyes lock. Stell's got her poker face on but a tiny muscle in her jaw flickers and I know she's clamped her teeth together.

'Where did that come from?'

Stell shrugs. 'So, do you?'

'Good God, no! You've nothing to worry about there, princess. I thought I explained all that.'

'When was the last time?'

'Last time what?'

'That you slept with her.'

I look up at the ceiling and frown. 'I honestly don't remember.'

'Like, weeks, months? More?'

'Oh God. A year or more.'

'Really? No slip-ups? You know, bottle of wine and: oops – never mind, it doesn't count anyway?'

'No. It's not like that. You have no idea!'

'If you say so,' says Stell – and I have no idea whether she believes me.

We don't have sex.

TWENTY-SIX

Stella

So now it's me on the receiving end of George's lies. The knowledge makes me angry until, slowly, it recedes, making way for an older and wiser me to rise from the ashes of my 'George 'n' Stell' dream. And, as I learn to live with what I now know, I start to think about that old saying, 'knowledge is power'. I may look serene as I go about my business, as I run my company and continue to date George, I may look normal to everyone who crosses my path, but I know that, deep inside, I am damaged.

I'm a damaged woman who has knowledge and power.

Oh, George.

And yes, I accept that, from the outside, this affair has train-crash written all over it; I accept that any sane woman would run away as fast as they could. But let's not forget that, ultimately, this is George we're talking about. My George. Yes, an older and wiser Stella may have emerged from the conversation in that hotel room, but a shadow of the teenage girl is still in my heart, too, and she's still hoping that this imperfect version of the man with whom she's supposed to be might somehow blossom into the man she knows he could be; the man he should be.

And, ultimately, I want to see where this goes; to see how George lets it play out. Now that there's a level playing field once more, is it me he'll choose, or Ness – or will he mess us both about? Call it an experiment, if you like, but I can't let it go. Just as people are drawn to car-crash TV and horror movies, I can't turn away.

I want to have a baby with you.

We don't see each other for a week or so, then, when George calls again, both nothing and everything has changed. To be fair, he makes an effort. If I didn't know about the baby and the miscarriage, I'd quite possibly be blown away by the energy he puts into making our stolen moments together absolutely perfect. The sex is fantastic and – he doesn't question it any more – always unprotected. The attention to detail on our dinner dates is touching: cars pick me up; reservations staff and maître d's know to expect me; we visit a series of restaurants he's hand-picked because he knows I'll like them. Always, though, at the back of my mind lies the question of why he no longer speaks of leaving Ness. There's no longer a baby. So what's he waiting for? *Actions, Stella. Actions speak louder than words.*

It's around this time that I develop a pain deep in my jaw. After knocking back anti-inflammatories like Smarties for a fortnight, I go wearily to the dentist expecting the worst: root infection; a long course of invasive treatment.

'Tell me,' the dentist says after he's examined my mouth. 'How would you rate your stress level at the moment?'

'Oh, the usual. About a five out of ten.' It's actually about a twelve out of ten, but I don't see stress as a bad thing in the way that most people do. If it was a three, I'd be dead through boredom.

'Hmm,' says the dentist, straightening up and tilting the lamp so it's no longer shining into my eyes. 'I wonder. I can't see any evidence of infection or any problem with your teeth *per se*.' He pauses. 'How are things at work? Going well?'

'Oh, the usual – you know how it is.'

'And, forgive me for asking – how are things in your personal life?' He picks up my file and squints at it. 'Are you married?' Before I have time to ask why he's asking, he points at me. 'That's it! You're clenching your jaw. The moment I asked you that, your jaw clamped down. I suspect that that's what's causing your pain.'

I'm speechless.

'I don't need to know the answer to the question, but I think we've found the problem,' says the dentist.

'No root canal?' I clench my jaw experimentally. It feels familiar.

'No root canal.'

'So, if that's what's causing this pain, what can I do about it?'

'Obviously, try to be aware. Stop yourself from doing it as soon as you realise what you're doing. Massaging the area can help. And, ultimately, try to identify what it is that's causing you to do it, and eliminate it. Though that's not always possible!' The dentist laughs.

Eliminate it? I imagine myself toting a machine gun.

'Sports,' the dentist adds. 'Anything that can help reduce stress and tension in your life. Yoga, maybe? They're not for everyone, but meditation and deep-breathing techniques can help. Or just joining a gym, so you have some sort of physical release.'

I take his advice. There's a gym near my office. I try a few things before I discover kick-boxing and it's like coming home. I don't always go to class: sometimes I just get my gloves on after work and punch and kick the bag over and over, harder and harder, left, right, left, right, faster and faster. My jaw pain recedes. I've never been so fit in my life.

One bright February day, a frost on the ground that morning yet the promise of daffodils in the air for the first time in what seems like a wet, grey for ever, George brings up the topic of us finally spending a night together. I sit at the bureau of our hotel room in my silk petticoat, looking out through the window at the teeming street below. Heat wafts up from the radiator making strands of my hair fly and, down below, cars in all colours sit in traffic alongside white vans, while motorcycles and cyclists weave in and out, seemingly oblivious to the laws that govern the rest of the traffic. My breath fogs the glass. I feel George's hands on my bare shoulders. They're big hands – strong – and his fingers instinctively find the dips that welcome pressure from his fingers. I lean back into his body, enjoying this little massage.

He bends his head down so his lips are close to my ear.

'Come away with me – for a weekend,' he says. 'I want you to myself.'

The breath stops going in and out of my lungs. 'A weekend?'

'Yes.' The pressure from George's fingers gets stronger. 'A nice hotel. Maybe somewhere near the coast. A big four-poster bed. An open fire. Country walks. Sea air, and a night in each other's arms.' He groans. 'I just want to wake up with you in my arms. What do you think?'

What I think is: *Why haven't you left Ness?*

Down on the street, the light turns green and the lane of traffic begins to move. Through the double-glazing, I hear muffled shouts; the sound of cars hooting. What else do I think? I think, *No way am I putting myself in that position again. The last time I offered to spend a night with you, you ran home to your wife.* I turn around to face George, forcing him to drop his hands and take a step back. He perches on the end of the bed. He's in his pants, nothing more, and it makes him look boyish and vulnerable. I remember, for a second, the boy on the pile of coats.

'George. I…'

'I promise nothing will get in the way. Nothing.'

My eyes narrow as I look at him and I nibble the inside of my cheek. I know he means what he says, but experience proves he's not always able to deliver, even if he does have the best intentions. I picture myself alone in a country hotel, lying on a four-poster bed, waiting for a George who never turns up. I close my eyes, draw my breath inside myself to summon up my strength, give my head a tiny shake and exhale. I won't let him hurt me again.

'Sorry.'

George's face falls and, again, I see the boy.

Did you really think I'd say yes? I want to add, *after what happened last time*, but I leave it unsaid. He knows.

'It's OK,' he says. 'I just wanted to do something really special for you, that's all.'

And this is where my mind starts to work. There's a charity Valentine's ball that I've been invited to. They're counting on the auction to raise desperately needed funds and I'd like to go – just not on my own. In my head, I see myself entering the ballroom with George on my arm. Gorgeous George in black tie. Us at the top table, maybe. Already I start thinking about what I'll wear. Red, obviously.

'Can I tell you what I'd really like?' I say to George.

He looks up, his face full of hope. 'Of course.'

I tell him about the dinner. 'I'd really like you to come as my partner. But could you get away on Valentine's Day? Or will Ness want to do something?'

Am I testing him? Maybe. But George is laughing. His gratitude for this scrap I've thrown him after refusing to indulge his countryside dream is so embarrassing I look away. 'Stell. I've told you. We're like brother and sister! Valentine's Day doesn't even register in our house.'

'Because I can't be let down.' I get up and stretch my arms above my head while I look around the room for the crumpled heap of my skirt.

'I know. Listen, what charity did you say it was?' I tell

him and he smiles again. 'Actually, that's perfect. My firm's a major benefactor, so it won't look too out of place for me to be there too.'

I really wish you hadn't said that, George.

'So it's a date?' I ask, stepping into my shoes.

'Yes,' he says. 'It's a date.'

TWENTY-SEVEN

Stella

I don't mean for us to get caught. Really, I don't.

The Valentine's event is in the ballroom of a hotel on Park Lane, and George picks me up from my apartment in a car. My scarlet gown is the epitome of understated glamour, and it makes me smile to think it took less than an hour to pick. I called on the services of a personal shopper in the end – briefed her, tried on a shortlist of dresses in my lunch hour and chose the most show-stopping gown. No fuss. No drama. When George saw me he stopped – he actually stopped – then he put his hand over his heart and did a funny little bow.

'Stell. You look breathtaking,' he said. It was the result I wanted. He, too, scrubs up well. His dinner jacket is well cut of expensive fabric, and it fits like a made-to-measure. Perhaps it is. I don't ask. George opens the car door for me and I step carefully inside, arranging the skirt of my dress carefully so it doesn't get stepped on. George runs around to the other side and scoots in next to me. He takes my hand.

'I've never been so proud to be with someone,' he says. 'You really are the perfect woman.'

I smile and kiss his cheek.

After some time stop-starting in Saturday-night traffic, we join the line of vehicles approaching the drop-off point for the hotel ballroom. A valet opens the door and I step out, arranging my dress as I do so. George takes my arm but then sees that a bank of photographers lines the red carpet, waiting, presumably, for the famous faces invited tonight. Some minor royal is the guest of honour. George lets go of my arm and takes a step back.

'You go ahead,' he says. 'Let them get your dress from every angle. I don't want to cramp your style.'

I look at him for a second, confused – I wanted to arrive on his arm – then I realise: he doesn't want to be photographed entering the event with me in case Ness – anyone, I guess – sees the pictures.

'Sure,' I say, and walk ahead. Mentally, I picture my hands in their red boxing gloves smacking into a boxing bag with George's face on it: left, right, left, right. My smile, as the cameras click, is frozen.

Inside, the ballroom is stunning. Everything, from the table linen to the chairs, is silver, white or glass, giving the effect of a glittering snow palace. The only exception to the icy theme are huge spheres of red and white flowers that hang from the ceiling on silver chains. I catch the scent of magnolia, rose and lily. The effect is stunning: the organisers have really done themselves proud. A waiter asks my name and offers to show me to my table. The whole point of my bringing George tonight was so I didn't walk in alone. I clench and unclench my jaw.

'I'll wait for my partner,' I say. 'He's just coming.'

'Miss Simons,' says a deep baritone voice behind me. I turn and find Nicholas Lazenby, the chief executive of the charity tonight's bash is supporting. He's a portly bloke but he looks dapper in his dinner jacket.

'Nicholas!' I lean in to air-kiss his cheeks. 'Is Joan here tonight?'

'Yes, yes. She's fussing about the flowers. You're here alone?' he asks.

I mention George's name. 'It's a work thing,' I say. 'Thought we may as well sit together.' I give a little laugh, irritated with myself for protecting the liar. It's an unintentional slip.

'Ah, Wolsey, the old mucker!' says Nicholas. 'One of my key benefactors.'

'I know. He was so proud of last year's fundraiser. It was a record amount, wasn't it?'

Nicholas positively beams. 'Yes it was! Nine hundred and seventy thousand, give or take the odd penny. Wolsey's really changed things for us. I'm hoping they'll beat that next year – should they choose to do another fundraiser for us, of course.'

'Oh I'm sure they will. You know George – loves a challenge.'

'That would be incredible. The work we're doing – it's so important.' Nicholas' eyes mist over and I know he's thinking about the children his charity helps: the never-ending tsunami of displaced children who need clothes and food and medicines and life-changing surgery.

'Lazenby!' George slaps Nicholas on the back.

'Ah,' says Nicholas, 'the man himself. Wolsey, old boy! How the devil are you?'

They chat for a minute, then George takes my arm and, together, we find our table and introduce ourselves to the others already there with no explanation of our relationship. I know none of the people there. Other benefactors of the charity, I assume. We make small talk: what brings you here? How long have you been involved with the charity? Wasn't the traffic horrendous tonight? At least it wasn't raining! And, all the while, I'm aware of the ladies at the table focusing on George: he is handsome; clearly the best-looking man at the table, perhaps in the room. I place my hand over his on the table.

TWENTY-EIGHT

George

There's a diamond bracelet Stell likes in the auction catalogue. It's a reproduction of a vintage piece in 18-carat gold sprinkled with diamonds and I see her catch her breath as she looks at the picture.

'Let's go and see it,' she says, so I go with her up to the glass case, and it's as if her eyes come alive.

'I can already feel the weight of it,' she says, circling her wrist with her thumb and fingers. 'It's as if I owned it in a past life. It needs to belong to me.'

'Are you going to bid?'

'Yes,' she says. 'Up to a point. I've set myself a limit. Is there anything here you like?'

'Not really. I could hang the signed football shirt in the office, I suppose, or there's a nice voucher for a weekend away: country house hotel, champagne, butler, spa...' I look sideways at Stell but her eyes are still on the bracelet.

The auctioneer calls us all to attention and the bidding starts. I join in for the fun of it and manage to bag the football shirt as well as a signed cricket bat – it's all for charity and

I always like to support Lazenby. We go back years. The bracelet's the last item, and Stell fidgets constantly.

Finally, the bidding starts and I watch in admiration as she bides her time, waiting for the pace to slow before she raises her paddle for the first time. Soon, it's just her and another bidder – a guy who looks quite serious about winning. There's a woman at his side fanning herself with the catalogue. I see her give Stell a tight smile and imagine the bracelet will be for her.

'Fifteen hundred?' asks the auctioneer. 'One thousand, five hundred pounds?' Stell nods.

He looks at the other bidder. 'Do I hear sixteen hundred?' The other bidder nods.

They ping-pong back and forth as the value reaches and then passes two thousand pounds. Stell continues on for an extra hundred pounds.

'Two two?' asks the auctioneer. 'Do I have two thousand two hundred?'

The other man nods. The auctioneer turns to Stell and she shakes her head and slumps back in her seat. The look on her face destroys me.

'The diamond bracelet is sold for two thousand, two hundred pounds. Going…'

I jump up. 'Two thousand five hundred!'

I'm aware of heads turning and my name ricocheting about the room – it's good entertainment, I guess, not to mention good publicity for the firm. Stell looks at me, her hand over her mouth.

'Two thousand five hundred from the gentleman at Table

One,' says the auctioneer, then he turns again to the other bidder, who shakes his head.

'Going, going, gone.' The auctioneer raps his hammer. 'The diamond bracelet is sold for two thousand five hundred pounds. Congratulations, Mr Wolsey.'

Applause breaks out and, auction over, an assistant comes to escort me to the back room so I can pay and pick up the bracelet. Stell's right – it's stunning. I watch as the assistant places it reverentially in a velvet box and closes it with a satisfying click.

'Congratulations again, sir. It's a fine piece.'

Dessert's been served as I walk back out with the box. Some sort of mini cheesecake concoction, artily arranged with a wafer of white chocolate, gold-crusted, standing out from the top like a sail. Half of the table have started eating, the others are presumably waiting for me but, as I come back out, one of the men at the table starts to clap. As I reach the table, everyone joins in so I give a little bow.

'Thank you. Thank you.'

Stell's fiddling with her spoon, drawing a pattern in the blobs of sauce that decorate the plate. Surely she knows the bracelet is for her, not Ness. I place the box onto the table next to her, and take my seat.

'You can pay me back later,' I say, and everyone laughs.

She opens the box and touches the bracelet gently with her fingertips. The she takes it out and holds it up, letting the light refract off the facets of the diamonds.

'Pass it around!' someone says, and I see how reluctant she is to let go of her new treasure but, still, she sends the bracelet around the table to be pored over with gasps.

'Do you mind if I… ?' asks one lady. She fastens it on her wrist. 'Oh, it suits me! It's like Cinderella and the glass slipper,' she says. 'Maybe it's supposed to be mine!'

Stell glowers at her. Reluctantly, the woman takes it off and the bracelet continues its circumnavigation of the table until it's back with Stell.

'Try it!' says the lady, and Stell lays it across her wrist but I stop her.

'May I?'

I take the bracelet and slowly fasten it around her wrist, aware that everyone's eyes are on us. I can see the faint movement of her pulse. Although entirely non-sexual, it's one of the most erotic moments of my life. Stell then holds her arm up to show the table and there's a collective sigh of appreciation before spoons are picked up and the attention turns once more to dinner.

'Do you like it?' I ask Stell quietly.

'Yes. Very much. Thank you. Excuse me a sec.'

She pushes her chair back abruptly and stands up.

TWENTY-NINE

Stella

I leave the ballroom through the heavy double doors and walk down the carpeted corridor aware of the weight of the bracelet on my wrist. What was he thinking?

I use the bathroom, then, as no one else is there, I take my time checking my hair and looking at my dress in the mirror. I hold up my arm and twist and turn so the bracelet sparkles in the mirror. I don't actually want to go back to the table. The evening's over as far as I'm concerned. I have no desire to eat dessert. I pull open the bathroom door and walk straight into George. He reaches for my hands; holds both of them in his.

'Hey, princess. Pleased with your bracelet?'

'Of course. Thank you.' I look at it twinkling. 'But you can't give this to me. Ness is bound to find out.'

'I'll tell her you paid me back. You don't have to, of course.' He laughs. 'I was just saying that, you know, for the table, because…' His voice trails off.

Everything feels wrong. I pull my hands gently back from George's. I don't want this beautiful bracelet to be associated with lies.

'What's wrong?' he asks.

I look down. George's shoes are super shiny tonight: a man of details. He lifts my chin with his fingers and I see a passing couple look over curiously.

'Are you uncomfortable with me buying it for you? Listen. Why don't you take it as proof of a promise? A promise bracelet?'

'A promise of what?'

'That I'm leaving her. That we're going to have that future together.'

I don't say anything. We've had promises before. What I want is action. There's a steady trickle of people in the corridor now – people are starting to leave.

'I know I've said it before,' George says, 'but I mean it. You've been incredibly patient, Stell. You've been amazing, and I want to make you a promise, right here and right now, that I'm leaving Ness. Will you accept this bracelet as a token of my love, and as a promise?'

Out of the corner of my eye I see a flurry of activity; a little posse of people walking fast – the minor royal's leaving; behind her, there's the glint of light on camera lens. I make my decision.

'Well—' I smile '—when you put it like that, how could a girl resist?'

George steps closer and I tilt my face up to his for a kiss that's so tender it feels as if it contains all the love in the world. In my peripheral vision, to the right, cameras flash.

THIRTY

Stella

I'm not surprised, then, to see an article about the ball in the paper the next morning. I scroll through the pictures, skimming over who was there and who wore what. George makes the cut and, posing alone on the red carpet in his dinner jacket, his thick, dark hair swept back with pomade, he looks every inch the movie star. I take in the image for a second, remembering the fury I'd felt walking the red carpet alone, then it's with a sense of inevitability that I reach them: multiple images of the headline guest gliding down the corridor after the ball – with George and I kissing in the background.

The focus is not on us of course but, for those who notice, the fact that the kiss was a private moment away from the theatre of the ballroom makes the images all the more compelling. Without having been there, you wouldn't be able to tell if it was a brief peck on the lips or a longer kiss, but my eyes are closed, which, in visual terms, speaks volumes.

I tap on the first image and enlarge it a little. Although you can't see the man's face fully, it's obvious to me that it's George, though to recognise him, you'd have to know his suit, his shoes, his hair and the shape of his body. And the most obvious thing to the general public is that the woman George is kissing is a brunette, not his famously blonde wife.

If Ness sees the image, she'll know.

'Oh no,' I say without any feeling, expanding the image to get a better view. My dress looks awesome.

I'm this far in when the phone rings.

'Stell!' George sounds panicked, his breathing ragged. 'Have you seen the paper today?'

'I have,' I say. There's no point in lying.

'Oh my God. She's nipped out to Waitrose, but she'll read the paper as soon as she gets back. She's going to look at that story. She knows it's my charity. She's going to see the pictures. What am I going to do?'

'Calm down,' I say. 'You can't see your face and they haven't named you. It could be anyone.'

He exhales loudly. 'Oh God! How could I be so careless?' There's a pause as the inevitability of being caught, and of Ness's reaction, sinks in. 'It's over, isn't it?'

George's voice breaks, and there's nothing much I can say to comfort him. He's probably right – he'll have to leave Ness now. I examine my new bracelet, turning it this way and that. He made a promise last night; I really can't understand why he's quite so panicky.

'I'm sorry,' I say. 'But look at it this way: you were going to leave her anyway, weren't you? It's just perhaps more sudden than you imagined.'

'Oh God!'

'I'm really sorry it happened like this.' I pause, noting that not a single part of me feels sorry for him. 'Look, if I can do anything, if you need somewhere to stay…'

'I may have to take you up on that,' George says. Then, 'Shit. She's back,' and the line goes dead.

I sit for a minute on the sofa, my breathing faster than usual. Could this be it? The day I finally get George back. February 15, 2015. I like it.

*

While George faces Ness, I pace around the apartment, fiddling with things, till I realise that the only way I'm going to burn off my nervous energy is by throwing some punches at the gym. Nothing beats the release of lashing out. There's no class on but my trainer's there.

'Whoah, you're on fire today,' he says, as I let the punchbag absorb my energy. The gym resounds with the whack of glove on bag. 'You want to try a little sparring?'

'Really?' I'm bouncing on my toes, sweat dripping off me.

He slips on his gloves, passes me the headgear, and holds his hands up. 'Give it to me!'

Jab, jab, straight right; jab, straight right, left hook. I'm dancing around him, unleashing myself, my arms flipping out, straight and strong as I dodge his blows. It feels amazing when my fist connects with his body. I think about nothing except where the next punch will land: George and Ness are out of my mind; my focus is on the feel of my heart pounding; the blood pumping through my veins; my muscles, tendons and ligaments working in perfect unity. This is my escape. My sanity.

I'm out for about an hour and a half, I suppose. Then I walk home, the motion seeming too slow, too easy, after the high-octane pace of the boxing ring. It's a gentle wind-down, and only then does the thought of George seep back into my mind like a toxic gas. I start imagining what might be going on at his house; that posh house on the hill in Richmond. I see Ness showing George the iPad; watching him scroll through the pictures. George, grey in the face, stopping before he reaches that picture; handing the iPad back to her. Ness scrolling and tapping, handing it back to him, her face icy. Would there be tears? Shouting? Recriminations? Does he tell her everything? Or just that he's leaving?

I dip into a newsagent and buy a hard copy of the newspaper. Posterity and all that.

*

After I step out of the shower, I see a missed call. Ness. I'm standing looking at her name on my phone when it rings again. I pick up.

'Stella?'

I wait.

'I know it wasn't your fault,' she says in a monotone hung with defeat. 'It's who he is. He's never been faithful to me. Never. He's a shit.' There's a static silence. 'Good luck.'

The line goes dead.

*

It's late when I hear a tap on the door. I'm on the sofa, reading: *How To Tell Toledo From the Night Sky.* It's a brilliant book, the symmetries of its plot about predestined lovers not lost on me, and I resent having to put it down.

I open the door. There's something hollow about George, and he's carrying an overnight bag. As I lock the front door behind him, he drops his bag in the hall, goes straight into the living room and collapses onto the sofa. It feels strange to see him sitting on my sofa. It's as if the space in the apartment has shrunk; as if a George-sized chunk has been taken out of it. Furthermore, he's sitting where I usually sit, and I'm now not sure where I should sit myself. George doesn't make any move to hug me or kiss me, so I perch one cushion along from him on my cream sofa and wait for him to speak.

'Do you mind if I…?' he says eventually, waving a hand feebly at the apartment.

'If you stay? Of course not.'

There's a silence. I see muscles working in George's jaw.

'Sod's Law, isn't it?' The words burst out of him.

'What's Sod's Law?'

'Random shot, and we're in it.'

George groans, head in hands. I fuss around in the living room, straightening things that don't need straightening. Then George sits abruptly upright again. 'I bet it was Bunny Larsen.'

'What?'

'Bunny Larsen. She's got it in for me.'

'Who?'

'Photographer I used to know. Oh God. It was her. I'd put money on it.'

'Umm – why?'

George shakes his head. 'Oh God. Bunny bloody Larsen. We have a little history, put it like that.'

'While you were with Ness?'

'Oof.' Delivered with an eye-roll, it's an admission. 'Just a night. She's hated me since.'

'Hated you after a one-night stand? When she knew you were married? That's a bit extreme. What was she expecting? Marriage and kids?' As I say it, the irony of my own situation isn't lost on me.

'Maybe it was a bit more than one night. Few weeks, maybe. I honestly don't remember. It wasn't anything major.'

'Were you unfaithful to Ness a lot?'

George looks at me sideways, a smile playing at the corner of his mouth. 'I bet it was Bun,' he says. 'She'd have known it was me. I'm sure she works as a freelancer these days. You know, selling society pics to the highest bidder.'

'So – if it was "Bun"…' I can't say the name without putting the quote marks in my voice '. . . if it was her, why wouldn't she have named you in the caption? Made sure she twisted the knife?'

'Not her style. She's clever. Subtle. She'd know that this would get back to Ness, but there's no dirt on her for naming and shaming.' He shakes his head. 'Clever girl. *Touché*, babe.'

I take his words like a punch in the stomach.

'Anyway,' George continues. 'The damage is done. Ness

knows it was you. She recognised you.' George closes his eyes. 'I really stuffed up, didn't I?'

I get up and walk over to the window. *Yes*, I think. You stuffed up the moment you slammed that door on me when I was eighteen and pregnant. You stuffed up again when you got Ness pregnant while promising me a future. But not today – today is not a stuff-up. Today's a correction, not a mistake.

'That's why she threw me out. I think if it had been anyone else,' George says, unaware of the bombshell he's just dropped, 'we might have been able to get through this – write it off as a moment of madness, a mistake – but the moment she realised it was you, she knew. She just knew.' George makes puppy-dog eyes at me. I think he thinks he's flattering me; trying to make me feel like he wouldn't have wrecked his marriage for anyone else – Bunny Larsen, for example.

'She knew what she was up against,' George says. 'Is it that obvious I'm in love with you?'

I give him a tight smile. George jumps up and paces the living room. It looks wrong; he's too tall, too big in my space. I think about the last time he was here; the time I found out Ness was pregnant. He stops and puts his head in his hands.

'What have I done?'

'Well, if you play with fire…' I get up suddenly and head towards the kitchen. 'Drink?'

'Got any whisky? Single malt?'

'Wine or vodka.'

'Wine.'

I pour two large glasses and take them back into the living room, where George is once more on my spot on the sofa. I sit down next to him and we both take a sip. George slumps into the back of the sofa. His eyes close. I lean forward.

'Can I ask you something?' I say.

'Sure.' He doesn't even open his eyes. Suddenly I'm furious that he's come here, assumed I'll be sympathetic and not even kissed me hello. Subconsciously, my hands curl into fists, itching to punch again.

'If you hadn't got caught,' I say, choosing my words carefully, 'when were you planning to tell Ness?'

George opens his eyes slowly and says something I don't hear. I don't need to: the look on his face says it all and I finally realise, once and for all, that it was a game to him.

Nothing more than a game.

PART II

ONE

Stella

10 months later

The wedding is perfect. Seventeen years after I planned it, my wedding to George Wolsey finally takes place, exactly as it always should have done.

Yes, I said exactly as it always should have done.

All day there's a smile on my face. People assume it's because I'm so happy to be getting married 'at last' – spare me the pity – and, of course I'm happy, but it's more than that: it's a smile of satisfaction that things are finally working out how they always should have done. It's a sense of things finally coming full circle.

'I don't get why you want a church wedding when you don't go to church,' George tells me when I let him in on some of the plans. 'You're not usually such a hypocrite. And, trust me, church weddings aren't all they're cracked up to be. Been there, got that T-shirt. Ha!' He rubs his hands together and laughs in a way that makes me all the more determined to do it.

'I just do,' I say. 'I can't explain it.'

And I can't. How can I explain the notebook? The hours spent alone in my bedroom as a teenager imagining what my wedding to George would be like? True, I've updated the dress and the cake's now in another league, but George gazing into my eyes as we say our vows at the altar is an image I've held close to my heart for the best part of two decades and I'm not going to miss out on it for the sake of being called a hypocrite. By George of all people.

It's a big wedding, but many of the guests are George's work acquaintances: clients and hangers-on. People, I presume, he wants to butter up with a free feed and the suggestion of intimacy. There's not many from my side. Sitting with notepad and pen, I can't think of many people I care to share the day with. Neither of us have much in the way of family, and George's brother, Harry, doesn't come.

'He's on holiday,' George says when I ask why. 'In the Lake District. Camping.'

I shrug. 'Priorities, eh.'

It's not me who invites the press, though. I'd never be that cruel to Ness.

'Oh,' George says to me a week before the wedding, 'my PRs have managed to get *Hello!* to come and take some pics of you before the wedding. Is that OK?'

'What do you mean by "before"? You mean like a week before, or literally on the day?'

'Oh, on the day. You know the type: luscious photos – big single-page images. You in your dressing room, doing up your dress, drinking a glass of champagne, having your hair done. Staged shots, of course. Paid. You don't mind, do you?'

I raise one eyebrow.

'Please, Stell? It would go a long way to…'

And I know exactly what he's getting at: he got a fair bit of bad press when he left Ness. The cheating husband abandoning his long-standing wife: the red tops had a field day, and would it be cynical for me to say that Ness milked it? Her brave, 'coping' face was plastered on almost every weekly as she talked about George's favourite recipes and how she's moving on, making pot dinners for one or some such crap. We both know that George's PRs will be desperate to turn that bad press around.

'What about Ness?' I ask. 'Isn't that rubbing her face in it?'

George shrugs. 'I'll give her a call. Square it with her. She knows the drill. She'll understand.'

It's my turn to shrug. 'Personally, I wouldn't do it. But it's your ex-wife and your business. Do what you like. Just ask them not to send "Bunny Larsen" to take the pictures.' I make rabbit ears with my hands and a Bugs Bunny face as I say this.

And so the day is perfect. From the moment I step over the threshold of the church and see George running his hand through his hair at the altar to the moment we fall into bed together that night as Mr and Mrs, I know everything's going to be all right. George and me, we may have had an unconventional route to the altar, we may have had our ups and downs, but I don't regret a thing and who was it who said 'all's fair in love and war'?

It was George, wasn't it? All that time ago. It was George who said that.

TWO

George

The first disagreement Stell and I have after our wedding is the old chestnut about where we're going to live. Ness's fleeced me in the divorce, so I'm keen to stay at Stell's but, after a few months of dancing around each other, even I have to admit her place is too small for the two of us and we start talking about where we might move to. I want to stay in Hampstead. It's a great spot, and I'd assumed she was happy there too, but suddenly, out of nowhere, Stell starts banging on about moving to the country.

'Really?' I say, searching her face for clues that she's joking. We both run companies in the heart of London. Why would we want to move to the country? 'We're not going to start growing our own veg and keeping chickens, are we?' I ask, as a picture of her feeding chickens in a pair of wellies with an anorak over her nightie comes to mind.

She tuts. 'Not the "real" country. I don't mean cut-off-in-the-winter country. Just somewhere where I can see more than a patch of sky at a time but we can still get into London easily.'

'We live next door to Hampstead Heath!'

'Yes, but… it's the sirens, too. And the pollution. The noise. The city. The *people*!' She shudders and starts typing into the search engine. 'Look, just don't argue with me. OK? You'll love the country. I'm going to take a step back from work, stick around at home more and finally start writing my novel. We'll have more space, fresh air…I want it for us, *and* for our children.' She looks up and smiles at me as she says that, and I see that I've lost already.

'Okaay,' I say slowly. 'Country it is.' But, even as I'm saying the words, I'm feeling like I've just been pushed into a corner. Is this what life with Stell's going to be like? Note to self: pick your battles.

Stell smiles again. 'Let's start looking around the end of the Tube lines. How about here?' She taps the screen. 'Look at all that green on the map, and you could be in the West End in under an hour.'

'Well, it's closer to Harry,' I say, leaning in to see better and imagining a life where I get to see a bit more of my brother. Stell's eyes narrow. She swipes across London and taps another area.

'Or how about here?'

'What's wrong with being closer to Harry?'

Stell looks up and gives her head a little shake. 'It's nothing to do with Harry. I just want us to have the best country experience we can with easy access to central London and this Tube line is more reliable than the other. You always hear there are delays on that line on the travel news, don't you?'

She searches the new area a little, but it fast becomes

apparent the houses there are not ticking her boxes. She moves back to the original search area.

I play along for a bit, thinking she might run out of steam when she realises that the type of house she'd like simply doesn't exist in a country setting. But, as the days go by, instead of diminishing, her dream gathers momentum like a runaway train and I start to realise I've underestimated what Stell's like when she wants something. She's a dog with a bone. She starts talking about the both of us working from home more and I know she's imagining us locked away together in some sort of country idyll, just the two of us and, later, the kids. And, as we go through house listing after house listing every evening after work, I see her compare the reality with the dream and I see that there are no matches, but still she doesn't give up. She's tenacious when she wants something. I give her that.

'What about this one?' I ask, pointing at a place called The Lodge. 'Look! It ticks every box.' *On your rather long list*, I want to add. I admit it, I'm feeling smug with The Lodge. A Grade II listed nineteenth-century house, it's within a stone's throw of the end of the Metropolitan Line; it's got enough bedrooms for the non-existent kids as well as an office for us (her? I can't picture me working from home). It's got a garden. And it's gorgeously higgledy-piggledy – all nooks, crannies and beams. It's even got a big, black Aga. More than anything, it looks homely.

Stell closes her eyes and I know she's comparing the image of the house to the image she carries in her head.

'Nope,' she says, screwing up her nose.

I sit back. 'Why? What's wrong with it?'

'It's too old.'

'We can do it up a bit. Look, the kitchen's new – they've just done it in keeping with the style of the house.' We both look at the terracotta tiles on the kitchen floor and the exposed red-brick wall and I think about Stell's colour palette of neutrals. Okay, maybe it's a little garish.

'It's vile.' Stell shudders and continues scrolling.

'I think we should go and see it.'

Stell glowers at me, but I scroll back up and jot down the number of the estate agent, give them a buzz and arrange a viewing.

*

Stell comes with me but it's apparent from the moment we get in the car that she's not going to give The Lodge a fair chance. She scowls her way around it, wincing and even pretending to gag at one point.

'What's wrong with you?' I hiss at her behind the estate agent's back.

'It reeks of dogs. Centuries of old, wet dogs. Can't you smell it?'

'It just hasn't been lived in for a bit. It's a little musty, but nothing opening the windows wouldn't cure. Try to look at the bigger picture. Please?' I catch her by the shoulders and give her a little kiss. She shakes me off.

'Expensive to heat,' she says. 'Probably not been wired since the turn of the century.' She looks around. 'Plumbing's probably about to break. Rising damp. You want me to carry on?'

'That's what the survey's for.'

'Why waste your money? I hate it. I may say "country", but this is not what I have in mind.'

We follow the agent up a narrow staircase that creaks underfoot. Halfway up, I have to duck my head under a beam to follow a winding little corridor up two higgledy steps and then down four uneven steps to a bedroom that sits on its own. It has small, mullioned windows that look out at the garden and is done up in shades of blue.

'Study?' I say, turning to Stella.

She turns and exits the room. We continue on up the stairs. The bedrooms are colourful and flowery. Stell barely gives each one a look before backing out.

'Well,' I say, as we climb back in the car, 'you certainly get a lot of house for your money, and I think it's lovely.'

'But…'

'Work with me, OK? I know that kitchen wasn't your style. But we can lay parquet over the flooring and paint the brickwork white. And the bedrooms – that was all cosmetic stuff. We could make it work. I think it was charming and very homely.'

'You think, you think,' says Stell in a nasty tone and I look sharply at her. Then she laughs. 'Just kidding. Let's keep looking?'

THREE

Stella

At last, a house that's perfect. I thought I'd never find it – but here it is: a listed barn that dates back to the twelfth century, except it's been gutted and completely refitted. Every room in the L-shaped building has double doors facing onto a sunny courtyard; behind the house there's a large, self-contained garden. The ultra-modern kitchen is so high-tech it makes the one in my London apartment look dated, and every room is an exercise in light, glass and airy space. More importantly, there's plenty of room for a couple of children, even as they get older. I don't plan on moving again.

Furthermore, the house is in the heart of a village – exactly what I want – but only a mile away from the last Tube on the line. It's the country/city compromise I've been looking for. *Yes*, I think, as I walk around the property with the estate agent: *this is The One. But how am I going to persuade George?* I double-check the listing I'm carrying around with me.

'So, about the price,' I say to the estate agent. 'Is there any flexibility on that?'

The estate agent shakes his head. 'I'm sorry. A house as

unusual as this? As well done-up? No. There's plenty of
interest, and the vendors rejected an offer yesterday of one
point two mill. They're not going to settle for less than one
point four. Though I expect they'll get the full asking price,
which is...' he checks his papers '. . . one point five.'

'Really? I mean...' I look around at the fields of sheep,
the cows and the woods that border the bottom of the garden.
'It's in the middle of nowhere.'

The agent laughs. 'It's what we call a "rural paradise".
This village is highly sought-after. There's a very good
community spirit here. Socials, fayres, a wonderful library,
a fantastic doctor's surgery and a pub that's the centre of
everything – but still within reach of central London. They
don't call it the "stockbroker belt" for nothing.'

I suck my cheeks in and look around. It's so quiet I can
practically hear my hair growing. It is exactly what I'm
looking for, but I'm not keen to tell the estate agent that.

'Most people moving to this area are looking for a better
quality of life,' says the agent as if I don't know that. He looks
about twelve and I guess he still lives with his parents; has
never bought a property of his own. There's something about
his pinstriped suit that I don't like; that and the fact that he's
lecturing me like a schoolteacher really doesn't help.

'They've done their time in London; earned their money,'
he says. 'Then they look up one day, in the City or wherever,
and wonder what it's all for. I see it all the time. Suddenly
they want big skies, birdsong, fresh air and neighbours who
say hello, not sirens at bedtime and stress, stress, stress.
It's personal, I suppose, if you want a friendly village or

to keep yourself to yourself. But look at the house.' He waves his arm towards the building. 'They spent half a mill on the refurbs and landscaping alone. Just look at the quality of the work. You can see they haven't skimped. I mean, the kitchen was imported from Italy. The floors are all solid wood. There's no laminate in there. It's all top of the range stuff.'

'Hmm.' He's right. It's why I love it so much.

'Look, if this is beyond your budget, I've other places. I just don't think we should waste anyone's time putting in an offer of anything less than one point four.' He gives me a sympathetic look. 'You liked The Lodge, didn't you? I can get that for you at a million.'

'I'm afraid The Lodge just wasn't "us",' I say.

'Oh, that's a shame because it's on at a really good price. Owners need a quick sale – they might even come down further. Well, look, why don't you go and have a think, have a chat to Him Indoors, and let me know what you want to do. But, if you're interested in this one, I'd advise moving fast. There's a lot of interest.'

'Give me a minute,' I say. I pull out my phone and dial George as I walk away from the estate agent. My heart's beating fast; I can't lose this house.

'Hey,' I say when George picks up. 'I'm really sorry. Bad news about The Lodge. It's been sold.'

'Oh shame – what was the offer? Can we beat it?'

'No. Deal's done. It's off the market now.'

George tuts. 'We should have moved faster. Locked them in. I told you to do that! If we have to live out in the sticks, that's the kind of place I'd like. Not one of those city places pretending to be a country home.'

'Mmm. But I've found another house, same sort of price, that I think you'll like. Silver lining and all that.'

'Really?' I can hear the disbelief in his voice. I suspect George thought I'd never find a house that I'd like. I've already rejected so many properties he's started calling me Goldilocks: 'This one's too big; this one's too small'. He's hoping, I think, that I'll give up the country dream so we can stay in central London, closer to his work, his friends and the goddamned motorcycle club Ness let him spend every other weekend with.

'Just a minute,' George says to someone at his end. I hear his footsteps; imagine him hunched over his phone, walking away from a meeting. 'Sorry. Crazy busy day. So what's it like? Is it similar?'

'Yes. It's a twelfth-century barn conversion. I sent you the details – remember?'

'Umm, yeah, maybe. Is it modernised?'

'What do you think? Its twelfth century!'

'Oh. Well, if it's what you want…' His tone is doubtful.

'Thanks, darling. You'll like it. Trust me. Big rooms, loads of space. A garden.'

'OK. Why don't we take a second viewing at the week-end?'

'That's the thing. There's a lot of interest. We've got to move fast. I'd like to put in an offer today. We can always retract it if you don't like it.'

Someone's talking to George at the other end of the line.

'Princess, I've got to go. If it's within the budget then go for it.'

'OK. Bye.'

I walk back to the estate agent. He's just getting off the phone himself. We start to speak at the same time.

'I'd like to put in an offer on this place,' I say.

'I'm afraid someone's just put in an offer,' he says.

'What?' I ask. 'How much? Was it accepted?'

'One point four. Yes, it was.'

'Call them back. Tell them one point four five.'

The estate agent raises an eyebrow. 'Are you sure? I thought your max was a mill.'

'Do it, please.'

The agent makes the call. 'Very well,' he says, 'I'll let her know. Hold on.'

He shakes his head. 'No deal.'

'How much?' I said. 'Ask them how much to get it off the market.'

'Asking price,' he says. 'One point five million and they'll take it off the market.'

'One point five and there's no more viewings, no more offers?'

He nods.

'OK, done. One point five subject to survey.'

The agent winds up the call and shakes my hand. 'Congratulations, Mrs Wolsey. It's a fantastic property and I hope you'll be very happy there.'

FOUR

George

The door to Stell's apartment has barely closed behind me when she appears in the hallway, a huge smile on her face. She's barefoot and casual, just the way I love her. I scoop her into my arms, whirl her around and kiss her slowly on the mouth.

'Good evening, Mrs Wolsey,' I say when I put her down.

'Good evening, Mr Wolsey,' she says. She takes my hand and leads me towards the kitchen.

'So we have a house?' I say. 'At last!' I dance a little *cha-cha*. Marrying Stell's made me feel ten years younger. It may have been Stell who pushed for us to get married, but now I see that Ness and I were stuck in a rut of familiarity – with Stell, everything's new and exciting again. And now we're through the property disagreement, I realise I haven't been this happy in ages. I dance over to the counter feeling like Fred Astaire, pick up the property listing and flick through the images. There's a lot of gleaming white space. The barn conversion looks more like a hospital than a home.

'Are you sure about this?' I ask. 'It's very modern. Are you sure it isn't too cold?'

'I love it.' Stell pulls a bottle of champagne out of the fridge. 'You will too, when you see it in the flesh.'

I turn back to the front page and then I see the price.

'One and a half million? Blimey. They took a big knock!'

'No. They took the asking price.' Stell says this as if it's obvious. 'I started low but had to go up. As I said on the phone, there was a lot of interest.' She untwists the wire on top of the bottle and starts to remove the foil.

'Hold on, hold on. You agreed on one point five million?'

'Yes?' Stell raises an eyebrow at me and pops the cork. 'Cheers!'

'But…'

She stops what she's doing and looks at me impatiently. 'It's perfect, George. You want us to be happy, don't you? Besides, you said this was fine. I emailed you the details, remember? And you said that if I liked it, we could do it. And I liked it. So…' She shrugs, and starts to pour the champagne.

'But, Stell… I didn't know it was one and a half million quid! Jesus!'

'Oh, come on: the price was on the listing. Of course you saw it. Don't be so melodramatic! This is our new home.' She hands me a glass. I take it but put it on the counter without tasting it. Stella hangs a teaspoon in the neck of the bottle and puts it back in the fridge. Then she straightens up and looks at me. We stare at each other for a few seconds and I feel we might be heading for our first proper argument.

'Princess,' I say gently. 'I'm not being melodramatic. It's just too much. I've freed up a million quid. It's more than enough for a lovely house. I can't go higher at this point. I'm sorry.'

Stell looks away. I go over to her and touch her arm, trying to make eye contact, but she won't look at me. I pull her face gently back and kiss her nose, which is all I can get.

'I just want us to start our new life together on the right foot.' I pause. 'Ness isn't exactly being understanding about all this. My liquid assets are stripped right back. She squeezed me for all she could get.' I think about the deal she nailed me to, citing my unreasonable behaviour. Aside from the business, of which I'm the chief shareholder, and my offshore investments, I'm pretty much starting out again, aged thirty-four. 'I just don't want to start off with a debt around our necks. Maybe we should look for somewhere smaller.'

'We'll need space for the children,' Stell says. 'I don't want to move again. A smaller house would be a false economy. Think of the stamp duty.'

'But don't forget all the other costs. You know – curtains and carpets and…'

'Shutters.'

'OK, shutters. Even worse. And furniture – shed-loads of furniture looking at the size of it – and heating and main-tenance.' I snort a laugh. 'I mean, Jesus, Stell, I think most people could find a pretty nice house outside London for a million quid.'

'OK,' Stell says. She turns her back to me and rummages in a kitchen cupboard. 'Look, if we can't afford it, I under-stand. I misunderstood you. I'll retract the offer.'

'Maybe we could find a cheaper place – a bit older, maybe a bit more homely, like The Lodge?'

'But we didn't like the style of The Lodge,' Stell says. 'It was too small, remember? The rooms were too higgledy-piggledy, and you hit your head on the beams.'

'I liked The Lodge.'

But Stell shakes her head at me. 'No. You forget. The Lodge stank of dogs.' Her nose wrinkles and she grimaces as she says it. 'Other people's dogs! There were no built-in wardrobes. I told you about the barn conversion and you loved the sound of it. Now, please, even if we're not celebrating, let's at least drink the champagne now I've opened it.'

She picks up my glass and hands it to me. 'Come on, let's sit down.'

I follow her to the living room, wondering how two peoples' experience of the same event could be so different. I thought I'd made it clear how much I liked The Lodge – though apparently not. I'm shocked that Stell's committed us to paying one and a half million for a house, but it's she not me who flops onto the sofa as if our conversation has drained her. I put my glass on the dining table and walk over to the window. Outside it's dark and the lights of London twinkle below the sodium haze. What's just happened? I'm not entirely sure. I turn back to the room.

'I have no memory of any of this: seeing the house details, talking about the price. I don't remember any of it,' I say.

Stell takes a sip of her drink and looks at me over the rim of the glass, her eyes narrowed; calculating. 'Really? You want to see?'

She doesn't wait for a reply. She picks up her phone and scrolls a bit, then holds the phone out to me. 'Look. Here you go.'

I read the email she's showing me: It's one and a half million but looks perfect, what do you think? And above that is my reply: It's a stretch but, if you like it, go for it. I just want you to be happy.

I hand the phone back to her. 'I didn't send this.'

'Um?' She laughs. 'Who did? Scooby Doo?'

'It wasn't me.'

'Yeah, yeah, Shaggy.' Stell laughs, but then she frowns, and I think about how busy I've been lately… how distracted.

'Oh… maybe I did…' I shrug. Surely I would have noticed something this big. But then, maybe not. I do just want Stell to be happy. I want to buy her her dream house.

Stell smiles at me. She jumps up, comes over and starts kissing my cheek; lots of tiny butterfly kisses.

'Oh George,' she says. 'You crazy cakes. It's OK. We'll let the house go. But what are we going to do with you? Having senior moments and you're only thirty-four!'

FIVE

Stella

I have to work quite hard on George.

'I really don't want a huge mortgage,' he tells me as we sit together at my dining table and go through the figures. 'Been there, had that millstone.' He rubs his neck and gives me one of his boyish grins. 'I'd really like to be able to buy our home outright… are you able to help? Do you have any spare cash lying about?'

I laugh. 'I would if I could. But every penny of my money is tied up in the company. Sorry.'

George sighs and rubs his chin. I wait. It's obvious his mind is whirring.

'Well,' he says after some time, 'I did inherit some money when Granny died. It's all tied up in investments, but I could potentially free it up. It's a big chunk.'

'Is it enough?'

He nods. 'Yeah. It would get us through.'

I clap my hands together. 'Perfect!'

'It might take some time, though. It's in a bond and I'm not sure when it matures. If interest rates have gone up and it doesn't mature any time soon, I'll have to sell below par. It's probably better to wait till it matures.'

'We don't have time. If we don't finalise this quickly someone else is going to snap up the house.'

'I know, I know…' George rubs his temples. 'But I need to speak to my broker.'

'Even if you sold below par would it be enough?'

'Yes. I imagine so.'

'Great! So, could you borrow the amount in the interim? Get a quick loan or something?'

'A loan shark? Please.'

I tut. 'Of course not.' We sit in silence for a minute. 'By the way,' I say slowly, as if the idea's just struck me, 'how much did you raise at the charity event in November?'

'About a million. Why?'

'And all of that money's with the charity now?'

George looks at me. 'No, most of it's still in the company account. I'm waiting for the last pledges to come through before I transfer it.'

I raise my eyebrows at him but George still doesn't get it: his eyes are searching my face.

'When does Nicholas expect the money to arrive?' I ask.

'He's pretty relaxed about it. If he knows it's coming, he doesn't push for it. Anyway, he's overseas at the moment, out in the field. What are you thinking?'

'Well…' I exhale. 'So technically it could be possible for you to borrow what we need for now from the charity account – perhaps give Nicholas the balance – and no one would be any the wiser. Right?' I can't read George's expression. 'God, don't look at me like that. I wasn't saying you should *steal* it – just borrow it until you release your funds from the bond.'

George is staring at me. 'Well, I suppose last year it did take a few months to get the money to him because we were waiting till we got the last of the bigger pledges…'

'OK… so you could even just say that you're waiting for a pledge to come in. Nicholas will neither know nor care as long as he gets the money in the end? It's not stealing.' I take off my glasses and smile at him. 'Look, it's only an idea. But I don't see the harm in it and I can't see any other way.' I pause. 'Or is there something else? Are you worried about putting the house in joint names if it's your money we're using to buy it?'

George frowns and shakes his head. 'No.'

'I have no issue with you keeping the house in your name,' I say. 'Give me a lasting power of attorney in case anything happens to you, but it can all be yours. I trust you. We're a team! Like we were at school. George 'n' Stell!' George smiles and I see that this does make him feel a little better. I wonder if he, too, remembers the pile of coats. I lean over and give him a kiss.

'This is the perfect house for us. We'd be so happy there. I just know it.'

He pulls me to him. 'OK, princess, let me think about it.'

SIX

George

And I give it a lot of thought. I really do.

I weigh it up for the best part of the morning, pacing up and down my office, listening to the conflicting voices in my head and, ultimately, what I come out with is this: as Stell said, it's not stealing; it's borrowing. I don't have a dishonest bone in my body; I'd no more steal from a charity than I would kill a puppy. What we're talking about here is a short-term loan that no one will ever know about. What is it they say? 'If a tree falls in a forest and no one's around to hear it, does it make a sound?' Of course it doesn't. I won't even remember borrowing the money in a year's time, let alone five years' time. It'll be a far bigger regret to have let this house that Stell loves go; to have to compromise; settle for less. I see us moving again in two years; I see Stell always hankering after the house that got away.

And it'll be fine. Everything always works out fine in the end.

So, I go online and shift half a million quid of the charity money into my own account without giving it a second thought. Lazenby's a mate: when he gets back from his trip,

I'll explain, make sure we're all upfront about it. When I pay it back, I'll even add on an extra five grand out of my own pocket – in lieu of interest, if you like.

And then we buy the house, and I feel good about it.

Stell throws herself into fitting it out the moment the sale goes through. For the next couple of months, she's up to her ears in swatches and samples, and it's a cold Saturday in February by the time she finally takes me to see the place. The bare trees that line the roads of West London are stark against the electric blue of the sky and, for the first time since New Year, I get that giddy sense of hope buzzing in the air. We turn onto the A40, which, amazingly, is clear, and anticipation crackles between the two of us – I honestly feel like a teenager again. I crank the music up loud and we sing along like a couple of schoolkids as I open the throttle and ease the car up to the speed limit. When the song ends, Stell turns it down and puts her hand on my leg.

'Sixteen years and we're finally together,' she says. 'As we always should have been. I love that it's going to be just the two of us: George 'n' Stell, finally living our country dream.'

I give her hand a squeeze. 'By the way, did I tell you I've even found a motorcycle club nearby? I can ride out with them every weekend. I think I might enjoy the country, after all.'

Stell doesn't reply so I turn the volume back up and we sing along again, laughing at the silly voices we each put on. Stell directs me once we leave the A40 and it's not long before we turn into the village. Stell's alert in her seat, head swivelling this way and that like a meerkat.

'This is it! This is Main Street, where everything is. And we're just… just down here on the right. Next right!'

I almost miss the turn – it's more of a lane than a street.

'Private access,' says Stell. 'Leads only to our house.'

I pull up outside the house. With walls that are a mix of red brick and black timber, topped with a thatched roof, it's a dark-looking building from the outside, and not entirely what I would have imagined from what I've seen of the interior. Maybe she's been bluffing me about the glass and steel. Honestly, if it's more rustic inside than modern, I'll be pleased. Give me a good set of ceiling beams, an Aga and a bit of oak, and I'll be happy.

'Ta-da!' says Stell, as she pushes me through the front door and the first thing that strikes me is the smell. It smells like every five-star hotel I've stayed in; some sort of blend of cedar wood, bergamot and jasmine. In the hallway I see a glass jar of those scented sticks and I get what she's trying to do with them. The place smells clean and fresh, but it doesn't smell like home.

Stell nudges me down a polished concrete corridor towards the kitchen, and I see at once that the entire place really has been gutted and refitted. She flicks some switches and spotlights come on in the ceilings; electric blue lights along the base of the kitchen cabinets.

'Do you like the lights? I love them!' Stell says and I nod because she's so enthusiastic; so proud of what she's done but, as I look around the kitchen, I can't see anything except a glistening sink and a quad of identical-looking ovens built into the cabinets. No fridge, no dishwasher. But Stell pulls open a few doors and I see that everything's been hidden among the gleaming white panels.

'Where's the Aga?'

Stell gives me a little nudge. 'Don't you like it?' Her face is lit up like a little girl, and I feel bad for teasing her. 'It's a great kitchen!' she says. 'Trust me.'

She doesn't wait for an answer before hustling me out of the kitchen and down the corridor past a study and a dining room to the staircase.

'I want to show you upstairs first.' She flicks her eyes to the glossy concrete floor. 'Underfloor heating, by the way.'

'Phew.'

'We can put a runner down if you find it too austere.'

We look at a couple of good-sized bedrooms done in fifty shades of neutral, then Stell leads me into the master bedroom.

'Wow,' I say again. It could well have been Stell's room from her apartment transported here: the same shades of white and soft grey. I get why she likes this colour scheme, it's clean and easy on the eye, but a huge part of me is disappointed. It's so impersonal. I wanted to see something of Stella in our bedroom; some passion, some colour. Ness had her faults but she was always a noisy riot of colour, her personality imprinted on everything in our house. Stell's idea of 'home' tells me nothing about her and it leaves me wishing for something that shows me who she is; something more than this perfect exterior. If I'd have opened the door and found a jungle of greens, browns and fiery reds, I'd have had her on the bed right away.

'And now,' Stell says, 'close your eyes.' She takes my arm and leads me to another room. 'OK, open them.'

I realise at once that this is the nursery. A cot takes pride of place in the centre of the room, a white mosquito net centred above it. For some reason it makes me think of *The Sleeping Beauty*: a room for a prince or princess to sleep in splendid isolation. The baby's not being limited to neutrals, though – here, Stell's allowed a little yellow to creep in in a cheery pattern on the curtains and also on the cot bedding. There's a multicoloured mobile hanging above it, too, and a plastic sheep gizmo thing at the foot of the bed.

'Night light. Plays lullabies,' says Stell, as I go over to see what it is.

By the window there's a stylish white nursing chair and a folded grey blanket. Stell squeezes her hands together as she looks at me.

'What do you think?'

I pull her to me and hug her. 'It's perfect. Great job.'

'Do you mind that I chose the cot already?' she asks.

'No. Not at all. Should I?'

'The woman in the shop thought I was being presumptuous. She practically told me not to count my chickens, the dried-up old bag. But we'll make it happen, won't we?'

I stroke her hair. 'If anyone can make it happen, princess, we can.'

SEVEN

Stella

'What on earth were the movers thinking?' I say as I open the cupboard above the kettle expecting to find the coffee and tea, but find myself staring at condiments and spices. 'Did they put any thought into how they filled the cupboards at all?'

'Not everyone's a cook,' says George. He's at the kitchen table in his leathers with the morning's papers. It's our first Saturday in the new house and we're slowly learning that, while the kitchen might look immaculate on the surface, the unpackers have thrown our new supplies higgledy-piggledy into the glossy white cupboards.

'Yes,' I say, opening random cupboards to try to find the coffee, 'but unpacking is their job! They should know how to do it! They do it for a living, for pete's sake! I can't bear it.' I start pulling packets of tea and coffee out of the cupboard once I find them sitting alongside the tomato paste and rice. 'I'm going to redo it. The whole kitchen!'

'Hang on, hang on,' says George, finally looking up from the sports page. 'If we're going to do it, we should do it properly. Let's draw up a plan of what should go where. Ergonomics. Not only should it look nice, but it should be efficient, too.' He stands up and stretches. 'Right, if you'll excuse me, I'm off to meet the local MC. They're planning a ride into the Chilterns.'

I turn to look at him. 'Oh. How long will that take?'

'A few hours. More if we stop for lunch.'

'Oh.' Pause. 'And the kitchen?'

'I'll help you later.'

I turn back to the cupboard and pull out a few more things. 'OK. Don't worry. I'll do it myself.' I'm speaking into the cupboard. 'Have fun.'

George doesn't move for a minute, then I hear him put his jacket back down and his boots cross the kitchen floor. He slides his arms around my waist and kisses my neck.

'Would you like me to stay at home?'

'Well. It is our first weekend at home together. And the kitchen does need to be done.'

'Then I'll stay.'

I turn in his arms and kiss his lips. 'Thank you.'

I get a piece of paper from the study and settle myself next to George on the bench seat, leaning in close to his body. He quickly sketches out a three-dimensional plan of the kitchen. I watch his hand, fascinated, as the pencil makes deft marks on the paper. Out of nowhere, a diagram appears.

'Right,' he says. 'Are we agreed that the kettle and the coffee-maker go here?'

I nod.

'Then the tea and coffee need to go in this cupboard.'

'Agreed.'

'And it makes sense to put the dishes and glassware in the

cupboards above the dishwasher, wouldn't you agree? And the saucepans in the drawer under the hob?'

'Spoken like a scientist,' I say.

We work our way around the plan of the kitchen, then, when it's complete, and we're happy with where everything is stored vis-à-vis where it'll be used, we pull everything out of the cupboards, and start sorting it.

'I'm looking forward to getting to know people in the village,' I say while we work.

'You'll have to make friends for both of us,' says George. 'Scope people out.' He chuckles.

'Why me? Why not both of us?'

'I'm going to be quite busy at work.'

'At home, though? I'm thinking pub lunches, afternoon siestas…'

George doesn't even turn to me. He gives an ironic little laugh. 'The lunches will have to wait. Maybe pub suppers.'

'Why? Where will you be?' We said we'd both work at home at least half the week.

'At the office, princess. I've so much on at the moment, I need to be there. We're pitching for a major new client.'

'But the company's doing well, right?'

'Yes. But this is business. It's pride. This company would be a major feather in our cap – it'd lead to more business. It's how it works.'

As if I don't know that.

'I know what we planned,' he says. 'But work's crazy-busy and I need to be there.'

Finally, George turns to look at me. I'm standing stock

still, a brand-new cast-iron saucepan in my hand, thinking: *George, broken promises*. For a second, anger pulses through me and I have the insane thought to whack him over the head with the Le Creuset. I'm breathing hard and I clench my teeth together to try to hide it.

'Don't look like that,' George says. 'It won't be for ever.'

'But you promised. You said…' I hate my tone. It sounds whingey. Needy. I'm not needy. I don't do needy.

'I know what we said,' says George. 'But look, the house cost more than we planned. No one pulls in a new client like I do. They need me in the office. For now. Once we're through this – once the new client's on board – I can ease off. But for now, see it as an investment in our future.'

I slip the pan into its designated drawer underneath the hob, taking the moment to close my eyes for a second, and take a deep breath.

'Yes,' I say, as I straighten back up. 'Of course.'

George comes over and puts his arms around me. When he speaks, I can feel his mouth moving against my hair; the heat of his breath on my scalp. 'I know you just want me here, all to yourself.'

I push him away and turn back to the array of kitchenware that's still spread out all over the units. 'Come on, let's get this done and maybe we can get to the pub at some point today.' I pause. 'That is if you're not *working*.'

'Ha ha, very funny.'

'I was thinking, by the way,' he says after a pause, 'we could throw a house-warming party. It would be a great way to get to know people. They must be dying to see what was done to the house during the refurbishments. We could let them in to have a look around.'

'You make it sound like the Queen opening up Buckingham Palace!'

George laughs and flushes, clearly pleased with the analogy. 'Yeah. Something like that. What do you think?'

'Good idea.'

'We could just invite the whole village. How many do you think live here? Two hundred? Three hundred?'

'Easily.'

'Fantastic! We'll blow them out of their sleepy little beds – show this village how to parteee!' George dad-dances around the kitchen. 'Maybe you could get into the coffee mornings; inveigle your way into the "in" crowd – find out who's who; make sure they get invited.'

'Yes. I'll go to yoga at the village hall. There's coffee after. That's where I'll get the gossip.'

'Yoga? Not kick-boxing?'

'I feel a gentler sport might be the way forward if I'm trying to…' I pat my tummy, and George smiles.

'You love a plan, don't you?'

'I do, hon. I do.'

EIGHT

George

Stell looks incredible when she comes downstairs later that evening. She's wearing a tight cashmere sweater, black leather jeans and high-heeled boots that make her hips swing when she walks. I've not made much of an effort myself: we're only going to the pub. She stops by the door to shrug on her coat and I give her a little wolf whistle. 'Nice. You're going to give the village girls a run for their money.'

She gives me a smile and holds out her arm. 'Shall we, Mr Wolsey?'

As we walk together down the lane, I try not to trip or land my foot in a puddle. The lane's not lit and it's hard to tell where the potholes are. Stell's clutching my arm, even less steady than I am.

'Maybe flats next time, princess,' I say as she teeters. 'You ain't in Kansas now… or rather, you are in Kansas now!' She rolls her eyes at me. Truth is, I quite enjoy having her hang tightly on to my arm; it's so rare that she needs me. I clutch her a bit tighter. On the wind, I pick up the smell of cows or horses – some sort of shit anyway. Stell breathes it deeply into her lungs and then breathes out with her eyes closed and her face lifted to the night air.

'It's different to London,' she says. 'but I like it. Just smell that fresh, country air. I can feel it going down into my lungs, expelling all those city fumes!'

'It's because it's so bloody cold. That's why you can feel it going down into your lungs!'

'It's going to be nice having a local, where everyone knows us.'

I suddenly get a flash of my local in Richmond: my drinking buddies round the bar; the late-night lock-ins; the sing-songs with Ness; the band who used to let me bang the drums while Ness bashed out the old favourites on the piano. We were a great double act.

'I guess.'

We turn onto Main Street and walk past a couple of shops to the pub.

'Bingo,' says Stell, pulling open the door. 'It's so close!'

Inside, it takes my eyes a moment to adjust to the light. It's an average pub: traditional; nothing special; but the open fire crackling down one end is a nice touch. There's a handful of people at the bar, and several of the dining tables and booths are taken. I point Stell to a vacant table then head to the bar for our drinks.

'You new around here?' asks the barman as he pours my pint and a whisky chaser.

'Yep. Just moved in.'

'Ah. To the barn?'

'Exactly.'

'Jolly good, jolly good. Nice to see it lived in again.' He shakes his head. 'Thought the work would never finish. Trucks and lorries up and down the lane at all hours bringing mud all over the street.' He tuts. 'Anyway. Happy with it?'

I nod. 'Certainly. It's been done well.'

While he waits with the glass still tilted under the pump, the man holds out his spare hand. 'I'm Derek, by the way. Landlord.'

I shake his hand. 'George. George Wolsey. Pleased to meet you.'

Derek raises his eyebrows. 'Anything to do with Wolsey Associates?' He sings a line or two from one of my current ads.

I sing along with him, ending with a flourish, then grin. 'Yep. I am the one and only Wolsey.' I give him a mock bow.

Derek nods slowly and places my pint on the counter. 'Welcome to the village. Now what's your rather lovely lady wife drinking?'

'A large glass of Sauvignon, cheers. Hang on, let me introduce you. Stell!' I call across the pub. 'Come and say hello!'

God, she looks good as she walks over. I'd say there are ten or so other women in the pub, some younger than Stell, and none of them holds a candle to her. There's something of the Angelina Jolie about the length of her legs and the look in her eye. Her hair's scooped back in a messy bun and, with her face framed against her her roll-neck sweater, it shows off both her cheekbones and her lips. The diamond studs I bought her glitter in her ears. She's gorgeous, and the best thing is: she has no idea herself. Hand on heart: she's perfect for me.

'Derek, this is my wife, Stella.'

Now I'm used to men appreciating Stell's looks but I'd have to be blind to miss the way he looks at her. I swear his mouth falls open and, for whatever reason, my hackles rise and all the good feeling I had about him recognising me evaporates. Then Stell holds out her hand for Derek to shake but he does that poncy thing where he takes it and kisses it.

'Enchanted,' he says, and Stella only goes and blushes.

'Will you be eating tonight?' Derek asks without taking his eyes off her.

'We'll take a look at your menu, certainly,' I say briskly and Stell gives me a funny look, as if to say: *We came out for dinner, why are you being so weird?*

'Why don't you grab a table while there's still one available, and I'll bring over the menus?' says Derek.

'Don't trouble yourself. I'll take them,' I say.

*

The food's nice and Derek doesn't bother us. Maybe he picked up on my irritation, but he sends over a waitress to take our orders and, after another beer, I manage to enjoy my steak pie and chips. Stell's more critical of her salad, like she's writing a review in her head.

'Dressing's a bit oily,' she says, poking a lettuce leaf with her fork. 'The beetroot was non-existent and I barely saw two bits of walnut.'

'But it's good?'

'It's OK. No great shakes.' She sighs. 'It's such a shame. They've a trapped audience here. If a pub like this had someone like me consulting on the menu it'd be unstoppable.'

'Like the River Café.'

Stell laughs, and we take our time over one, then two, bottles of red wine, and then I have treacle pudding and custard – custard! – while Stell has a coffee. I yawn.

'Early night, Mrs W.? I'm exhausted.'

'I was thinking about a nightcap.'

'Let's go home. I need my bed.' I stand up and Stell follows suit.

''Night!' calls Derek across the pub.

'That's nice, isn't it?' says Stell as the cold air hits us outside. 'Being known by the landlord? I like that. He seems really nice.'

'Yeah, "really nice". I saw you blushing when he slobbered all over your hand. Don't get too "known by the landlord"!' I stumble a little then, and realise I've drunk more than I thought.

Stell laughs. 'Oh I don't know… if you're going to be at work all the time…' She skips a little ahead of me, swinging her hips and flicking her hair. 'I've always fancied having a go with an older man… seeing what a silver fox is like in the sack… I mean: all that experience!'

She turns back to me and she's laughing. I know she's joking yet, from nowhere, a red rage courses through my body. Ness was never like this. Ness knew her place. In two steps, I'm on Stell, and we struggle as I try to grab hold of her by her upper arms. For a moment, we're both grappling in the street. Then I get her and I give her a tiny shake, my face close to hers. Her eyes are saucers in the white of her face.

'George! Get off me! What are you doing?' Stell struggles, but I've got her hard by the biceps. I give her another tiny shake.

'Don't you *ever* joke about it! OK?' I'm shouting. It's suddenly imperative that I get this message through to her. I've given up everything – my house, my wife, almost all of my money in that sham of a divorce settlement – to be here with Stell. She has to know what a sacrifice I've made. She has to know she can't mess me about.

'I never want you to speak to him again!' I hiss at her and she flinches as some of my spit lands on her face. She tries to rub it off with her shoulder.

'Yes, George.' She speaks slowly and nods sarcastically. 'Yes, never speaking to the pub landlord: that'll work. Dream on!' She wrenches herself free of my arms and runs towards the house. I break into a sprint and grab her but we both go crashing to the ground.

'For fuck's sake, George! What's got into you?' Stell scrabbles in the mud and wet leaves to get up. I jump back up. I've banged my elbow and my knee.

'Stell. I'm so sorry.' I try to touch her but she jumps away and scurries towards the house without looking back. I catch her up at the door and bundle through it after her as she tries to slam it in my face. In the hall, I grab her and spin her around to face me.

'I'm sorry! I'm sorry. I love you! OK?'

She stares at me. We're both breathing hard, scraped and covered in damp patches from the fall, covered in leaves and sticks and smears of mud. Then I lean forward and kiss her, hard, and then I'm practically eating her I'm so hungry for her. I claw at her clothes, desperate to feel the warmth of her bare skin, to feel the weight of her tits in my hand. I wrestle with my jeans then I tear off her boots and wrench down her leather trousers and then I've hitched her up against the wall, her legs around my waist and I'm slamming into her and we're both gasping and I come hard inside her.

My God, that woman.

NINE

Stella

George goes upstairs when we've recovered ourselves while I fix my clothes and hobble into the kitchen. What the fuck was that all about? It was a side of George I've not seen before. I sit at the island for a minute or two, head in hands, and try to examine how I feel.

How dare he? How dare he treat me like that? I sit in silence for a good few minutes, thinking. Then, shaking my head, I pour us each a glass of water and follow George upstairs. He's already in bed.

'Here, take these or you'll have a sore head tomorrow.' I hand him his water and a couple of tablets, and watch while he takes them.

'Thanks, princess,' he says. 'That was amazing, by the way.'

'We'll talk about it in the morning.'

I take back his glass but, by the time I've hung my clothes, he's fast asleep. I stand and look at him as he snores on the out-breath as well as the in-breath. Lying there, smelling of booze, George looks like any soon-to-be middle-aged man – there's no hint of advertising's golden boy there now

– and, for a fleeting moment, I wonder what someone else's middle-aged bully of a husband is doing in my bed. He's put on weight lately, carrying it in the pudge in his face, his torso, backside and fleshy thighs. Although his general outline is familiar, it's as if it's blurred – blended – and I don't like it one bit.

But then look what he ate and drank at the pub. Where does he think all that rubbish goes? George used to be so lean, so fit. He used to care about how he looked. Is that it? Now he's got me, he's letting himself go? I resolve then and there to put him on a diet. It'll be hard for him: I know how much he likes his food.

Is it a punishment for the way he treated me tonight?

You tell me.

TEN

George

I come to slowly, unsure for a few seconds of where I am. Light oozes between the shutters and I'm aware of a throbbing pain in my head before I'm even fully conscious and I lie still, desperate not to make it worse. I haven't had a headache like this in years: it's quite a party trick of mine to know just how much I can drink before a hangover is inevitable. I'm famous for it at the office, actually: the last man standing; the first man in at 8 a.m. So what happened last night?

I think back. We went to the pub. Quiet night. Dinner, a beer or two, a bottle of wine – or was it two? I can kind of picture myself asking for a second one. Then? Oh my God! The sex! I remember the sex. Despite my head, my dick stiffens at the memory and I allow myself a moment to remember the feeling of Stell clinging to me, rammed up against the wall while I thrust into her.

But what led to that? Was there some sort of scuffle? It's hazy. Something to do with the bloke in the pub? I'm naked – which is usual – but, out of the corner of my eye, I see my clothes in a crumpled heap on the floor which is not like me.

I usually manage to get them at least on the chair; folded, even. I buy nice clothes. I look after them. Was I that drunk?

Slowly, gently, trying not to hurt my head any further, I roll over and look at Stell. She's on her side, sleeping the way that makes her hair kink in the morning, and she looks really peaceful. I enjoy watching her sleep: I love the way her eyelashes curl onto her cheeks and the sandy pink of her lips – slightly parted in sleep – her nose, the paleness of her skin, the little freckles she hides every day with make-up, even the fuzzy, warm scent of her. I can still smell a version of her perfume from last night, top notes missing now, like ghosts. I like the faded scent, but it disorientates me for a moment, especially in my state, because it used to be Ness who had the cosy, slept-in, morning smell while Stell was always fresh perfume and lipstick, applied for our dates. I still can't quite believe that everything's out of the closet now – no more creeping around, no more lying.

Stell's eyes flutter and open. She doesn't move; just lies there staring back at me, through eyelids that I see now are puffy.

'Morning.' My voice is a croak. 'Jesus, what did they put in that wine?'

Stell's hand moves to her forehead, her fingers exploring. 'Ow.'

'I think that bloke spiked our drinks!' I try to laugh but it hurts too much.

Stell moves her hand away from her head, moves her head a little, and I see a bruise, angry and purple, on her temple; a stain on the satin of her skin.

'Whoah!' I say. 'That looks sore. Are you OK?'

She closes her eyes and lets her head fall back on the pillow.

'When did you get that? Not last night?'

She rolls over and faces me; props herself up on one elbow and I see properly now the extent of the bruise; the puffiness of her eyes.

'What happened?'

She shrugs.

I think back again. I remember more detail this time, but there are still blanks – the latter half of the evening is definitely hazy, but I can picture Derek behind the bar; I remember the way he'd slobbered over Stell; the rush of anger that had coursed through me; Stell teasing me; goading me, and shame oozes through me as I remember how jealous she made me feel. As if Derek, with his paunch and his thinning, greying hair, would ever stand a chance!

'Was it when we… ?' I smile, but she doesn't smile back. 'It must have been then. You must have bumped your head.' But even as I'm saying it I'm remembering the position we were in and I know her forehead wasn't anywhere near the wall. I reach out to touch her arm, but she jerks it away.

'I didn't bump my head.'

Another memory leaps into my mind's eye: us tussling in the mud. 'Oh God! We fell over, didn't we! My elbow's sore, now I come to think of it.' I rub at my arm. 'You must have hit your head then.'

Stell sighs. 'Does it matter?'

'You've got a bruise the size of Africa. Of course it bloody matters!'

'Can we just drop it? The bruise is inconsequential. What we do need to talk about is the bigger picture about what happened last night, which is your insecurity. You were drunk and jealous. I mean, really, George. You were out of control. I've never seen you like that before.'

'Must have been off my head. Sorry.' I grin at her: sheepish, I hope, but she's looking at me in a way I've never seen before. As if she's shying away from me. She puts her hand to the bruise and looks so sad that I suddenly can't breathe.

'Do you remember what happened? How you got the bruise?'

She just looks at me with those eyes.

'Stell? Tell me.'

She closes her eyes. 'Can we just not talk about it? It's bad enough as it is without hashing over it.'

She turns her back to me, gets out of bed and goes into the bathroom, closing the door behind her. I try the door: it's locked. I knock.

'Stell… hon… open up. What are you saying? That I did this to you?'

Silence.

'Stell, come on! Please!' I lean my head against the door. How did we come to this? We're barely married two minutes and now she's got a bruise and she's locked me out of the bathroom. I feel like a complete shit; unworthy. I hear her pee, then the flush of the toilet, the gush of water as she washes her hands. Then the door opens, forcing me to scramble upright.

'An apology would be nice,' she says, walking past me, 'then let's leave it at that.'

'I'm sorry! Of course I'm sorry! You've no idea how sorry I am!'

I spin around and watch her slide open the wardrobe door and rifle through her clothes. And then I see a mark on her arm. Four semicircle marks on her bicep, to be precise. I pick up her arm and she watches me as I examine it. There's a larger mark on the inside of her bicep. Matching marks on her other arm. My eyes meet hers and I let her arm drop. My head's pounding; my vision cloudy and I feel giddy, like I might even throw up. I lean against the wall for support.

Stell turns back to the wardrobe. 'Look, in the grand scheme of things, it's not important,' she says. 'There's zero chance of me running off with Derek, so let's just agree today that you're going to learn to control your jealousy and anger, and then pretend it never happened. OK? It's fine.'

'It's not fine. It's far from fine! You're covered in bruises!' I realise I've raised my voice, but domestic violence in any shape or form is not something I do. Ever. There are things I may be, but a wife-beater is not one of them.

Stell spins around, her hands up and her eyes wide with – oh my God! – fear. 'Whoah. Chill out! You have such a temper. It's not good.'

'I'm sorry, but I don't believe I hit you! I wouldn't do that!'

'But you don't remember?' She stares at me, challenging me.

I hang my head. 'No.'

She looks at the bruise in the mirror, tracing around it with her finger. 'Look. It was an accident. And I don't want to talk about it. There's nothing to say.' Her tone is final, like there's lots she's not telling me; lots she'll never tell me. 'I just hope no one from the village saw us fighting. I'd be so ashamed.'

My heart's thumping. 'I didn't hit you.' I take a step towards her, wanting to pull her into my arms, stroke her hair, comfort her, apologise, make things right again, but she sidesteps me.

'I'm so sorry,' I say. 'If it was my fault, I'm so, so sorry. But I don't remember. I don't remember anything at all after coming upstairs.'

Stell takes her clothes into the bathroom and shuts the door again. I slump onto the end of the bed and wait. It's the first time she's ever shut me out while she's getting dressed. Is she punishing me?

Or is she scared of me?

The door lock clicks open. 'I just don't think you should drink so much,' she says when she comes out. 'It doesn't help. And I'm really worried about your jealousy, your anger *and* about the fact you can't remember much of last night.'

'But – I love you. I'm sorry I got jealous. It's just I've given up so much to be able to be with you, I couldn't bear to see a prick like that landlord slobbering over you and you looking like you enjoyed it. You understand that, don't you?' I look at her but she's got her hands on her hips and a frown on her face.

'I'd never harm you,' I say. 'You know that, don't you?' I try to catch her arm and again she shies away. I feel like a fool following her around, naked. I'm so frustrated I want to shake her to get her to understand and then I realise that I shook her last night. It comes back to me: me shaking her on the way home from the pub. Did I shove her, too? Bash her head on the wall in my rage? Punch her?

Did I?

'You promised it wouldn't happen again,' Stell says. 'And I believe you, so it's fine.' She looks at me, hands on hips. 'Please let's just pretend it never happened.' She releases her hair from her clip and pulls the front so it falls over the bruise. 'Look. I can put make-up on it, too. No one need know.'

Suddenly, I'm swallowing back tears. 'I'm so sorry. So, so sorry.'

Finally, she comes over to me and stands right in front of me. I stare at her, taking in her face, her beautiful face, then she leans forward and kisses my cheek.

'Let's put it behind us and move on,' she says. 'Please?'

ELEVEN

George

Stell goes downstairs and I sink back onto the bed, my head in my hands. Never in my life have I felt so ashamed.

And so confused.

I'm not perfect – this I know – but I'd never deliberately harm a woman. If there was one thing our parents managed to ingrain into Harry and me, it was not to lay a hand on a woman. But I know I have both a jealous side and a bit of a temper, especially when I've had a few. And Stell knows how to push my buttons. She's much feistier than Ness. But was I really so drunk that I pushed her, hit her or smashed her head on something? Why was I so angry? That Derek bloke was hardly God's gift.

I try to imagine what could have happened. She was teasing me about Derek in the lane. That I remember. But it's what happened at home that I can't remember, and that she's not telling me. Did she do something stupid like a striptease and pretend it was for Derek? I can almost see her flicking her lingerie around in the bedroom and dancing, licking her lips, gyrating her hips and moaning 'Derek' to piss me off. Is that what happened after we came upstairs? Or did she call his name when I fucked her?

Did I hit her?

I don't remember.

I have the sense I'm standing on shifting sand; an unnerving feeling that there's way more to what happened last night than what Stell's letting on; that she knows more than I do.

I get up and pace up and down the room. Ness never gave me any trouble like this. She was always the model wife. We had our roles and we stuck to them. Obviously, I was the leader: I decided where we went, who we saw, what we did and when we left, and she was happy to follow. It was how it was and it was never questioned. I breathe in deeply through my nose as I accept that this might not be the case with Stell. In my fantasies of life with her, I always imagined her in Ness's role: slightly subservient. Magnificent, maybe, but never challenging; never questioning; never provoking. I always saw it as a partnership – with me as top dog.

I may have to revisit that idea. It's a new, and altogether unpleasant sensation.

I scrabble in my bedside cabinet for Panadol, hoping it will take away the pain if not the shame, then get into the shower. The water cascades down my body as if it can wash last night away. But whatever happened, one thing remains: why can't I remember it? Why can't I remember anything beyond coming into the bedroom?

I throw on my clothes, squirt cologne on my face and realise that, to add to my woes, I can't find my wedding ring. If it's not on my finger, it's always by the sink and it's nowhere to be found. Tutting to myself, I head downstairs, where Stell's sitting in the kitchen with a coffee and the iPad. She looks up and gives me a smile.

'Coffee's done.'

I lean down and kiss her hair. 'Thanks, princess.' I pause. 'And – again – I'm so sorry.'

She holds her hand up. 'It's over.'

'I just want to ask you one thing.'

'OK?'

'Do you think I should be worried that I don't remember what happened? It's like I had a blackout. And there are other things I've forgotten, too.'

Stell sucks the inside of her cheek. 'I don't know. You've had a stressful year, what with the divorce and the house move… What is it they say? Those are two of the most stressful life changes a person can go through? I guess it's understandable that you're forgetting things. I wouldn't worry too much.'

'Hmm. But…'

'But what?'

I sigh. 'Oh, I don't know. It's just not like me. That's all.' While we're talking I move around the kitchen, picking up papers and moving things about, trying to find my wedding ring – it's a chunky platinum band that tells the world how married I am, and Stell hates me being without it. I have a quick look at the hall table and the sink by the downstairs bathroom.

'Looking for something?' she asks when I come back into the kitchen.

I shrug and pour my coffee. 'No.'

She appears to look directly at my left hand and I steel myself for her to notice, but she doesn't.

'How about we go out for breakfast?' I say. 'Take a little drive into the countryside and find somewhere new to try?' I rub my hands together. 'I could just murder a Full English.'

Stell's lips flatten and she shakes her head just a little. 'I don't think that's a good idea. Sorry to say it, but you need to start taking care of your weight. I'm going to put you on a diet.' She taps the iPad. 'I've been working out a plan for you. If you stick to it, you should lose one or two kilos a week.'

'What does it entail? Cabbage soup?' Even as I say it, I'm thinking I'll do anything – anything at all – to prove to Stell that I love her; to make amends for what happened last night. From now on, what she says, goes.

'Nothing like that. Lots of protein. Carbs only if you've exercised. No carbs at night. No sugar.'

'Okaaay...'

'Give it a try, George.' Stell gets up and comes over, puts her hands on my waist and squeezes what flesh she finds. 'You've got to get a grip on this or it's only going to get worse.'

I move her hands off my waist and hold them. 'All right. So no breakfast.' I do a fake sniff. 'What shall we do today then?'

'Let's go for a walk, then I'll make you something healthy for lunch.'

TWELVE

Stella

I'm just putting the last of the things back in the kitchen cupboards a few days later when I hear a key in the front door. I look at the oven clock: 11.15. It can only be George. I haven't left the kitchen since he left the house at seven-thirty this morning and, for an insane second, I have the sense that I've been caught doing something I shouldn't. I give my head a little shake as I close the last cupboard door. I wasn't expecting him back till much later this evening.

The door slams, then George's footsteps thud down the passage. He bursts into the kitchen and I can tell at once that something's wrong. His face is grey and his hair ruffled, as if he's been running his hands through it all morning. He looks surprised to see me standing in the kitchen and, for a second, my absurd feeling of guilt returns.

'Hey,' I say. 'You're early.'

George makes straight for a cabinet and rips open the door. He doesn't find what he wants, so he pulls open the next one, then the next.

'Where's the whisky?'

'And hello to you, too,' I say. 'Would you like a coffee?'

'Where is it?' George is still opening cabinets, leaving open the doors I've just closed. I walk over to a cabinet, extract the whisky bottle and hand it calmly to him. George then opens the cupboard above the dishwasher.

'What the… ?' he snaps. 'Now where are the glasses? I thought we did all this! God. I give up!'

He slams the cupboard, untwists the cap of the bottle and raises it to his mouth.

'Stop! Stop it!' I leap to the cabinet where the glasses are kept and hand him a tumbler. 'Here. You're clearly upset but don't take it out on the kitchen.'

George pours himself a good slosh of whisky and downs it in one, then pours another, all the while shaking his head – whether to do with the fact he couldn't find the whisky or his day I've no idea.

'Are you going to tell me what this is all about?' I say. 'Why are you home? What's going on?'

George stands across the kitchen from me. 'Been chucked out of the office, that's what's going on. Chucked out of my own bloody office!'

'What?'

George pulls at his hair. 'They found out about the money.'

'What money? The loan?'

George throws another whisky into his mouth, wincing as he swallows.

'Yep. One of the trustees called the office to ask when the money from the fundraiser was coming. Can you believe it? Last year it was months before we handed it over. Talk about Sod's Law! The one time—' George bangs his fist on the counter as he says the word '—the one time I do something like this!'

'But… but how?'

'So the trustee speaks to my accountant. The accountant checks the account and sees I've withdrawn five hundred grand. He tells the trustee he must have received this money and suddenly I'm standing in my own accountant's office like a schoolboy explaining that I "borrowed" half a million quid of charity money to buy a house!'

'But it was just a loan?'

George scrubs at his eyes and, when he looks at me, he looks hunted.

'Maybe I could have got around my accountant. But he'd already told the trustee that I'd withdrawn the money. I mean, why wouldn't he? He thought it had been lost in transit, not that his CEO had nicked it.' George is still pulling at his hair like he wants to rip it out.

'But now you can explain? Surely? Nicholas is a friend, isn't he?'

'Well, if it were up to him, maybe. But there's a bigger story going on here. Lazenby was away, and the trustees jumped on it. It turns out the charity's been defrauded of money by quite a few benefactors and there's a much bigger investigation going on. It's a criminal offence: "charity fraud". Lazenby's had to cut short his trip. He's furious.'

I step towards George and try to hug him but he shrugs me off.

'The media's bound to get hold of this. What am I going to do?' George is pacing the kitchen, running his hands through his hair. 'But you know what hurts the most? I've been accused of stealing from the charity I work my arse off to support!' He takes another swig of whisky.

'That's ridiculous.'

As George stares at me, he blinks several times and I realise he's holding back tears. 'It's not, though, is it? I took the money. I took it.' He turns away from me.

I trail a finger on the countertops. 'Look,' I say. 'This isn't fraud; it's a loan. What you've done isn't a crime. I'm sure if you explain what happened and give them a date when you'll pay back the money, you can clear this up amicably.'

'As I just said, it's too late. It's now part of a bigger investigation so the moment this came up it was like a red flag to a bull. Lazenby's too trusting. And, in my case, there's no grey area. Even a five-year-old could see that I withdrew the money from the company account and didn't pay it in to the charity account. It's all there in black and white.' George puts his head in his hands and moans.

I shake my head. 'That's so unfair! The others were presumably stealing while all you did was borrow.'

'It's all the same on paper. God. After that fundraiser! How much work did I put into that thing? I didn't eat or sleep for weeks.' George smashes his hand into his forehead. 'It's crazy! I love those kids. I love making their lives better.' He turns to face me. 'I shouldn't have done it. I shouldn't have taken the money. It's that simple. If I were them, I'd be investigating me, too.' He looks broken.

'It's my fault. I'm so sorry. I should never have suggested it.'

'But I did it. No one forced me to. I could have tried to talk to the seller – told them when the money would be ready. I could have got a proper loan.'

'I'm so sorry.'

George takes a deep breath and pours himself another whisky. 'So now I've been kicked out of the office. As soon as the board found out, they had an emergency meeting: they feel it's "in the company's best interests" for me to be out of the way till it's cleared up; they don't want the company's named to be smeared – and quite rightly. They don't want the publicity, or the liability. Not only is Lazenby's lot going to involve the police, but my own board has a forensic accountant coming in to check *all* the books for other irregularities and I'm suspended till it's done. God, Stell, it could be months!'

'It's probably not as bad as you think. People know you're a good guy, and that's got to count for something.' I try to hug George again but he's stiff in my arms so I let go of him and go to the window, where I look out at the garden, unsure what else to say.

'I'm sure it won't be for long. They'll see that you've never done this before… you haven't, have you?' It's a joke but the look George gives me is filthy.

'How much business will we lose over this? What will this do to my reputation? To the firm's reputation?' He's almost wailing.

I pick up the whisky bottle. It's about two-thirds full. 'Are you finished with this?' I pop it back in the cabinet, then I pick up his glass, rinse it and put it in the dishwasher.

George slumps over the kitchen table. 'Now what? What am I going to do now? Work is my life. It's everything.' He looks at the clock. 'It's not even midday. What am I going to do all day? Every day? How am I going to get through this? I can't even imagine.'

'Oh, come on!' I rub his back. 'It won't be that bad. You still have me.'

THIRTEEN

George

I clatter downstairs in my biking boots the following Saturday morning. It's an overcast day for my first ride with the motorcycle club but it's forecast to stay dry and that's all I care about. Having missed out on the previous ride, I literally feel like a little boy on Christmas morning. We're heading out before the traffic gets too busy, and aiming for a long route that'll take us out for lunch and back mid-afternoon. The thought of this ride has kept me going all of this shitty, shitty week. I could really do with the camaraderie.

'Morning!' I say to Stell, who's at the kitchen island in her pyjamas. 'Great day for it!'

She nods. 'I guess. Your oatmeal's in the fridge.'

Even the thought of choking that joyless gruel down my throat doesn't get me down this morning and I pull up a stool to the island and dig in.

'Now don't go blowing your diet in the pub if you're out for lunch,' Stell says. 'Remember, no carbs. Nothing fried. And certainly no chips. Look for something like soup, or vegetables and protein.'

It feels odd – mundane – is that the right word? – to

have Stell talk to me like this. She was my temptress, my seductress, my thrill, not my keeper. I guess I'd imagined the excitement of the affair would remain in the marriage.

'Yes, Mum.' I shove my chair back to drop my empty bowl in the sink. 'Do you mind…' I nod at the sink '. . . it's just I need to get going.'

'It's fine.'

I go outside and open the garage. There, under its cover, is my Ducati. Even though I've owned it for a couple of years now, I still get a thrill every time I see it or hear the roar of its engine. I bring the bike round to the front of the house and close the garage. Back inside, I gather my things.

'Did you see my phone anywhere?' I scan the countertops.

Stell looks up and shakes her head. 'Sorry. Did you leave it upstairs?'

I run up the stairs, conscious of the time. The phone's not on the bed, the bedside table, the dresser or in the bathroom. I dash back down the stairs and tear about the kitchen lifting things.

'Where is it? I can't see it anywhere.'

'Shall I call it?' Stell asks. She picks up her phone and dials. 'It's connected… it's ringing…'

I stand still, straining to hear.

'Don't hang up!'

I run back upstairs to listen in the bedroom but the silence is unbroken.

'Shit!' I slam back down the stairs. 'Where is it? I had it! It had it right here! I know I had it. I left it on the island when I went to the garage!'

Stell shrugs and holds out her phone. 'Do you want to take mine?'

'Thanks, but no. I need mine. All the info I need is on the WhatsApp group; all the contacts, everything. I don't have the guy's number – nothing!' I slam the kitchen counter as I realise that, without my phone, I can't join the ride. I don't know where the meeting place is – last night I'd received a pin in a map but I didn't look at it properly so I have no hope of remembering where it was, and I don't have anyone's numbers anywhere except in my phone.

'Shit! Shit shit shit!' I run back out to the garage and look around for my phone: nothing. I check my pockets again as I walk back into the house. Nothing. Not even in my jacket pocket.

Stell sighs. 'So, now what?'

'Now I can't go! That's what!' I sink onto a stool and drop my head into my hands to hide my disappointment. I feel Stell's hand on my arm.

'It's OK,' she says, leaning into me and rubbing my shoulders. 'There'll be other times. You can go on the next ride.'

I look up. 'You don't know how much I wanted to go. I missed the last one. But it's not just that. Where's my phone? I left it here! I know I did.' I slam about the kitchen once more, lifting things, moving things. I even open the kitchen bin and poke my hand in there.

'Oh for God's sake, give it a rest, will you?' Stell snaps. 'That was your work phone, wasn't it? We'll get you a new one. New number so no one can bother you. We can go right now if it makes you happy.'

I don't say anything.

'Maybe it's a blessing,' Stell says and I can tell from her voice, even though she's still behind me, that she's smiling. 'You can escape from all those calls asking what's going on. And now we can do something together today. Silver linings and all that.'

I sigh. That's not the point. For such a clever woman, she can be so dense.

FOURTEEN

Stella

Later that week, George and I decide to walk into the village. He has a meeting with one of his managers from work. The guy's ostensibly coming to collect some paperwork, but I know George is hoping he'll be able to give him a little update on what's going on in the office, as well as some insight into what people are saying behind the scenes.

'My name'll be mud by now,' George says, as we walk down the lane towards Main Street. It's damp out, and the scent of wet vegetation hangs heavy in the air, mixed with the unmistakable pong of manure. Apart from George's voice, I can hear only the suck and crunch of our matching wellies on the muddy lane, and a chorus of birdsong that makes me wonder what birds have to be so happy about every single day.

'Everyone will hate me now,' says George. 'I mean, who in God's name steals from a children's charity to buy a million-pound house? The tabloids will have a field day.'

'The news isn't public yet, though, is it?'

'Nothing spreads faster than a secret.' George scuffs his feet along as we walk. 'You can't expect people not to gossip. It's human nature.' He kicks despondently at a random stone, aiming it into the bushes that line the lane and, all of a sudden, I'm eight years old again, watching him doing exactly the same thing as we walked home from school. For a minute I have the strangest sense of time looping and curving around us like visible trails of vapour; of George and I walking through time, holding hands. George and I, together for ever. But time… perhaps it has a strange way of warping things.

'What happened to "innocent until proven guilty"?' I say.

'I took the money. Guilty. Even if I pay that money back today, my name will be permanently smeared. More than anything else – more than the awards and the ads – people will always remember this when they hear my name. It's word association. It's how people's brains are wired. People will never remember that it was a loan and that I paid it back. I'll always be "George Wolsey – yes, him: the one in that charity scandal. Was he ever cleared? I don't remember…"'

I tut. 'Stop thinking like that. This will all blow over. Today's news: tomorrow's chip paper.'

'They don't even use real newspaper any more.'

'God, George.'

We reach the crossroads where the lane meets the main road.

'Where will you be?' George asks, nodding towards the road lined with shops and businesses. 'I'm going to be in the café.'

The village is as yet untainted by coffee shop chains: the café is a husband-and-wife business, the treats baked daily by a rota of village ladies. Service can be slow when a lunch rush is on, but nobody complains. The one time I waited nearly half an hour for a prawn sandwich with a side of slightly soggy crisps, I found myself thinking about *The Emperor's New Clothes* – a conspiracy by the villagers never to mention the bad service. They wouldn't survive two minutes in London.

'How long will you be?' I ask.

'An hour maybe?'

I look at my watch: mid-morning. 'The pub? I might have a little wander down the road and stop there for a coffee. Maybe we could have lunch there when you're done?'

'OK, great.'

I give George a soft kiss on the cheek. 'Good luck.'

'Thanks.'

I wander down Main Street, dipping in and out of shops. There's a fair mix: as well as the café, there's a gift shop, a boutique, a couple of charity shops, a bakery, a butcher's, a small grocery shop, a Post Office and a couple of estate agents among other things. It doesn't take me long to make my way down the street and back. At a loss for what to do, I head to the pub.

Derek's behind the bar again and, today, there's a slightly older man sitting on a bar stool chatting to him. Aside from that, there's a handful of ladies in brightly coloured activewear drinking coffee – the post-yoga coffee group, I presume. I walk up to the bar and stand a little way down – but not too far – from the man on the bar stool, and ask Derek for a coffee.

'Welcome back,' he says with a smile. 'How's the other half? Off working?'

I blink. 'Oh, he's um… he's taking some time off right now.'

Derek raises his eyebrows and nods.

'Nice if you can afford to. "Taking time off." Oh yes. We've a few doing that around here through no choice of their own right now. Job market.' He sucks air in through his teeth. 'Not so good in the pub business, either. Hanging on by the skin of our teeth, most of us landlords. Those supermarkets and their cheap booze. Anyway, it'll be nice to see more of both of you.'

I smile and take out my purse. 'Thanks.' I don't mean to mislead him but neither do I want to explain George's situation to all and sundry.

'That's three quid,' says Derek. 'I'll bring it to your table.'

'Actually,' I say, 'I think I'll stay here at the bar.'

I've spotted a rack of newspapers. I amble over and pick a broadsheet, then return to my seat at the bar. The man sitting at the bar catches my eye and smiles. I give him a little smile back. He's older; well dressed – a pinstriped shirt, tie and casual jacket. Small, silver-framed glasses.

'He's harmless,' says Derek, following my gaze. 'Stella, meet Dr Grant. Dr Grant – Stella Wolsey. New to our neck of the woods.'

Dr Grant gets up and comes over to shake my hand. 'Pleased to meet you.' I get a feeling not dissimilar to the one I get when I walk through the Customs Hall at the airport: a feeling that I'm being professionally assessed. But then I remember the shadow of the bruise on my forehead. I touch my fingers to it. I thought my hair hid it, but maybe not as well as I imagined.

'Looks like that took quite a crack,' says the doctor.

'Oh, it's nothing.' I shrug. 'Walked into a door! These things happen.' I give an ironic little laugh.

'Yes… yes. Indeed they do,' says Dr Grant without laughing.

Derek places my coffee on the bar and I busy myself pouring in milk from the jug he's placed next to it.

'Actually,' I say to Dr Grant, 'do you have a practice here in the village? I need to get a repeat prescription and, obviously, we're new to the area so I'm not registered anywhere.'

'Oh yes, no problem. Just pop along to the surgery any time in office hours. It's just off Main Street.'

'Thank you.' I take a sip of my coffee, blowing on it a little as it's hot.

'So,' says the doctor, 'did I hear you saying your husband's taking some time off work?'

'Yes. Yes, he is.'

'That's good. We all need some time out.'

'Well… it wasn't entirely his own choice.'

'I see,' says Dr Grant.

'He's still adjusting, to be honest. He has his ups and downs. Understandably.' I pick up my cup and blow gently on the coffee. I get that Dr Grant's being friendly and concerned, and I get that this is a small village, but I'm unused to talking about my situation with relative strangers.

'Does he play golf?' Dr Grant asks.

'He hasn't really had time up till now. Maybe he'll take it up.'

Dr Grant nods. 'Might see him at the links.'

'You may well.'

The doctor peers at me one more time, then says, 'Well, if you'll excuse me, I'm due at the surgery. Lovely to meet you, Stella. No doubt we'll see each other around.'

'No doubt we will.'

Dr Grant is just gathering his things when the pub door opens and George bursts in, squinting in the dingy light. He sees me at the bar and crosses the pub with long strides.

'Hey,' I say. 'How was your meeting?'

He shakes his head dismissively. 'Are you ready?'

I look at Dr Grant, then back at George. 'Weren't we going to have lunch?'

'Let's go. Now.'

'But…' I feel the eyes of the yoga group on us. Dr Grant stops moving.

'Now!' says George, and I remember his anger last time we were in the pub so, averting my gaze lest I incense him further, I slide off the bar stool, pick up my handbag and follow him silently out of the pub.

FIFTEEN

George

Two days later, I'm sitting in a greasy little café across the road from Lazenby's office, a cappuccino in front of me as I fiddle with my new phone, trying to set it up the way I like it. I've lost all my old contact numbers, my photos, my WhatsApp groups – everything – but, as Stell said, I guess there's a silver lining in that the incessant flow of calls from clients wanting to know what's going on with the investigation has stopped.

I'm waiting for Lazenby to leave work, at which point I'm going to ambush him. I want to sort this out with him, man to man. My plan perhaps isn't the most elaborate, but it's a plan, nonetheless, and I didn't get where I've got in life by sitting around doing nothing. Look at the way I won Stell back that day I waited outside *her* office. And what else can I do if Lazenby refuses to take my calls?

But Stell, I know, would disagree, so I told her I'm seeing my mate Phil for a drink. I can just imagine Stell wagging her finger at me: 'There's a reason he's not taking your calls, George, and that's because he doesn't want to speak to you.'

But me and Lazenby go back years. What's he going to do? Blank me?

I shift on the hard seat and think back to the time I waited for Stell in that Greek place. God, look at us now… so near but so far. We're together but it's not how I thought it would be. I imagined… I don't know… an image of Stell and I making love in her apartment fills my mind; the smell of her skin and the feel of her endless legs wrapped around me. I can even smell those scented candles she used to put around the place.

Yeah, I guess I imagined there'd be more sex; more togetherness. I imagined us travelling into London together; sitting side by side reading the papers on the train as we rattled our way into central London. I know she said she was going to scale back her work, and I understand her reasons why she has done, but I didn't realise it would be quite so sudden and quite so extensive. It's slightly scary how into village life she's getting. But I admire her for trying. I really do. But me? I liked the idea of commuting to London – being a part-time villager with one foot there and one in London – and now that's taken away from me for the foreseeable future. And what will people think when they find out about this thing? I don't want to use the word 'scandal', not even in my head, but that's what it is. It's almost laughable. Here I am, one of the most respectable people I know, at the heart of a charity scandal.

Respectable? There's a voice in my head that reminds me that I'm an adulterer. That's not respectable. I pack that thought back in its box and put it away.

Across the road the door opens and my body tenses. It's Lazenby. I leap up and dash across the road, catching him just as he slows to cross a side road. He stops and I grab his arm.

'Lazenby! Hey, how are you?'

He takes a step back. 'Wolsey.'

'How was your trip?'

'Look. I don't think…'

'I need to talk to you. Please let me explain.' I give him the 'honest George' look; the one the clients love.

Lazenby's looking all pinched and drawn in. 'I've seen the accounts and it doesn't look good, Wolsey.'

'Hands up, I took the money! I've never tried to hide that. But it was a loan! I was going to pay it back. With interest! I was releasing capital from an investment and – oh God – I know I shouldn't have done it, but I did, and… I wanted to tell you but you were uncontactable.' I search his face to see how he's taking this and all I see is that he's not making eye contact with me. 'Can't I just pay it back and we'll be done with it? I never meant any harm.'

Lazenby ushers me into the side street so we're out of view of the main road.

'I'm sure you probably didn't mean any harm. But it's gone too far now. It's out of my hands. I was away and the trustees acted without me. Had I been here, it might have been different – I'd have spoken to you.'

'But I'd never cheat a charity. You know that, don't you?'

Lazenby looks at me and suddenly I see myself through his eyes: someone whom he thought he knew, who did, in fact, take money raised for charity to buy a house for his new wife. I'm despicable. I hang my head.

'There are two problems,' he says. 'One: this is part of a bigger investigation and you've been tarred with the same brush, and two: you took such a huge amount of money. The others might have creamed off a few thousand here and there, but you took half a million quid! I'm sorry, but in no world does that look good.'

'I'm not a thief. I was going to pay it back.' I sound pathetic. In this moment, I hate myself: standing on a side street trying to justify myself.

Lazenby shakes his head. 'The trustees want to bring in the police, as they have every right to do. And I really shouldn't be speaking to you about it. I'm sorry.' He looks around furtively as if expecting to be caught talking to a criminal.

'Can you get them to remove me from the case before it goes that far? Say it was all a big misunderstanding, if I pay back the money now?'

Lazenby rocks back on his heels. 'It's a big ask, Wolsey. A big ask.' I'm hanging on to his every word while he strokes his chin. 'But, pay back the money and I'll try, all right? Give a cheque to me in person. No promises.'

'Is there anything else I can do?'

'If I were you, I'd get legal advice. You'd be well advised to have your ducks in a row if this goes to court. You know charity fraud is a criminal offence? You could go to jail.'

Jail? An image of Stell suggesting I borrow the money that day in the kitchen comes to mind. She'd never have suggested it if she'd known what the penalties could be. God, how life can turn in a heartbeat.

'Do you think it will go to court?'

'The case as a whole? Yes. There's been widespread fraud against us, I'm sorry to say. But your part of that?' He shrugs. 'I'll do my best for you with the trustees but, once it's with the police, I don't believe there's a lot I can do. It's up to the CPS to see if they have enough evidence against you.' He pauses and I think about what evidence they have: it's all there. It just depends if they believe my motives were good.

'Get some legal advice,' says Lazenby. 'That's what I'd do.'

*

The trains are up the spout so I have a couple of pints in a pub by the station while the service gets back to normal and I get my thoughts in order. How has it come to this? I'm not a criminal! I breathe in deeply through my nose and squeeze my eyes shut, my fingers pressing on my temples to counteract the tension headache that's been building all evening.

'You all right, mate?' the barman asks. I nod and he nods back and, for a minute, I feel he understands. But of course he doesn't know. No one would understand what's happened to me and why; how an innocent desire to buy my wife a house has spiralled into a potentially criminal case and cost me my job. I feel like such an idiot. At the end of the day, I counted on the fact that Lazenby was a friend and would understand, but I see now that he's scared. The fraud has happened on his watch and he's got to go through the correct channels to get justice. I'm just a shrimp who got tangled up in the net. What was I thinking?

My train gets in around 10.30 but I'm still too wired to sleep. I flop on the sofa with a beer but my mind's still mad as a bag of frogs so I chase the beer with a couple of whiskies while some car-crash TV show plays out in front of me. When I turn off the lights to go upstairs, I see Stell's left a big glass of water on the counter with my cholesterol tablets, a note and a smiley face: 'Don't forget these.' I smile, grateful to be reminded: at least someone still loves me.

SIXTEEN

George

Stell's alarm jolts me awake the next morning, but I sink back to sleep almost immediately. It's only when she touches my shoulder and gives me a bit of a shake that I start to claw my way back to the surface.

'It's morning,' she says. 'Did you hear the alarm?'

I squint at my watch and see that it's gone seven and, for a minute, I think I'm late for work. I start to sit up, remember I'm not going to work, then I remember why I'm not going to work and I slump back on the pillow with a feeling of such utter devastation I have to stop myself from sobbing out loud. My head's foggy and all I want to do is hibernate till this whole thing has blown over.

'Morning,' I croak.

Stell's lying on her side facing me, unsmiling. 'How are you feeling?'

'Uh.'

'I'm not surprised after last night. I half expected you to throw up again.'

'What?'

'I suppose there was nothing left to come up.'

'Who threw up? Me?'

'No, me.' She tuts. 'Of course you!'

'What?' But even as I say the word, I move my tongue in my mouth, and catch the acrid taste of old alcohol. I think back. I'd had a few drinks: two pints at the station, then a couple of beers and a whisky at home. That I remember, and trying to be quiet as I came upstairs – and then? It's a blank.

'What happened?'

'You came upstairs, bashed into the furniture, threw up in the bathroom, and passed out on the floor.' Stell speaks matter-of-factly, as if cataloguing these events at a police station. 'I was worried you might choke on your own vomit so I cleaned you up and got you to bed. Not easy, I can tell you.' She shakes her head and looks away.

'What?'

'Did you drink the water I left for you? If you're drinking that much, you really should try to rehydrate a bit before you come to bed.' Stell swings her legs over the edge of the bed and sits up.

'Yeah, I drank it.'

'Then you must have had a right skin full with Phil if that didn't help.'

Phil? I close my eyes to disguise my confusion. Was I with Phil last night? I have no memory of that, either, and it takes a minute for me to recall that that was because I'd told Stell I was seeing Phil when I was actually going to see Lazenby. When did my life become so complicated? I press on my temples, trying to erase the pain in my head.

When I open my eyes, Stell's standing with her hands on

her hips looking down at me. It's then that I see it: a fresh bruise on her arm, the telltale shape of fingers, and dread clutches at my throat.

Not again.

I swallow, bile rising.

'Say what you like,' Stell says. 'I know what I saw last night – you clearly had more than a couple of pints. You want to see the towels I used to clean up? I can get them for you.'

I shake my head. 'Did anything else happen? Did we argue? Was I obnoxious?' I try to laugh but the sound doesn't come out.

She sighs. 'Obnoxious? Yes, that's a good word for it.' She holds her upper arm, covering the bruise. 'You don't remember, do you?'

'What did I do? Did I hurt you?'

She shakes her head dismissively. 'Look, George. I really think you should see Dr Grant.'

'About my memory? Or—'

'Yes, about your memory.'

'Do you think it's a problem? I don't get it. I don't get why it's happening.'

'That's why you need to see the doctor. It's very worrying.'

I take a deep breath. 'Stell. Princess… can I ask you something? Are you afraid of me when I've been drinking?'

She looks away. She doesn't need to answer; it's written all over her face and shame sweeps through me. How could I do this to her?

'I'm so sorry. I'm going to get rid of all the whisky right

now. From this day on, I won't touch the stuff.' I try to take her in my arms but she steps aside.

'How can you forgive me? I can't forgive myself. Come on. Let's go and get rid of the whisky right this minute.'

She laughs bitterly. 'Good luck with that!'

'What?'

'Well, there's not a lot left.'

'What do you mean? I had three bottles. I've drunk, maybe, one? I'm going to pour them all down the sink.'

'You had three bottles. I think you still have three bottles.' She pauses. 'It's just that they're empty.'

'Rubbish. Come on. I'll show you. This I do remember.'

I lead her to the kitchen.

I open two cupboards before I find the one with the bottles. I pull out the whisky bottle and stare at it in shock. It's almost empty. I look back in the cupboard for the other two but all that's there is the bottle of tequila Phil brought back from Mexico.

'Where are the other two?'

I look at Stell and she raises an eyebrow and looks towards the glass recycling box, where two empty bottles stand tall. I go over and pick one up.

'No.'

'Clearly yes.'

I shake my head at the empties. 'I have no memory. None at all.'

'I can imagine. I don't know how you do it. Your liver must be mush.'

'Oh my God, Stell.' I turn away to hide my shock. 'I hadn't

realised it had got this bad. I'm so sorry. I'm so, so sorry. That's it from now. I'm not drinking any more. I promise you that here and now.'

'Don't be daft. You don't have to quit completely,' she says. 'Just know when to stop. I really don't want any more…' Her voice trails off and she waves her hand vaguely towards her forehead. 'This isn't how imagined it.' Her voice breaks. 'Where will it end, George? Where?'

'I'm so sorry. I'm so, so sorry. There's nothing else I can say, is there? I'm just… it won't happen again.'

'I hope not,' she says.

'Look, I've been thinking. About my memory loss. Do you think I should start keeping a diary? I could use it to double-check what actually happened each day.' I wait but Stell doesn't reply. 'Or does that sound mad? Am I losing my mind?'

Stell looks thoughtful. 'No, it doesn't sound mad.'

'So do you think I should do it?'

'If you think it'll make you feel better, why not?'

*

In the shower, I trawl over and over what happened last night but I still can't remember anything beyond putting the key in the lock, having a few drinks while I watched television, and coming up the stairs. I turn the water to its hottest setting and scrub my body with the loofah as if I can somehow scrub the shame and self-loathing from me; as if the action might let me somehow emerge from the shower a new person. Through the steam, I see Stell come into the bathroom and I wipe a circle of steam from the door so I can see her. She opens the laundry basket and picks out a bundle of crumpled towels, gagging slightly then squeezing her lips shut as she scoops them into her arms. I turn away and let the water cascade over my face.

SEVENTEEN

Stella

Five-thirty the next day, there's a screeching noise in the garden – a fox or a cat, maybe. It wakes me from a muddled dream, and then the first birds start to squawk and my brain starts up its whirring. Next to me, George is snoring. I lie still, thinking. It's possibly too early to test, but my period's late and the packs of pregnancy tests I've bought are burning a hole in the cupboard.

Shall I, shan't I?

Can I wait another day or two?

I get up and go into the en suite, closing the door softly behind me. From the bedroom, the snoring continues.

With shaking hands, I rip open a box and pull out the test. I give the instructions a quick glance to remind myself for how long I need to hold it in the stream of pee, then I sit on the loo and get on with it, capping the test afterwards and placing it face down by the sink. Determined not to look at the results until it's developed, I open the bathroom cupboard and stare at the contents. Tick tock. Tick tock. My eyes roam over my supplies: razors, tampons, nail polish remover, make-up remover, cleansers, eye creams, serums, night cream, little glass bottles of essential oils, medicines. I pick up my sleeping pills and count them: not many left. I'll have to get some more from Dr Grant. Surely that's three minutes up now. I wait another couple of minutes to be absolutely sure the test will have developed and then I pick it up.

'Not pregnant.'

The breath goes out of me. The hope. The light. I feel the words like a slap in the face and I slump down the wall until I'm sitting on the bathroom floor, the test in my hands. How can *she* get pregnant and me not? We've been having unprotected sex for months now. Lots of it! But the lack of pregnancy is clearly not George's fault, given his track record. And Ness is the same age as me. I treat myself well; I eat well and take the vitamins. Why can she get pregnant by accident and I can't even with a systematic plan? I pull myself up and look in the mirror.

What is wrong with you? I ask myself. *Why can't you get pregnant, you freak?*

EIGHTEEN

George

Stell and I aren't talking much since the other night. The atmosphere's strained. I try, but she's all monosyllables and closed-eye sighs. I can't say I blame her; I just wish I knew how to put it right.

Mid-morning, she goes out to pick up groceries, and I wander from room to room, fiddling with things; unable to settle. For the first time in my life, I don't like myself, and I no longer know how to be alone. The remorse I feel about the way my marriage is panning out is oil in my veins, oozing through me, clogging me up. How can I put things right? *Actions*, George. *Actions*. Show her you love her. Stell hates mopping floors – really loathes it – so I decide I'll make it my job: cleaning the house will be my penance. I grab the mop, fill up a bucket with hot water and bleach, and set to work on the floors of the kitchen, hallway, stairs and bathrooms.

And, as I work, moving the mop left to right and right to left, drawing a trail of lemon-scented bleach across the polished concrete, I think. Aside from the state of my marriage, there's the not inconsiderable issue of how I'm going to get the money I've promised Lazenby. I straighten up for a second, slightly breathless from the activity, and wipe my forehead. It's still two months till my bond matures and my broker's adamant that I shouldn't sell below par – clearly he's never been faced with the possibility of a jail term. But then it hits me: the reason why I no longer have half a million quid lying about could also be the solution. Ness. Without stopping to think, I pull out my phone and dial her number. It rings five times.

'Hello, George,' she says carefully and the sound of her voice hits me in the solar plexus. It takes me a second to recover.

'George… ?' she prompts.

'Hi. How are you?' I ask. 'How are things?'

'Good, all good, thanks. How are you?'

'Oh… I've been better.' I pause. 'Have you heard about the court case?'

'Have I heard?' She laughs.

'Of course you've heard.'

'The whole of London's heard. You're the best gossip anyone's had lately. What made you do it? What were you thinking?'

I close my eyes. 'God. It was all a misunderstanding. I didn't actually *steal* the money. I'd never do something like that. You know that, don't you?'

She doesn't say anything.

'Ness! You know I wouldn't steal money from a children's charity, don't you?'

Micro pause. 'Yes. Yes, I do.'

I exhale. The familiarity of her voice falls on me like balm.

'Are you OK?' she asks. 'It can't be easy.'

'I'm all right, thanks. Coping. But I wanted to ask you a favour.' I speak quietly: it feels naughty to be standing here in the house I share with Stell, speaking to Ness. It's like a reversal of all that happened previously; the creeping around I did with Stell while hiding from Ness. I go to the hall window and look out at the lane, watching for the car. 'You know the money you got from the divorce settlement?'

'Yes,' she says carefully.

'I wondered if I could, well, borrow half a million. To pay the charity back.' I pause but she doesn't say anything. 'Look, I have the money in a bond. It's just going to be a few more weeks till it matures and – oh God – Ness, it looks like there could be a court case and it'll look so much better if I've paid it back. At best it could mean I won't get dragged to court. At worst, it'll look good in court. Basically, I have to find it. Half a million quid.'

'But you don't have it?'

'Not accessible, no, I don't.'

'So, what you're saying is that, if you pay back the money, Lazenby – it was Lazenby, wasn't it? – can somehow try to stop the case going to court?'

'Yes. You know I could go to jail?'

'I heard. Is that true? Or just Chinese whispers?'

I sigh. 'Yeah. Apparently. Although I really doubt it would happen. But it's just all so rubbish. Lazenby told me to pay back the money asap and he'll do his best to get me out of the court case, but he can't make any promises. Meanwhile, I'm off work for the foreseeable future.'

'Living the country dream,' says Ness.

'Hardly.' I regret saying it the moment the word leaves my mouth. But, instead of taking the chance to gloat, Ness glosses over it and I'm grateful to her for not picking up that ball and kicking it right back at me.

'So, what do you think? Could you lend it to me?' I pause. 'Please?'

She sighs. 'When do you need it and when can you pay me back? You *will* pay me back, won't you?'

'Scout's honour! I need it as soon as you can get it, and I can pay it back within eight weeks, maximum. Is that doable?'

'I suppose so.'

'Oh, Ness. Thank you! Thank you so much. If there's anything you ever need, please just call me. Anything.'

'How about a husband? I seem to have lost mine.' The words sting, but I hear a smile in her voice.

'Point taken,' I say. 'But seriously, thank you for helping me out.'

'Well, you may have treated me like crap, but that doesn't mean I want to watch you go to jail.' She laughs and the sound triggers memories that flicker through me in the space of a heartbeat: Richmond, parties, our white-sand honeymoon in Mauritius.

'Oh Ness. I…'

I feel like a complete shit, is what I want to say. Compared to you, willing to help me out when all I did was cheat on you and humiliate you, I feel like the biggest shit on the planet. I open my mouth to say it but a car turns into the lane: Stella. I jerk back from the window.

'I've got to go. I'm so sorry. Can we talk later?'

'Stella's back? How ironic,' says Ness.

When Stell opens the front door, I'm mopping the floor.

NINETEEN

Stella

Compared to kick-boxing, the yoga class is interminably slow but I enjoy it far more than I think I will, especially as the other participants don't take it so desperately seriously. There's chat and even friendly laughter as one woman collapses while balancing on one leg. With spiky, hennaed hair, multiple piercings and the compact, muscular body of an athlete, the teacher's not at all what I imagined. She makes a point of helping me ease my limbs into contortions designed to de-stress, detox and unwind. And, as we lie on the floor with our eyes closed at the end of the ninety minutes, I'm woken by someone else's gentle snore from a sleep that stole me unawares. I feel, to my surprise, energised, balanced and taller as I wipe down the mat, roll it up and tuck it into the storeroom. Afterwards, Jude, the teacher, invites me to join the class for a coffee.

'It's a bit of a tradition,' she says.

'Sure.' I shrug, and join the raggle-taggle group heading down the high street. It's nice to enter the pub with people for a change; for a moment, I feel like I belong to something. I

take a seat with the group and, within a minute or two, Derek
is out from behind the bar and over with his order pad.

'The usual, ladies?' he asks.

'And one extra for our new recruit.' Jude smiles at me.

'I've already had the pleasure of meeting Stella,' says
Derek. 'Americano?'

'Yes please.'

'So what brings you to our village?' the teacher asks once
Derek's back behind the bar, and everyone's eyes swivel to
me. I don't suppose they get a lot of new blood here and I feel
it's a seminal moment: it's now that opinions will be formed
and alliances made. Given the mid-morning timing of the
class, none of these women can currently be career women.

'We moved from London,' I say. 'We wanted a change
of pace.' I look around the faces – they're hanging on to
every word. I lean forward a little, confidentially. 'We want
to start a family.'

The sentence has its desired effect and coos of approval
ripple around the table.

'You're in the right place,' says the lady who lost her balance in the class. Her name's Angela. Her face is pretty but
tiredness hangs under her eyes and I see it, too, in the hollows
of her cheeks. 'This is a lovely place to bring up children.'

'Do you have any?'

'Three.' She nods. 'Five, four and two.'

The table erupts into a conversation about the 'wonderful' village school and nursery versus the pros and cons of
sending children to the bigger schools a car-drive away. The
village nursery, I learn, provides a home-cooked lunch for its

little charges. It's not cheap, I also learn, but the meals are made using hormone-free meats, wholegrains and organic produce.

'And what's the alternative?' one woman asks. 'Rice crackers, Waitrose hummus and endless bloody carrot sticks that never get eaten?' All the women collapse in laughter and I nod along, deciding that I, too, will send my children to the village nursery with the hormone-free, organic, cooked lunches. I almost forget I don't yet have any children.

'And your husband?' asks Jude. 'Will he be commuting?'

I take a deep breath, still unused to explaining George's circumstances. I'm saved, though, by Derek, who brings the tray of coffees.

'Don't you go scaring off our newest recruit with your questions.' He gives me a big smile and starts to unload the coffees from the tray. As I'm passing them out, I see Jude's eye rest on my right arm. For a minute, I can't think why she's looking at it, then I glance down and remember the bruise. I'd caught her looking at it during the class but now I realise she can see it far more clearly.

'Everyone got the right coffee?' I ask. The women around the table nod and busy themselves with their coffees and then their attention is back on me. I lean forward with a smile.

'So what's village life like? What do I need to know?'

'It's so friendly,' says a woman called Rachel. 'You know that saying: "It takes a whole village to raise a child"? Well, that's what it's like. Everyone's in and out of each other's houses. I know that my son – he's eight – I know that if he falls off his bike down the other end of the village, someone there will patch him up and send him home. It's that friendly.'

'And safe,' says Angela.

'Yeah. It's so safe,' says Rachel. 'We don't have any crime here. Don't even need a Neighbourhood Watch: we all take care of each other.'

The women laugh.

'It's like going back to the 1950s,' Rachel continues. 'The men are men – real men – not those namby-pamby, touchy-feely types you get these days. Have you seen those "man-bags" some blokes carry these days?' She shudders. 'None of that here. Our men are the sort who look after their women and their families.' She's on her soap box and everyone's nodding. These men are sounding a little like cultural dinosaurs to me but I can hardly say that. 'I mean,' says Rachel, 'that bruise on your arm.' She nods at my arm and, again, I clasp my hand over it defensively. 'You see anyone here with a mark like that and if these guys thought someone was messing with you – my goodness, I pity that guy.'

My smile is tight and Rachel's hand flies to her mouth. 'Oh God! I never meant to imply anyone was messing with you; I was just giving an example!'

There's a stricken silence, just for a second, then, 'You and your big mouth,' says Angela, and everyone laughs. Biscuits crunch; china clinks.

I take a deep breath, close my eyes, then open them. 'Oh, come on, give the guy a chance! It's just… difficult for George right now. He's not working at the moment, and he's not used to being home all day, every day. I understand completely what he's going through.' I frown. 'He drinks a bit. You know what it's like… but… everything's fine.' I smile brightly at the women around the table and they look at me in silence, no idea of what to say next. 'Everyone has bad days, don't they?'

I rub my hands together and grin at them. 'Aw-kward! I'm sorry. I've already said too much…' I let my voice tail off as I look around the table and the women nod solemnly.

'Don't worry,' says Rachel. I wonder if she wishes she'd never brought up the topic. The others echo her. 'Our lips are sealed.'

'If you need to talk,' says Jude quietly, placing her hand on my forearm.

'What's said at the pub stays at the pub,' says Angela.

'Thank you,' I say. 'I loved the class by the way – is it just once a week?'

TWENTY

Stella

'So how long have you been having trouble sleeping?' Dr Grant asks me in his consultation room later that morning.

'Oh, it started around the time George and I decided to move house. What with work – I run my own business – quite a big business!' I give a little self-deprecating laugh. 'And the move, there was a lot to keep track of and my brain doesn't know when to stop.' I don't for a minute think Dr Grant will question it. But...

'Hmm,' he says, steepling his hands under his chin and narrowing his eyes at me through his silver glasses. 'Strong sedatives such as these—' he picks up the empty box I've brought in '—are a great short-term aid, but – and, call me old-fashioned if you like – they're not a long-term solution. Personally, I'd like to get to the bottom of what's causing the problem and tackle that. Maybe look at some ways you can learn to calm your mind. Meditation techniques can be very useful.'

'Of course. I do try, but... goodness, I just have so much on my mind at the moment. We've only been married less than a year and – ah, how to put it? It takes a bit of adjustment, doesn't it? Learning to live with someone?' I laugh. 'Sometimes I'm just awake with my worries and my anxieties and I just get into this cycle of sleeplessness and I need to break it.'

'Anxieties, you say? About anything in particular?'

'Oh, just marriage stuff. I'm sure every newly-wed goes through this… George can be – how to put it – "difficult"? He's a high-achiever.'

Dr Grant raises his eyebrows. 'But everything's all right, I hope?'

I rub my bicep where the bruise is subtle, but still there. 'Of course it is. Everyone has their moments, don't they? It's obviously a period of adjustment when you're used to being on your own… anyway, we're trying for a baby.' My voice is bright.

'I see.'

'That'll smooth things over, I'm sure. We'll be so busy we won't have time to argue!'

Dr Grant inhales then exhales. 'Do you both want to start a family?'

'Yes. Absolutely. I'd say pretty equally.'

'Good. Because I'm sure you've heard the term "Band-Aid baby", and that's not a solution for anything.'

I laugh. 'No, definitely not a Band-Aid baby.'

'OK… Just be absolutely sure.' He rubs his hands together. 'So… these sedatives. Would you say you take them every night?'

'No! They're my last resort. I only take them for a couple of nights when I've had a few sleepless nights and I need to get out of a rut. You know, break the cycle?' For a second I almost have an out-of-body experience: I see myself sitting in the doctor's office practically begging for this prescription. If I'm not careful I'll be on my knees in a minute.

'Hmm,' he says again. 'I see. So you wouldn't seem to be at risk of developing an addiction. Because that's a risk with this tablet. It's reasonably addictive. And, if you're trying to conceive…'

'Oh no. I don't have an addictive personality,' I say. 'I've never smoked! I can give up booze at the drop of a hat. In fact, I often do Dry January.' I laugh.

'Well, of course,' says Dr Grant, 'that's the other thing: these tablets must *not* be mixed with alcohol. The pills will depress your central nervous system and, despite what many people think, alcohol's a depressant, too, so the effect of mixing the two can cause all sorts of problems and – well, in some cases, even be fatal. So, you must never take these if you've been drinking. Even just a couple of glasses of wine. All right?'

'Of course. Understood.'

'And, of course, if you're trying to conceive, both of you would ideally be looking at limiting your alcohol intake. Does your husband – George – does he drink much?'

I sigh. 'Whisky's his poison. But I'm trying to limit that already because I don't like what it does to him.'

Dr Grant raises his eyebrows but I suddenly feel disloyal to George for talking about him behind his back so I give him my best 'everything is absolutely fine' smile.

He looks thoughtfully at me for a moment, then opens

up a page on his computer and holds his fingers over the keyboard, ready to type.

'I'll just give you two weeks' worth,' he says and I exhale, aware suddenly that I've been holding my breath.

'Then you can come back to me and we'll reassess. Meantime, let's try to look at a long-term solution. Will you look into relaxation techniques?'

'I've joined the yoga class at the village hall! In fact, I've just been!' I wave at my yoga clothes.

'That's a good start.' The printer whirs and Dr Grant hands me the prescription. Mission accomplished.

TWENTY-ONE

George

Ness and I have a bench on Richmond Green. We don't own it – it's not carved with our names or anything – but it's where we sat the evening we moved into our house all those years ago. After spending the day keeping out of the way of the movers, we'd bought sandwiches, crisps and a bottle of wine, and eaten our picnic supper on the bench as the sun went down. It had been June, the sun reluctant to go, and the light had lasted for ever, casting longer and longer shadows across the grass as I'd wound my arm around Ness's shoulders and we'd imagined what this new chapter of our lives might bring. I'd tasted success by then, and I remember that feeling of invincibility; I'd felt as if I could – and would – conquer the world, our Richmond house being just the start of it: the control centre from which the arms of success would spread.

I remember, too, the giddy feeling of love I'd had for Ness back then. I'd forgotten about that.

I remember all this as I walk towards the bench. Ness isn't there, but then I see her walking towards me from the opposite direction, our red setter, Pepper, on a lead. Ness sees me and gives a little wave, then there's that awkward moment when we're both still walking towards each other and neither of us knows whether to maintain eye contact. Ness's hair is loose and flying behind her as she walks and I get the absurd feeling that we're in a movie; a score of violins playing in the background, and that I should run towards her, scoop her in my arms and twirl her around… I have to remind myself that we're divorced, and then why we're divorced.

Why are we divorced?

Ness arrives at the bench a few steps before I do. Pepper leaps towards me, jumping up on me, straining at the lead and pawing my clothes, licking every part of me she can reach, so ridiculously pleased to see me.

'Down, girl. Down!' I say, petting her head, then I stand up and look at Ness.

'Hey,' she says.

'Hey.' I stand and look at her. She's dressed down – in far more casual clothes than she ever wore when we were together, and she looks well – really well. Younger, happier. Gone are the designer clothes and the high heels; the huge handbags and the bright lipstick. She looks lovely. So fresh. She's wearing Converse, and her perfume smells of garden flowers. She holds out a foil package.

'What is it?' I feel her eyes on me as I peel open the foil. 'Oh my God, did you make this?' It's a huge slice of Victoria sponge, its layers oozing with buttercream and jam. I take a huge bite and speak through the crumbs. 'It's so good. Thank you! I haven't had cake in how long?'

Ness flushes. 'It's no biggie. I still enjoy baking, even

though it's for one these days.' She shrugs, then watches me eating. 'You lost weight, by the way.'

'In a good or a bad way?'

'Just don't lose any more. That's all.'

I crumple up the foil and aim it at a nearby bin, stupidly happy when I score in front of Ness. 'You want to walk, or sit here for a bit?'

'Better walk,' she says, and I know what she means. It doesn't seem right to sit on 'our' bench.

I hold out my arm. 'Madam?' She takes it and we set off along the path I've just walked, Pepper trotting along beside us like the old days.

'So what are you up to these days?' I ask. 'Dating anyone?'

'I'm working as a teaching assistant.' She smiles and dips her head. 'Primary. I started volunteering at a local school, you know, just for something to do. And I liked it so much, I started working towards getting some qualifications so I can move up the ladder a bit.'

'Wow, that's fantastic!' Now she mentions it, I can see how good she'd be in the classroom. She always was so patient, and so good with people. But she didn't answer my other question. Is that an admission that she is dating someone?

'Why don't you train to be an actual teacher?' I ask.

She sighs. 'I'd love to. But you need a degree. So I'd have to do a B.Ed. I'd be looking at three or four years, full time.'

I raise my eyebrows at her. 'So, do it!'

'Do you really think I could?'

'Yes.'

I let go of her arm, take her hand in mine and squeeze it. 'Should have done it years ago.'

'I couldn't,' she says, giving me a sideways smile. 'Too busy helping someone build his empire.'

I feel it like a blow to the stomach. 'And look how I repaid you.'

'It's OK.'

'No, it's not OK.'

'George, what's done is done. Don't beat yourself up about it.'

'It's hard not to, now I have all this time on my hands to think about things.'

'Why don't you get a job? Something local, I mean? Just to give you something to do? Volunteer somewhere, or learn a new skill? If I can do it…' She smiles and I notice her dimples. I always liked her dimples.

'I was hoping to be back at work quickly.'

'But what if you're not? What do you do all day?'

I shake my head. 'You're right. It's not a bad idea.'

'You're at your best when you're busy,' she says, and two things strike me: one, how well she knows me and, two, if this could be why I keep losing both my memory and my temper. We walk in silence for a moment while I mull this over. For the first time in my relationship with Ness, I feel like the inferior one – and that's another alien feeling.

'Can I ask you something?' I say.

'Of course.'

'Why did you agree to help me? I just don't get it. After the way I treated you, after all that I did…'

Ness smiles. 'Look. For what it's worth, we were together for fifteen years. You were my husband. I have the money, and I don't want to see you in trouble.'

'Is it really that simple?'

She shrugs. 'Yes.' She reaches into her pocket and pulls out a cheque and a piece of paper. 'I hope you don't mind but my lawyer's drawn up a receipt stating the terms of repayment if you wouldn't mind signing.'

'I don't need to read it, do I?'

Ness smiles and I know I trust her. I take the cheque, sign the paper and hand it back to her.

'Thank you so much.'

'You're welcome.'

We walk on again in silence. We're almost back to where we started, and there's still one thing on my mind.

'Anyway, back to my original question,' I say. 'How's your love life?' I rub my hands together, telling myself that my interest is nothing more than friendly concern.

We stop walking and stand by the bench. Pepper's lead plays out as she snuffles around the base of a nearby tree. The irony of us being here, talking about who Ness is dating, isn't lost on me. What would our younger selves, those optimistic kids with their crisps and their wine, have said had we told them this is how we'd end up?

Ness sighs. 'Oh, you know. I go on dates now and then.'

'But no one special?'

She sighs again. 'There's this guy, Peter, one of the teachers from school – a department head actually! We went out for a while, but...' She shrugs.

'It didn't work out?'

'Oh I don't know. He wants marriage, kids, but I just…'

'Don't?'

She smiles.

'Been there, done that?' I ask.

'Yes and no. I haven't given up on having kids… but whether he's the right guy… I just don't know.'

'Well. Don't jump in unless you're sure.'

'I won't.'

'Good girl.' I pull her into my arms and give her a hug. 'Thank you so much for the loan. I really appreciate it.' I can smell the clean scent of her hair and, as I let her go, we pause for a moment, our faces close together, and I look at her mouth, free of lipstick. We freeze for a moment, unsure what the new rules are, then I touch my parted lips gently to hers for a fraction of a second. The kiss is both chaste and erotic in equal doses.

'Thank you,' I say.

'Any time,' she says.

TWENTY-TWO

Stella

As soon as I open the front door, I can tell George isn't home. The house has that silence about it; that feeling you get that, by coming home and making noise, you're disturbing something. I throw my keys and handbag onto the hall table, and go through to the kitchen. There's a note on the counter: a hand-drawn cartoon of a train with a tiny George sitting inside one of the carriages with the newspaper. Underneath, George has written 'Nipped into London. Back after lunch.'

The answering machine light is blinking. I press play and the sound of a man's voice fills the hallway, its timbre somehow similar to George's despite the distortion by the machine:

'Georgie-P, it's me. What's happened to your phone? It's always off! Hiding away with the wife, eh! Just wondering how you're getting on. Do we have the patter of tiny feet yet, and by that I mean dogs not kids – ha!' There's an awkward pause then he continues, 'Did I miss the house-warming? Let's try to get together. It should be easier now you're the right side of London! So, let me know when you're around to sink a few pints and catch up. It's been too long. Right, bye.'

George's big brother Harry. Five years older and effectively from another planet. Though maybe not these days. I lean against the doorway and remember how George and Harry were like chalk and cheese growing up: George the sensitive one despite his physical strength; George happy to have a girl for his best friend, and Harry, the typical alpha male. Seemingly so much older, and so out of touch with George and I that I hardly knew him. Harry would swing in and out of his parents' house with various friends and, later, girlfriends, in tow, pinching George's cheek, throwing punches at him and calling him Georgie-Porgie – but now? It suddenly strikes me that they've reversed their roles. Harry's now a respected psychologist – married to his scholarly work – while George is the one who strung two women along; getting one pregnant while planning a life with the other... where would that have gone had George not got caught that night at the dinner? A shiver crawls over my skin. It's behaviour I'd have traditionally expected from Harry, not from George. I press delete and watch as the red light stops blinking.

TWENTY-THREE

George

The house is quiet when I get home and I take the stairs two at a time hoping to get out of my jeans and jacket before Stell gets back so I don't have to explain to her what I was doing in town. But I realise the moment I reach the bedroom that she's already there. She steps out of the shower, a towel wrapped around her body, just as I enter the room.

'What's up?' she says, looking at my clothes. 'Where did you go?'

She kisses me softly on the lips. It's an invitation, I think, and usually I'd be on her like a wolf while she's all soft and warm from the shower but not today. I sink onto the edge of the bed and watch as she picks out a pair of pants and steps into them. She puts on a matching bra and I see that she's trying harder, putting on a bit of a show for me, flicking her hair about and bending over to show me her cleavage as she settles her tits in the cups. It's a typical Stella come-on but today it just doesn't hit the spot.

'Where were you?' she asks when she realises I'm not moving. 'You didn't see a solicitor dressed like that? Come on, tell me! Or were you out with your girlfriend? A walk in the park and a bit of lunchtime slap-and-tickle?' She pauses. 'Don't forget I've met you before!'

My breath catches. I look at her but her eyes are dancing. She's laughing, teasing me, completely unaware of how close to the bone her joke hits. Then she comes close and looks me up and down – almost examining me – and I realise I'm holding my breath, hoping, hoping, hoping that there's no trace of Ness on me – *How could there be? We didn't do anything!* – no perfume, nothing. But Stell focuses on my shirt, leans in and carefully picks a crumb off my shirt. She looks at it closely then pops it in her mouth.

'Cake?' she asks, eyebrows raised.

I lean back on the bed and let my forearms take my weight. 'I was sorting out the payment for Lazenby. Got peckish. So shoot me.'

'You managed to get hold of the money?'

'Yeah.'

'You liquidated the bond early?'

'Yeah. Anyway, look, I was thinking. What do you think about me getting some sort of a job?'

'A job? What sort of job? You have a job!'

'Just something small. To get me out of the house; give some purpose to my day. Some volunteer work, or part-time work in the village.'

'But why?'

'I can't sit about all day – it's driving me crazy. I miss the camaraderie of work; the banter.' I pause. 'I'm best when I'm busy.' Ness's words. 'I just want something to do.'

'Hang out with me.'

'I… I just want to get out a bit.'

Stell sighs. 'When we were talking about moving out of London, I had this idea in my mind that we'd be spending more time together; cooking together; going for long walks; bringing up our baby together… Do you remember how we used to fantasise about it? I thought you wanted that, too.' She laughs bitterly. 'Or have you realised I'm a monster?'

I frown. 'Of course I want to spend time with you. This isn't about you and me, or even you – and of course you're not a monster! It's about me doing something productive with my time.'

Stell steps into her jeans, leaving them undone, and pulls a silk shirt from the wardrobe. 'I just would've thought that taking a two-bit job in the village might be a little beneath Mr Advertising, that's all.'

'It's an academic discussion at this point, anyway: I asked around on my way back from the station just now but no one wants me. No one wants George Wolsey!' I laugh to detract from the hurt.

'Where did you try?'

'The pub. But Derek said he had nothing.' I walk over to the window. 'Tried the gift shop, too. I quite fancied selling tea towels and soaps for a few hours a week. Keep my mind off things.'

'And?'

'No-go. And the coffee shop, too, so it looks like you're stuck with me, after all.'

'Why don't you focus on the house-warming party? Consider it a project?'

Ah yes. The famous house-warming. 'Do you think people would still come? Some must know by now...' I picture the villagers and try to imagine if they'd care. My London life is so remote from their concerns. 'They would, wouldn't they? Free booze and they'll be dying to see what was done to the house.'

'Yeah, they'd come. They won't have heard about your "work issues" yet. It's another world out there.'

'Fingers crossed they won't ever.'

Stell does a silent cheer. 'Yay. That's the spirit. But the party: you could make it amazing – come up with a theme, get a band and a dance floor. I can do the catering.'

'Yeah. I guess it'll keep me busy. And you don't have time to do it, do you?'

She shakes her head. 'I'm trying to tie up a lot of things so I can slow down in case...' She puts her hand on her belly and, as I look at her, I realise that she's still standing there with her jeans and shirt undone, wanting to get pregnant and looking for all the world like some Amazonian Victoria's Secret model, all glossy hair and tits. I'm still curiously aroused after kissing Ness so I lift her hair and kiss the back of her neck, then work my way around her collarbone.

'I'm going to start writing my novel, by the way.' Stell tilts her head so my lips can work their way up her neck.

'Maybe I could get used to being at home...' I whisper because I know this is what she wants to hear. She turns in my arms and presses herself against me as her hands slide over my skin.

'Maybe,' she whispers with her lips on mine. 'Maybe you'll find that staying at home isn't such a terrible thing…'

She pushes me back onto the bed and straddles me. 'Maybe, if you stick around, you'll find that I'm actually way more fun than selling scented bloody candles…'

TWENTY-FOUR

George

I've always believed there's no time like the present so, the very next morning, Stell and I are in the kitchen with our coffees, hand-writing the invitations for the party. In front of me is the ring-binder file I'm using to collate all the plans – and, God knows, I've been up since dawn so there are plenty of those.

'I don't know why we couldn't just print the invites off the computer,' Stell says, opening and closing her fingers. There's a smudge of ink on her index finger from the fountain pen. 'I could have designed a really nice invite and printed it off: done.'

'It looks more personal this way,' I say, shaking out my hand. I'm left-handed: writing with ink is really tricky for me – I have to bend my arm around the script to make sure I don't smudge it. 'We want to give a good impression. I want every single person we've invited to know that we've thought specifically about them, not just done a mail drop.'

'But this *is* a mail drop.'

'Maybe. But it's a personal one.'

'We don't even have half the names.'

'That's not the point. The point is that they'll each receive a hand-written invitation through their door. That'll go a long way to making people like us. Trust me.'

'Whatever you say,' Stell says. 'It's your bash.'

I get up. 'Another coffee?'

'Sure.'

I look at the kitchen counter for a moment. 'Did you move the coffee-maker?'

Stell laughs. 'What a strange question!'

I point to the counter. 'Wasn't it here before?'

'No! What are you like?'

I rub my eyes. 'Must have been imagining it. It's just I thought…' I shake my head. 'Never mind.' But no, this really bothers me. 'Actually…' I pull out my phone and open the camera. I open the line of cupboards and stand back to take a couple of pictures of the contents and of where things are on the work surfaces.

'What on earth are you doing?'

'Taking photos of where things are.'

'Why on earth?'

'I swear, things are never in the same place. But then I don't know if I'm imagining it or just remembering wrong. I spend a lot of time thinking about it. I'm going to sort it out once and for all.'

'What are you saying? That some fairy comes in and moves stuff?' Stell's proper-laughing now. She pretends to pray. 'Oh, dear kitchen fairy, while you're magicking things around the kitchen, pretty-please would you also load the dishwasher?' She looks at me sharply. 'Did you seriously just take pictures?' She gets up and peers at my phone over my shoulder. 'You did!'

'So what?'

She looks at me as if I'm a complete lunatic and suddenly I see myself standing there in the kitchen photographing the coffee-maker and I see how ridiculous it looks.

'OK,' I sigh, deleting the images. 'It's just… I don't know. I don't know what's going on in my head these days.'

'Have you had any more memory lapses? Have you been writing your diary?'

I shrug. 'Yeah. There've been a few things I don't remember, but nothing major like those nights.'

'I wonder what's causing it. You're not taking any medications other than your cholesterol stuff?' Stell taps her fingers on her lips. 'Something that reacts badly with alcohol?'

I cluck my tongue. 'No.'

'Maybe it's just the stress,' she says. 'I hope you don't mind, but I did some research. Memory loss can be linked to stress, anxiety and depression.' She pauses. 'But then I think it started before all this stuff with your job happened, didn't it?'

I shrug again. 'I'm sure it's nothing. Like you say, probably just stress.'

'I hope it's nothing more serious.'

'Like what? Alzheimer's?' I roll my eyes then put on a doddery old-lady voice. 'Darling… darling… I love you so much… what was your name again?'

She tuts. 'No. Not Alzheimer's, you prat. Like a stroke or something.'

'What?'

'Apparently memory loss can be a symptom of a "silent stroke" or even a brain tumour. I'm just worried, that's all. Maybe it's worth getting yourself checked out.'

The coffee machine beeps. I rinse and refill the cups in silence.

'There's a nice doctor here – Dr Grant,' Stell says. 'No harm in getting a quick appointment just to rule out any underlying conditions. Wouldn't you rather just know? I mean, if it's something major, it's better to catch it early. Right?'

'It's nothing. I'm just tired and, as you said, a bit stressed. As you can imagine.' I rotate my shoulders backwards and realise how much tension I'm carrying in them.

'But you never know. And—' she looks at me coyly, flutters her lashes '—I'd kind of like you not to conk out on me.'

I smile back at her. 'All right.'

'All right what?'

'All right, I'll see the doctor. OK? See what he says. But I think it's kind of pointless.' I plonk her coffee down on the island.

'Thanks, darling. And for the coffee, too.' Stell smiles at me, a huge beam, and somehow I'm left with the impression that I've just been played though, for the life of me, I can't think how or why.

TWENTY-FIVE

Stella

'It's going to be a great party,' I say as George and I walk down the lane towards the village to hand out the invitations. There's warmth in the sun today but it's fleeting, turning chilly every time a cloud passes over. 'Are you pleased with the arrangements?'

'Yes, I think so. Thanks for coming up with such a great menu.'

'I enjoyed planning it. I hope I haven't gone overboard. I can't wait to see the LED dance floor. Do you think people will dance?'

'After a few drinks, yeah, I reckon.'

We walk in silence for a minute. From the direction of the village I can hear music and a voice, amplified by microphone, encouraging people to 'roll up, roll up'. We turn the corner and see tented stalls lining the street. People are milling about chatting.

'Oh it's the village fête today! I'd completely forgotten.' I pull the stack of party invitations out of my bag and give George about ten from the top: Rachel, the yoga girls and Dr Grant are all in his section. Rachel helped me get everyone's addresses. I've got the bulk of the anonymous ones I'm going to push through every door.

'Right, see you back here,' I say. George gives me a kiss and turns up the road while I head towards the bustle of the market. There's all sorts going on under the tents: local produce for sale, cakes, face-painting, some bric-a-brac on sale for the local animal shelter. Dressed in jeans, a sweater and an olive body-warmer, Rachel's manning the stall.

'Hi. How's business?' I ask.

'Oh, you know,' she says, casting her eye over the goods for sale. It's a table of other people's junk, really. Rows of tatty paperbacks, dog-eared toys, some DVDs, glassware, a set of crockery, a few bits of costume jewellery, a few garments on wire hangers and a new hairdryer in a box. I don't even pretend to look.

'How are you?' Rachel asks. 'Everything all right?'

'No complaints.' I smile. 'Can I get you a cuppa?'

'Oh I'd love one, cheers. Let me get you some money.'

'No, not at all. My treat. Since you're doing your bit for the community.'

'Well, thank you.'

I potter through the market, chatting to those few people I know, then stand in the queue at a catering truck. It's selling hot dogs, doughnuts and candy floss as well as hot drinks and the queue straggles down the street. Small children yank at their parents' hands.

'Pleease?' I hear. 'Why can't I have candy floss?'

'You know what you're like on sugar, darling.'

I wouldn't be so mean to my own child, I think, looking at

the mother's stony face and at the child's right leg wobbling back and forth with desire, if only I ever get a chance to have a child. Sometimes it seems as if the whole world pops out babies without so much as thinking about it. Except me.

I order two teas and head back to Rachel.

'Thank you so much,' she says. 'So, have you had a good look around? We always get a good turnout for the fêtes. The whole village comes together. I love them, especially the summer one in June. The weather's usually better. It often ends up with everyone bringing drinks out from the pub. Derek sometimes sets up a Pimm's table. That's always fun.'

'Sounds lovely.'

'It is.' Rachel looks around at the busy scene and smiles.

'I'm handing out invitations to our house-warming party today,' I say.

'You've decided on a date, then?'

'Yes. April first.'

'April Fool's Day?'

'Ha. Yes, I guess it is. But it's a Saturday and I'm hoping the weather'll be good enough.'

'It's outside?'

'Sort of. We've booked a marquee, just in case.'

'Wise.'

'George has your invitation. He's putting it through your door.'

'Thank you.'

'Do you think you'll be able to come? You and your husband, of course.'

Rachel fiddles with the stock on her table. 'I'm not sure. I'll have to check my diary and get back to you.'

I shrug. 'Sure.' Then I see George walking down the street towards us, his hands devoid of invitations. As I watch, he pulls his phone out of his pocket and thumbs in a message. He's smiling as he does it, a million miles away from Main Street. His phone's back in his pocket by the time he reaches us, but the smile remains.

'Oh, here's George now,' I say.

'Pleased to meet you.' Rachel nods but doesn't take the hand George is holding out.

'The pleasure's all mine,' George says giving her his megawatt smile, and I know what he means – I know this is one of his stock phrases – but, somehow, with Rachel here in the village, it comes across as smarmy. Rachel gives me a weak smile.

'Right,' she says, fiddling with things on the stall even though there are no customers. 'Must be getting on. See you around.'

TWENTY-SIX

George

Stell's out of bed like a rocket on the morning of the party; no lie-in, no snuggles, even though we've got almost twelve hours till kick-off. I follow her down to the kitchen. Given she's a caterer, I'd have thought she'd be calmer than this; more of a pro. Ness certainly was. But Stell's all over the place, won't sit still, keeps getting up and jotting things down. Her nervous energy would light up the whole of London.

'What about power sources?' she asks. 'For the band? They'll have an electric guitar and a keyboard. Microphones and so on. Have you got that covered? And what time is the marquee coming? Will it be up in time for the dance floor to be fitted?'

I catch her as she orbits the kitchen and hold her by her wrists. 'It's all under control. Trust me. I know what I'm doing.'

She shakes me off and sits down with a leg bent under her. She's sucking a pen and flicking through my lists. 'Yes maybe, but in *my* domain: we're giving over the kitchen to the chef. We won't have access after he sets up – I mean, we will be able to get in here if we need to, but we can't count on this as a usable space. The bar will be set up outside, yes?' I nod. 'So we need to get all the drinks out before the chef arrives.'

'Princess, you worry about the catering. I'll sort out everything else. Trust me. It's going to be the party of the century, and I'm in control.'

And I'm proud of this one. At the top of the garden, there'll be a glow-in-the-dark lounge that gives the feel of a Scandinavian vodka bar: in daylight, the sofas will look white but, as the sun goes down, they'll glow with LED lights: blue, yellow, green and pink. The bar itself will glow electric blue. Behind the bar, the spirits will be set up with optics. In a bank of fridges, I'll have bottles of wine and beer lined up, labels to the front, like glass soldiers. But the *pièces de résistance* will be two large ice bowls that take pride of place on the bar. Fifteen minutes before the party starts, the barman will fill them with ice and a hundred and fifty miniature bottles of champagne for guests to grab and drink with straws.

Waiters will circulate with the food. I run through Stell's menu in my head: we'll start with *arancini* with roasted pepper dipping sauce, then move on to the more substantial things: fish and chips in mini paper cones, mini bowls of mushroom risotto, lamb skewers, mini burgers and roast beef on tiny roast potatoes. At the bottom of the garden, there'll be a marquee, which is where the band will play. Inside, there'll be a stage and an LED dance floor, surrounded by incidental bar tables and clusters of gilt chairs and dining tables for those who'd rather sit. I bet the village has never seen anything like it.

Stell takes a deep breath. 'You're right. And I do trust you. It's just that I want everything to be right for you.'

'I know what you mean.' I'm on a high all day as we get everything in place. I haven't been this busy since I was suspended, and it feels great: me doing my thing and Stell doing hers. It's how it might be if we were still in London; still working.

*

By seventy-thirty, Stell and I are standing by the bar.

'Shall we?' I say, looking at the mini champagne bottles that stud the ice bowl like spikes on a hedgehog. All are opened, straws peeping temptingly out of the tops of the bottles.

'It'd be rude not to,' Stell says, smiling at me.

'Quality testing, of course.' I pick a bottle from the bottom of the display and hand it to her, then take one for myself.

'Cheers, Mrs W.'

'Cheers.'

We clink bottles and Stell slides onto a bar stool. 'Nice outfit,' she says. 'You look great.' A pause. 'Where's your wedding ring, by the way? Why aren't you wearing it?'

'Oh.' I look at my left hand, massage the ring finger. 'It's, um, upstairs, I think. You want me to go get it?'

She shakes her head. 'No. I was just wondering.' She pauses. 'I've put a sign on the front door telling people to come around the back, by the way, just in case they don't hear the music,' she says. Even so, her eyes flick to the garden path every few seconds. It's contagious: I find myself doing it too.

'Stop it,' I say. 'They'll find their way. Just relax. Enjoy yourself. All the hard work's done.'

'Before it all gets going, I just wanted to say well done for organising such a great party. It'll be talked about for years to come.'

'I hope so.'

'I'm surprised your brother isn't coming.' Stell's examining her nails.

'I didn't invite him. He's so busy. He wouldn't want to traipse down here for a house-warming.'

Stell frowns. 'He'd have loved to come. He practically invited himself.'

'You spoke to him?'

'No. But he left that message a while back. I told you: he called the house. You were supposed to call him back?'

Fear lurches through me: not again. Stell peers at me. 'Are you all right?'

'I've got a minute, haven't I? I just need to do something.'

'OK. Be quick!'

I run to the study, and open my diary on the computer. I do a quick search for 'Harry' and the entry comes up immediately – it's the day I met Ness: 'Got the money to pay back Lazenby today' and there, at the bottom, there's a note: 'Call Harry.' The air goes out of my lungs. I don't know if I'm glad to have this record or not. It makes me realise how difficult I must be to live with; how patient Stell is. I shut off the computer and go slowly back out to the garden, wondering whether or not to admit what I found.

'Everything OK?' she says, smiling and I'm about to tell her about the diary when a voice hails us from the corner of the house.

'Hello, hello.'

We both turn and then Stell slides off her stool and starts walking towards the man who's appeared. He's slightly older and dressed in slacks and an open-necked shirt with a cardigan. There's an awkward moment when I'm not sure if she's going to shake his hand or kiss him but she goes for an air kiss, which he receives rather awkwardly, his manicured fingers grasping her shoulders.

'Dr Grant,' she says, turning to me, 'this is my husband, George.'

I hold out my hand and, for a minute, I don't think Dr Grant is going to take it but he does and we shake hands formally.

'I think we saw each other in the pub, but pleased to meet you properly,' Dr Grant says.

'Likewise. Always good to know the doctor! Now what can I get you?'

'What have you got?' Dr Grant rubs his hands together.

'Everything.'

'A whisky would be great, thank you.'

I put my empty champagne bottle on the bar and ask the barman for two whiskys. 'Neat, thanks.'

'George,' Stell says quietly. 'Whisky?'

'Maybe I'll have a glass of red wine,' says Dr Grant.

'No, it's fine. Really it is. Just the one,' I say to Stell. 'I'm keeping the good doctor company.. I'll switch to beer after this. I promise.'

Stell smiles at me. 'Thanks, sweetheart.' Dr Grant's eyes flick from Stell to me and back.

'I'm trying to cut down,' I say.

'Good, good. Everything in moderation,' says Dr Grant.

I pick up the two drinks and hand one to him.

'Cheers.' I take a sip, loving the familiar burn of the liquor in my mouth. God, I've missed my whiskys.

'Good stuff,' says the doctor.

'So what's your wife – Marjorie, isn't it? – up to tonight?' Stell asks.

'Oh, she, um… she had to babysit for our grandson.' Dr Grant looks at the bar as he says this, examining it as if it's the most interesting thing in the world. 'I like what you've done with the drinks,' he says, nodding towards the ice bowls. 'Never seen that before. Are you settling in well?'

'I hope so,' Stell says. 'We've met a few people. It seems like a friendly village.'

'It is,' says Dr Grant. 'Very close-knit.' He speaks slowly, putting weight behind his words. 'We look after each other.'

'I like that. I think!' Stell smiles at him.

'Not many people here yet then?' Dr Grant asks after a pause.

'No. Not yet. You're the first. It's still early.'

'Hmm.'

There's a silence while the three of us stand around stiffly.

'Did you catch the news today?' Dr Grant asks but then

he continues before either of us has a chance to reply. 'Did you see that Taylor bloke finally got two years?'

He's referring to a domestic abuse case that's been rumbling on in the papers.

'Yes,' I say. 'Coercive control, wasn't it? Unbelievable what he did to her! Brave woman to go to the police.'

'He'd broken her down,' says Dr Grant. 'He'd completely wiped out her confidence and any sense of self-belief.' He shakes his head. 'She believed everything he told her. I tell you, if I got my hands on that man... if he walked into my surgery...'

'You wouldn't know, though,' I say. 'These people are clever. To the outside world that marriage probably looked perfectly normal.' I give a little laugh. 'I bet no one who knew him would have guessed what was going on at home.'

'There are signs,' says Dr Grant. 'My own father did this to some extent with my mother. Although it's only just being recognised by the law, it's not a new thing. I grew up watching it. Once you know what to look for...' His voice trails off.

I look at Stell. She's staring at her champagne bottle, picking the damp label a little. Then she looks up. 'It's so sad,' she says. 'That poor woman. What must it have been like for her?'

'Anyway, it's all over now. Taylor's in jail where he belongs and hopefully she can start to pick up her life again.' Dr Grant shakes his head. 'It'll be a slow process, though.'

The waiter appears with a tray of *arancini*.

'Canapé?' Stell asks Dr Grant.

'Thanks.' He takes one and pops it into his mouth in one go. 'Mmm. Good,' he says. 'Couple more of those and I won't need my tea!'

Stell and I take one each. The outside is crispy and the cheese inside is perfectly melted. After the low-carb diet she's had me on, it's like manna from heaven. I take another.

'Are you expecting many people?' Dr Grant asks.

'Everyone within a three-mile radius.'

'Speaking of which: darling, have you checked your phone?' I ask.

Stell picks up her phone. 'Oh no! It's on silent.' She types in her passcode. 'Oh, Rachel's messaged… Rachel from yoga? Ah, she can't come. One of her kids is sick. Shame.' The phone updates and WhatsApp pings two more times. 'Oh no. Angela can't make it, either.'

'Never mind,' I say. 'There are plenty more.'

Sure enough, we hear voices. Around the corner of the house, a couple with two teenagers appears. Behind them, there are two more couples, slightly older, who appear to have come together. Both groups pause for a minute as they take in the marquee and the LED bar, which is now lit up. I can see their lips moving as they comment to each other and it's obvious from their low-key outfits that this isn't really the kind of thing they'd been expecting.

'Welcome,' I say. I hold out my hand. 'George Wolsey.' I have to stop myself from adding 'Wolsey Associates' and, without the label of my job, it feels as if I've been robbed of my identity. Now I'm no different to any other man.

Both couples shake hands with Stell and I and introduce themselves before saying hello to the doctor.

'There's a band,' Stell tells the teenagers. I can tell she doesn't want them hanging out with us. 'Go and have a look in the marquee if you like. They're all set up.' The teenagers slink off and, within minutes, the lounge music stops and I hear the first beats of the drum strike up. The band may only do cover versions of popular hits but they're good. The women of the two couples start clicking fingers and mouthing lines to the songs as they stand at the bar sipping their champagne. I can see how the alcohol's relaxing them; they're getting used to the setting; starting to feel at home. The chef also picks up the pace, sending canapés faster. Another family with older kids arrives. They all seem to know each other and those children, too, disappear into the marquee. Dr Grant stands up.

'Excuse me but I must get back to the trouble and strife,' he says. 'Nice to have met you.' He shakes my hand then takes Stell's hand in both of his.

'Take care,' he says.

*

It's properly dark when one of the guests suggests that we, too, move towards the marquee. She rubs her hands up and down her arms.

'Brr. Nights are still chilly.'

I look at my watch. Nine-thirty. The woman's right: it is parky but I've been insulated from it by the champagne. I'm at least six mini bottles down. I try to calculate what that is in terms of glasses, and fail. Not a whole bottle, surely.

'Thank you so much for inviting us,' says one of the women and I see that she's a little tipsy now – she's lost the inhibitions that made her nervous when she arrived. 'We feel quite honoured.'

'Yes,' says the other. 'Your party was quite the topic in the village.' She raises her eyebrow at the other woman and they exchange a look.

'You're so welcome!' Stell says.

'Oh, I love this song! Let's dance!' says one of the women. 'Come on!' She grabs her bottle and starts to shimmy towards the tent and we all pick up our drinks and follow as if she's the Pied Piper.

Inside, the snug warmth of the tent makes me realise just how cold it is outside. The teens are dancing and the mums plonk their drinks on the tables and go straight over to the dance floor. Left alone, I see Stell dither for a second and I know she'd rather sit with the men than dance with the women. Captured there in the half-light, there's something very *Titanic* about the scene: the band playing on while the ship of our party sinks. Stell catches my eye and gives me a tiny eye roll, then she puts her drink on a table and joins the women on the dance floor. I rub my hands together and ask the husbands what I can get them to drink.

TWENTY-SEVEN

Stella

When the police arrive, walking up to the dance floor in full uniform, it's clear that George thinks they've come to join the party. First, he joshes with them as if they're strippers, then he starts offering them drinks. I dash over to stop him from making even more of a fool of himself.

'Evening, officers,' I say. 'How can we help?'

'We've had a complaint about the noise.'

'It's only just gone eleven,' George says.

'Lower the volume, or turn it completely off, please.' The officer is mealy mouthed. George mimes 'turn it down' to the band and they stop playing.

The singer comes over. 'Don't want any trouble. We don't "do" trouble.'

'Neither do we,' I say. 'Let's call it a night.' We'd only booked the band till midnight anyway.

George turns back to the police. 'Has someone complained?'

Out of the corner of my eye, I see our guests gathering their coats and grouping together ready to leave.

Look,' says the officer looking around. 'It may well be

a case of sour grapes. Nice party like this. Someone not invited. But the law's on their side.' He taps his watch. 'After eleven, it's got to be turned down or off.'

'We were just finishing up anyway,' I say.

'Don't let us ruin the party. Just keep the music down now.'

George sees the officers out then sorts out the band while I try to rally the guests into another drink but the mood's broken and there's nothing I can do to stop the three families heading towards the garden path. When they turn the corner, George plucks another mini bottle of champagne from the ice bowl.

'What a disaster! Who called the cops?' he says, swigging half the bottle in one mouthful and slamming it back down on the bar. 'So much for the whole village coming! So much for this being the party of the decade! Ten people came. Not three hundred! TEN!'

I gather together some of the empty bottles. 'I wonder why. Are you sure they got the invitations?'

'We handed them out ourselves. Can't even blame it on the post!'

'Well, we had a few who gave reasons. The ones I know from yoga had excuses.'

'But what about the others? Do you think it's because they've heard about the investigation?'

'Of course not. It's probably something completely unrelated – maybe it was sour grapes over us buying the house. Maybe there was someone in the village who wanted it and we pipped them to it. Remember someone had put in an offer before us. I don't know. But it would have been a great party had people come.'

'It's my fault. It's all because of me.' George is shaking his head. 'I put a curse on everything these days. I can't do anything right.' He gets a glass of water and surveys the mess in the kitchen. 'Let's leave this for tomorrow. I'm going to bed.'

I give George a quick kiss. 'Don't blame yourself. I'll be up in a sec. Just finishing up here. Wait for me.'

I bin the uneaten canapés, then lock the back door, turn off the lights and head up to the bedroom. George is lying on the bed, fully clothed. I slip off my shoes and snuggle into his arms, placing little kisses all over his face.

'Don't let it get to you,' I tell him between kisses.

George turns his face away and runs his hand through his hair. 'Sorry, Stell. I'm tired.'

I roll onto my back and sigh. 'Are you still thinking about why no one came?'

'Free food. Free booze. Why didn't they come? Sod those stupid villagers and their stupid conceits.'

'Maybe there's more to it. Maybe they saw my bruise the other week, put two and two together and made six. You know what villages are like.'

He stiffens. 'What?'

'It's possible. You heard Dr Grant going on about how the village looks after each other. Maybe they think… Oh, I don't know.' I stare at the ceiling.

'The one on your head? But you told them it was an accident, right?'

'Of course. But there was also the hand mark on my arm. The girls at yoga saw that.'

'From that night outside the pub?' George flushes.

I chew my lip. 'Not that one. There was another one a bit later.'

'What? When?'

I look at him. 'You know! There was that night when I tried to take the whisky away from you?'

George shakes his head.

I sigh. 'Why aren't I surprised? Anyway. The girls at yoga saw it. I forgot it was there and wore a vest.'

George collapses back on the pillows.

'Oh great, so now I'm a wife-beater. For God's sake! I'd never touch you! You know that don't you?'

'Of course!'

George's face collapses. 'I can't do anything right any more. I'm an out-of-work criminal who steals money from children's charities – oh, and did I mention that I beat up my wife in my spare time?' He groans. 'All I need now is for Ness to release a kiss-and-tell book about how I used to beat her up too! No wonder no one came to the party! I'm a low life!'

He leaps out of bed, slams out of the room and thumps down the stairs. I hear the kitchen cabinets banging as he hunts for the whisky, then the sound of the glass and the bottle on the granite work surface. Sleep takes me after that: it's been a long day.

TWENTY-EIGHT

George

I come to slowly the next morning, expecting the whack of a hangover with each new degree of consciousness but, when the headache does start to register, it's dull and bearable; not as bad as I deserve. I shift slowly. Stell's still asleep. What was I thinking, mixing champagne, whisky and beer?

Oh God, the champagne. I squeeze my eyes closed, and exhale. Why on earth did I tell the barman to open all the bottles before the guests came? What a waste. And what in God's name happened last night? The disaster that was the party slams into my consciousness like a missile, ripping apart all the hopes I'd had for it. It was supposed to be a celebration – an announcement of our arrival in the village, an investment, not a public embarrassment. Oh, yes, Stell: you said the party would be talked about for years. Sure it will! For all the wrong reasons. What's become of my life? Suspended from the company I own; branded a thief. Not just a thief – someone who stole money from a children's charity. The injustice of it makes me squirm in the bed, as if finding a new position could make it all go away.

I press my hand to my chest, feeling the thud of my heart.

I breathe in and out a few times, trying to ease the tension. I haven't even got work to lose myself in. How long will this investigation take? Will it go to court? And how much damage will the case do to the firm? In my head, I see clients deserting us like rats. I need to get back to work. My heart's thumping again. This is new. I never had this feeling that my heart's going to jump out of my chest before, but I get it almost every day now. Could it be high blood pressure? Or a heart condition? Maybe I should see the doctor. That Dr Grant bloke. He seemed all right. I could ask him about my memory, too – keep Stell happy. Why didn't people come to the party? I close my eyes, and then I remember what Stell said last night and coldness sweeps through my veins.

Bruises. She said I gave her more bruises.

And as if that's not worrying enough on its own, there's also the fact that I can't remember giving them to her; that I've been having these full-on blackouts where I can't remember swathes of the evening. It's one thing not remembering where the things are in the kitchen and losing things like my phone and my wedding ring (oh God, my wedding ring!) but having these blackouts can't be normal. And I don't drink that much. I really don't. So what causes them? A brain tumour?

I slip out of bed as quietly as I can and step into shorts and a T-shirt. The house is warm – Stell's way more extravagant with the heating than I would be – and go downstairs. My laptop's in the study. I open it up and wait, tapping the desk while it fires up. As soon as the search page comes up, I type in 'blackouts' and learn from Dr Google that I was right: blackouts can be caused by drug side effects (no), epilepsy (no), excessive alcohol consumption (surely not!) or brain damage. OK, I'll see the doctor.

Next I Google myself. If the investigation has hit the media, maybe that's why people didn't come to the party. The screen fills with writing. *George Wolsey, accused, children's charity, funds, stolen, investigation, fraud.* There are pages of articles. Pages and pages. How did I not know this? All the broadsheets have the story; the headlines in tabloids, blogs and God-knows-what sites are more speculative. There's even a Twitter hashtag for it. I click on one headline and scroll through the story, the tightness in my chest making my breathing shallow. How could I have thought this wouldn't make the papers? Does everyone know? I'm a social pariah. This is why people didn't come. Who wants to say they're going to George Wolsey's house?

I reach the reader comments at the end of the article: 'what a low life', 'what scum steals from a children's charity?', 'thief'. I shut the page but the words are branded on my brain. I can't un-see them now. How did it come to this? I'm the founder of the Britain's edgiest advertising agency – I'm the golden boy of advertising for God's sake – and I practically pioneered corporate social responsibility. I championed women's rights long before it was trendy. I put the spotlight on worthy causes that usually miss the limelight. Hundreds of thousands of people follow me on social media. I'm a good person. I was going to pay interest! I almost can't bear the weight of my head in my hands. How do you move on from something like this? It'll stick to me for ever. I'll always be 'George Wolsey – oh yes, wasn't he the one with the thing from the charity? You know? Who took the money?'

Bruises. She said I gave her bruises.

Without thinking about what I'm doing, I pick up my phone and dial Ness.

'Hey,' she says, sounding sleepy. An image of her lying in our bed, all warm and soft, imprints on my mind. 'How was the party? It was last night, wasn't it?'

'Oh, fine.'

'OK, what happened?'

I sigh. 'It wasn't like one of ours. Let's leave it at that.'

She laughs. 'Don't be hard on yourself.'

'Anyway, look, can I ask you something? Sorry to drop this on you first thing in the morning… and I'm sorry if it sounds like a weird question… but did I ever hurt you when we were married? Shove you around? Or make you feel scared?'

'Of course not! What a strange question!'

My whole body collapses with relief. 'Really? Nothing? I never pushed you or shoved you or hit you? Not even when I was drunk?'

'No. You could be forceful, and worse if you'd been drinking heavily, but you never lifted a finger to me. Ever.'

'I'm so glad to hear that. You have no idea how glad.'

Ness pauses. 'Why do you ask? Is everything OK with Stella?'

'Oh God. I don't know. I don't know what's going on.' Ness doesn't say anything and suddenly I'm desperate to talk to someone – anyone, even if it's my ex-wife. She knows me better than anyone. Better than I know myself these days.

'You're the last person I should tell.' I give a bitter laugh.

'I don't mind.'

Silence.

'For what it's worth,' Ness says eventually, 'I always thought there was more to Stella than meets the eye. And I don't say that in a bitchy way. I'm not sure you ever saw it, but I did. Others did, too.'

'What do you mean?'

'She can be quite manipulative.'

'Really?'

Ness sighs. 'Yes, George.'

'Anything else?'

I hear Ness breathe in, then she sighs again. 'Look. You're right. I'm not the right person for you to have this conversation with. I'm sorry.'

Shit.

'No, it's me who's sorry,' I say. 'I'm really sorry.' I say the words, and I'm not really sure she understands what it is I'm apologising for: it's not just for this conversation, it's everything. I'm apologising for everything.

TWENTY-NINE

Stella

George isn't in bed when I wake up on the morning after the party. I stretch in the bed enjoying the feel of the sheets on my skin. Stripes of sunshine slash the room through the shutters and it's obvious that it's one of those bright spring days that reminds you of the potential of summer. The house is silent: George must already have finished cleaning up downstairs. I do some gentle yoga stretches then shower slowly, drawing the steam deep into my lungs and breathing it back out again before stepping out, wrapped in my towel.

Downstairs, I stop short at the kitchen door. George isn't there and last night's mess is untouched. So where is he? There's no note to say he's gone out, much as I'd welcome a flaky *pain au chocolat* from the bakery this morning, and there's no sign of any coffee having been made. So little do we use it, it takes me a moment to remember that we have a study and, indeed, that's where I find George, head in hands, laptop open on the desk.

'Morning, darling,' I say, kissing the top of his head. As I do so, I see what he's been doing. I don't need to read the article over his head – I'm familiar with the gist of them.

'Never do that.' I give him a little shake. 'Never Google yourself. You should know that.'

He looks up slowly and I'm shocked how rough he looks. He's aged. Just since this business with the investigation started, he's aged fifteen years, maybe more. The skin hangs across hollows beneath his eyes; he looks gaunt; hollow; red-eyed and slightly crazed.

'George. These are not facts. Most of this is opinion. No one has the facts. They're just speculating.'

'I'm despicable. Honestly, Stell? I wish I could die. The world would be a better place without me.'

I try to take his hand but he snaps it away.

'Don't say that,' I say. 'Don't ever think that.'

'But I gave you bruises, didn't I? You can't deny that.'

I stay silent.

'As I said: despicable.' George rams his fist into his palm. 'It's true, isn't it? No one came last night because they all know. They know I stole money and they think I shove you around.'

'Stop it. There could be any number of reasons why people didn't come. And probably not even one reason for every-body. It's just a coincidence.'

George's fist slams the desk this time, making me jump. 'Seriously, Stell? Some coincidence!'

I've never seen him so low, so desperate. 'Look, how about I make us lunch? A roast chicken? Roast potatoes?'

He shakes his head irritably. 'Not hungry.'

'What? You've got to eat. Look at you! You're skin and bone! Whether or not you eat lunch isn't going to change a thing on there—' I nod at the screen '—or in the village, so let me look after you a bit. Come on, let me take care of you.'

George doesn't reply so I put my hands on his shoulders and massage a little. He doesn't respond to my touch so I step away again.

'Right. I'm going to go and start clearing up the kitchen and then I'm going to make some coffee and put the lunch on. Either you can sit here and stew or you can come and help me.'

*

The smell of the chicken brings George to the kitchen as I knew it would. He fixes us each a drink as I prepare the vegetables. By the time I serve the roast, I can see his shoulders have relaxed a little. I wouldn't say he's his usual perky self, but his energy seems better. He always was annoyingly like a Weeble – you can push him down but he'll always bounce back up.

'How is it?' I ask as he takes his first forkful of food. It's the first full roast I've done for him in a while; the first time I've let him off his diet.

'Really good. Thanks for cooking.'

I smile at him. 'How are you feeling?'

'Well. I've been thinking.

'And?'

He chews, swallows, then continues. 'This isn't me. Sitting here letting people take potshots at me. This is not how I operate. I need to take control.'

I raise my eyebrows at him and wait. I know there'll be more. He'll have come up with a plan. This is so George. Hope in the face of adversity. Positive thinking. He's a walking version of one of his own Technicolor ads.

'I'm giving Lazenby the money in person on Monday. Then I'm going to get some legal advice, just in case he doesn't manage to get my name taken out of the case before it goes to court.'

'OK,' I say slowly.

'I just want to be prepared for what might come next.'

'You really don't want it to go to court,' I say. 'If they charge you under the Fraud Act, the maximum sentence is ten years.'

I can see from his face that George didn't know that. He pales.

'Ten years?'

'Yes. If you look at it from their point of view, it's what they call "confidence fraud".' I pause. Am I sounding as if I know too much about this? 'You conned people into thinking they were giving you money for charity, then you spent it on a house. You have to admit, from their side, it looks really bad. Even if they accept you were going to pay it back, you could end up paying a huge fine, as well as court costs.'

'What?'

'I'm no lawyer, obviously. I'm sure yours will know better than I do. But it's possible you could lose everything. Your savings, the company – your house in Richmond.' I pause. 'This house.'

'Ah,' says George. 'Not the house in Richmond.'

'How come?'

'I signed it over to Ness. When we divorced. It's all in her name.' He actually sounds pleased with himself.

I keep my breathing steady. 'You didn't tell me that.'

George shrugs. 'I didn't think you'd be interested in the ins and outs of my divorce settlement. I told you she fleeced me.' He laughs. 'And she did!'

There's something almost like admiration in his voice. I close my eyes. 'But this house is in your name. You could lose this house.' I look around the kitchen. 'After all we've done to make it our home. This kitchen. Our bedroom.' I pause. 'The nursery.'

George reaches for my hand and squeezes it. 'It won't come to that. I promise.'

He attacks his food with relish, smacking his lips and rolling the wine around his mouth. I try not to let the sound of his chewing irritate me but now I've noticed it, it's all I can hear, so I get up and turn on the radio in the hope that it'll drown out the sound.

'Oh by the way,' says George, swallowing and wiping his lips with his napkin. 'I spoke to Harry.' He pauses, but I don't say anything. 'I've arranged to meet up.'

'When? Where?'

'Next Friday.' He holds his hand up and smiles indulgently. 'Don't worry. I'm not expecting you to cook. I said we'd meet him in a pub, what do you think?'

'Lovely.' I get up and scrape the remains of my plate into the bin.

THIRTY

Stella

After George leaves for London late Monday morning, I empty out the remaining champagne bottles, fill the car boot with the empties and drive to the recycling centre. On my way back, I turn into the Tesco car park. I'm choosing apples one by one, carefully checking each for bruises, when I hear footsteps behind me. A male voice booms out.

'I hear it was a good night!'

I turn. 'Hello Derek!'

'How's the head this morning?'

'Been better.' I smile, tie my bag of apples and place it in the trolley. 'So, why didn't you come? If you don't mind me asking.'

Derek's voice takes a magnanimous tone. 'Would have loved to have come, thank you for asking, had we been invited.'

'But you were!'

Derek shakes his head.

'Are you sure?'

'Sure as eggs. We were wondering what you had to do to get an invitation.'

'But we invited everyone. The whole village was welcome.'

'Not the story I heard. Did many people come?'

I chew my lip. 'Now you mention it, no they didn't. We were wondering what we'd done to offend so many people.'

'How about not invite them in the first place? That'd be why they didn't come.'

'But George…' I stop talking, my mouth hanging open. 'Ahhh.'

'George what? Invited the wrong village?' Derek cackles.

I tut. 'George was supposed to put them through everyone's doors. I gave them to him myself. But… oh God.' I shake my head. 'Oh no, it must have affected him more than I realised.'

'What?'

'Oh nothing.' I sigh and look around to check no one I know is nearby. 'Just… please can I ask you to be discreet?'

Derek inclines his head as if this is a given.

'The fact is, he's not taking time off work through choice.' I pause. 'I presume you've heard about the investigation hanging over him?' Derek nods. 'He must be ashamed,' I say. 'You know he wasn't even able to get a part-time job to keep him busy. It takes its toll.' I realise I'm rubbing my upper arm and stop doing it. 'You know what these alpha male types are like sometimes. He never wants anyone's pity. I bet that's what happened.' I give myself a little shake. 'Anyway, please accept my apologies. You were actually top of our list. But now we seem to have alienated the whole village when our point was to make friends!'

'I wouldn't worry too much about it. I'll spread the word a little for you, if you like.'

'Umm. Thank you, but… it's kind of delicate? I wouldn't want George to think everyone knew our business. Or that he felt ashamed.'

Derek pats my arm. 'Of course. Understood. Subtlety's my middle name.' He taps the side of his nose with his finger. 'Trust me.'

We part company and I head over to the phone shop where I pick the cheapest pay-as-you-go smartphone I see, and a new SIM, too.

'Would you like a package?' asks the sales lady. 'We have some great deals.'

'No. Thank you. It's just going to be a spare. In case my husband loses his. He can be such a doofus sometimes.'

The woman laughs. 'Nothing worse than being without a phone, right?'

THIRTY-ONE

George

It's only 5 p.m. when I finish with the solicitor and I feel pretty good when I step out into the street. Instinctively, I pull out my phone but my finger hesitates over Stell's name. She'll just expect me to come straight home. I call Ness instead.

'Hey!' I say. 'I just wanted to let you know Lazenby was really glad to get the cheque. Thank you.'

'You're welcome. So, is that you off the hook?'

'I'm not sure. But I've just seen a solicitor and he says it should go some way, especially as Lazenby's going to give me a character reference, too.'

'That's great! I'm pleased.'

'Maybe we could go out one night? So I can thank you in person?' As soon as I've said it, I realise I've overstepped the mark. 'Only if you want to!' I add.

Ness clears her throat. 'No, it's fine. Really.'

I hang up and, again, am struck by Ness' generosity of spirit. This is a woman who dedicated fifteen years of her life to helping me build my business; a woman whom I thanked by screwing around behind her back. A woman who almost gave me the baby I want so badly; who didn't hesitate to help me when I needed it. I don't like to think about the fact that Stell could easily have come up with the cash.

I cross the street and walk slowly into Russell Square. The sun's starting to dip below the tops of the buildings and the light has that magical early evening feel about it. After being stuck for so long in the village, I feel that special buzz of London. There's something about it that, I don't know, enthuses me. It's a prickling in my veins, a buzz in my stomach – I feel like I'm a teenager getting ready for a party: I don't want to go home, and I have the sense that anything could happen.

Inside the park I find an empty bench and think about what I'm going to do. It's a long time since I've felt like this. Life in the country's nice enough, but it's, God, I don't know, suffocating? Being there with Stell all the time. Yes, she's magnificent – a little voice says 'too magnificent?' and I slap it down. I need a bit of space now and then. The smallness of village life... it's just... Richmond was great. I used to kid myself we lived in a village but it wasn't really a village at all. A village in the city. But this – this is real village life and the minutiae of it feels like pondweed wrapping itself around my ankles and dragging me down. That prick of a pub landlord. That Nazi woman with the gift shop. Yoga mornings! I try not to think about my kick-boxing Stell enduring the yoga mornings just so she can meet people. And those people all forming opinions about me and Stell and not coming to the goddamned party. I'd have been all right if I had my job – if I'd been able to come into town every day – but being home all day, every day...

And then there's the blackouts. What the hell's going on with that? I rub my temples. Can I really be drinking so much I've killed my brain cells? Or is it something worse? But I've forgotten so much stuff lately I've started trying to hide it. Like in the kitchen. I can never remember where things are kept, even though Stell and I put it all there ourselves. It's like someone else's kitchen every time I walk in. Sometimes I stand there and try to imagine the most logical place for the coffee cups and open that cupboard and it'll be the whisky. But when I want the whisky it's never there. One week the kettle's on the left of the sink; the next it's on the right – or so it seems. It makes me so unsure of everything. I dread going into the kitchen now. I'm always second-guessing myself: was that really there yesterday? Or not? And every time I check my diary there are things – admittedly small things – that I don't recall happening. I don't tell Stell any more. I'm like an alcoholic trying to hide the extent of my problem. Not that I'm an alcoholic.

I'm not.

I can't believe how quickly I got through the whisky the other week. When Stell showed me the empties. Shit.

Speaking of which, I know what I want to do tonight. A drink. With Phil. I haven't seen him for ages. I imagine us in a pub, some beers – God, it's been so long since I've had any 'guy' time. I don't even get to see my colleagues these days. I pull out my mobile and call Phil. He's free. Brilliant.

*

'Cheers. So how's life in the country?' Phil asks. 'New wife, new house… all good, I hope?'

I take a long pull of my beer. It's cold and goes down well. It could get messy tonight and I don't care. How to answer that? Living the eternal bachelor life right in the heart of London, Phil's one of my oldest friends. He knows me pretty well.

'Yeah, it's good.'

'You got the babe.'

I laugh. 'It's all relative, mate.'

'I never thought you'd leave Ness, to be honest. You and her…' His voice trails off. 'So what happened? You had an affair? Got caught, right?'

I fill Phil in on the details. He makes the right noises.

'And so, the country? How's that going? You were always such a city boy.'

'I'd be all right if I was still working. You've heard, right? About the investigation?'

Phil looks at his beer. 'Yeah. People talk…'

'It's killing me, mate. That's why I'm in town. Paid back the money and got myself a brief.'

'Good you've paid it back, but I have to ask: why did you do it? You must have known how it would look. Stealing money from a charity.' He shakes his head. 'That's pretty low!'

I sigh. 'It was only ever supposed to be a loan. Stell and I were buying a house. I needed to move quickly. I had no liquid cash after the divorce so I borrowed it from the charity account for a couple of months.'

'OK. So what happened? How come they found out?'

'Just bad luck. A vigilant trustee sticking his nose in.' I run my hand through my hair and exhale. It's so good to talk to Phil. 'I don't know what shit's going on in my life at the moment. It's just started to fall apart. It's like – I don't know – there's this curse on things suddenly.' I laugh at how pathetic I sound. 'Not a curse. But it never used to be like this.'

'Like what?'

'Well, having a potential criminal case hanging over me for starters. But it's more than just that. I thought I'd be sorted once I moved in with Stell but now it's my health. I get this tightness in my chest…' I realise I'm sounding like a whingey old man. 'My memory. You're my age, aren't you? Do you forget stuff these days?'

Phil laughs. 'Yeah. All the time.'

'Like what, though?'

'My name. Where I live.' Phil laughs.

'Seriously.'

'What are you forgetting? Things like walking into a room and forgetting what you came in for? That's normal.'

'No. Where things are in the kitchen. Conversations. Events. I lose stuff. I put things down and I can't remember where they are. Phone calls and messages. I could go on.'

'Hmm.'

'There are text messages. Emails I have no memory of sending.'

'But you sent them?'

'Yeah.'

'What else?'

I stare at my beer. Can I tell him about the bruises? I'm so ashamed.

'Whole evenings. Stell will be funny with me the next day and I don't know why. Then she'll remind me we had a row or something. There was one night I got so drunk I threw up, but I have no memory of it at all.'

Phil sits back. 'Wow. That's not good. Are you drinking? Like, much more than usual?'

'Not more than usual. You know. I'm no saint, but the odd whisky or whatever. Not a lot. I'm actually trying to keep off it because – well…'

'What – "well"?'

I look at the bar, suddenly shy. 'Well apparently alcohol stops the little fellas swimming or something.' I look at Phil, feeling somehow as if I'm confessing to a monstrous crime. 'We've been trying for a baby.'

He looks sideways back at me. We don't usually talk so intimately. 'Well, look at you! I never thought I'd see the day!'

He ribs me and I take it. It's this that I've missed up in the village with Stell. I love that joshing, that teasing, and the beer tastes so much better in the pub with my mates than it ever does with Stell. Before I know it, the bell for last orders has rung and we're the last ones propping up the bar. Phil knows a cocktail bar around the corner that'll serve till 1 a.m. and we bundle over and start on the Jägerbombs. I have no defence: it seems like a good idea at the time, though I realise my thinking may be skewed and, at the back of my mind, I can picture Stell pacing the kitchen, looking at the clock, gnashing her teeth and wondering where I am. But I'm having a brilliant time and I know she'll want me to have a bit of fun. Let my hair down and all that.

'One for the road,' Phil slurs when we're several Jägerbombs down. 'What time's your last train anyway?'

I look at my watch and burst out laughing. 'Gone!' I put on a station announcer voice. '"The vomit express has left the station." I'd say it was halfway home by now.'

'Crash at mine.'

'Nah. There's a night bus.'

He looks at me and we both crack up. It's as if it was the funniest thing anyone's ever said. Phil bangs his hand on the bar, whimpering, 'Night bus! Night bus!' through tears of laughter. I haven't laughed like this in ages – my stomach muscles are aching and my face is wet with tears.

'One for the road, mate,' Phil says when we've both calmed down, 'and you're coming home with me.'

I don't argue. He lives close enough to walk. But I do pull out my phone and, with clumsy, drunken fingers, prod in a message to Stell: *Sorry, hon. Met up with Phil. Missed the last train. Am crashing at his. Love u X*

It's 1 a.m.

THIRTY-TWO

Stella

George comes in whistling. It's a bright morning and, under different circumstances, we might have been preparing to have people over for lunch – nipping out to the butcher to pick up a joint, par-boiling potatoes to roast, making batter for Yorkshire puddings, preparing vegetables, setting the table with the crystal glasses. I think I'd have done an apple crumble and my fingers rub together subconsciously as I imagine rubbing the cold, hard butter into the flour and sugar to make the crumble topping. And custard. I'd have done custard – rich and creamy with those luscious vanilla pods I found at the new organic shop.

By twelve-thirty we'd be opening the wine to breathe – inhaling the scent of a nice Bordeaux and pouring ourselves a snifter before the guests arrive, clinking our glasses together and maybe having a bit of a kiss. But no. I'm sitting in the kitchen with nothing inside me except three strong coffees, feeling as if I've been hit by a truck. My head's thick and my eyes are scratchy – I haven't dared look in the mirror for fear of what I'll see. I'm hunched over the table, my shoulders up by my ears, the tension in them impossible to shift – and in he comes through the front door, whistling a cheery little tune. Then, before I've really had a chance to finalise what I'm going to say, he's here in the kitchen, beaming at me, his arms full of tulips. He looks tired, as if he's trying to hide a night of no sleep.

'Hey, gorgeous!' he says. 'How are you? I picked these up for you on the way home. They had buckets of them at the station – got you a bunch in each colour. I know they're your favourite.'

He's right: they are. Their colours make me feel optimistic about spring and the potential advent of summer and its deep blue skies, but today I give the tulips little more than a cursory glance. George puts them down by the sink and comes over. He bends over me and tries to kiss me, but I don't look up – he kisses my hair instead, then gives it a little stroke. I shake his hand off.

'What's up? Are you OK?'

I push him away. On the table in front of me is my phone. I glare at it but he doesn't understand.

'Is something wrong? Have I forgotten something? Were we due somewhere?' I don't respond. 'It's not your birthday, is it?' He looks upwards, as if trying to recall. 'Our anniversary? Can't be. What is it, Stell?'

'What's up?' I say slowly to the table, then I look up at George and repeat myself. 'What's up? What do you think is up?' I slam my hand on the table with my last word and it's as if all the anger inside me explodes in his face like a volcano. 'Let's see, George. What do you think is up?'

He pulls out a chair and sits across the table from me, his hands clasped in front of him.

'You're pissed that I stayed out?'

'Goodness, George, you're good. Got it in one.'

'But... but I messaged you.'

'Oh yes,' I scoff. 'You messaged me. That makes it all right then, does it?'

'Well – umm – yes? I mean, I'm sorry it was so late, but at least you didn't need to worry.'

'At least I didn't need to worry. Yes, that's very thoughtful of you. Thank you. I suppose I should be grateful for the fact that I knew exactly where you were and what you were presumably doing. Without your wedding ring on, if I may say so.'

George looks at his hand and frowns. 'I'm really sorry. I lost it ages ago. I was going to get it replaced, but...'

I raise my eyebrows at him.

George rubs his temples. I imagine he's got a headache – drunk too much, slept too little and is having trouble following the conversation – but I don't feel any sympathy.

'Look,' he says. 'I'm tired. I've no idea what you're getting at. I missed the last train. I told you that. You got the message, didn't you?'

'Oh yeah. I saw it. I don't know why you bothered sending it. As if I could have got any sleep after that!'

'After what? What are you talking about?'

I shove my phone over to him. 'This! After this, how was I supposed to get any sleep?'

George picks up my phone and taps the screen to bring it to life. As he reads the message, his mouth drops open and he starts shaking his head.

'No! I didn't send this!'

I shrug. 'What am I supposed to think? It's come from your phone. See: George Wolsey.'

'But my phone was with me all night!'

'I rest my case.' I grab my phone back from where George has dropped it on the table. '*Guess who I've bumped into?*' I read out loud. '*Grabbing a quick bite with Ness. Won't be late!* Won't be late, eh? Well, I suppose technically you're not late.' I look at my watch. 'You're actually reasonably early. And then—' I open another message. 'Oh, here it is: *Missed the last train – going to bunk at Ness's.* Great, George. Absolutely great. Thanks for that. As I said, I'd almost rather have not known where you were. Then maybe I could have got *some* sleep!'

'Stell.' George shoves the chair back and starts pacing the kitchen. He's running his hands through his hair. 'I don't know what's happened. I don't know how you got that message, but I promise you – hand on my heart – I didn't meet Ness. I haven't seen Ness for over a year! I was with Phil! I came out from the solicitor's. It was a lovely evening, I felt like going for a drink so I called Phil. Yeah, things got a little out of hand and for that I apologise, but it was his house I crashed at and that's what I told you – here, look!'

George grabs his phone from his pocket, scrolls to the text messages. 'Look! Here it is!' He shoves the phone in my face. Indeed, there is a message saying he's missed the train and is crashing at Phil's. I push the phone away.

'I don't know what you've done with your phone – if that even *is* your phone – but I know what message I got from you last night and that's all that matters. Maybe you were so drunk you deleted it. Or maybe you realised you shouldn't have told me. I don't know. I don't know you at all sometimes.' I shake my head. 'So what did you and Ness do – top and tail? Offer to sleep in the spare room?' I laugh bitterly and carry on before George has a chance to reply. 'In what world did you think that would be all right? In what world is it OK to spend the night with your ex-wife *at her house*?' I'm shouting now. I get up, too: we're standing at opposite ends of the kitchen, each of us with our back to a counter. 'What's going on?'

George is shaking his head. 'Nothing! Nothing's going on! Don't make this something it's not.' But even as he speaks, I see something in his eyes as he mentions Ness and it knocks the breath out of me: he's seen her. I'd bet my life on it.

'For fuck's sake, George! How much more do you want me to take? The jealousy, the temper, the blackouts, the bruises – and now Ness? If you're not going to keep your end of the deal, I can't do this. I can't!' I grab my bag and keys and bang through the front door, slamming it behind me.

*

I slow down as I reach the end of the lane and turn into Main Street, and my anger dissolves as fast as it had built in the kitchen. It really is a beautiful day, and the cherry blossoms are in full bloom – probably only a few days to go before they start falling. The wisteria's starting to come out, too, and I breathe in the scent of the earth, the flowers and the

ANNABEL KANTARIA

distant smell of horses. The air up here is so clean compared to London, it feels like a tonic. But what is it that George is hiding? Has he really seen Ness? I don't doubt what I saw in his eyes. Is he having regrets about leaving her? About marrying me? After all I've put up with from him? The thought throws me, and then there's a tap on my shoulder.

'Lovely morning, isn't it?' says Dr Grant. 'Hello.'

'Morning. Yes. I was just thinking the same. The cherry blossoms are beautiful. The village is so pretty.'

'Hmm. It's probably a bit late now but, down by the wood – you know at the end of Main Street? – we get a carpet of bluebells in early April. It's quite a sight – our hidden treasure.'

'I'll look out for it next year,' I say with a smile. I do like Dr Grant. We chat about flowers a little. I never thought I had it in me to like a flower that wasn't in a vase. Sometimes I surprise myself.

When the conversation lulls, Dr Grant gives a little cough.

'Sleeping better?'

'Oh – umm, off and on. I might need to get another prescription.'

'OK. Well, come into the surgery and we'll have a chat about it.' He pauses. 'I just saw your other half walking up from the station, by the way. Lovely flowers.'

'Oh yes. He brought tulips. My favourite.' Big smile.

'Not guilt flowers, I hope!'

I look at the pavement, then back up at Dr Grant. He's not stupid. Given the time and the fact George was in a suit, it must have been pretty obvious that he was coming home the morning after. I give a little shrug.

'He missed me. He had a boys' night in London last night.' Another smile. 'Stayed over… you know how it is. But I don't mind. At least there was no snoring!' I pause. 'No, I'm just joking. I'm lucky to have him!'

I look away as I say this but, even so, I feel Dr Grant looking at me. I know that he's weighing up whether to say something or not. He looks down and then back up at my face. I can see what he's thinking.

'I hope everything's OK?'

'Yes. Yes of course!' Now I give the doctor a really bright smile and a little laugh. 'Gosh, everyone argues, don't they?' I roll my eyes. 'Show me a couple who say they never row and I'll show you a pair of liars!'

Dr Grant leans forward and touches my hand. 'I'm always here if you need to talk.'

THIRTY-THREE

George

Stell slams the door and I collapse at the kitchen table, my head in my hands. What happened last night? I remember leaving the solicitor's; calling Ness. There was a plan about meeting up, then I met Phil. I did meet Phil, didn't I? I remember the conversation, the bar, laughing. But what did I do after that? Did I rock up at Ness's? I was drunk – really drunk – and it wouldn't be my first blackout so it's feasible. Unlikely, but feasible, and so unnerving. It's as if other people know more about my life than I do; like I'm experiencing only 80 per cent of my life, and relying on others to fill in the gaps. And so, speaking of gaps, I pick up the phone and dial Phil's number. No response. Conscious of how often I'm doing it these days, I call Ness. No reply there, either, so I send a message: *Strange question, but did we meet up last night?*

In the study, I switch on the laptop. While it fires up, I wipe my hands on my trousers, aware of the clamminess of my fingers. As soon as I can open the browser, I type in 'memory test' and pick one of the ones that comes up: matching animals. I click through them feeling as if I'm in primary school and my score at the end is 89 per cent. That can't be bad.

Did I see Ness last night?

A part of me likes the idea that I might have done.

*

I find Stell in the pub. She's sitting with a coffee and the papers at a big table by the bay window. A sunbeam's falling on her hair and it looks as if she's in her very own spotlight. Her sweater's too big for her – she's shoved it up her arms a little and I can see her narrow wrists, her long, slim fingers clasped around the paper, and the diamond bracelet I bought her catching the light. As I watch, she raises a hand and pushes a strand of hair back behind her ear and I see better the profile of her lips. The whole effect gives her a vulnerability, a fragility, that makes me want to scoop her up, wrap her in cotton wool and make sure that nothing bad ever happens to her. I walk over to her. When my shadow falls onto her paper, she looks up.

'Hey.'

'Hi,' she says.

I indicate to the table. 'May I?'

She shuffles along the bench seat in silence, making space for me to sit next to her. This is good. Better than I imagined. I sit next to her and take her hand. She lets me. Again, better than I'd hoped. I pick up her hand and kiss it gently. Her skin smells of the hand cream she keeps by the bed. I can picture the tube with the red and blue logo; the way she sometimes screws the cap back wonky because her hands are greasy with cream. Unbidden, the thought comes into my head of the things she sometimes does to me with her hands greasy with cream, and I have to stamp on that thought at once.

'I'm sorry, princess,' I say. 'I don't know how you got that message, but you have to believe me: I didn't see Ness and I certainly didn't stay with her.'

She sighs – it's a long sigh but not altogether a bad one. Is she leaning a little into me, or am I imagining it? 'It's OK,' she says slowly, and I barely believe my ears. She looks solemnly at me, her eyes latching on to mine. 'I've been thinking.' She sighs. 'Look – even if you did see Ness, the point is you're mine. You made your choice, and you chose me.'

'I did.'

'I should remember that.'

She's being so understanding I feel like a complete louse. 'You shouldn't have to make yourself remember that!' I say. 'I shouldn't put you in a position where you have to remind yourself that I chose you. It should be obvious to you every minute of every day.'

She smiles at me and I can't resist pulling her to me, hugging her to my chest and kissing her forehead.

'I'm so sorry,' I say.

'I'm not going to say it's OK because it's not,' she says. 'But promise me one thing?'

'Yes?' I'll do anything. Anything!

'Will you go and see Dr Grant? Just ask him what could be the cause of your blackouts? It might be something simple

– something really simple that could be easily fixed. And I don't want us to continue this…. this "roller coaster" of highs and lows when you don't remember. I hate drama. You know that.' Her voice softens. 'I hate fighting with you.'

'I will,' I say. And I mean it.

*

When Ness replies to my message later that evening, I take my phone into the bathroom to read her reply but I needn't have bothered. 'No, we didn't meet,' she says, simply, and I have the sense that I'm edging across a rope bridge. I'm way out over a steep ravine, and someone's cut the bridge behind me.

THIRTY-FOUR

Stella

Friday evening. George appears in the kitchen door and slings his jacket over the back of a chair. He's dressed, ready to go, and is rolling up his shirtsleeves as he speaks. I catch a waft of his cologne and notice that he's shaved, too. When did he last see Harry? I guess it's been ages but, even so, George's eagerness to see his big brother makes me pity him a little. Clearly the power balance in the relationship is a little skewed.

'Come on! We need to leave in twenty minutes!' George says.

'Just a minute.' I'm on the iPad. Not doing anything important, just flicking about on Facebook, trying to summon up some enthusiasm for the evening ahead.

George looks pointedly at his watch. 'Do you need a shower?'

'Yeah.'

'Well, please go and do it or we're going to be late.'

I sigh and close the iPad. 'OK. Going, going. What shall I wear? I haven't seen Harry for years.'

'Something. Anything! Just be yourself.'

'OK.'

I take my time getting ready. I can hear George's shoes pacing about on the concrete floor downstairs and his impatience amuses me.

'Are you ready yet?' he yells up the stairs but he doesn't wait for a reply; he bounds up them and appears in the bedroom as if to check I really am dressing. I see he has his jacket on.

'Nearly done,' I say. 'Which earrings?' I hold two different ones up by my ears. He barely looks at them; just says. 'Left.'

'My left or your left?'

'Yours!'

'This one? Oh, I was thinking it might be too "evening-y". Although I suppose it is an evening…'

'Sweetheart.' George sounds strangled. 'Please. They're both nice. Just pick one.'

'All right, all right.' I fasten my earrings, slip on my shoes, grab a clutch. 'Right. I'm done.'

George turns of the lights and follows me out of the bedroom. I run down the stairs but, a couple of steps before the bottom, I fall, landing awkwardly on my ankle.

'Ow!' I clutch it and rock backwards and forwards, trying not to cry. 'Ow! Ow! Ow!'

'Oh my God, Stell, are you all right?' George is beside me in a flash. 'What happened? Did you just miss the step? Here, here, let me look.'

I let him gently ease my leg out in front of me. Already I can see there's some swelling as the flesh is starting to bite into the delicate strap of my shoe. George undoes it and frees my foot, holding it tenderly.

'Can you move it? Wiggle your toes.'

I do. George then moves my ankle gently this way and that.

'I don't think it's broken. Probably just a sprain. Let me get some ice.'

He comes back with a pack of frozen peas and places it carefully on my ankle.

'What are we going to do?' he asks. 'Shall I call a taxi?'

I squeeze my eyes shut. 'George. I can't come! I can't walk like this. Look at it. I'm not hopping into central London.'

I watch his face change as he realises we're not going anywhere. He takes off his jacket.

'You can still go,' I say. 'Please don't ruin your evening on my account. Harry will be waiting.'

George helps me to stand and support me as I take a step or two, but my ankle gives out. I lean against the wall, panting.

'Ow. I can't put any weight on it. But go. Go on, you'll be late.'

George passes a hand over his brow, smoothing out the frown that's there.

'No, sweetheart. It's fine. I'll stay with you. Let's get you up and get that leg elevated.'

I lean heavily on him as we shuffle to the living room. He settles me on the sofa, and fusses about, propping me up with cushions and asking what he can get me.

'Is it feeling any better?' he asks. 'We might have some bandage. I think we should strap it up tonight.'

'Stop fussing,' I say. 'I'm a big girl. Fussing isn't going to salve your conscience.'

'What d'you mean?' He honestly looks baffled. I stare at him and he stares back. 'What do you mean?'

I look down. 'Well, if you hadn't been in such a hurry...'

'If you hadn't been so slow! We were late!'

'Five minutes, maybe, but you didn't need to shove me down the stairs.'

'Shove you?' George's mouth hangs open.

'OK, not shove, but you were on top of me. Your foot hit the back of mine. That's what knocked it out from under me.'

'No!'

I nod. 'Yes. But, look, let's not hash over what happened. I'm fine.'

George shakes his head. 'No. I was three steps behind you.'

'Maybe. I wasn't counting. But you were coming down faster than I was. And you have big feet! You didn't even feel it, did you? But I felt you whack my foot out from under me. Anyway, look, there's no point in going over it now. As you say, it's not broken so all's well that ends well. Why don't you go and see Harry? I'll be fine here.'

George stays.

THIRTY-FIVE

George

It's not difficult to get an appointment with Dr Grant. He takes private patients and, thankfully, my health insurance is still valid. The waiting room is small and a little shabbier than I would have expected – the chairs a little worn, the magazines well thumbed – but I'm not there long before the receptionist calls me in. Dr Grant's writing something when I knock on the door and enter the consulting room, and he doesn't look up so I choose one of the two chairs adjacent to his desk and sit down. While I wait, I look at my hands. My ring finger looks bare without my wedding ring. I cross my arms so it's out of sight.

After a minute or two, Dr Grant looks up.

'So. George. What can I do for you today?' he asks, raising his eyes over the line of his glasses. No pleasantries. It seems abrupt but I'm kind of glad about that. It's good to keep personal and business matters separate.

'There are a few things.'

'OK?'

'The main one is my memory. There are things I just can't remember.'

The doctor laughs. 'It happens to the best of us.'

This wrong-foots me a little. 'I've started having black-outs. That's not normal, is it? If it was just forgetting things, I wouldn't be here. Trust me – I never go to the doctor!' I laugh. 'Avoid them like the plague!'

'OK, OK. Can you give me any examples?'

'Well, several times I've come home after a night out and I can remember a certain portion of the evening but nothing after that. Nothing at all. It's as if I was unconscious. Stella tells me things that have happened and I have no memory.'

'Hmm. Would you typically have been drinking when these episodes occur?'

'Not more than usual.'

'Would you say you're a heavy drinker?'

'All due respect, doctor, but it's not to do with alcohol. I know my limits.'

Dr Grant looks at me over his glasses.

'There's general memory loss, too, when I haven't been anywhere near a drink. Losing things. Not remembering text messages and emails that I sent to my wife.'

'I see. And this causes a problem between you, presumably?'

'Exactly. That's why I'm here. She asked me to see you, to be honest. She's worried.'

'So you've forgotten about text messages you've sent? Is there anything else?'

'Not remembering where things are kept at home – it's like living in a stranger's house sometimes.' It sounds feeble when I say it out loud and I half expect him to make a joke about it. 'It's very disorientating.'

'I see.'

'I've been keeping a diary.'

'And?'

'Often what I remember happening doesn't match what I've written in the diary.'

'I see. And Stella asked you to come and see me?' Dr Grant is nodding as if he finds this point particularly interesting.

'Yes.' I try to keep the impatience out of my voice. 'So, is there any sort of test you can do to see what's causing it? I've ruled out epilepsy, alcohol and drug use, which leaves brain damage. Do you think it could be a tumour? Do I need a brain scan?'

Dr Grant tuts. 'First, let me get a little more background. On a scale of one to ten how would you rate your current stress level?'

'Mmm. About an eight.'

'You're not currently working, are you?'

'No. That's part of the stress.' I cross my legs and uncross them. What I say to a doctor is confidential, isn't it? I shift on the seat. 'I've been suspended from work for the time being, pending an investigation.'

'That sounds serious.'

'Oh, it's nothing. A "misunderstanding".' I shift on the seat. 'Look. I took some money in good faith – a really short-term loan to tide me over. I was going to pay it back with interest. I shouldn't have taken it. But I didn't steal it.'

'I see. And how do you feel about this?'

'Pissed off.'

'Well. I'm sure if you acted in good faith then your name shall be cleared,' says Dr Grant rather dismissively. 'But, in the meantime: you say you feel…' he pauses '…annoyed?'

'Yes. Annoyed.'

'Anything else?'

'Let down. Disappointed. Anxious. Actually—' and I don't know why this hasn't occurred to me before '—could that cause my heart to thump? It's been thudding a lot lately. Almost feels like it's going to jump out of my throat.' I smile. 'I thought I was going to have a heart attack, too. As well as the brain tumour.' I give a laugh to show I'm not entirely serious.

'It's quite possible that the pounding is caused by anxiety,' says Dr Grant. 'I can arrange for you to have an ECG. But, I'd like to go back to these negative feelings you're experiencing: would you say there's anger there?'

'Yes. Yes, I guess so. Towards the company and the way they've shafted me. They know I wouldn't do something like this.'

'Okay.' Dr Grant looks at his notes and then back up at me. 'So how do you deal with this anger that you feel?'

I sit back in my seat and cross my arms. 'What do you mean how do I "deal" with it?'

'Well, do you have some sort of release for your anger?'

'Like?'

'Oh I don't know. Some people go running, or take up some sort of sport. Go for long walks.'

'I run. Always have.' Even as I say it, I realise I haven't been running since we moved to the village.

'OK, good. Anything else? Do you have any hobbies that get you out of the house?'

'I have a bike. A Ducati.' I can't say it without smiling. 'I ride that.'

'Hmm. Anything else?'

I shrug. 'Not really. I don't usually have any spare time for hobbies.'

'So no golf or anything like that? Pool? I don't know what games you youngsters play these days. Foosball?' He twiddles his hands as if playing table football. I shake my head.

'Yoga? Meditation?'

'Nope.'

'OK. And friends. Do you have many close friends? Who you see regularly?'

'Well, I had my work colleagues till recently. We were a close team. Work hard, play hard – you know how it is.'

'But you don't see them at the moment.'

'No.'

'Anyone else?'

'Well, I had friends where I lived before: my MC – motorcycle club.'

'Hmm.'

Dr Grant lapses into silence and I fidget on the chair. I'm aware that the picture he's painted of me is very negative: no job, no hobbies, no friends, angry and frustrated and a bit of a drinker. Am I really that pathetic a figure? Where did George the golden boy go? I remember how I used to leap out of bed in the mornings, ready for another day at work; how ideas used to bombard me day and night. What happened?

'Hmm,' says Dr Grant again. He's looking at me thoughtfully. 'Let's just do a quick check of your memory. Can you tell me the months of the year in reverse order?'

I rattle them off.

'And count backwards from twenty to zero?'

Again, I manage without stumbling.

'OK, look,' says Dr Grant, 'I'm not concerned about your memory loss at this stage. I think the stress you're under is taking its toll. And we'll book you in for an ECG if that gives you some peace of mind. But I am concerned about the impact your anger and frustration are having on your home life.' He glowers at me as he says this and I get the feeling he's trying to imply something. 'You need to find an outlet. Take up a hobby, even if it's just while you're out of work. See friends outside of your work circle. Try to reduce your stress levels.'

'So I don't have a brain tumour?'

The doctor leans back in his chair and steeples his fingers. 'I sincerely doubt it. But, if you're concerned about what you're forgetting, I'd keep up with the diary. Try to spot any patterns – if memory loss occurs only after drinking, for example, or when you're feeling stressed. And come and see me again and we can take it from there. In the meantime, my advice is to get yourself a hobby.' He stands up and holds out his hand and I realise my appointment is over.

THIRTY-SIX

Stella

Given I'm stuck at home with my sore ankle for a few days, it seems a good time to really make a start on the novel I've been meaning to write since I scaled back my office work. I settle myself on the sofa with the foot elevated, stare blankly at my notebook and wait for the ideas to come.

They don't.

I drum my fingers on the sofa and look around the room. Why can't I do this? Why can't I write a novel? I was brought up to believe I could do anything and the lack of progress annoys me; it irritates me like a tiny stone lodged in my shoe. Not hurting; just annoying. Giving me jaggedy edges where things should be smooth. I know what the book's going to be about but, in all the time we've been in the village, I haven't got down a single word, not even a title.

I've been procrastinating, of course. Everyone wants to write a book – and I've realised, since moving house, why it is that most people never actually start. It's because it's difficult. A bit like ice-skating, maybe – it looks effortless enough but when you actually get those things under your feet for the first time you realise how much strength and balance goes into making it look quite so easy. But this is where that stone irritates me: I'm not used to finding things difficult. And with a book, even if you have the idea and the time, it's still unbelievably hard to get that first chapter written down. Every time George has been out – which hasn't been a lot, to be fair – I've Googled how to start writing a novel. And an inspirational sentence I've come upon today – 'Start where you are. Use what you have. Do what you can' – has given me a bit of an epiphany. Now, sitting here in the sunny living room with the patio doors open and the sound of birdsong drowning out the radio, it's made me realise that all I have to do is begin. I take a deep breath, pick up my pen and write on the first page.

'Diary.'

I stop as soon as I've written that because I can't think what to write next. Diary of an Abused Wife? I cringe. Diary of Domestic Violence. Too dull. Diary of a Marriage. Also dull. Diary of Doom. Oh God, this is hard.

What would make someone want to pick it up and read it? It's quite a dark story I plan to write, about a woman who's trapped in her house by her husband. I got the idea after Dr Grant started talking about the Taylor conviction at the party. I couldn't stop thinking about how the husband must have deliberately set about to erode all of his wife's self-confidence and self-belief until she truly believed that she shouldn't leave the house. How can that happen? How can two people live in such a warped version of reality?

I decide to finish the title later. I enter the date, and then I start to write: 'He's angry all the time. So angry, I'm afraid for my life.' I bite my lip. It's going to be good.

THIRTY-SEVEN

George

I get a job. Stell comes in one day, her face glowing. She looks so happy she's practically walking on air as she bounces into the kitchen.

'Guess what?' she says. 'Derek's agreed to give you a job at the pub!'

She grabs me by the wrists, pulls me to my feet, and plants a showy smacker of a kiss on my cheek. 'You're welcome,' she says.

'What sort of job? Behind the bar?'

'He didn't say.'

'How did you get him to agree? He was so anti employing me when I asked.'

'I just fluttered my lashes,' she says as if it's the most natural thing in the world to bat your lashes and get what you want. I can see why Derek agreed. There's something about Stell that just kind of railroads you into doing what she wants. An innocent expectation, maybe, that you'll do what she wants; that 'no' just isn't an option. And then there's the fact that he fancies her.

'It's only a trial, though. Unpaid,' Stell says. 'So I thought I'd give you an allowance.'

'An allowance?'

'You know, so you feel like you're earning something. Aren't you going to say thank you?'

I lean over and kiss her. 'Thank you.'

'Right. You'd better get dressed. He's expecting you at midday for the lunch crowd.'

'So soon?'

'Why waste time? I know how much you wanted a job.'

I change out of my shorts into chinos and a shirt, and head off to the pub. Derek's behind the bar. He looks me up and down as I stride over to him.

'Looking very smart,' he says.

I smile. 'Thanks for this. I appreciate it.'

'I'm only doing this because your lovely wife asked me,' Derek says.

Our eyes meet. 'I know.'

Derek lifts up the bar and I step towards the gap, but we almost collide as he comes out.

'Where are you going, sunshine?' he says. 'Kitchen's this way.'

'Of course.' I follow Derek through a door into the kitchen, then out the other side into a cramped anteroom where there's an industrial-sized sink, a couple of dishwashers and a pile of dirty dishes and glasses on a draining board.

'Dishes there. Sink. Bin. Soap. Dishwashers.' Derek points to each item. 'You scrape the dishes, rinse them, stack them. Put the tablet in. Turn on the dishwasher. When you run out of dishes, you come outside and clear tables. If both machines are busy, you wash by hand. Got it?'

'Got it.'

'House rules: no flirting. No chit-chat when you're out front. No dilly-dallying. No drinking, not even if someone offers to buy. Water's on the house, and one meal per shift, eaten out here, not front of house. Got it?'

I nod. 'Got it.'

'Three day shifts a week: eleven to six. Three night shifts: six to eleven. Rota will be behind the bar. One month's trial, then minimum wage, cash in hand. Sorted?'

'Sorted.'

The door bangs shut after Derek and I turn to face the pile of dirty dishes.

*

I'm exhausted by the time I leave the pub at six. The sink's a little too low for me and my shoulders ache from stooping over it and bending to load and unload the dishwashers. I can't believe how many people come to the pub for lunch; how many plates, glasses and cups they get through. My hands feel rough from the detergent and the sickly smell of the dirty dishes feels like it's lodged in my nose for ever. I've leaned in someone's leftover ketchup and it's stained my chinos. My attempt to dab it out with water only made it worse.

I've got to do it all again tomorrow.

As I walk down the lane, I kick at random stones, aiming

them into the bushes while I try to find the bright side. The commute is short. Ha! I kick another stone way too hard and it hits a tree trunk, sending birds flapping upwards. It may not be in London, but it's something for me to do – something to get me out of the house.

But, oh my God, it's not easy. How did my life come to this? A CEO washing dishes in a village pub? I try to tell myself that it's a learning experience – that it'll help me grow as a person – and a part of me likes that, but mainly I just feel ashamed. Ashamed that my career's stalled so suddenly and so publicly. All I've known so far is success after success. I step up to the front door and, blimey, Stell must have been waiting for me because the door opens before I've even got my key out.

'Darling!' she says, coiling her arms around me. I really don't know what she does all day because she's wearing one of my shirts, knickers and little else from what I can tell. Her legs look amazing, but all I want to do is collapse on the sofa with a whisky. My whole body aches.

'How was it?' she asks when she lets go of me.

'Exhausting.' I try to walk to the living room but she heads me off into the kitchen.

'Oh, come on! Don't be like that! I'm so proud of you! I got some champagne to celebrate!'

I look at her, her eyes shining. But I really am knackered. I slump onto a chair at the kitchen table. Why is she spending money on champagne, after all that got wasted at the party?

'No need for champagne. Save it for a real celebration.'

'But you have a job!'

'I'm washing dishes for free, Stell!'

If she's shocked I'm not behind the bar, she doesn't show it. She gives me a massive smile.

'Don't be like that. I said I'd give you an allowance, and here it is: ta-da!' She picks up an envelope that's on the counter and waves it at me. 'Your first pay packet!'

She grins at me and I wonder if, for all her time in catering, she's ever been down the messy end; if she has any idea what it's like to scrape other people's half-eaten food into a bin: the chicken bones, bits of pie crust and oil-soaked salad leaves; the sweet stickiness of stale ketchup and the slop of congealed gravy.

'You won't be on trial for ever and you won't be washing dishes for ever,' she says. 'It could be the start of a whole new career for you – for us.' Stell opens the fridge, pulls out the champagne bottle and starts to undo the foil. 'You could learn the ropes at the pub then maybe we could buy a pub together. Just imagine it: me cooking and you behind the bar. Oh God, I can picture the menu already… We'd be a husband-and-wife team. It'd be so cool… I can see us locking up after hours, just the two of us having a drink together and unwinding; talking about the punters.' She stares into space and sighs. 'The kids helping out when they get older; learning the value of hard work. A real family business. It'd be amazing. Maybe it's time to think about a new career, George.'

'I have a career. I don't need a new one.' A pub, for God's sake!

'Well, that rather depends on what happens with the investigation, doesn't it?' she says sharply as she pours two glasses of champagne. She turns and hands me one. 'Gosh, I don't mean to say that you won't be able to go back to work. But who knows what impact the negative publicity is going to have on business… or if it ends up going to court and then there's court costs…' Her voice trails off. 'Anyway, cheers!'

'Cheers.' The champagne tastes acidic and I put the glass back down. All I want is a whisky. I've been thinking about it all afternoon. Stell's clattering about the kitchen, pulling dishes out of cupboards and packets out of the fridge.

'I love that we're so happy,' she says, arranging something on a dish, and I think I must have misheard her. Happy? Making the most of a bad situation, perhaps, but happy? I raise my eyebrows at her. She pops an olive into her mouth.

'Look at us, I mean. We're living the dream. Finally together. Gorgeous house. Trying for a baby. Both of us working locally – me working from home; flexible hours; no commute. And finally writing my book! Yes! I started it! I could even pop into your pub to see you for lunch! Ha! People would *die* to have our life.' She takes a mouthful of champagne and swills it around. 'I know there's, you know, the "unpleasantness" with the charity thing but you have to look at the bigger picture, which is that we're so *happy*.' She bends down and gives me a hug from behind before placing the dish of olives in front of me. 'Thought you might be hungry after your day at work…'

I stare at her as she burbles on, pottering about the kitchen as she talks. She's making it sound as if we're some magazine idea of perfection. Does she really believe this, or is she trying to persuade me? I stare at the table while she goes on and on.

'I thought I was happy before – you know, before we got together – but now I see that I wasn't happy at all. My life was so two-dimensional without you. And look at what we've built together in such a short period of time. I mean, it's not so long ago we were sneaking around in hotels.' She looks at me from under her eyelashes. 'Back then I would never have imagined we could have built all this together. You must be so proud…'

Proud? *Proud?* My life is falling apart. My life is in pieces. Everything I've known is broken. Something inside me snaps. I bang the table.

'Stop! Just stop right there!'

Stell spins around to face me, the champagne in her glass slopping over the lip and her eyes wide with surprise. 'What? Are you OK?'

'Just stop this talk of living the dream.' I try to calm myself but I can hear my pent-up fury in the tremble of my voice. 'Stell. Don't get me wrong. It's great that we're together. It really is. But living the dream? Sweetheart. I'm suspended from work – suspended from working at the company I own; the company I've spent my life building. I've been caught taking money from a charity and could potentially be facing a long and expensive court battle. I might lose everything – not least this house!' I sweep my arm across the table, sending the olives flying. The dish smashes onto the floor and it pleases me to hear the crash; to see the broken shards and the splatter of olives on the gleaming floor. 'This is not living the dream. It's living a fucking nightmare!'

Stell looks shocked for a second but then her face composes itself quickly.

'Aww, it's sweet that you're so sensitive,' she says, 'but don't be like that. Don't focus on the negatives.' She pauses. 'Think beyond that. Look at what you *do* have.' She smiles at me then, when she realises I'm not saying anything, she carries on. 'The house. Our life in the village, the friends we've made…'

She steps over to me and touches my arm but I shake her off and turn away. She has to understand this. She has to understand how hard this is for me.

'A house bought with stolen money! *Stolen* money! A house I don't even like – yes, Stell, I don't *like* the house – OK? It's cold, it's sterile. It's like living in a bloody hospital. And I miss London. There. I've said it. All right? Maybe I'm not cut out for village life.' As I say it, an image of my old house in Richmond pops into my head and, with it, Ness – an image of Ness alone inside it: wonderful, admirable Ness, studying for her future. Were we really so unhappy? I loved that house. I really did.

Something passes across Stell's face; she breathes in deeply and it looks as if she's drawing herself in ready to hit me but then she exhales, shakes her head and laughs.

'Oh, George! It was you who wanted this: not me! I was the one who didn't want to leave London,' she says. 'It was *your* dream to live in the countryside!' She points her index finger at me as she talks and she looks so confident, so sure of herself, that an icicle of dread slides through my veins: is she right? Was it me who drove the move to the countryside? I get that eighty:twenty feeling again, the sense that other people know more about my life than I do. Is this something else lost in the haze of my memory?'

Stell shakes her head at me. 'I didn't even want to sell my apartment, remember? I thought this might all be a big mistake but you wanted it so badly, this "country dream". But anyway—' she faces me, a bright smile on her face now '—the main thing – and what we must remember, crazy cakes – is that we're in this together.' She puts her hand to her forehead where the bruise is long faded and when she speaks her voice is quiet. 'You're so lucky to have me. No one else would stick with you through this.'

And I think: Ness would.

PART III

ONE

Stella

Roast fillet of beef. Roast garlic. Yorkshire puddings. Roast potatoes, carrots and beans. A gravy so rich my mouth's watering as I stir it on the hob. Traditional, safe, homely food: a treat of fat and carbs for George. He can afford to eat it now, I think. Sometimes I catch sight of him unawares and his gauntness surprises me. The paunch is almost gone, though it's unfortunate the weight loss has had such an effect on his face.

I set the table for dinner – not the kitchen table: the dining table. The best crockery. The crystal glasses. Bordeaux in a decanter, but only one wine glass. Sparkling water with slices of lemon, lime and orange in a crystal jug. A trail of tea lights leading from the front door to the dining room. The door on the latch. I want George to open the front door and 'discover' this dinner – to breathe in the aroma of beef cooking, and to follow the trail of tea lights to where I'll be waiting in candlelight in the living room.

I step back from the table and look at my watch. I'm ravenous. It's been a challenge timing the beef just right – George likes it medium-rare and I don't want it to dry out. He called to say he was going to be an hour later than he'd originally said but, still, I readjust everything to accommodate. Nothing will ruin tonight. I check the meat, turn down the oven and head upstairs. All that's left for me to do is shower, dress, light the candles and wait for him to get home.

After my shower, I massage body lotion into my skin, then open the wardrobe. It's just a formality, really because I know what I'm going to wear: silk underwear, cropped blue jeans and a cream silk shirt. Bare feet, loose hair, a spritz of perfume at my throat and wrists. When I'm ready, I look at myself in the mirror. I may have put on a little weight since then, but other than that, I look almost identical to how I looked the night George first came to my apartment. The night I found out that Ness was losing the baby.

He won't notice of course.

TWO

George

Lazenby calls. Like the guillotine, it's brief.

'Wolsey. Bad news, old boy. The trustees are like rabid dogs on this case. Nothing I could say would influence them. Your name's going forward along with the others. It's in police hands now. Sorry.'

My solicitor is just as discouraging. 'There's no easy way out of this now,' he says, shuffling his notes.

My thoughts are morose as my train takes for ever to make its way out of London: stop-start-stop-start with more of the stop than the start. No matter what happens, the damage to my reputation is done. Who's going to trust a company director who 'borrowed' money from a charity? I've lost all credibility as a fundraiser, which hurts almost as much as the damage I've done to my business. I bury my face in my hands. Why did I do it? Why? For the hundredth time, I run through that moment in the kitchen when Stell suggested I use the charity money. What was I thinking?

I just wanted to buy her the house. I wanted her to be happy.

And now, whatever else happens, my business will

probably never recover. No one wants to be associated with a company that has a scandal hanging over it. I'm toxic. Maybe I should walk away. Give the company a chance to move on without me. Even as I think it, something dies inside me. It's *my* business; my life's work. I don't want to run some two-bit village pub. There's only one person who'll understand. I call her.

'How did it go? The meeting with the solicitor?' Ness asks.

'Oh God. It's not looking good. Absolute best scenario: the Crown Prosecution Service drops my part of the case due to lack of evidence. Worst scenario… well, there are several of those, ranging from a fine and having to pay court costs, to ten years in jail.'

Ness gasps. 'Oh come on now! It won't come to that! You've paid the money back already.'

'The fine could be hundreds of thousands. Short of selling the company – which I really don't want to do – I don't have any more money,' I say. 'The only asset I have left is the house.'

'You'd have to sell that?'

'The court might force me to.' I pause. 'Look, I don't want to ask but needs must. You couldn't… ?'

'Bail you out again? I'm sorry, George. I gave you everything I could. But there is something you might be able to do…'

'What? What are you thinking?'

'Is the house in your name?'

'Yes.'

'Well, I imagine if you put it solely in Stella's name, they couldn't come after you. I'm no lawyer, but isn't that what people do in these situations?' She laughs. 'I get all my info from the tabloids. You know that!'

My mind's racing a hundred miles an hour. Could it work?

'I'll look into it,' I say. 'Thanks, hon.' I realise my mistake as the word slips out but Ness doesn't correct me and a little flame of hope ignites inside me that she liked the endearment. 'Thanks for listening to my problems, and for being so patient with me.' I pause. 'Were you always this lovely?'

I wait but she doesn't reply.

'You were, weren't you?'

She sighs. 'Sometimes, George, people don't see what's right in front of them.'

I hang up and drop my head into my hands. What am I doing with my life? It's like I've lost the ability to make good decisions since the school reunion. Things were fine before then. Boring, maybe, but fine. I look at my watch and my heart sinks: I'm going to be late and Stell's going to go ape-shit. She said something about a special dinner and, with her, that means something timed to perfection. She gets really uptight about food. It all has to be absolutely 'so'. It's her job, I suppose. It's how I am at work, too.

Was.

It's hard to be that dedicated when it comes to clearing dirty plates.

I wonder what tonight's all about. Something special, clearly. I can hardly dump it on her that the case is going to court. It's ironic, really, that Ness is the only one of the three of us who'll keep her house. The train pulls in and I move off it, through the village and down the lane to the house like a zombie. I put my key in the lock, push open the door and step straight into a tea light, which upends, sending hot wax pooling out onto the concrete floor and nearly setting light to my trousers.

'Shit!'

I look around for something to blot it up with, then decide it'll be easier to scrape it off when it's cooled. There's a row of tea lights and they lead down the hallway to the living room. I stand for a second looking at the effort Stell's gone to and try to summon up enthusiasm for the kind of evening she appears to have in mind. Romance couldn't be further from my mind. I breathe in and count to ten, then slowly exhale and walk down the corridor. At the threshold of the living room, I pause and run my hands through my hair feeling suddenly nervous. There's always a motive with Stell. What's all this about?

I push open the door. The room jumps and flickers in a mass of candlelight. At the heart of it, Stell's reading a book on the sofa. The twinkling light makes her eyes sparkle and gives a soft glow to her skin; she looks radiant. I catch, too, a whisper of her scent on the air. She puts down her book and smiles.

'Hi,' she says.

'Hi.'

I walk around the sofa to her and bend to kiss the top of her head. Her hair smells of flowers and I breathe it in. She turns her face up to me and we kiss for a minute, then she twists herself up until she's standing. She's barefoot, which makes her look small and vulnerable.

'How was your meeting?' she asks.

I take a deep breath. 'Fine.'

'Really?'

I sigh. 'Not really.'

'Could we lose everything?'

I look at her face, so earnest and trusting and hesitate. 'No.'

She knows I'm lying.

'Come on,' she says, 'let's not talk about it now. Tonight's a special night.'

She ushers me onto the sofa and comes back with a whisky and a plate of nibbles.

'You're allowed one,' she says, referring to the whisky, and I notice that she doesn't have a glass.

'What are you drinking?'

'Oh, mine's in the kitchen,' she says.

'Dinner smells amazing.'

'Roast fillet of beef.'

I smile at her. 'Yorkshire puddings?'

My mouth's already watering. It's been so long since she's let me eat anything as rudely unhealthy as batter.

She nods. 'And potatoes.'

'Mmm.' I roll my eyes upwards, imagining the taste and texture of such treats. 'So what's tonight about?' I look around the room. 'What's all this in aid of?'

'I have something to tell you.'

My blood runs cold but Stell's smiling. She sits down next to me and takes my hand.

I search her face for clues. 'What? What is it? Has something happened?'

'You could say that.'

'What?' The tightness in my chest comes back, constricting my breathing.

She looks down and then back up at me. 'Are you ready?'

I nod, swallow.

'George,' she says, 'I'm pregnant.'

THREE

Stella

He cries, of course.

'Really?' he asks, searching my face with his eyes, looking I imagine for clues that this is some sort of joke. But why would I joke? Is there any reason why I'd joke about this?

'Yes, really,' I say.

He wraps his arms around me and holds me tight against his chest as he strokes my hair. 'I can't believe it,' he says. 'Finally. I just can't believe it.'

Then he takes my hand and gently sits me down on the sofa like I'm fragile as a newborn lamb, and that's when I see his tears glinting in the candlelight.

'Stell,' he says but doesn't continue. 'Stell.'

He rubs my back and it's as if he no longer knows what to do with me; how to touch me; like he's frightened he'll break me, so I pull him down till we're lying squashed together on the sofa and I kiss him deeply and run my hands over his back, and he resists for a second, like I'm some sort of virgin, but then he groans and suddenly he's hungry for me, his kisses deepening as his hands slide over my waist, over my belly, and then he's slowly undoing my shirt and bra, and kissing me all over, breathing 'I love you' into my ear.

'I love you,' he whispers, 'I love you, I love you, I love you.'

He trails kisses across my belly, then he's undoing my jeans and I'm lifting my hips to let him slide them off. I undo his belt and he stands up to drop his trousers.

'Is this OK?' he asks as he lies back down. 'Are we allowed to?'

'I want you to.'

But now I feel his hesitation; the awkwardness in his touch. I run my hands over him, trying to lead him on, but he resists.

'What's wrong?' I breathe into his ear. 'It's fine. Really it is.'

George pulls me into his arms and settles my head on his shoulder. 'But what if it's not? I couldn't bear it. I couldn't bear for anything to happen to our baby.'

'Really, it's OK.'

I stroke his chest as we lie in awkward silence for a minute.

'I can't do it, Stell,' he says. 'Not while it's so new.'

My mood changes in a flash. I'm not going to beg for sex. I untangle myself from his arms, stand up and step back into my clothes.

'You're right,' I say as I pull my shirt back on. I keep my back to him to hide the tears of frustration. 'The dinner's ready anyway. I don't want the beef to spoil. Come on, get dressed. We'll go and eat.'

My smile's too bright, my voice too brittle, but George – more fool George – he doesn't notice.

FOUR

George

I shove the kitchen door open with my backside and am hit by a wall of sound. The buzz of chatter fills the pub – it's five-thirty on Thursday and Derek's 'mummy and me' supper promotion's going down a storm: the place is a sea of kids and mums taking advantage of the deal: a three-course supper from the kids' menu, and a free glass of wine for mum. Even the garden's rammed with kids rampaging over the climbing frame and swarming the sandpit while their mums try their best to ignore them in the late afternoon sun. I've been boomeranging in and out of the kitchen, picking up dishes and glasses, wiping spills and sweeping up forgotten fries. Both dishwashers are on as I head out again to collect more plates, and I see Stell at the bar, an empty wine glass next to her. I'm shocked: it's barely a month since she told me she was pregnant.

I go over to her. 'Hey.'

'Hi! You must be clocking off soon – I thought we could grab something to eat.'

'Here?'

'Why not?'

The pub's the last place I want to be when I clock off. I have a Pavlovian reaction to the stale-beer, old-food smell of it now: the association with dirty plates makes me want to throw up.

'How about the Indian?' I say.

Stell wrinkles her nose. 'I really don't feel like spicy food.'

'OK, all right. Whatever you want.' I look at my watch. 'Half an hour to go.'

'Here you go.' Derek places a glass of white wine in front of Stella with a flourish.

'Thanks.' She picks up the glass.

'Another?'

She puts the glass down without taking a sip. 'Yes?'

I reach over to take it from her but she slaps my hand away and we stare at each other. In this moment, she looks hostile – it's as if she's challenging me. The school reunion comes to mind: the way Ness had let me take her glass simply because her period was late. We hadn't even known there was a baby then, and she let me protect her.

'Are you… are you sure you should?'

Stell looks at Derek and shrugs.

'Let her be,' says Derek. 'It's Thursday. A girl needs to let her hair down.'

'But, Stell… you know…'

'Know what?' she says.

'Maybe not the best thing to be doing.'

She looks at Derek, picks up her wine and takes a deep swig.

'I'll do what I want,' she says and I stare at her. What's

come over her? My child's inside her body; our child is depending on her to keep it safe – she's going to be a mother!

'Hear, hear!' says Derek, then he turns to me. 'Haven't you got work to do? It's in the rules: no chit-chat. Remember?'

'OK, OK.' I turn my back on the two of them. Is it non-alcoholic wine? Is she playing a joke on me? It's only half an hour till I clock off: I'll talk to her about it then.

FIVE

Stella

George's face is tight when he comes over at six. There are two empty glasses next to me now and he points at them.

'What's going on?'

'I know,' I say. 'Can't get the staff these days. Where's a good dish-clearer when you need one?'

Derek overhears and snorts a laugh. 'Can say that again, ha ha.'

'Seriously, Stell!'

'Can I get you a drink?' I ask George.

'Looks like George here could do with one,' Derek says. 'Lighten him up a bit. On the house.'

George's mouth opens but no words come out. I can see he wants to have a drink but something's stopping him. He takes a deep breath and pulls himself up tall.

'Thank you, Derek. But I think we should get the bill and get Stella home.'

I roll my eyes at Derek.

'Come on, Stell,' George says. 'You've had more than enough. Let's get going.'

He takes my arm and pulls me to my feet. I shrug him off. 'But I want another one.'

Now we're standing and glaring at each other. I'm embarrassed that this is playing out not just in front of Derek, but in front of Dr Grant and his wife, who've just come in and are further down the bar. I can see that George is furious: he's struggling to compose himself and a vein throbs at his temple.

'Now!' he says, and grabs my arm. He throws some notes onto the bar. 'That should cover the bill. But we're leaving *now*!'

I freeze and George yanks my arm so hard I stumble and lose my footing. 'Come on!'

'Is that all right with you?' Derek asks me.

I wrench myself free of George. 'What's got into you?'

He glares at me as if he's trying to tell me something. 'You *know* what's got into me.'

Tears prick behind my eyes. 'George. Not now. Not when I feel like this. Please.'

Derek comes around the bar now and steps in between me and George.

George's lips flatten. 'Move. She's my wife and I'll deal with this.'

'Now, you listen up!' Derek says. 'This is my pub and I will not have you manhandling anyone on my property.' He looks George up and down. 'Men like you, you make me sick!'

'Men like what exactly?'

Derek takes a step towards George and squares up to him. 'Men like you! If you want to shove anyone, shove me.

Picking on a woman. Knocking them around.' He shakes his head and I get the feeling that if he could spit on George, he would. 'Loathsome. You're lucky I haven't called the police on you.'

George takes a step back, his hands in the air. 'Whoah. There's no shoving going on anywhere. I'm just trying to look after her. I want what's best for her.'

'You want what's best for her?' Derek's tone is scathing. 'Don't you think she's the best judge of that?'

'Clearly not!' George says, pointing to the wine glasses. 'Look, what are you doing even serving her? She's pregnant!' He sobs. 'She's pregnant with my child!'

There's a stunned silence. Derek turns to look at me and then back at George. It feels as if the entire pub is listening. Derek steps back from the two of us.

'Well… congratulations,' he says.

I look up and my eyes are wet. 'Not here, George. Not now. Let's go. Please.'

We leave the pub in silence.

SIX

George

Stell marches home ahead of me. Neither of us says a word. She opens the front door and lets it slam in my face so I have to get my own key out. I look for her in the kitchen, living room and study, then climb slowly up the stairs. She's curled in the foetal position on the bed, her back to the door.

'Stell…' I sit at the foot of the bed and touch her leg. She pulls it away from me. 'Stell, sweetheart, what just happened?'

Silence.

'I'm sorry I said that you're pregnant, but the guy practically accused me of knocking you about. I wanted him to understand that there's nothing more precious to me than you.' Silence. 'You know that, don't you? You and the baby. You're my everything.'

The bed shakes and I realise that she's crying. I kneel next to where her head is and stroke her hair away from her face.

'Stell, what's the matter? Is it so bad that he knows?'

Her crying intensifies. I want to take whatever it is that's bothering her, pull it out of her and throw it away.

'Stell, what is it? You can tell me.'

She takes a deep breath and then whispers with her eyes closed. I strain to hear. 'You've forgotten, haven't you?'

My entire body goes cold and I get this out-of-body feeling, as if I'm watching the scene from above. 'Forgotten what?'

'I lost the baby, George. You know I did!'

'What? What are you saying? I don't understand. Stell!' I try to lift her face; to turn it so I can look into her eyes and see that she's somehow joking, but she pulls away and turns her face into the pillow.

'George, please! This is difficult enough as it is.' She starts crying again.

'No! What are you talking about?'

'I told you last week, I started bleeding…' She puts her hand on her tummy and closes her eyes. 'Don't make me explain it all again. You know all this.'

'No! No, I don't!'

'Oh God. George! It's too much. I can't deal with this! Not on top of the miscarriage. Please tell me you remember.' She's got her hand over her mouth now and I can see that the fact I've forgotten is distressing her as much as losing the baby.

'Princess.' I reach out to her; stroke her, any bit of her I can get: her hair, her shoulder, her upper arm, her hip. I smooth her hair around her ear but still I can't see her face. 'I don't understand.'

But, as I'm stroking her, I'm thinking back over the past month: she'd been quiet; slept a lot; stayed in bed more than usual, but I'd put it down to her being tired with the pregnancy. But why don't I remember her telling me that she was bleeding? I'd have taken her to the doctor; gone with her to hospital. God, I've been through all this with Ness! I know what to do.

'Do one thing for me,' she says. 'Check your diary.'

'OK.' I kiss her cheek, her forehead; try to hold her head in my hands. 'Princess. Can I hold you?'

She moves up a little and I climb onto the bed next to her, take her gingerly in my arms and stroke her hair and her back. 'There, there,' I croon as if she's the baby. 'It's OK. Everything's going to be all right.'

I say it as if I mean it.

SEVEN

Stella

I take a bath, then make my way downstairs. George is sitting at the kitchen island staring into space. He looks like a shrunken version of himself. When he sees me, he stands up and folds me gently in his arms.

'How are you? Is there any pain?'

'No. It's OK now.'

'I'm so sorry.'

I tighten my arms around his waist, noticing as I do how I can clasp my own wrists behind his back he's so thin. 'It's OK.'

'Thank you for saying that. But it's not, is it? Nothing's right. And I don't know how to put it right.'

I pull away and hold his hands. 'We'll work on it. Together. That's what this marriage is all about. It's a partnership.'

His face is so hopeful I can't bear to look at it. 'I'd love some tea if you feel like making it.'

With something to do, George snaps into action. 'Go and sit in the living room. I'll bring it.'

'Thanks.'

I flop onto the sofa. I'm cosy in my pyjamas and have

that sense of release that comes after crying. When George comes in with the tea, though, I realise the toll all that's happened lately must be taking on his well-being. He looks haggard, with grey shadows sitting on his face and deep lines running from his nose to the corners of his mouth. I think about the fraud case, the stress that must be causing him, the loss of his job and now the news of the failed pregnancy and another memory lapse, and I almost feel sorry for him. I can't imagine what it would be like to be beaten when you're already down – and the memory loss must be terrifying. He sits down next to me on the sofa, runs his hands through his hair and sighs.

'How are you feeling?' he asks.

'Like the boat's been rocked, but it's still afloat.' I give him a weak smile.

'Good.'

'Did you check your diary? Is it there?'

He closes his eyes as he nods, his face utterly beaten. I press my hand over my mouth and when George looks up at me again, we stare at each other silently acknowledging how bad this is.

'What are you thinking?' George asks.

I take a deep breath. 'I'm relieved everything's out in the open. Admitting there's a problem is half the battle, isn't it?'

'I guess so.' George sighs again, and runs his hand through his hair.

'I wondered why you didn't say anything about it the next day.' I put my hand on George's leg and stroke it absent-mindedly. 'I was expecting you to be more sympathetic, but then, when you didn't mention it – when you left me to go through it on my own – I just thought it was your way of dealing with it.'

'Oh God. You must have thought I was so unfeeling. No. I just had no memory of the conversation.' We stare at each other. 'And you're completely sure? About the baby?'

I nod.

'Oh God. I'm so sorry.'

We lapse into silence. George's eyes search my face. 'It's bad, isn't it?' he says, his voice breaking. 'What's happening to me?'

'We can move forward from this,' I say.

'How? How can we? It's just… sometimes I feel my life is spiralling out of control. Everything's going wrong. Everything.'

'No. Don't think like that. I've been thinking. Do you want to hear?'

I look sideways at him and suppress a smile: he's hanging on to every word. If I told him to dye his hair blue, he'd ask which shade.

'OK, first,' I say, 'they say you're most fertile in the months following a miscarriage, so…' I give him a shy smile.

'You want to try again so soon?'

I nod.

'OK. If you're sure…'

'I am.' I stare at my teacup. 'And there's one more thing.'

'Yes?'

'It's about the house. It's been on my mind a lot. Maybe it's even why I…' I rub my stomach and leave long enough for George to realise what I mean. 'I've been quite stressed about it. About the fact that we could lose it.'

'OK…'

'You were protecting me when you said there was no way we could lose the house, weren't you?'

He has the decency to look guilty.

'Well, look. Before all this happened with the baby, I checked out the situation with a lawyer myself. I guessed you'd be focusing on the court case with yours, and not looking so much at the bigger picture.'

'True. And?'

'Well, it seems that you could be liable for a fine and possibly court costs. And, if you can't pay, the court would be within their rights to force you to sell the house. Our house. It's in your name. It's your asset.'

George rubs his chin. 'So… ?'

'Well…' I take a deep breath. 'The solicitor recommended transferring the house into my name for the time being. We can transfer it back the moment the case is over. But what that means is that they can't make you sell it.'

'Hmm.'

'I'm just telling you what the solicitor told me.'

George doesn't say anything.

I exhale. 'I know. I don't like it either. But it's what he said we should do. I just thought I'd throw it out there.'

I get up and walk to the window, keeping my back to George. When he doesn't say anything, I dab at the corner of my eye.

'I'd really miss this place. I's our first home together. Look at the garden. It's coming into its own now. The flowers look so beautiful. I can just imagine us out there with a cup of tea... a little toddler chasing after bubbles in the sunshine. A little boy, maybe, in a little stripy romper suit.' I turn and face George with a smile. 'But it's fine. We'd find somewhere else. We'd be fine wherever. Even if we had to downsize to an apartment. All that matters is that we're together.'

George is rubbing his neck, massaging it and tipping his head backwards, rolling it around.

'And what about the firm?' he asks. 'Could they make me sell my shares in that? The firm I've built from scratch?' His voice is thick with disbelief.

'Ah. We spoke about that, too.'

'And?'

'He recommended we set up an offshore company – owned by me for the time being – and keep the shares there. They'll be untouchable. We can change the company directorship back to you later.'

George snorts. 'Untouchable and probably worthless when this has dragged through the courts.'

'They won't be worthless. We'll get a good PR onto it. You'll bounce back, trust me, and then we'll transfer the shares back to you, good as new. Promise.'

EIGHT

George

So, today Stell said she'd seen a solicitor and he recommended putting the house and company shares into her name so the court couldn't come after me if I'm fined or ordered to pay costs. But, God, would it be such a disaster if we had to sell this house? It's full of bad memories, it's too big for us and I never liked it in the first place.

I sit back and reread what I've just written in my diary. It's enough for today. I really don't want to transfer the house – it seems rather extreme, and I'm wondering what prompted Stell's solicitor to tell her to do that. I didn't even ask who she used – someone in London, I suppose. I close the document and look over to Stell – she's across the kitchen island from me, working on her book. She's obsessed with writing it by hand in a notebook. Says the physical act of writing makes her more creative – whatever floats her boat. We've the radio on Jazz FM and the back door's open to the garden. I take it all in: on the surface, it's a scene of peaceful domesticity but I can't settle. My mind keeps going back to what Derek said at the pub earlier: 'Men like you make me sick!' He thinks

I push Stella around. I shove the chair back and stand up. If I go now, I should catch him before the lunch rush starts.

'Just going out for a walk.'

Stell barely looks up. 'OK. Take your time. I'm busy here.'

'How's it going?'

'Great. I'm really enjoying it. I think I could be on to something.'

I walk down the lane composing what I'm going to say to Derek in my head. When I get to the pub, he's polishing glasses behind the bar and, thankfully, there are no customers. I stand opposite him at the bar and wait for him to look up. When he sees it's me, he opens his mouth but I hold my hand up to stop him.

'Look. About what happened yesterday.'

Derek doesn't put the glass he's holding down. 'What about it?'

'I just wanted to clear the air. Tell you my side of the story.'

'Think I know your side of the story.'

'No. Let me say this: I've never pushed Stella around. I've never hit any woman and I never would. I don't know where you got that idea from but it's insane.'

Derek looks hard at me. 'If you say so.' I can tell from his dismissive tone that he doesn't believe me at all.

'I'm not that kind of guy, Derek.'

'If you say so.'

I turn and move towards the door, but then he speaks again.

'She asked me to give you the job, you know.'

'I know.' I start to walk back towards Derek but don't go as far as the bar this time.

'She's very good to you,' Derek says.

'I know.'

'Loves you too much, if you ask me.'

I bow my head. I know all this.

'You have issues, mate,' Derek says. 'Sort your life out before someone does it for you. Mark my words.'

I close the door quietly on my way out.

NINE

Stella

I'm so engrossed in my writing I barely notice when George gets up and goes for a walk. I'm really enjoying writing by hand, feeling the glide of the pen over the paper and the sound of the paper crinkling as I turn to a fresh page of the notebook. I'm trying to get inside the head of my protagonist – the woman whose husband chips away at her self-esteem and her sense of self, making her believe that he's her only protector. But, inside the house, he doesn't protect her, he abuses her. She doesn't know who her enemy is, and increasingly feels she's going mad. As I write, her emotions flow through me. I sigh and wince and clasp my hand to my mouth as I reread what I've written, but my thoughts are interrupted by the ring of the doorbell. Chiming out in the silence of the house, it sounds almost rude.

I look through the peephole before I open the door. It's Dr Grant.

'Hello,' I say. 'What can I do for you?'

'Good morning, Stella. I hope you don't mind. I was just passing and thought I'd call in to check that you were… that everything was… OK. After yesterday?'

Ah. The pub. I really shouldn't have let that scene get out of hand. There's a trailing cobweb on the doorframe. I blow at it then look back at the doctor. 'I'm fine, thank you. All's good.' I give him a big smile. It's fake.

'It's just – again, forgive me – your husband said you were expecting?'

I smile. Really fake.

'And, well… look, can I come in?'

'Sure, of course.' I laugh to disguise the reluctance that's seeped into my voice. 'How rude of me, I'm so sorry. Please come in.' I step back and lead Dr Grant through to the kitchen. 'Coffee?'

'I'd love one, thank you.'

Dr Grant will never understand that my making him instant coffee instead of ground coffee is my way of saying he's interrupted me from something I would rather be doing and, as I spoon the granules into his cup, I realise that my book's still open on the counter and that Dr Grant is looking at it.

'Oh, excuse me.' I zip over to it and close the notebook. 'You caught me in the middle of something. Please, take a seat. So, what can I do for you?'

Dr Grant sits at the island. 'I just wanted to check if everything is all right. You were drinking quite heavily last night, and… in your condition… I say this both as a doctor and, I hope, as a friend – well, you know you should avoid alcohol. Certainly in large amounts.'

'I'm not pregnant.'

'Oh! Forgive me! It's just I thought I heard…'

'You did. George said it. But I lost it.' Dr Grant stiffens.

'Oh, nothing too traumatic.' I wave my hand, unwilling to accept the sympathy. 'It was over barely before it started. Early days. I hear it's very common.' I pause. 'I'd told George but he'd forgotten.' I look at Dr Grant and he's hanging on to every word. 'He's been having a little trouble with his memory lately.' I give a little laugh. 'Anyway, look, can I get you a biscuit?'

Before he has a chance to answer I go to the living room to retrieve the biscuit tin. While I'm there I see the sofa cushions are all crushed from where George and I sat yesterday, so I take a minute to straighten them, and then I straighten the rug, which is no longer aligned with the coffee table. Then I pick up the biscuits and head back to the kitchen. Just as I reach the doorway, I see that Dr Grant has opened my book and is reading again. I take a few steps quietly back and watch while he absorbs what's on the page, then I clear my throat as I approach again, giving him time to shut the notebook quickly and pull over the newspaper that's next to him.

'Here we go,' I say, tipping some biscuits onto a plate.

'How did George take the news? About the baby, I mean.'

'He's OK, I think. Disappointed, obviously.'

'He's keen to have children?'

'More keen than I am, if that's possible!'

'I see.' Dr Grant takes a sip of his coffee, then sighs. 'It's a difficult time. Can put a lot of stress on a couple, especially given what else is going on with his job and the memory issues.' He looks directly at me. 'Are things all right between you both?'

I nod vigorously. 'Yes. Everything's fine. Really. Really

fine.' I get up suddenly and open a kitchen cupboard. 'Would you like any other biscuits? Anything at all? I'm sorry, these are all I have. I thought I had more but I wasn't expecting you and I haven't been shopping.' I'm talking too fast.

'Stella.' Dr Grant's voice is firm and I turn to face him.

'Yes?'

'If you need anything – anything at all – please remember that I'm here, and that you can talk to me in complete confidence.'

Silently, I nod.

TEN

George

After I leave the pub, I walk straight down Main Street, past the end of the lane to our house, and continue on down the road that leads past the woods and out of the village. I don't know that I'm turning into the woods until my feet take me off the pavement and onto the pathway that snakes between the trees. Branches heavy with the new leaves of early summer hang low and I bend every now and then to avoid being whacked in the face, but I'm not taking in the scenery, just keeping my body in motion as I try to sort out my thoughts.

Derek's words come back to me and I cringe. His hostility jars me. I'm one of those people that everyone likes: jovial, easy-going, popular. It's who I am, and the feeling that the village – not least the pub landlord and the doctor – is against me unsettles me. But how? How has my life come to this? Why am I even being judged by a bunch of people I barely know? Why do I care what they think?

The path opens out to a series of small ponds and I stop for a moment to take in the sight of the sun reflecting off the flat surface of the water. Insects buzz back and forth over the water but nothing breaks its surface. It's so still that the canopy of trees is reflected almost perfectly, like a mirrored underworld. How have we not been here before? It's so tranquil; such a great spot.

I start walking and, with my body back in motion, I think back to when I first got together with Stella. I was always a moth to her flame in a way that no one else understood. Even back at school, Stell could be prickly and cool to the point of seeming disinterested. There was always an independence about her; a feeling that she didn't need me; that she chose to be with me because she liked me – nothing more, nothing less. And I guess, if I'm honest, I liked the fact that I was the only one who got to know her. Stell had no friends at school; she couldn't give a fig about the other girls, was aloof, stand-offish, happy in her own company, and I liked that about her. I liked that I was the only one who fascinated her enough to keep her coming back. It's not that I had any shortage of offers from other girls – 'easier' girls, I guess – but Stell was a challenge and, when we were together, she was so warm. Even now, walking in the woods my dick stiffens at the thought of how warm Stell was when we were alone as teenagers; how accommodating. Being with her was like cracking a soft-boiled egg, getting through the shell to the softness inside.

The other girls – God. I shake my head as I remember. They were all posture: all legs and lips and lashes, but when it came to the crunch, they wouldn't give out like Stell did. Stell gave me everything and asked for nothing. Other girls wanted a kiss and a fondle, then wouldn't do more unless

we were a 'couple'; they wanted to be 'dating', they wanted
to be 'exclusive'; they wanted everything packaged and
sewn up. Stell was different. She took what I offered, gave
from her soul, and left me feeling she couldn't give a damn
whether or not I came back. I smile despite myself. Why
couldn't I just choose the easy option?

But hang on, I did. I chose Ness. Pretty, popular Ness.
Ness who knew how to play the game, and, boy, we played
it together: the parties, the events, the lifestyle. She has an
easy charm that Stell lacks; a way of disarming even the
prickliest of clients. Emotional intelligence. Ness has it
in spades and I used it to bag clients I was having trouble
reeling in.

'Come to dinner,' I'd say. 'Just a casual supper at my
house,' and I knew that Ness would work that charm and
the account would be in the bag by morning. Ness was, to
all intents and purposes, the perfect career wife. Stell – Stell
wouldn't have given a damn about that. She wouldn't have
cared.

And then a sobering thought: did I get where I was
with my career partly because Ness was there, supporting
me, showing me off, suggesting parties, hosting dinners,
schmoozing the right people? Is it because I'm without her
that my life has fallen apart?

Ness was such a good egg.

There's a bench by the pond, its wooden seat, scarred
by decades of penknives, dappled with sun and shade. I sit
on it and rest my head in my hands as I stare at the lake.
Dragonflies – or are they damselflies? – dance over the

water, zipping back and forth like their lives depend on it. The sun is warm on my back.

I didn't know what I stood to lose.

But Stell. The moment I saw she'd signed up for the school reunion, I knew I was in trouble. I'd followed her career in the media – that meteoric rise to success she'd had with her catering firm, from delivering hand-prepared lunches to offices within a square mile to being the most talked-about, the most popular private catering company in London. I was thrilled for her success; desperate to talk to her; desperate to see for myself the woman she'd become... because... if I'm honest with myself, because Ness was too nice, and I was bored.

And when I saw Stell that night – ignoring me as she always used to – I was lost. She wasn't interested and that was irresistible: adult Stell was more of a challenge than she ever was at school. I shake my head as I think about the ways in which I chased her and tried to win her over. Those lunches I sent. The car. Getting that bloody first edition. The clumsy way I'd slid the hotel key card to her. But it had worked, hadn't it? And here we are.

But?

I can't put my finger on what it is. But something's not right.

ELEVEN

Stella

I'm still writing when George gets back. He walks into the kitchen and stands there without saying anything. I feel his eyes on me so I finish the sentence I'm writing and look up.

'Hey,' I say, cocking my head and smiling. 'Good walk?'

'Yeah. Went down to the woods.'

'Lovely.'

There's a pause and it seems awkward. George's energy is weird. It's like he's thinking more than he's talking, which is not like him at all. I look at his left hand.

'Still haven't found your wedding ring?'

He looks at his hand. 'No.'

'Sure it's not in the bathroom? I thought I saw it by the sink. It's been there all week.'

'It's not there. All right?' George's voice is snappy.

I hold my hands up in a mock surrender. 'OK, OK. I was just asking.'

George comes over to the kitchen island. 'I'm going to write my diary.'

'OK.'

He opens up the laptop and I hear him type in his passcode then the double-click of the mouse as he calls up the document. Through my lashes, I watch his face as he reads.

TWELVE

George

At least things are black and white in the diary. I log into the computer, click on the document to open the diary, and reread my last entry.

Today Stell saw a solicitor and put the house and company shares into her name so the court couldn't come after me if I'm fined or ordered to pay costs. What would I do without her?

My stomach's full of cold, hard lead; my lungs have no air in them. I sit and stare at the screen. Did I type this? I look at Stell – she's writing away, completely oblivious, and suddenly I feel so alone. I no longer feel it's Stell and me against the world. It's just me going quietly crazy. I breathe quietly in and out through my nose, trying to calm myself. Did we go to the solicitor? Which solicitor? I remember Stell telling me about the meeting she had with him, the advice he gave, but I'm one hundred per cent certain that we didn't go to a solicitor together. I was still thinking about whether I wanted to transfer the house – and the business! – wasn't I?

But I'm the man who forgot his wife lost their baby.

And then I remember the lasting power of attorney I gave

Stell when we married. She doesn't need my signature. She could have done this without me even there. But did I agree to it?

When I feel I'm calm enough to keep my voice steady, I speak. 'Hon, did we ever decide if we were going to put the house in your name?'

She looks up and smiles. 'You and your memory, crazy cakes. Yes. We did.'

'Ah. And we did it?'

'Yep. All done. One less thing to worry about.' She smiles again and turns back to her book.

I try to keep my voice even. 'OK.'

I close the document, log out of the computer and go upstairs. I need to speak to someone who's outside all of this – someone who can give me an objective view. But, aside from Phil and Ness, I realise I haven't been in contact with anyone since I got married. I'm cut off from my work colleagues for obvious reasons, and I've moved away from all my local friends: my mates in Richmond and my motorcycle club. Then I lost my phone and, with it, all my numbers. I've still not managed to make a ride with the local bike club. My social circle is non-existent.

There's a phone by the bed. I stare at it for a minute, then I pick it up and dial Harry. He may have his faults, but he's family and, right now, that's what I need. And a little voice inside my head reminds me, too, that he's a psychologist; that he might be able to help in a way I neither understand nor want to admit.

'Hey stranger,' he says when he picks up. 'How's things?'

'I need to talk to you. Do you fancy meeting in London this weekend? Bit of a boys' night, just you me?'

'This weekend? Umm…'

'Please?' I sound desperate, even to myself.

'Are you OK?'

'Yes. Fine. Everything's fine. Just: please?'

'OK, sure. But don't cancel on me again this time.'

'I won't. I promise.'

Harry laughs quite bitterly, as if he knows something I don't know, and I hang up, already planning. I go to the bathroom. There, exactly where I always leave it, on the counter next to my sink, is my wedding ring.

THIRTEEN

Stella

For the first time since this whole thing started, I think I may have overdone it. As George gets up and leaves the kitchen, I see in his face that something's shifted; he's starting to question what I tell him. He knows we didn't agree to transfer the house into my name. I throw my pen down. Still, maybe I've done enough now – put enough wheels in motion – for this to continue on its own momentum.

There's nothing George can do about the house or the business now. He has no power to change it back to his name, and it's only fair, isn't it, that I have a house in my name if Ness has one in hers? You'd think I was asking a lot, wouldn't you? A husband who's happy to be at home with me, and ownership of my own home? If George had played fair from the start of all this, I wouldn't have had to go to these lengths. It's all his fault. All of it. He's brought it on himself.

But where's it all going to end? I think back to the cold winter's morning when I'd had lunch with the charity trustees. Jail wasn't a part of my plan. I'd been sure Lazenby would forgive George once he paid the money back, which he'd said he was able to do – it was a loan, after all – and they're such good mates. Old boys' network, and all that. The fact that he was suspended from work was a nice addition because it gave me more time to play with him, but what I hadn't realised was that the CPS would get involved; that there was a bigger case in the frame.

That was just unfortunate.

I hear George's footsteps coming back down the stairs and along the corridor and quickly pick up my pen. I suck the end of it and stare into space. When I snap my eyes to George as if coming down out of my thoughts, I see at once that he's found his wedding ring. He speaks with no introduction, as if he's been planning what to say.

'I just want to tell you that I don't recall agreeing to put the house in your name. I was actually still thinking about it.' He pauses. 'I just want that to be said. So there's no misunderstanding.'

'OK.' I shrug. 'But you should tell Dr Grant about it. It's not good that you're forgetting such big things now. Important things.'

'Stella. I didn't agree to it. That's what I'm saying.'

I raise my eyebrows at him. 'What does it say in your diary?'

'Exactly what happened: that I didn't like the idea of it and was thinking about it.'

I watch his face as he says that. Only a tic near his eye gives away the fact that he's lying. But we already know that George is a good liar. So what else is he lying about? Was he with Ness when he went out this morning? Did she come up to see him? There's a new spark of energy in his demeanour and I know it's got something to do with her. He forgets how well I know him.

'OK,' I say slowly. 'Maybe you wrote the diary before you decided to do it. But you did agree to it. We were sat at the kitchen table after dinner – had you been drinking? Yes, I think you were on the white wine the night I cooked those chicken kebabs, you remember the peri-peri ones? – and you said you didn't like the idea but it made "perfect sense".' I imitate his voice as I say that bit. 'But I understand that you don't remember. Look, I was just trying to help. Do the right thing. I'm sorry.' I hold my hands up, palms facing him. 'I'm sorry I even got involved. Would you prefer it if I stepped right out of this and let you handle it on your own? With your "solicitor"?' My voice is contemptuous. His solicitor's done nothing about getting the case dropped so far. How difficult can it be when he has good character references and has already paid the money back?

George tuts. 'Don't be like that.'

'Like what?'

'So dramatic.'

I scoff. 'I'm not being dramatic! You're the one marching in here making melodramatic declarations. If you ask me, it just makes you look more crazy than you already are. But, look—' I lower my voice '—I'm just trying to ride with this as best I can. It's not easy, and I'm sorry if I got it wrong.'

George stares at me for a minute.

'I'm seeing Harry on Friday,' he says. 'On my own,' and my heart literally jumps.

'Where?'

'London. He's coming down. It's about time we had a good catch-up.'

I suck the top of the pen and look at George through narrowed eyes.

'Oh that's a shame. We'd talked about going away, hadn't we? I was hoping we could have a nice weekend break down by the coast?'

George shakes his head. 'Another time. I'm not messing Harry around again.' He turns abruptly and leaves the room.

My smile is tight. 'Lovely.'

FOURTEEN

George

'What's happened to you?' Harry asks when we meet in town on Friday night. 'She's a chef? Isn't she feeding you?'

'What do you mean?'

'Look at you: you're skin and bone!' His eyes search my face and I sense he wants to say something about that, too, but he holds off, which is unlike Harry: it must be bad. I do look tired – this I know – tired and grey – and the weight loss doesn't help. I can't believe I went along with Stell's stupid diet. She kept telling me I was paunchy and I believed her even when I could see that I was losing too much weight. The truth is, I felt so guilty about that bruise on her head, I'd have done anything to please her.

'I was going for "lean and distinguished",' I say.

Harry laughs dismissively. 'But, seriously, Georgie-P? What's she doing to you? So much shagging you don't have time to eat?'

I sigh. 'Hardly. The court case? You must have heard.'

'Yeah. So you nicked a million quid or something?' He makes his fingers into the shape of a pistol, shoots me – 'Boom!' – and blows the imaginary smoke off the gun.

'It wasn't a million! Half that! And I didn't nick it. It was a loan. A short-term loan. That's all it was ever meant to be. And, for the record, I've paid it back.'

I tell Harry everything, starting with the court case and working through everything I feel's gone wrong in recent months from the party to losing my memory. Although he's trained to listen, it's not easy talking to Harry to begin with because he makes it clear that he simply doesn't believe the tale of woe coming out of my mouth. And, to be honest, even to me, my monologue of whingey complaints sounds pathetic. I feel like a kid telling tales to the teacher: 'And then she said this, and then she said that.' But, as I talk, Harry's heckling reduces and then stops, and I can see, as he tilts his head and taps his lip, that his interest is piqued. That alone makes me feel validated.

'But you remember none of these things?' Harry asks when I've told him everything that comes to mind.

'OK. How's your memory otherwise?'

I shrug and Harry snaps some current affairs questions at me; then asks things about our childhood.

'Eight out of ten short-term and nine out of ten long-term,' he says. 'Does that make you feel as if you're losing your memory?'

'Not really.'

Harry leans back in his chair and steeples his hands. 'I'll tell you why you don't remember any of these things – not least hurting your wife – *hurting your wife*, George – it's because they didn't happen.'

Tears spring out of my eyes from nowhere and I wipe

at them with the back of my hand. Harry looks away. It's pathetic. I'm pathetic. But the relief to hear that said out loud almost drowns me. I'm not sure I believe it but it's what I want to hear: it's my life raft.

'I can't imagine hurting her,' I say. 'You know what Mum and Dad were like about anyone who hurt a girl. Remember when you kicked that girl – Suzie? – in a fight and Mum frogmarched you to her house to apologise?'

'And grounded me for a month.'

'Exactly. I thought she was going to explode she shouted at you so much; I honestly thought her brains were going to burst out through her ears.' I pause. 'I'd never hurt a woman. But Stell showed me the bruises. Told me about the arguments we'd had.'

'Bruises, schmoozes. I wouldn't put it past her to bash her own head and blame you for it.'

I look away. I desperately want what Harry's saying to be true, but I don't see how it can be. Harry has his own agenda: he's never liked Stell, and he's never seen how we are together now, as adults – how perfect we are. The woman he's describing isn't the Stell I know. But…

'Why did you leave Ness anyway?' Harry asks. 'She was so good for you – just what you needed, but you had to balls that up. Couldn't keep your pants on, eh? Oh God, Georgie.' Harry shakes his head. 'I know I shouldn't speak badly about your new wife and I know you've had a thing for her since you were yay high, but I'm sorry to tell you that Stella Simons is not a well-balanced individual. There's always been something about her. You see enigmatic; I see cold.

She has no friends – never did. Have you ever noticed that? It wouldn't surprise me if she has psychopathic tendencies.'

'What?'

'I bet she'd score quite highly on the scale.'

'No!'

'Let me see. Is she cold? Well, you might not think so, but I'd say she is. Ruthless? Don't answer. Calm? A good planner?'

'That doesn't mean she's a psychopath!'

'Of course it doesn't. But all these things together, added to what you've already told me…' Harry exhales, shaking his head. 'Let me guess: it was her idea to borrow the money from the charity, wasn't it?' My mouth falls open. 'She knew it was the wrong thing to do but she still suggested it,' Harry says, nodding at me. 'Typical of a psychopath. And then, once you were caught, how was she? Full of remorse and sympathy?' Harry looks at me. 'Did she offer to try to help you pay it back? No. Did she offer to help in any way? I didn't think so. Did she try to belittle the trouble you were in? Make you feel it wasn't such a big problem?'

I stare at Harry.

'Have you ever noticed how she likes to control everything you do?' Harry asks. 'Who you see? What you eat?' He strikes his hand to his head. 'She runs a catering company, doesn't she? Oh God, it's so textbook it hurts. I'd love to do a case study on her! I'd have a field day. She probably became a cook only because she wants to control what people eat. Psychopaths gravitate towards certain careers.' Harry holds up his fingers and counts them off. 'CEO, lawyer, media, sales, surgeon, journalist… um… I forget the others… police, and guess what? Chef. Oh look, there we are: a chef who's CEO of her own company.' He laughs. 'It's classic!'

'Come on! Now you're being ridiculous!' I say, but I'm thinking about the diet she put me on.

'Am I? Have you ever argued with her about what she cooks for you? Said chicken when she says duck?'

I shake my head. Unending weeks of salad. No carbs. No sugar. No fat. No fun.

'You should try it. She won't like it one bit. She'd be like a balloon when you stick a pin in it, fizzing away into the distance till she's a screaming speck on the horizon.'

We both stare at our beers for a moment. I'm reeling at what Harry's saying. I'd like to believe it but it's so far-fetched; so typical of Harry to come up with such a ridiculous idea. Yet maybe there's a seed of truth in it. It was Stella's idea we move to the village, not mine. She chose the house, not me. And now I see that she possibly – probably – lied about me saying it was OK to buy it. I don't remember her showing me the details. I'd have questioned it from that moment. It's not my kind of house. I loved The Lodge. God, if I were to believe Harry, it would make Stell a monster.

'And you know what else?' Harry says, pointing at me. 'She's manipulative. Have you noticed that? Do you always have to do what she wants?'

Manipulative. Ness also said she was manipulative. 'No.'

'Let me ask you a question: apart from tonight when you're with me, when did you last do something for yourself?

Just you and your friends? Your bike group, or whatever it is you do?'

I take a deep breath in. Oh God. Both times I tried to join the new MC, I ended up staying home and doing something with her instead. My blood runs cold. Did she take my phone that morning? It was on the kitchen island. I know it was. And then her fall on the stairs the night we were supposed to meet Harry. I've been over it a million times and I know I didn't trip her. I was nowhere near her.

I push back my seat and stand up. 'Just going for a wee.'

In the Gents, I go into a cubicle and sit on the seat, head in hands, as I go over what Harry's been saying. I don't want to hear it and I do want to hear it. I trust Harry's expert opinion but then he's never been fond of Stell. Could it be that he's just enjoying shooting her down for fun? Making me look a fool? Having a laugh over a few beers at his baby brother's expense?

Back at the table, Harry takes a sip of his beer, smacks his lips, then puts the glass back down.

'I was just remembering how she used to pop up in floods of tears or with some sort of family crisis every time you were supposed to be going out without her.'

I'd forgotten about that.

'I've been thinking about it while you were in the bog. Gas-lighting. That's what she's doing.'

'What?'

'Psychological term. Messing with your sense of reality. Manipulating you.'

'Oh, please.'

'God, you're so naïve, Georgie. Google it.'

'But why? Why would she do that?'

Harry scoffs a laugh. 'Because it's who she is. It's what she does. It's fun for her. It's sport.'

'But she loves me. I don't get it.'

'Maybe she has an agenda. I don't know what's gone on between you two. I haven't seen her since she left school.'

Something strikes me. 'But what about my diary? Everything that happens is written there in black and white.'

'She changes it. Simples.'

'It's password-protected.'

Harry rolls his eyes at me. 'And? You think a password's a problem for an act like her? *I* could guess your password.'

'But the fact remains that I'm still having blackouts.'

Harry leans back, tapping his fingers on his lip. 'Tell me, do you have any prescription medication in the house?'

I shake my head. 'No. Only Stell's sleeping tablets. But I don't go near those.'

Harry thumps his fist on the bar and beams at me. 'Bingo.'

'What? I don't take them.'

'Or so you think. Is there any way she could be getting them into your food or drink?'

I don't reply. I'm thinking about the fact she cooks all my meals, and about all the chances she has to drug me should she so wish – and then it hits me: the nights she's left my choles-terol tablets out for me; nights when I've been drinking. What if they weren't actually my cholesterol tablets? I was usually worse for wear. I wouldn't notice if they were slightly different to usual. But she wouldn't do that? Surely she wouldn't?

'Those prescription sedatives are strong,' says Harry. 'If you mix them with alcohol, you could easily end up with memory loss, confusion and blackouts – there's a plethora of side effects you could be experiencing.'

'Pounding heart?'

Harry nods. 'Georgie-P, I think you've just found your answer. You're not losing your mind.'

But I'm shaking my head. Stell wouldn't do that! Anyone knows it's dangerous to mix sleeping tablets with alcohol – but then… the blackouts…

'I don't believe it. I just don't. She wouldn't do this. You can't possibly think she would – God!' The scale of what Harry's implying is impossible to get my head around. She loves me! 'You've always liked your conspiracy theories. But this is my life we're talking about.'

Harry takes a final swig of beer. 'Maybe I'm wrong, little bro. But maybe I'm right. Why don't you start another diary? A secret one. Somewhere where she won't find it. Write it in your own handwriting so she can't change it – unless forging hand-writing is one of her life skills.' He snorts as if that might be entirely possible. 'Compare it to the one on the laptop. That's what I'd do.'

*

Stell's in bed when I get home. I don't know what to make of what Harry's said. The further the train clickety-clacks me away from central London, the more ridiculous it seems and, by the time I'm home, I've discounted 99 per cent of what he said. His own marriage never worked out: he's just jealous I got a second stab at it and he didn't. I fire up the laptop and, with fingers that feel like thumbs thanks to the beer, start typing.

Saw Harry tonight. He made me realise how I've lost myself a little lately; reminded me of who I am. He reckons I haven't lost my memory at all. 'Gas-lighting.'

With the number of clutzy typos I make, even those four sentences take five minutes so I stop there. Bedtime.

FIFTEEN

George

The kitchen smells of fresh air and coffee when I come down in the morning. Stell's at the island with the papers. She's wearing a little summer dress with flowers on it and has one leg tucked under her and the other dangling from the stool, long and bare. Her ballet pumps are next to the stool as if she's kicked them off to walk barefoot in some imaginary meadow, and the back door's open. It's one of those glorious days when the sky's as blue as anything on a Pantone chart and you really feel the summer's arrived.

'Morning, darling.' Stell untangles her legs, comes over to me, snakes her arms around my waist and kisses my lips as she presses herself against me. 'I didn't wake you in case you needed a lie-in, but there's coffee ready if you want it now you're up.'

'Thanks.' I disengage from her and go over to the coffee machine.

'How's Harry?' she asks.

'Fine.'

My sleep was sweaty and fractured – the stuff of nightmares. The first thing I did when I woke up was check the sleeping tablets in the bathroom cabinet. The sticker said the prescription was recent but there were only four tablets left and I've never been aware of Stell taking them. As far as I know, she sprays some arty-farty lavender spray stuff on her pillow and sleeps like a log. I'd popped one out and brought it down to compare with my cholesterol tablet. Almost identical. So is there any truth in what Harry said? In any of it?

'Did you sleep well?' My tone is light; I keep my back to her.

'Yep.' She's back at the newspaper.

'No sleeping tablets?'

'No.'

'I saw them in the cabinet the other week. Prescription, right? Do you use them often?'

She slaps the newspaper shut. 'What is this? Twenty questions?'

'I was just wondering. They can be addictive.'

'Don't worry. I barely use them and I'm not addicted. Did you have a good time last night?'

'Yes. Was good to catch up.' I busy myself pouring the coffee. Has she seriously been drugging me?

'I'm popping out in a bit,' Stell says. 'Do you have any plans?'

'No. I think I'll just potter at home today. There's a bulb in the bedroom needs changing and I want to de-clog the bathroom sink.'

'Great.'

She disappears off to gather her things, then kisses me goodbye. The door slams behind her and then I sit and soak up the silence of the house. More uncomfortable than usual in the house, I have the strangest sense that I'm a zoo animal, out of my natural habitat and here entirely for someone else's amusement.

'But that's nonsense,' I say out loud. I get up and rinse out my coffee cup then rifle through the drawers in the utility room looking for spare light bulbs. None there – then I remember the cabinet in the hall, which has become a gathering ground for odds and sods. I find the key in the bureau and open the cabinet: bingo – light bulbs galore. Stell's a sucker for ensuring we never run out. I rummage around, and open a Tesco bag. Inside are loads of white envelopes. I pull one out and I know as soon as I see the hand-written name what it is. The breath goes out of my lungs: it's an invitation to our house-warming party. Judging by the heft of the bag, the majority of the invitations are in there: the ones Stell was supposed to deliver. So that's why no one came. Nothing to do with me at all. I'm still standing there barefoot in the shorts and T-shirt I slept in when I hear footsteps and voices outside the front door. I freeze, the bag clutched to my chest. The doorbell rings and I bundle the bag back where I got it and lock the cabinet quickly, gripped with the ridiculous feeling that I've been caught red-handed snooping through someone else's belongings.

'She said he'd be here,' says a woman's voice outside the front door.

'Try again.'

The doorbell rings again, twice this time, then the letterbox rattles. I leap into action before they peer through and catch me standing there.

'Coming!'

I open the door and take a step back as I see a sea of faces gathered like carol singers. Only they're not singing; they're looking serious. There's Derek, Dr Grant, that woman Rachel, and some woman with loads of facial piercings. Before I can get a word out, Derek speaks.

'George. We're here to stage an intervention.'

I'm speechless. An image of a drug addict shaking on the floor with his friends gathered around fills my mind. What does this have to do with me?

'Can we come in?' Derek starts moving towards the door as if I've invited him into the house and, automatically, I stand back and let him. One by one the group files past me, none of them meeting my gaze. Derek walks purposefully; Dr Grant has an aura of importance about him; Rachel holds her chin high; the other woman's eyes look anywhere but at me.

'Where shall we…?' Derek asks, and I indicate towards the living room. They troop down the hallway and I close the front door and follow. None of them sits down. They all face me and Rachel loops behind me and stands by the living room door. I'm blocked in. Did they discuss this beforehand? Did they plan how they were going to corner me in my own home?

'What's all this about?' As I put my hands on my hips, I catch a whiff of my own sweat and wish I'd had time to shower and dress. It makes me feel at a disadvantage before we've even begun.

'It's an intervention,' says Derek.

'But… for what?' Seriously, not the drinking?

'May we?' Derek indicates the sofas and I nod. He pulls a chair to the middle of the room and they seat themselves on the sofas facing it.

'Please,' says Derek, indicating that I should sit in the chair.

'Are you going to tell me what this is about?'

'Dr Grant,' says Derek, and Dr Grant clears his throat.

'We believe you're harming Stella and we want you to know we're here to help. Obviously this could ultimately be a police matter but Jude here—' he indicates to the woman I don't know '—thought we should try to intervene before the police are involved.'

'Appeal to you as a reasonable man,' says Rachel.

I bristle. They're a bunch of village vigilantes. 'And do you have any evidence?' I ask.

'She came to yoga with bruises,' says Jude.

'We've all seen her bruises,' says Rachel.

'They were handprints,' says Jude. 'Clear as day.'

'What makes you so sure I caused them?' I ask.

'I've seen you get rough with her,' says Derek.

'Hardly!'

'I know what I saw,' he says, nodding.

'But none of this is evidence! It's all supposition.'

'That's why we're warning you before going to the police,' says Rachel. 'We wanted to give you a chance to give your side of the story.'

I look at them one by one. Dr Grant is still now he's said his piece, his face a picture of self-righteousness. Funny how your perception of a person can change in an instant.

I'd imagined he was a professional and upstanding member of the community; now I see him as a man past his prime; a bored, interfering busybody. And, as for this village: I don't care what Stell says, we're selling this house and moving back to London. I hate this place; I loathe these meddling, interfering busybodies.

'I suspect you didn't want to take it to the police because you have no evidence,' I say. 'And you have no evidence because nothing's happened. This is outrageous.' My voice rises. 'I've never raised a hand to Stell, and I never would.'

'Ah, but we do have evidence,' says Derek.

I swivel to look at him. 'What "evidence"?'

Dr Grant steps forward. 'Her diary.'

'What diary?'

'I happened to read some of her diary. It's a catalogue of domestic abuse.' He levels his chin as he looks at me, as if challenging me to some medieval duel.

'She doesn't write a diary,' I say.

'She was writing it in the kitchen when I came over,' says Dr Grant. 'She left it open on the counter.'

'And what did she say in this "diary"? That I push her around? That I hit her?'

'Yes. Some things like that. But that you control her. Tell her what to eat and what to wear. That you stop her from going out.'

'Oh please,' I say. 'You've all seen Stella out and about. Don't be ridiculous. That wasn't her diary! That's her book. A novel she's writing. It's fiction!' Then Harry's words finally crystallise in my head. The penny drops. 'She set me up! She planned all this! She wanted me to look guilty!' I whack my hand to my head. 'You have to believe me. I haven't done anything! She set me up!'

I look at them one by one, trying to make eye contact, trying to get one of them on my side, but they're all staring at me as if I'm a two-headed gorilla and then, from behind me, I hear Stella's voice.

SIXTEEN

Stella

'What did I set up?'

George spins to face me. There's panic in his eyes and it doesn't suit him. Hemmed in by the villagers on the sofas, and still unwashed from sleep, he looks like a caged animal; ragged around the edges and slightly insane. He's a far cry from the smooth George who seduced me in London. But then he should have thought of that, shouldn't he? He should have thought of that before he got Ness pregnant while telling me he loved me.

'These *friends* of yours are accusing me of domestic violence,' George says, 'but you and I both know I've never raised a hand to you!' He's almost shouting and he looks like a lunatic. Rachel's eyes are wide. 'You set me up! You wanted them to think this!'

I shake my head and go over to George. I stand in front of him and place both my hands gently on his forearms. 'Darling, what are you talking about? Why would I do that?' I give his arms a little squeeze then whisper, 'Come on, honey. Calm down. You're sounding a little deranged.'

George shakes me off. 'What the fuck's going on, Stell?'

I turn to the group and shrug. 'I haven't set him up with anything. I don't know what he's talking about. What's the problem? Maybe there's been some sort of misunderstanding.'

Dr Grant says, 'I'm so sorry, Stella. We were just trying to help by confronting George about the way he treats you.'

'The way he treats me?'

Dr Grant coughs. 'Yes.'

'What do you mean?'

'I hope you forgive me but I read your diary. Just a couple of pages. That day I visited. You left it on the counter. I know it was wrong but I couldn't stop myself and – well, now I'm glad I did.'

'My diary?'

'You don't write a diary!' George says, and I hold up my hand.

'I read your diary,' Dr Grant says again, as if to wipe out George's words.

'Hang on,' I say. I dash to the kitchen and pick up the notebook in which I'm writing my novel. On the front, there's the title I never got around to deciding on: 'Diary'. I hold it up for Dr Grant to see. 'This?'

Dr Grant nods. 'Yes.'

I burst out laughing, perhaps slightly too raucously, but I'm genuinely finding this funny. Those people with their serious faces, thinking they're saving me from my husband, who couldn't actually harm a fly. It really is funny when you think about it. My laughter is the only sound in the room. Do I look unhinged? Maybe.

'George is right,' I say, straightening my face. 'This isn't my diary. This is a novel I'm writing. Based on the case we spoke about at the party, Dr Grant. The domestic abuse case that had just been tried? Where the guy went to jail? I decided to do a fictionalised version from the point of view of the woman.' I'm trying to catch Dr Grant's eye; trying to make sure he's understanding what I'm saying. Out of the corner of my eye, I see that Derek's shaking his head, Rachel's mouth is hanging open and Jude, my yoga teacher, is rubbing her eye.

'Honestly, it's not a diary,' I say.

Dr Grant takes a deep breath and stands up, brushing at his trousers as he does so.

'There's no need to lie, Stella,' he says when he straightens up. 'You're with friends, and you can speak the truth. There's no need to hide any more.'

'But I'm not hiding anything,' I say.

'I told you!' says George. 'You've got the wrong end of the stick. You're lucky I'm not calling the police on you. Now, if you…'

'Just know that we're here for you.' Dr Grant looks intently at me as he says this, and the others stand. Rachel and Jude start to edge towards the door. 'Any time, day or night, you can come to any of us. OK?'

'Thank you. But, really, there's no need!'

'Right,' says George. 'If that's everything cleared up.' He opens the living room door forcefully and stands by it like a bouncer while everyone files past him. 'I trust this will be the last of this nonsense. An apology would be welcome. When you're ready.'

'Sorry,' says Rachel, her eyes downcast.

'We're here any time you need us,' says Jude.

'I know what I saw,' says Derek.

'Remember, Stella, any time at all,' says Dr Grant.

George closes the front door quietly, then turns to face me. We stare at each other for a moment and I can't read his expression. Then he pushes past me and races straight up the stairs.

SEVENTEEN

George

I run up the stairs two and a time and close the bedroom door behind me. I can't be near her. I don't want her coiling herself around me, kissing me and whispering sweet nothings in my ear. Into my head comes an image of Ness: warm, welcoming and so genuine and it's as if the blinkers have come away. I can't stay here any more. I want my old life back so badly the emotion catches in my throat: my old house, my dog, my friends, my life. It's as if the past year has been a bad dream. I want to wake up in bed with Ness and find that none of this happened.

Think, George.

What was it that Harry said? Gas-lighting. I open my phone and type the phrase into the browser. The first sentence that comes up is from Wikipedia: 'Gas-lighting is a form of mental abuse in which a victim is manipulated into doubting their own memory, perception and sanity.'

I can't breathe. 'Doubting their own memory, perception and sanity.' I squeeze my eyes shut, not wanting to read any more. The months that I've been in the house with Stella run through my mind like a film. Memory loss. Blackouts. Losing things. The whisky that disappeared. The party invitations that I found just now. Did she honestly forget to deliver them? Or did she deliberately sabotage the party? Did she want me to believe no one wanted to know me because of the investigation? Suddenly everything comes into focus; I see the last few months of my life from a completely different perspective and I stagger back onto the bed as my knees buckle.

Oh God. The investigation. It was her idea I borrow the money, and… was she the one who tipped off the trustees? She works with that charity. She had a lunch with the trustees. I remember her going! Could she have told them that I'd taken the money? Why would she do that to me? Why would she destroy our life together?

And then I remember the lasting power of attorney she mentioned so casually. Did she really plan this whole thing so she could transfer ownership of the house and my business to her name? I shake my head. She's a successful business owner in her own right. I pace the room again, filled with the sense that there's something missing: there's a link I just can't grasp. Why would Stell do any of this? I don't know, but what I do know is that I can't be with her a moment longer.

I pull out my overnight bag from under the bed, pull open the wardrobe doors and start whacking things into the bag. Clothes, underwear, toiletries – and then, as I stare unseeingly at the wardrobe, I freeze: outside the room, I hear Stell's footsteps approaching, one lighter than the other as she still favours the ankle she sprained on the stairs. I turn to face the door as the steps come closer, then I watch as the door handle slowly depresses. My heart's thumping so loudly I imagine she can hear it. I hold my breath and press my hand against my chest, but my traitor heart still thumps. Outside the window I'm suddenly aware of a blackbird singing, singing, singing, but on the other side of the bedroom door is something other than my beautiful Stell; something I no longer recognise.

'George?' she calls.

I run into the en suite and shove the door closed. All my body wants to do is put space between us but, in the bathroom, I'm trapped. I stand, helpless, at the sink. The footsteps get closer. Step, limp, step, limp.

'George? Are you there? Are you all right?'

I can't speak.

Slowly, oh so slowly, the door swings open. My throat's so tight my breath rasps. I lean on the sink for support and watch until there she is, standing in the doorway, her stone Buddha statue in her hands. She's breathing hard, too. She stares at me and I stare at her, but behind her I see in the periphery my bag on the bed and I know at once that she's seen it; that she's seen I'm packing; she knows that I know. She raises the statue with both hands, and I jerk backwards, scattering towards the toilet like a terrified kitten.

She smiles. 'Take it, George! It's heavy! I thought it would look better in the bathroom.' I realise she's holding out the statue and I come forward and grasp its cold weight in my hands. Do I have it in me to whack her over the head with it? To put an end to this?

But, as I hesitate, Stell turns and leaves the bathroom. Her eyes sweep over the packing on the bed as she leaves the room. I hear the click of the lock; the rasp as she withdraws the key, the chink of her dropping it elsewhere, then her footsteps receding.

She's locked me in. I sink onto the edge of the bed, my head in my hands, my breath still rasping. Think, George. Think, think, think.

But it's hard to think. My entire landscape has changed. Sitting here on the bed that Stella chose, locked in the bedroom that Stella decorated, in the house that Stella tricked me into buying, I realise I'm shaking uncontrollably. I've been a marionette whose strings she's jerking and now I'm trapped with a monster, left at her mercy. I get up and pace the room. At the window, I look out at the top of the garden, the fields and hedges beyond; over to the left, the woods. Could I feasibly jump and run? Just go and never come back? I imagine lowering myself down from the sill, then taking the six-foot drop. The bedroom is above the living room. What if she saw me? Would she chase me?

What have we become?

Then from downstairs, I hear a sound: the opening of the front door followed by its closing with a click. For a second I think she's left the house, then I recalibrate that information knowing what I now know: maybe she's tricking me into thinking she's left. If I break out, will she be waiting outside the bedroom door for me? With what in her hand? An image of her bludgeoning me to death springs to mind and I see crime scene tape outside the house; news reporters in the lane outside. Then I give myself a shake: *Get a grip, George. Surely she wouldn't kill you. Surely!*

With my ear pressed to the bedroom door, I strain to hear the sound of the garage door raising, of the car starting, but there's nothing, just silence and that infernal greasy blackbird chirping its annoying little lungs out. I cross the room and look again at the familiar garden; at its friendly coloured flowers and the grass still slightly depressed where the marquee had sat for the party, but now it's enemy territory: a branch in the hedge moves and suddenly I'm seized by the fear that she's out there, watching me from outside, plotting, planning – planning what? To burn the house down with me inside? I whack the shutters closed, bang, bang, bang, panel by panel, then I sink onto the floor, my head below the level of the window.

Think, George. Think.

I crawl to the bed, where my phone is, and dial Harry, still sitting on the floor, as if she's going to shoot me (with what?) through the window. My words tumble out as soon as he picks up.

'You're right! She's been gas-lighting me. I just looked it up. She's a psycho! She had this statue in her hand and I thought… Oh God.' I pause. 'I'm scared, Harry. I don't know what she's going to do next.' Tears spring from nowhere and I see myself – a middle-aged man crying on the bedroom floor – and I have no shame.

'OK, OK,' says Harry. 'What's happening now? Where's she? Where are you?'

'She's locked me in the bedroom and left the house. I think.' I wipe at the snot that's running down my face.

'Does she know you know?'

'I think so. I was packing. She saw my bag. What shall I do? Tell me what to do!' I'm sobbing. Self-loathing chokes me.

'This is the most dangerous time. If she knows you know. The stakes are way higher now. You've got to get out. Break the door down.' Harry's voice is urgent.

'What if she's still here? What if she's waiting behind the door?'

Harry exhales. 'It's a risk you've got to take. What's the alternative? You wait there till she chooses to let you out? Who knows what she's planning. Who knows how long that'll be. Better you break out now. She could leave you for days, till you're starving and weak. She loves to control you, remember? It's her modus operandi. You need to take back control.'

I realise the whimpering I can hear is coming from me.

'George!' Harry shouts. 'Get a grip! Come on! Get your shoulder against that door, or use that statue, and break it down. Go on, do it! Do it now! I'll stay on the line.'

I try. I throw myself at the door once, twice, three, four, five times, but it won't budge. From the phone I hear Harry's tinny voice.

'George! George!'

I pick it up again, panting. 'I can't do it! I can't get out! She's going to kill me!'

'Calm down. Come on, let's think. Do you have your house keys with you?'

I scan the room fast, not taking in anything, then again more slowly. I see them on the dresser.

'Yes!'

'OK. I'm coming over. Sit tight. Don't do anything. Just wait. I'm coming now.'

EIGHTEEN

George

I don't know how long it is till Harry calls again. It feels like for ever. I sit on the floor, below the height of the window, leaning against the bedroom wall and every fibre of my being is tensed, listening for the slightest sound: the strike of a match, the crackle of a flame, the click of a lock. My scalp prickles with the effort. I jump when the phone rings.

'I'm here,' says Harry. 'Where's your bedroom? Front or back?'

'Back.'

'OK, I'm coming round. Open the window and throw me the keys.'

'Ring the doorbell first. What if she's here? Hiding?'

'OK. But throw me the keys now.'

I open the shutters and there's Harry outside in the garden looking so bizarrely normal in his jeans and jacket. I fiddle with the window, wrench it open and chuck the keys down. Harry disappears down the side path and then the doorbell rings. I run to the bedroom door and listen for any movement in the house; any stirring but there's nothing. The doorbell rings again. Faintly, I hear Harry's voice.

'Yoo-hoo! Anyone home?'

A fist bangs on the door – bam-bam-bam – then I hear the key sliding into the lock and the door opening.

'George? Stella?' he calls, then suddenly he's on the landing and at the door.

'George. The key's not in the door!' There's a pause, then footsteps. Oh hang on, got it.'

As he slides the key into the lock I leap into the bathroom and peer out, ready to slam that door in his face – what if it's a trick? What if Stella's with him? But it's only Harry who steps into the room.

'She's definitely not here?' I ask. I'm shaking.

'I didn't see her. Come on, get your things and let's go.'

I grab my bag, take one last look at my marital bedroom – at the place where I was supposed to be so happy. Harry follows me out. On the landing, I freeze.

'Ssh. I heard something.'

We both stand stock-still, listening, then I creep towards the nursery. From inside comes the faintest sound. I strain to hear: a song, a lullaby… 'Twinkle, Twinkle, Little Star'. With my foot, I give the door a gentle nudge. It swings open. The room's empty, the lullaby coming from a battery-operated toy: the plastic sheep night light on the cot. Once I'm sure that the room's empty, I step across to the cot and click off the switch. The silence then is deafening.

'Come on.'

Harry and I clatter downstairs and straight out of the front door. I slam it hard behind me. Harry jingles his car keys.

'Right. Where to? You want to come back to mine?'

I shake my head. 'Thanks but no. It's the first place Stell will look for me. Can you take me to Richmond? To Ness.'

She'll understand. She'll take care of me.

NINETEEN

George

It's a long journey down to Richmond, but Harry doesn't say much. I spend the bulk of the journey telling him every single little thing that Stella did during our short marriage, from the diet she put me on to encouraging me to take the money. He nods along, unsurprised.

'And you were right,' I say. 'I'm sure she was drugging me. She had sleeping tablets. There were only four left and she never takes them.'

'What? She was putting them in your food?'

'No. She switched them with my cholesterol meds. She used to leave them out for me with a glass of water if I was out late. And it was always those times that I lost my memory of the night before. I never questioned it.' I feel physically sick when I think about this.

'Whoah. Mixing sedatives with alcohol?' Harry shakes his head. 'It's a dangerous game. Shit, George. But the main thing is you're out of it now. We've got to come up with a plan for you going forward. How you're going to get her claws out of you.'

'Hmm.' I lapse into silence and rehearse what I'm going

to say to Ness. I'll apologise, of course. In my mind's eye, I see myself on my knees in front of her, clutching her hands and begging for forgiveness, though I know it won't happen like that. But I need to apologise for the way I treated her when we were married. I can see it all so clearly now. How could I have been so cruel? I took her for granted, cheated on her, kept her down where I wanted her and didn't even let her pursue her own career.

And, while I'm thinking about all this, I remember that chaste little kiss we had on Richmond Green – how erotic it had been – and I wonder if there could ever be a day when Ness might even take me back; when I might be able to put right all that's gone wrong since the day I met Stella.

My body physically relaxes when we reach Richmond, and I exhale all my stress in several deep breaths. This is where I belong. This is my place. Whatever happens, I'm going to move back here; get a place on my own – whatever. As Harry drives us through town, I feel like it's a homecoming; like the shopfronts are my friends. I'm looking out for people I know. It's a sunny day and, as we reach the crest of Richmond Hill, I catch sight of the river sliding through the city like a ribbon of silver light. God, how I've missed it, stuck out in the country – trapped in Stella's country dream. I've been brainwashed. I see that now. How could I have been so stupid?

Harry turns into the driveway and stops the engine.

'I'll wait here,' he says. I get out, rake my fingers through my hair, check my breath, then I walk up the drive and ring the doorbell, almost surprised that the sound of my heart banging doesn't bring her to the door. Like a schoolboy calling for his first date, I shift from foot to foot, and then the lock clicks and the door opens.

'George!' Ness does a double-take. 'What are you doing here?'

She's barefoot, in shorts and a vest, and there's classical music coming from inside the house. Haydn. The track makes my insides contract. Sunday mornings with Ness: music, coffee and the papers.

'Hey,' I say.

'Are you OK?' She looks at me in concern and we lock eyes for a moment. Her eyes. I'd forgotten how blue they are: 'irises like irises' I used to say. It's Ness who breaks the eye contact to nod at my backpack.

'What's up? Has something happened?'

'It's a long story. Can I come in?'

She motions me into the hallway and closes the front door behind me as I breathe in the smell of home. Pepper comes running, tail wagging, mad as a bag of frogs as usual, and I bend to pet her. It kills me that all this is no longer mine.

'Sit!' says Ness. 'Stay!' And Pepper does as she's told, cocking her head to look at me.

'You've trained her?'

'Yep.'

I drop my bag and Ness looks at me expectantly. I swallow, suddenly shy.

'So… the news is, I've left Stella.'

'Okaay,' Ness says slowly. 'And… ?' She holds her hand out, palm up.

'Oh God. I don't know where to start,' I say. 'You won't believe what I've been through; what she's done. But the first thing I want to do is apologise to you.' I pause. 'I'm so sorry. For everything. I see now what an arse I was when we were married. You have no idea how sorry I am.'

'George. I…' Ness opens her mouth to speak but outside the front door, there's a commotion. A man's voice shouting; the sound of running footsteps; a thud against the front door; and then someone banging on the door. Ness and I look at each other, eyes wide.

'What's going on?' Ness pulls the door open and I know on a primal level before my eyes fully process what they're seeing, exactly who it is who's outside; who it is who's struggling with Harry: Stella.

'I'm sorry! I couldn't stop her!' Harry's out of breath.

'So this is what you've been up to!' Stella spits at me. 'I knew it! I knew I'd find you here! I knew if I left you, this is where you'd run!'

For a moment, I stare at her. I stand stock-still and stare, taking in the full horror of what Stella is; at last fully comprehending all the ways in which she's tried to manipulate and destroy me, and it's only then that I realise what the missing part of the puzzle was.

Hatred. Stella Simons actually hates me.

She lurches towards me, but I shove past her and I run. Away from the madness. Away from the monster. I run down the steps. Down the driveway. As if demons possess me, I bolt straight into the road – straight into the path of a speeding white van.

'George!' Ness screams.

But Harry's there behind me and his weight slams into me, trying to push me away from the van.

Screeching brakes. Screaming. Blackness.

TWENTY

Stella

George doesn't die.

It's touch and go for a while. Internal injuries, a brain injury and bones broken in so many places they resemble putty. But I don't know that at the time. When I see his body fly up in the air, spinning in an arc against the bright, bright blue of the sky, and when I see him fall, shattered, onto the road with a crunch that still haunts me; when I arrive at his side and see the stillness that hangs over him among the chaos all around; when I see the snake of blood oozing from his mouth and the odd angles of his limbs, I think he surely can't survive. No human can survive such an impact. His brother, with his brain matter spilling on the tarmac, clearly hasn't.

But then I rally: this is George – my George! – he always bounces back.

Yes, he always bounces back.

And so, while a passer-by respectfully covers the remains of Harry's crushed head with her coat and while Ness falls to her knees over George, unable to do anything but scream his name, it is I who springs into action.

It's I who calls the ambulance; who speaks to the controller, gives the right address, stops passers-by from moving him. It's I who checks his airway and covers him with a blanket. And it's I who feels for a pulse, who looks up at Ness and nods, before she turns and vomits on the pavement. They say the first few moments after an accident are the most critical.

So, yes, it is I who saves his life.

I sleep in ICU with him until he's out of danger, the beep of his heart monitor lulling me to sleep. I lose track of time; the ICU becomes my underwater world of semi-darkness and whirring machines, and then, days later, he wakes from his coma, and I discover the most ironic thing of all: I discover that George has lost his memory.

TWENTY-ONE

George

'And this is the village doctor – Dr Grant,' says Stell.

I'm in hospital for weeks. Every day Stell brings in photos to try to spark my memory. Thankfully, the long-term stuff is fine: my childhood, family, and so on. Stell's told me that Harry died trying to save me and I find it hard to imagine how or why because we never were that close.

I even remember being married to Ness and running Wolsey Associates. It seems to be pretty much the last year that's been wiped. Stell's brought pictures of our wedding, our house and the village we live in but nothing's firing the synapses; it's like looking at someone else's photos. I take the picture she's holding today and examine it: it's an older man, nicely dressed, wearing small, silver glasses. While I don't recognise him, I can see that being a doctor might suit him.

'He looks nice.'

'Yes. He's a good bloke. Sends his regards, by the way.' Stell holds out another photo. 'And this is Derek – the pub landlord.'

She watches me like a hawk while I scrutinise the picture.

I want desperately to recognise something; I can see how much it means to her and I really want to please her.

'Still nothing?' she asks. 'I thought you might have remembered him. We had good times at the pub.'

'And we will again, I promise.' I put the photo down and look at her; drinking her in from the long legs she's crossed so artlessly, up to that gorgeous dark hair. I still can't believe that Stella Simons – this beautiful, magnificent, complex woman – is my wife. I must have done something right in my past life.

'I know this is a long process,' I say, 'but, with your help, I'll get there. I will. Once you've told me things, I can remember them. It's not as if I have to write everything down just to remember who I am. It's just a gap in my memory, and it's only a year or so. Maybe it'll all even come back at some point. And this—' I point to my broken body '—the physio will get me there. They say I'll make a full recovery.'

Stell's smiling – a secret smile. Her whole face is alive; her eyes are dancing.

'What's up? Why are you smiling like that?'

'It's just something you said. About the pub.'

'What? About having happy times there again?'

'Yes.' She clasps her hands together as if she can't contain herself. 'I've got some news for you.'

'What is it?'

'It's about the pub! Derek's selling it, and I'd like us to be the new owners.'

'What?'

'You always wanted to run a pub. A gastropub to be

specific. This is perfect. The village is gentrified enough to enjoy my cooking. I'd cook and you'd be the landlord,' says Stell. 'It's a fantasy we used to talk about all the time – a dream we had.'

I shake my head, taking this in. Me? A pub? 'But what about my firm? My work?'

Stell looks down and fiddles with something on the arm of the chair; scratches at it with her nail.

'Look, this isn't going to be easy to hear but… before your accident, you were at rock bottom.' She looks up at me. 'Things weren't going well at work. You were being investigated for charity fraud.' I gasp and she holds her hand up. 'It's OK. It was all a misunderstanding. You didn't do anything wrong. The CPS dropped the case due to lack of evidence. You're in the clear.'

'Thank God.'

She reaches for my hand and pats it. 'It's weird how you've forgotten all this stuff. It's like you're a brand-new person; like I have to remind you who you are.'

'I'm so lucky to have you.'

She smiles. 'Anyway, about the pub. We have the money to buy it because, when everything was going pear-shaped with the investigation, you decided it'd be better for Wolsey Associates if you pulled out, so you sold the business.'

'I did?' I can see it would make sense, but a part of me is glad I can't remember this because I can imagine I wouldn't have been happy about selling my stake in a business I'd built up my whole life.

'So what do you think about the pub?' Stell asks. She tilts

her head and looks at me through her eyelashes with her hands clasped in prayer. On her wrist, a diamond bracelet flashes. 'Pretty please with a cherry on top?'

'Are you sure this is something I really wanted?'

'With all your heart. We used to dream about it, talk about it and fantasise about it – and now we're finally in a position to do it.' She really is breathless with excitement and all I want to do is give this woman who saved my life everything that she wants. 'What do you say? It'll just be a family venture: you, me and—' she pats the swell of her belly '—our baby. Maybe a dog. A fresh start. The villagers are all rooting for us. They can't wait for you to come home.'

'Wow,' I say. 'Seems like everyone's on our side. Look, I trust you. If this is what you say we wanted, then let's do it.' It feels good to be making decisions again.

Stell jumps up and flings her arms around my neck, then kisses my cheek.

'Thank you!' she says. 'We're going to be so happy. I just know it.'

Acknowledgements

This book owes the initial spark of its creation to a school reunion I attended myself twenty-six years after I left school. Like most people, I'd been in two minds about going – but I was curious to see how they all turned out – so I went.

And I'm glad I did because the strangest thing happened that night: I made a lot of new friends. Now I wish I could tap my teenage self on the shoulder as she skulks shyly about the playground with her nose in a book, and tell her: 'pay a bit more attention to her, and him, and her; they might turn out to be friends for life…' So, to all my old-new friends from school: thank you for accepting the hand of friendship in adulthood. It's wonderful to have got to know you at last.

As ever, I'm indebted to the team of people around me whose hard work and dedication go towards making my manuscripts the best they can be: to Luigi and Alison Bonomi; to my fantastic editor, Sally Williamson; to Charlotte Mursell, Alison Lindsay and all who work tirelessly behind the scenes at Harper Collins. There's always a special place in my heart for the team at the Emirates Airline Festival of Literature and Montegrappa, whose First Fiction competition in 2013 was my springboard to success: Isobel Abulhoul, Yvette Judge and Charlie Nahhas, thank you.

Thank you, too, to my little author posse here in Dubai: Rachel Hamilton and Charlotte Butterfield. Extra thanks to Rachel for those sweaty brain-storming meetings on roller-skates and for the patient reading of my first draft, and thanks to my core group of friends – my cheerleaders all around the world – who consistently lift me up.

Last but not least, thanks to my family. To my mum for always believing in me; to my wonderful husband, and to my ever-patient children.

The trip of a lifetime,
or the perfect murder?

Audrey Templeton has it all planned: she's going to spend her 70th birthday with her children Lexi and John, on a cruise around the Greek islands, where she'll tell them about their life-changing inheritance money.

But when Audrey fails to return to her cabin after the ship's White Night party, the crew carry out a full scale search that soon moves from inside the ship, to the deep waters of the med. With tensions rising between Lexi and John, they start to question not only how well they knew their mother, but whether they can actually trust one another.

After all, there are no police at sea…

HQ
One Place. Many Stories

The home of bold, innovative
and empowering publishing.

Follow us online

 @HQStories

 @HQStories

 HQStories

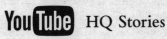 HQ Stories

 HQMusic